A KNIGHT FOR NURSE HART

BY
LAURA IDING

AND

A NURSE TO TAME THE PLAYBOY

BY
MAGGIE KINGSLEY

GW00689612

 MILLS & BOON®

FROM NURSE TO NEWLYWED!

Saying 'I do' to Dr Delicious!

Two nurses beyond compare
are showered in confetti and congratulations
when they fall for the men of their dreams!

A KNIGHT FOR NURSE HART
by Laura Iding

It takes a very special man to persuade Raine
to swap her uniform for a wedding dress:

A NURSE TO TAME THE PLAYBOY
by Maggie Kingsley

Fragile but feisty Brontë
reforms the sexiest doctor in town in:

A KNIGHT FOR NURSE HART

BY
LAURA IDING

First published in Great Britain 2010
Harlequin Mills & Boon Limited,
Eton House, 18-24 Paradise Road, Richmond, Surrey TW9 1SR

© Laura Iding 2010

ISBN: 978 0 263 87915 5

Harlequin Mills & Boon policy is to use papers that are natural, renewable and recyclable products and made from wood grown in sustainable forests. The logging and manufacturing process conform to the legal environmental regulations of the country of origin.

Printed and bound in Spain
by Litografia Rosés, S.A., Barcelona

Dear Reader

You met Emergency Nurse Raine Hart in THE NURSE'S BROODING BOSS, and I felt compelled to write her story. You may remember Raine as Elana's light-hearted and fun-loving friend—only now circumstances have changed, and unfortunately Raine isn't quite the same person as she was before.

Emergency Physician Caleb Stewart dated Raine for a few months, then they decided to take a break—mostly because Caleb couldn't quite get over his deeply rooted trust issues. Now he wants a second chance, but Raine isn't sure she can lower her defences enough to give him one.

Writing about characters who need to overcome massive hurdles in order to find themselves and to find love is always a challenge. This book was no exception. Raine and Caleb met at the wrong time, but in the end everything happened for a reason and they both grew stronger and closer to each other as a result.

I hope you enjoy Raine and Caleb's story.

Happy reading!

Laura Iding

PS I love to hear from my readers, so drop by my website at www.lauraiding.com and send me a message if you have time.

Laura Iding loved reading as a child, and when she ran out of books she readily made up her own, completing a little detective mini-series when she was twelve. But, despite her aspirations for being an author, her parents insisted she look into a 'real' career. So the summer after she turned thirteen she volunteered as a Candy Striper, and fell in love with nursing. Now, after twenty years of experience in trauma/critical care, she's thrilled to combine her career and her hobby into one—writing Medical™ Romances for Mills & Boon. Laura lives in the northern part of the United States, and spends all her spare time with her two teenage kids (help!)—a daughter and a son—and her husband.

Recent titles by the same author:

THE NURSE'S BROODING BOSS
THE SURGEON'S NEW YEAR WEDDING WISH
EXPECTING A CHRISTMAS MIRACLE
MARRYING THE PLAYBOY DOCTOR

CHAPTER ONE

"RAINE! You're here? Working Trauma again?" Sarah greeted her when she walked into the trauma bay fifteen minutes before the regular start of her shift.

Emergency nurse Raine Hart smiled at her co-worker. "Yes, I'm back. Working in the minor care area for a few weeks was a nice reprieve and a lot less stress. But I confess I've missed being a part of the action."

"Well, we sure missed you, too. And I'm so glad you came in early," Sarah said, quickly changing the subject from Raine's four-week hiatus from Trauma to her own personal issues. "I have to leave right away to pick-up my son, he's running a fever at the day care and there's a new trauma coming in." Sarah thrust the trauma pager into her hands as if it were a hot potato. "ETA is less than five minutes."

"No problem." Raine accepted the pager, feeling a tiny thrill of anticipation. She hadn't been lying, she really had missed the excitement of working in the trauma bay. She scrolled through the most recent text message from the paramedic base. Thirty-year-old female with blunt trauma to the head with poor vital signs. Not good. "Sounds like it's been busy."

"Crazy busy," Sarah agreed. "Like I said, we missed you. Sorry I have to run, but I'll see you, tomorrow."

"Bye, Sarah." Raine clipped the pager to the waist-band of her scrubs, and swept a glance over the room. It looked as if Sarah had everything ready to go for the next patient. She was secretly relieved to start off her first trauma shift with a new admission. She'd rather be busy—work was a welcome distraction from her personal problems. Raine was thankful her boss had kept her real reason for being away from Trauma a secret, telling her co-workers only that she'd been off sick, and then reassigned to Minor Care to work in a less stressful environment on doctor's orders. After three weeks in Minor Care, she was more than ready for more intense nursing.

So here she was, back in the trauma bay. Raine took a deep breath and squared her shoulders, determined to keep the past buried deep, where it belonged.

She could do this, no problem.

"No sign of our trauma patient yet?" a low husky, familiar voice asked.

She sucked in a harsh breath and swung around to stare at Dr. Caleb Stewart in shocked surprise. According to the posted schedule, Brock Madison was supposed to be the emergency physician on duty in the trauma bay tonight. Obviously, he and Caleb must have switched shifts.

"Not yet." Her mouth was sandpaper dry and she desperately searched for something to say. Caleb looked great. Better than great. Better than she'd remembered. But she hadn't been prepared to face him. Not yet. She hadn't seen him since they'd decided to take a break from their relationship just over a month ago.

She couldn't ignore a sharp pang of regret. If only she'd tried harder to work things out. But she hadn't.

And now it was too late.

Thankfully, before he could say anything more, the doors of the trauma bay burst open, announcing the arrival of their patient. Instantly, controlled chaos reigned.

"Becca Anderson, thirty years old, vitals dropping, BP 86 over 40, pulse tachy at 128," the paramedic standing at the patient's head announced. "Her GCS was only 5 in the field, so we intubated her. She probably needs fluids but we've been concerned about brain swelling, and didn't want to make her head injury worse."

Raine took her place on the left side of their trauma patient, quickly drawing the initial set of blood samples they'd need in order to care for Becca. Luckily, the rhythm of working in Trauma came back instantly, in spite of her four-week absence. Amy, one of the other nurses, came up on the right side to begin the initial assessment. One of the ED techs cut off the patient's clothes to give them better access to any hidden injuries.

"Raine, as soon as you're finished with those labs, we need to bump up her IV fluids and start a vasopresser, preferably norepinephrine," Caleb ordered. "Shock can kill her as much as a head injury."

"Left pupil is one millimeter larger than the right," Amy informed them. "I can't feel a major skull fracture, just some minor abrasions on the back of her scalp. It's possible she has a closed cranial trauma."

Raine's stomach dropped at the news. Patients with closed cranial trauma had the worst prognosis. When the brain swelled there was no place for it to go, often resulting in brain death. And Becca was too young to die.

Suddenly, she was fiercely glad Caleb was the physician on duty. Despite their differences, she knew he'd work harder than anyone to make sure their patient survived. Determined to do her part, Raine took her fistful of blood tubes over to the tube system to send them directly to the laboratory. En route, she noticed two uniformed police officers were standing back, watching the resuscitation. It wasn't unusual to have law enforcement presence with trauma patients, so she ignored them as she rushed back to increase their patient's IV fluids and to start a norepinephrine drip.

"We need a CT scan of her head, stat. Any other signs of internal injuries?" Caleb demanded.

"Bruises on her upper arms," Raine said, frowning at the dark purple spots that seemed to match the size and shape of fingertips. She hung the medication and set the pump to the appropriate rate as she talked. "Give me a minute and we'll roll her over to check her back." She finished the IV set-up and took a moment to double-check she'd done everything correctly.

"I'll help." Caleb stepped next to Raine, adding his strength to pulling the patient up and over onto her side, so Amy could assess the patient's backside. Caleb was close, too close. She bit her lip, forcing herself not to overreact at the unexpected warmth when his arm brushed against hers.

Memories of the wonderful times together crashed through her mind and she firmly shoved them aside. Their relationship was over. She wasn't the same person she'd been back then.

And they had a critically ill patient to care for.

"A few minor abrasions on her upper shoulders,

nothing major," Amy announced. Raine and Caleb gently rolled the patient onto her back.

"She's the victim of a domestic dispute," one of the police officers said, stepping forward. "Her husband slammed her head against the concrete driveway, according to witnesses."

Dear God, how awful. A small-town girl at heart, Raine had moved to the big city of Milwaukee just two years ago after finishing college. But she still wasn't used to some of the violent crime victims they inevitably cared for. She tried to wipe the brutal image from her mind.

"Raine?" Caleb's voice pierced her dark thoughts. "Call Radiology and arrange for a CT scan."

She nodded and hurried to the phone. Within minutes, she had Becca packed up and ready to go.

"I'm coming with you," Caleb said, as she started pushing the cart towards the radiology suite next door. Thankfully the hospital had had the foresight to put the new radiology department right next to the emergency department. "I don't like the way her heart rate is continuing to climb. Could be partially due to the norepinephrine, but it could also be her head injury getting worse."

She couldn't argue because Becca's vital signs were not very stable. Usually the physicians only came along on what the nurses referred to as road trips, for the worst-case scenarios.

As Becca's blood pressure dropped even further, Raine grimly acknowledged this was one of those times she would be glad to have physician support.

She was all too aware of Caleb's presence as they wheeled the patient's gurney into the radiology suite. There were unspoken questions in his eyes when he glanced at her, but he didn't voice them. She understood—this was hardly the time or the place for them to talk about the mistakes they'd made in the past. About what might have been.

She kept her gaze focused on their patient and the heart monitor placed at the foot of her bed. They were only part way into the scan when Becca's blood pressure dropped to practically nothing.

"Get her out of there," Caleb demanded. The radiology tech hurried to shut down the scanner so they could pull the patient out from the scanner opening. "Crank up her norepinephrine drip."

Raine was already pushing buttons on the IV pump. But then the pump began to alarm. She looked at the swollen area above the patient's antecubital peripheral IV. "I think her IV is infiltrated."

Caleb muttered a curse under his breath and grabbed a central line insertion set off the top of the crash cart the radiology tech had wisely brought in. "Then we'll put a new central line in her right now."

"Here?" the radiology tech asked incredulously.

Caleb ignored him. Raine understood—they couldn't afford to lose another vein. A central line would be safer in the long run. Anticipating his needs, she quickly placed sterile drapes around the patient's neck, preparing the insertion site as Caleb donned sterile gloves. Luck or possibly divine intervention was on his side when he hit the subclavian vein on the first try.

"Here's the medication," Raine said, handing over the end of the IV tubing she'd disconnected from the non-working IV.

The moment Caleb connected the tubing, she administered a small bolus to get the medication into her patient's bloodstream quicker, since the woman's blood pressure was still non-existent and her heart rate was dropping too. For a moment, Raine held her breath, but their patient responded well and her blood pressure soon returning to the 80s systolic. Caleb anchored the line with a suture and then quickly dressed the site.

But they weren't out of the woods yet. Worried, she glanced at Caleb. "Should we complete the scan?" she asked.

He gave a curt nod, his expression grave. One of the things she liked best about Caleb was that he didn't build a wall around himself to protect his emotions. He sincerely cared about his patients. "We have to. The neurosurgeons are going to need to see the films in order to decide whether or not to take her to surgery."

The radiology tech didn't look very happy at the prospect, but took his place to continue running the scan. Raine and Caleb together slid the patient back onto the exam table. She was startled when he took her arm, and instinctively pulled away. She winced when she realized what she'd done, knowing he'd done nothing to deserve her reaction. Her issues, not his.

His stormy gray eyes darkened with hurt confusion but she avoided the questioning look he shot her way. She felt bad about hurting him again, but at that moment her patient's heart monitor alarmed so she was forced to go over to adjust the alarm limits. The ten-minute exam seemed excruciatingly long, but they finally finished the procedure.

Caleb didn't say anything as they pushed the gurney back to the trauma bay. The moment they arrived, he crossed over to page the neurosurgeon to discuss the best course of action for their patient.

"Becca?" Raine glanced over at the shrill voice. She saw Amy bringing in a woman who looked to be a few years younger than their patient. "Oh, my God, Becca. What did he do to you?"

Raine had to turn away from the crying woman who clutched their patient's hand.

"Her sister, Mari," Amy said in a low tone. "I had to let her in because I'm betting Becca will be going to the OR ASAP."

"Of course you did," Raine said, but her voice sounded far away, as if she was speaking through a long tunnel. She'd wanted to be busy, but maybe she'd been overconfident. Maybe she wasn't ready for the trauma room just yet. Maybe she should have stayed longer in the minor care area of the ED, where they didn't deal with anything remotely serious.

Her eyes burned and she fought the need to cry right along with Mari. She turned away, to give them some privacy and to pull herself together. She went over to the computer to look up Becca's most recent labs.

"Raine? Are you all right?" Caleb asked, coming up to the computer workstation.

"Of course." She subtly loosened her grip on the edge of the desk and forced herself to meet his gaze, hoping he couldn't tell how emotionally fragile she was. It was far too tempting to lean on Caleb's strength. To confide in him. If things had been different...

But they weren't. Reminding herself that she needed to find her own strength to work through her past, she waved a hand at the computer screen. "Did you see these latest results? Her electrolytes are way out of whack."

He gave her an odd look, but then nodded. "Get her prepped for the OR. Dr. Lambert wants her up there ASAP."

"Okay." Raine abandoned her computer and jumped to her feet. She hurried over to Becca's bedside and told Amy and Mari the news.

Within moments she and Amy transported Becca up to the OR, releasing her into the hands of the neurosurgeons. There was nothing else they could do for now but wait.

Raine tried to push Becca's fate out of her mind since she and Caleb had done everything she could for the patient. But concentrating on her job wasn't easy. Especially when she could feel Caleb's gaze following her as she worked.

She could tell he wanted to talk. The very thought filled her with dread. She couldn't talk to him now, no matter how much she wished she could.

It was too late. She'd missed her chance to take his calls weeks ago. Better now to focus her energy on moving forward rather than rehashing the past.

What she and Caleb had once shared was over.

"Dr. Stewart?" He glanced up when Raine called his name. "I think you'd better check Mrs. Ambruster's chest X-ray. Her breathing has gotten dramatically worse."

Caleb scowled at the formal way she addressed him. They'd dated for almost two months, had shared more than one passionate kiss. He knew it was his fault that she'd requested a break from their relationship but, still, hadn't they moved well beyond the *Dr. Stewart* stage?

"Sure." A surge of regret washed over him. Seeing Raine again made him realize he'd never gotten over her.

Not completely. If only he'd handled things differently. If only he hadn't been such an ass.

He'd heard she'd moved over to the minor care area because she'd needed a break from Trauma. He knew full well she'd really needed a break from him.

And he'd missed working with her, more than he'd wanted to acknowledge.

He gave himself a mental shake. This wasn't the time or the place. He crossed over to the patient, who had come in with vague flu-like symptoms that he was beginning to suspect was something much more complicated. Using the closest computer terminal, he pulled up the patient's chest X-ray. Raine was right, the patient's breathing must be severely compromised as the X-ray looked far worse. He suspected the large shadow was a tumor and likely the cause of a massive infiltrate on the right side of her lungs, but she would need more of a work-up to be sure. "How much O2 do you have her on?"

"Six liters."

He frowned. "Crank her up to ten liters per minute and prepare for a thoracentisis."

Raine did as he asked, although he noticed she gave him a wide berth whenever he came too close.

He was troubled by the way Raine was acting. He regretted the way he'd overreacted that night and had tried to call her several times to apologize but she hadn't returned his calls. Did she still blame him? Was it impossible for her to forgive him?

Seeing her tonight brought his old feelings back to the surface. Along with the same sexual awareness that had shimmered between them from the very first time they'd met.

But as much as that sensation was still there, something

was off. He'd noticed right from the start of their shift how her usual enthusiasm was missing. Maybe it was just the seriousness of their domestic violence patient, but they'd shared tough shifts before. Somehow this was different, especially the way she seemed to avoid him whenever he came too close.

Maybe she was worried he'd ask her out again. And he had to admit, the thought had crossed his mind. More than once. Sure, he'd made a stupid mistake before, but didn't he deserve a second chance?

Apparently, Raine wasn't willing to grant him one.

He turned to their elderly patient, focusing on the procedure he needed to do. He put on a face mask and then donned sterile gown and gloves, while Raine prepped the patient. He lifted the needle and syringe in his hand and gently probed the space between the fourth and fifth ribs. He numbed the area with lidocaine and then picked up the longer needle used to aspirate the fluid. Slowly, he advanced the needle.

He hit the pocket of fluid and held the needle steady while the site drained. Once he'd taken off almost a liter of fluid, their patient's oxygen saturation improved dramatically.

"Place a dressing over this site, would you?" he asked Raine. "And we need to send a sample of this fluid to Pathology." Stepping back, he stripped off his sterile garb. Once she'd gotten the specimens sent to the lab and the patient cleaned up, he went back in to talk to the husband and wife.

"Mrs. Ambruster, I'm afraid your chest X-ray shows something abnormal and I believe whatever is going on is causing fluid to build up in your lungs."

The elderly couple exchanged a look of dismay. "What is it? Cancer?" her husband asked.

Caleb didn't want to lie but at the same time he didn't honestly know for certain what the problem was. He was impressed by the mutual love and respect this elderly couple displayed toward each other, something missing from his own family life. He tried to sound positive. "That is one possibility but there are others that could be less serious. I'm not a thoracic surgeon, but I'd like to refer you to one. I can arrange for you to see someone first thing in the morning if you're willing."

The Ambrusters agreed and he made the arrangements with the thoracic surgery resident. By the time he wrote the discharge orders for Mrs. Ambruster, the oncoming shift had arrived.

He was free to go home. But he didn't want to leave, not without talking to Raine.

He found her in the staff lounge, but stopped short when he realized she was crying. Immediately concerned, he rushed over. "Raine? What's wrong?"

"Nothing." She quickly swiped at her eyes, as if embarrassed by her display of emotion.

"Raine, please. Talk to me." He couldn't hide the desperate urgency in his voice.

There was a slight pause, and he found himself holding his breath when she finally brought her tortured gaze up to meet his. "Becca died. She never made it out of surgery."

Caleb grimaced beneath a wave of guilt. Here he'd been worried about himself when Raine was grieving over their patient. "I'm sorry, Raine. I didn't know."

"Doesn't matter. We did what we could."

The despair in her tone tugged at his heart. He wanted

to reach out to her, but knew he'd given up that privilege when he'd accused her of cheating on him.

He wanted to apologize. To explain he now knew he'd been wrong, but where to start?

"I have to go," Raine muttered, swiping at her face and attempting to brush past him.

"Wait." He reached out to grasp her arm. "Please don't go. Let's talk. About us. About where we went wrong."

"There's no point. What we had is over," she whispered, wrenching from his grasp. The hint of dark desperation shadowing her eyes hit hard. She hesitated only for a moment, before ducking out of the room.

Shocked, he could only stare after her. Something was definitely wrong. This wasn't just Raine wanting to take a break from their relationship. There was something more going on.

He'd screwed up before, but he wouldn't give in so easily this time. He was determined to uncover the truth.

CHAPTER TWO

RAINE drove home, wishing she hadn't lost control like that in front of Caleb. It was her own fault that he had no idea what she'd been through. No one did. She been too embarrassed, too ashamed. Feeling too guilty to tell anyone.

She was determined to get over the past, and she knew that moving forward was the best way to accomplish that. And if she regretted taking a break from her relationship with Caleb, she had no one to blame but herself.

Caleb had trust issues. But instead of trying to work through them, she'd broken things off. And then, when he'd tried to call to make up, she hadn't returned his calls.

Because by then everything had changed.

She'd thought she'd put the past behind her. But obviously she'd jumped back into the trauma environment a little too quickly. She'd taken off work completely for a week, and then had taken a three-week assignment in the minor care area, trying to ease herself back into the stressful working environment the way her counselor had suggested. Obviously, she had a way to go before she'd be back to her old self.

She pulled into her assigned parking space in the small

lot behind her apartment, threw the gearshift into park and dropped her forehead on the steering-wheel with a deep, heavy sigh.

Who was she trying to kid? She'd never be the person she had been before. Hadn't her counselor drilled that fact into her head? There was no going back. The only option was to move forward.

Firming her resolve, she climbed from the car and headed up to her second-story apartment. She smiled when her cat, Spice, meowed softly and came running over to greet her, rubbing up against her leg with a satisfied purr. She picked up the cat and buried her face in the soft fur. She'd adopted Spice from the local shelter a few weeks ago and had not regretted it. Coming home to an empty apartment night after night had been difficult. Spice made coming home much easier. And the cat gave her someone to talk to.

She threw a small beanbag ball past Spice—the goofy cat actually liked to play fetch like a dog—and tried to unwind from the long shift. But the relaxation tips her therapist had suggested didn't help and she still had trouble falling asleep. She'd taken to sleeping on her sofa, and as she stared at the ceiling, she thought about her counselor's advice to confide in someone. She knew her counselor might be right, but she just couldn't make herself take that step.

If she told one of her friends what had happened, they'd look at her differently. With horror. With pity. Asking questions. She shivered with dread. No, she couldn't stand the thought of anyone knowing the gory details. Especially when she couldn't remember much herself.

The one person she might have confided in was Caleb. If he'd trusted her. Which he didn't.

The events of that night when he'd looked at her with frank disgust still had the power to hurt her. She'd gone out to a local pub with a group of ED staff nurses and physicians after work. Jake, one of the new ED residents, had flirted with her. She hadn't really thought too much about it until the moment she'd realized he'd had too much to drink. He'd leaned in close, with his arm around the back of her chair, trying to kiss her.

Before she could gently, but firmly push him away, Caleb had walked in. She'd blushed because she knew the situation looked bad, but he hadn't given her a chance to explain. Instead, he'd accused her of seeing Jake behind his back.

She'd seen the flash of hurt in his eyes, but at the same time she hadn't appreciated Caleb's willingness to think the worst of her. She'd talked to him the next day, and had tried to explain. But when he'd sounded distant, and remote, she'd given up, telling him it might be best to take a break from their relationship for a while.

She'd been stunned when he'd agreed.

Pounding a fist into her pillow, she turned on the sofa and tried to forget about Caleb. With everything that had happened, she'd put distance between herself and her friends.

Her closest friend, Elana Schultz, had recently married ED physician Brock Madison. In the months since their wedding she hadn't seen as much of Elana. They were still friends, but Elana had a new life now with Brock.

When Elana had assumed Raine had taken the job in Minor Care to avoid Caleb, she hadn't told her friend any different.

It was better than Elana knowing the truth.

The next morning Raine's phone woke her from a deep sleep. She patted the mound of linens on her sofa, searching for her cellphone. "Hello?"

"Raine? It's Elana. I just had to call to tell you the news."

"News?" Elana's dramatically excited tone brought a smile to her face. She pushed a hand through her hair and blinked the sleep from her eyes. "What news?"

"We heard the baby's heart beat!" Elana exclaimed, her excitement contagious. "You should have seen the look on Brock's face, he was so enthralled. He brought tears to my eyes. You'd never guess he once decided to live his life without children."

"He was delusional, obviously," Raine said dismissively. "And that was long before he met you. I'm so excited for you, Elana. Did you and Brock change your mind about finding out the baby's gender?"

"No, we still want the baby's sex to be a surprise. But my due date is confirmed—five months and one week to go."

Raine mentally calculated. It was the seventh of June. "November fifteenth?"

"Yes, give or take a week. Brock is painting the baby's room like a madman—he's worried we won't have everything ready in time," Elana said with a laugh. "I keep telling him there's no rush."

"Knowing Brock, he'll have it ready in plenty of time." Raine tried to hide the wistful tone of her voice. Watching Elana and Brock together was wonderful and yet painful at the same time. They were so in love, they glowed.

If only she were worthy of that kind of love. She pushed aside the flash of self-pity. "Do you have time to meet for lunch?" she asked.

"Oh, I'm sorry Raine. I'd love to, but I agreed to volunteer at the New Beginnings clinic this afternoon. Can I take a rain-check?"

"Sure." Raine forced lightness into her tone. The New Beginnings clinic was a place where low-income patients could be seen at no cost to them. She'd volunteered there in the past, but not recently. "No problem. Take care and I'm sure I'll see you at work one of these days."

"I know, it's been for ever, hasn't it?" Elana asked. Raine knew it was exactly one month and three days since they'd worked together. Since her life had irrevocably changed. "You've been working in the minor care area and I've been cutting back my hours now that I'm pregnant. The morning sickness has been awful. Brock is being a tad overly protective lately, but I'm not going to complain. I'm scheduled to work this weekend."

"Great. I'm working the weekend, too and I'm back on the schedule in the trauma bay. I'll see you then." Raine hung up the phone, feeling a bit deflated. Not that she begrudged her friend one ounce of happiness. Elana had gone through some rough times, too.

Elana had moved on from her painful past, and Raine was sure she could too. One day at a time.

Since the last thing she needed was more time on her hands, Raine forced herself to climb out of bed. There was no point in wallowing in self-pity for the rest of the day.

She needed to take action. To focus on the positive. She'd taken to volunteering at the animal shelter on her days off, as dealing with animals was somehow easier lately, than dealing with people.

It was time to visit her furry friends who were always there when she needed them.

* * *

Caleb pulled up in front of his father's house and swallowed a deep sigh. His father had called to ask for help, after injuring his ankle after falling off a ladder. His father was currently living alone, as his most recent relationship had ended in an unsurprising break-up. Caleb was relieved that at least this time his father had been smart enough to avoid marrying the woman. With four divorces under his belt, you'd think his father would learn. But, no, he kept making the same mistakes over and over again.

Leaving Caleb to pick up the pieces.

He walked up to the house, frowning a bit when he saw the front door was open. He knocked on the screen door, before opening it. "Dad? Are you in there?"

"Over here, Caleb," his father called out. His father's black Lab, Grizzly, let out a warning bark, but then came rushing over to greet him as he walked through the living room into the kitchen. He took a moment to pet the excited dog, and then crossed over to where his father was seated at the table, with his ankle propped on the chair beside him. "Thanks for coming."

"Sure." He bent over his father's ankle, assessing the swollen joint, tenderly palpating the bruised tissue around the bone. "Are you sure this isn't broken?"

"Told you I took X-rays at the shelter, didn't I?" his father said in a cantankerous tone. "It's not broken, it's only sprained. Did you bring the crutches?"

"Yes, they're in the car." But he purposely hadn't brought them in. He'd asked his father to come into the ED while he was working, but did he listen? No. His father had taken his own X-rays on the machine he used for animals. Caleb would rather have looked at the films himself.

"Why did ya leave them out there? Go get 'em."

Caleb propped his hands on his hips and scowled at his father. "Dad, be reasonable. Take a couple of days off. Being on crutches around animals is just asking for trouble. Surely the shelter can do without you for a few days?"

"I told you, there's some sort of infection plaguing several of the new animals. I retired from my full-time veterinary practice last year, didn't I? I only go to the shelter three days a week and every other Saturday. Surely that's not too much for an old codger like me." His dad yanked on the fabric of his pants leg to help lift his injured foot down on the floor. "If you won't drive me, I'll arrange for a cab."

Caleb closed his eyes and counted to ten, searching for patience. He didn't remember ever calling his dad an old codger, but nevertheless a shaft of guilt stabbed deep. He'd promised to help out more, but hadn't made the time to come over as often as he should have. "I said I'd take you and I will. But, Dad, you have to try taking it easy for a while. Every time I stop by I find you doing something new. Trying to clean out the gutters on that rickety old ladder was what caused your fall in the first place."

"Well, someone had to do it."

This time Caleb counted to twenty. "You never asked me to help you with the gutters," he reminded his father, striving for a calm tone. "And if you'd have waited, I could have done the job when I came over to mow your lawn on the weekend."

His father ignored him, gingerly rising to his feet, leaning heavily on the back of the kitchen chair to keep the pressure off his sore ankle. Grizzly came over to stand beside him, as if he could somehow assist. "I'm going to need those crutches to get outside."

Arguing with his father was about as effective as herding cats. His father simply ignored the things he didn't want to deal with. "Sit down. I'll get them." Caleb strode back through the house, muttering under his breath, "Stubborn man."

He grabbed the crutches out of the back of the car and slammed the door with more force than was necessary. He and his father had always been at odds and the passing of the years hadn't changed their relationship much. Caleb's mother had taken off, abandoning him at the tender age of five. One would think that fact alone would have brought him and his dad closer together. But his father hadn't waited very long before bringing home future stepmothers in an attempt to replace his first wife. At first the relationships had been short-lived, but then he'd ended up marrying a few.

None of them stayed very long, of course. They left, just like his mother, for a variety of reasons. Because they realized being a vet didn't bring in a boat-load of money, especially when you were already paying alimony for a previous marriage. Or they found someone else. Or simply got bored with playing step-mom to someone else's kid.

Whatever the reason, the women his father picked didn't stick around. Carmen was the one who'd stayed the longest, almost three years, but in the end she'd left, too.

Yeah, his father could really pick them.

"Here are the crutches," he said as he entered the kitchen. "Now, be patient for a minute so I can measure them. They have to fit your frame."

For once his father listened. After he'd adjusted the crutches to his father's height, the older man took them and leaned on them gratefully. "Thanks," he said gruffly.

"You're welcome." Caleb watched his father walk slowly across the room, making sure he could safely use them. Grizz got in the way once, but then quickly learned to avoid them. Crutches weren't as easy to use as people thought, and Caleb worried about his father's upper-arm strength. But his father was still in decent shape, and seemed to manage them well enough. Reluctantly satisfied, he followed his father outside, giving Grizz one last pat on the head.

The shelter was only ten miles away. Neither one of them was inclined to break the silence as Caleb navigated the city streets.

He pulled up in front of the building and shut the car. "I'll come inside with you," he offered.

"Sure." His father's mood had brightened the closer they'd gotten to the shelter, and Caleb quickly figured out the elder man needed this volunteer work more than he'd realized.

More guilt, he thought with a slight grimace. He held the front door of the building open, waiting for his father to cross the threshold on his crutches before following him in.

"Dr. Frank! What happened?"

Caleb froze when he saw Raine rushing toward his father. She didn't seem to have noticed him as she placed an arm around his father's thin shoulders.

"Twisted my ankle, that's all. Nothing serious." His father patted her hand reassuringly. "Now, tell me, Raine, how's Rusty doing today? Is he any better?"

"He seems a little better, but really, Dr. Frank, should you be here? Maybe you should have stayed at home to rest." Raine lifted her gaze and he knew she'd spotted him when she paled, her dark red hair a stark contrast to her alabaster skin. "Caleb. What are you doing here?"

"Dropping off my father." He couldn't help the flash of resentment at how friendly his father and Raine seemed to be. She had never mentioned working at the animal shelter during those two months they'd dated. But here she was, standing with her arm protectively around his father, as if they were life-long buddies.

A foreign emotion twisted in his gut. Jealousy. For a moment he didn't want to acknowledge it. But as he absorbed the camaraderie between his father and Raine, he couldn't deny the truth.

His father had grown closer to Raine in the time since she'd pushed him away.

Raine couldn't believe that Dr. Frank was actually Caleb's father. She'd never really known if Frank was the retired vet's first or last name, and hadn't asked. They'd had an unspoken agreement not to pry into each other's personal lives. But now that she saw the two of them in the same room, the resemblance was obvious. Dr. Frank's hair was mostly gray, whereas Caleb's was dark brown, but the two men shared the same stormy gray eyes and aristocratic nose. Of course, Caleb was taller and broader across the shoulders but his dad was no slouch. In fact, she thought Dr. Frank was rather handsome, all things considered.

Caleb would age well, if his father's looks were any indication. And for a moment regret stabbed deep. As much as she needed to move forward, it was difficult not to mourn what might have been.

"What time do you want me to pick you up?" Caleb asked his father.

"I can give Dr. Frank a ride home if he needs one," she quickly offered.

Caleb's eyebrows rose in surprise, as if he suspected she had some sort of ulterior motive. Was he assuming she was trying to get back into his good graces by helping his father? If things were different, she might have been tempted.

"That's very kind of you, Raine," Dr. Frank said. She could have sworn the older man's gaze was relieved when he turned back toward his son. "There's no need for you to come all the way back out here, Raine will drive me home. Thanks for the ride, Caleb. I'll see you this weekend, all right?"

"Yeah. Sure." For a moment Caleb stared at her, as if he wanted to say something more, but after a tense moment he turned away. She had to bite her lip to stop herself from calling out to him as he headed for the door. "See you later, Dad," he tossed over his shoulder.

He didn't acknowledge Raine as he left. And even though she knew it was her fault, since taking a break from their relationship had been her idea, she was ridiculously hurt by the snub.

Trying to shake off the effects of her less than positive interaction with Caleb, she faced Dr. Frank. "So, are you ready to get to work?"

Caleb's father's glance was sharp—she should have known he wouldn't miss a thing. "Do you and my son know each other?"

She tried to smile. So much for their rule to stay away from personal things. "Yes, we both work in the emergency department at Trinity Medical Center," she admitted. "Caleb is a great doctor, everyone enjoys working with him."

"Everyone except you?"

She flushed, hating to think she'd been that transparent. Especially when she liked working with Caleb. Too much for her own good. "I like working with him, but I'm thinking of changing my career to veterinary medicine," she joked, in an attempt to lighten things up. "Maybe you'll give me some tips, hmm? Come on, let's head to the back. I think I should take a look at that ankle of yours."

"Caleb already looked at it." Dr. Frank waved her off. "I'm more interested in the animals. I'm going to need you to bring them to me in the exam room as my mobility is limited."

"No problem." Raine wanted to help, but as he deftly maneuvered the crutches, she realized he was doing fine on his own.

Dozens of questions filtered through her mind, but she didn't immediately voice them. Caleb obviously hadn't mentioned her to his father during the time they'd been seeing each other, which bothered her. Especially since he hadn't even talked about his father very much.

What else didn't she know about him? And why did it matter? What she and Caleb had was over. For good. No matter how much she missed him.

Dr. Frank didn't notice her preoccupation with his son. His attention was quickly focused on the sick animals.

She brought Rusty into the room, the Irish setter puppy they'd rescued three weeks ago. She'd fallen for Rusty in a big way, especially when everyone teased her that Rusty's dark red coat was the same color as her hair. But unfortunately the lease on her apartment didn't allow dogs, which was why she'd taken Spice, the calico cat, instead.

But when she did have enough money saved to buy a house, she planned on adopting a dog, too. Hopefully one just as sweet tempered and beautiful as Rusty.

"There, now, let me take a listen to your heart," Dr. Frank murmured as he stroked Rusty's fur. The dog had been in bad shape when he'd been picked up as a stray, and he'd shied away, growling at men, which made them think he might have been abused. Raine didn't know how long he'd been on the streets, but he'd been dangerously malnourished when he'd arrived. And he'd been sick with some sort of infection that had soon spread to the animals housed in the kennels near him.

She held the dog close, smiling a little when he licked her arm. "You're such a good puppy, aren't you?"

"He's definitely doing better on the antiviral meds we've been giving him," Dr. Frank announced, finishing his exam. "Let's move on to Annie, the golden retriever."

Volunteering at the shelter had saved her from losing her mind in her dark memories. Raine found she loved working with the animals. The hours she spent at the shelter flew by. She barely had enough time to run home to change, after dropping off Dr. Frank, before heading off to work.

As she entered the emergency department, she saw Caleb standing in the arena. When his gaze locked on hers, her stomach knotted with tension. Was she really up for this? Working in Trauma with Caleb? She quickly glanced around, looking for the charge nurse, determined to avoid being assigned to his team.

Unfortunately, there were only two trauma-trained nurses on duty for the second shift, so she had no choice but to work in the trauma bay. And, of course, Caleb was assigned to the trauma bay as well.

Her stomach continued to churn as she took report from the offgoing nurse. As they finished, a wave of nausea hit hard, and she put a hand over her stomach, gauging the distance to the bathroom.

She swallowed hard, trying to figure out what was wrong. Could she have somehow gotten the virus that seemed to be plaguing the animals at the shelter? She'd have to remember to ask Dr. Frank if animal-to-people transfer was even possible.

Sipping white soda from the nearby vending machine helped and Raine tried to concentrate on her work. They'd transferred their recent patient up to the ICU but within moments they'd received word that Lifeline, the air-rescue helicopter, had been called to the scene of a crash involving car versus train.

Sarah, the other trauma nurse on duty, was restocking the supplies so Raine used the few moments of free time to head into the bathroom.

As she fought another wave of nausea, she leaned over the sink and thought of Elana. This must be how her friend had felt with her horrible bouts of morning sickness.

Her eyes flew open at the implication and she stared at her pale reflection in shock. Could it be? No. Oh, no. She couldn't handle this.

Her knees went weak and she sank down onto the seat of the commode. Counting backwards, the sickness in her stomach threatened to erupt as she realized it had been just over four weeks since her last period.

CHAPTER THREE

DEAR God, what if she was pregnant?

No, she couldn't be. There was just no way she could handle this right now. Especially considering the circumstances under which she might have conceived. She shied away from the dark memories.

She didn't have time to fall apart. Not when there was a serious trauma on the way. Car versus train, and the train always won in that contest. She took several deep breaths, pulling herself together with an effort.

She couldn't think about this right now, she just couldn't. It was possible she had flu, nothing more. She had to stop jumping to conclusions. She'd been through a lot of stress lately. Far more stress than the average person had to deal with. There were plenty of reasons for her period to be late. And it wasn't really late. She could get her period any day now.

But the nagging fear wouldn't leave her alone.

She used the facilities and then splashed cold water on her face in a vain attempt to bring some color back to her cheeks. She stopped in the staff lounge to rummage for some crackers to nibble on as she made her way back to the trauma bay.

The pager at her waist beeped. She glanced at the display. *Thirty-five-year-old white male with multiple crushing injuries to torso and lower extremities. Intubated in the field, transfusing four units of O negative blood. ETA five minutes.*

Five minutes. She took another sip of white soda and finished the cracker. She couldn't decide if she should be upset or relieved when the cracker and white soda combination helped settle her stomach.

"What's wrong?" Caleb demanded when she entered the trauma bay a few moments later. "You look awful."

"Gee, thanks so much," she said sarcastically. "I really needed to hear that."

"I'm sorry, but I wanted to make sure that you're okay to work," Caleb amended. "The trauma surgeon has requested a hot unload. We need to get up to the helipad, they're landing in two minutes."

"I'm okay to work," she repeated firmly, determined to prove it by not falling apart as she had last night. Every day was better than the last one—hadn't her counselor stressed the importance of moving forward? She was living proof the strategy worked. "Let's go."

She and Caleb took the trauma elevators, located in the back of the trauma bay, up to the helipad on the roof of the hospital. At first the confines of the elevator bothered her, but she inhaled the heady scent of Caleb's aftershave, which pushed the bad memories away and reminded her of happier times. When they reached the helipad, they found the trauma surgeon, Dr. Eric Sutton, was already standing there, waiting. Lifting her hand to shield her eyes against the glare of the sun, Raine watched as the air-rescue chopper approached. The noise of the aircraft made it impossible to speak.

When the helicopter landed, they waited until they saw the signal from the pilot to approach, ducking well below the blades. The Lifeline transport team, consisting of a physician and a nurse, helped lift the patient out of the back hatch of the chopper.

"He's in bad shape, losing blood fast," the Lifeline physician grimly informed them. "In my opinion, you need to take him directly to the OR."

"Sounds like a plan. We can finish resuscitating him there," Dr. Sutton agreed. "Let's go."

In her year of working Trauma, she'd only transported a handful of patients directly to the OR. They all squeezed into the trauma elevator around the patient, Greg Hanson. She kept her gaze on the portable monitor, trying to ignore the close confines of the elevator as they rode back down to the trauma OR suite located on the second floor, directly above the ED.

The elevators opened into the main hallway of the OR. The handed the gurney over to the OR staff who were waiting, taking precious moments to don sterile garb before following the patient into the room.

"Caleb, I need a central line in this guy—he needs at least four more units of O neg blood," Sutton said.

They fell into a trauma resuscitation rhythm, only this time the trauma surgeon had taken the lead instead of Caleb. As Eric Sutton was assessing the extent of the patient's crushing leg wounds, she and Caleb worked together to get Greg Hanson's blood pressure up to a reasonable level.

She didn't know the circumstances about why Greg Hanson's car had been on the railroad tracks and as she hung four more units of blood on the rapid infusor, she found herself hoping this hadn't been a suicide attempt.

Being in close proximity to Caleb put all her senses on alert. But when his shoulders brushed against hers, she didn't flinch. She tried to see that as a sign she was healing.

"Here," she said, handing him the end of the rapid infuser tubing once he'd gotten the central line placed. "Connect this so I can get the blood started."

Caleb took the tubing from her hands, his fingers warm against hers. Eric and the OR nurse were prepping the patient's legs to begin surgery and the anesthesiologist was already putting the patient to sleep, but for a fraction of a second their gazes clung, as if they were all alone in the room.

"Great. All set," Caleb said, breaking the nearly tangible connection. "Start the blood."

She turned on the rapid infuser, rechecking the lines to make sure everything was properly connected. She took four more units of blood, confirmed the numbers matched, and then set them aside to be hung as soon as the other four had been transfused into their patient. She could see by the amount of blood already filling the large suction canisters that he was going to need more.

"Draw a full set of labs, Raine," Caleb told her.

She did as he asked, handing them over to the anesthesia tech, who ran them to the stat lab. She began hanging the new units of blood when the current bags were dry.

"I think we have things under control here," the anesthesiologist informed them a few minutes later. Taking a peek over the sterile drape, she could see Dr. Sutton was already in the process of repairing a torn femoral artery.

She was loath to leave, feeling as if there was still more they could do. But now that the anesthesiologist had put the patient to sleep, he'd taken over monitoring the rapid infuser, along with the anesthesia tech.

They really weren't needed here any longer.

Caleb put a hand on her arm, and she glanced up at him. The warmth in his gaze made it seem as if the last four weeks of being apart hadn't happened. "Come on, we need to get back down to the trauma bay."

"All right," she agreed, following him out of the OR suite. Outside the room, they stripped off the sterile garb covering their scrubs.

"Good work, Raine," Caleb told her, as they headed down to the trauma bay.

"Thanks. You too," she murmured, sending him a sideways glance. From the first time she'd met Caleb, there had been an undeniable spark between them. An awareness that had only intensified as they'd worked together.

His kisses had made her head spin. There was so much about him that she'd admired. And a few qualities she didn't.

Working together just now to save Greg Hanson's life had only reinforced how in sync they were. They made a great team.

Professional team, not a personal one, she reminded herself.

The nauseous feeling returned and she glanced away, feeling hopelessly desperate.

Impossible to go back and change the mistakes and subsequent events of the past, no matter how much she wished she could.

Caleb couldn't seem to keep his gaze off Raine. The adrenalin rush that came from helping to save a patient's life seemed to make everything around him stand out in sharp definition. Especially her. Raine's dark red hair, her pale skin, her bright blue eyes had beckoned to him from the moment they'd met.

She was so beautiful. His fingers itched to stroke her skin. Memories of how sweetly she'd responded to his kisses flooded his mind. Along with a stab of regret. If only he'd have handled things differently, they might have been able to make their relationship work.

His fault. She'd pushed him away, but it was all his fault. Because he'd jumped to conclusions.

Raine had tried to talk to him, but he hadn't been very receptive. And then Jake had come to apologize. Confessing that he'd had too much to drink and had made a pass at Raine.

So he'd called her back, prepared to apologize, but she'd refused to take his calls.

He wished, more than anything, that she'd talk to him. Allow him to clear things up between them. But instead she'd gone to work in the minor care area, located at the opposite end of the ED from the trauma bay.

He and Raine made a great team on a professional level. He shouldn't dwell on the fact they couldn't seem to make the same connection on a personal one.

"Where's my brother? Greg Hanson?" a frantic voice asked, as they walked past the ED patient waiting area.

Caleb stopped to address the young man. "He's in surgery. We can let the trauma surgeon, Dr. Eric Sutton, know you're here waiting for him."

"Surgery?" The man's expression turned hopeful. "So he's going to make it?"

"I'm sorry, but it's a little too early to say for sure,

although I think he has a good fighting chance," Caleb told him. He glanced at Raine, who gave a nod of encouragement.

"His vital signs were stabilizing when we left," she added.

"Good, that's good." The young man sighed. "Greg's wife and baby are being examined to make sure they didn't sustain any injuries. He risked his life to save them. His wife, Lora, panicked when her van got stuck on the railroad tracks. She didn't want to leave because the baby was in the back seat. He pulled her out of the car first, and then yanked the baby out just as the train hit."

He heard Raine's soft gasp. "Dear heavens," she murmured.

Caleb grimly agreed. The guy was a hero, and he could only hope the poor guy didn't suffer irreparable damage to his legs as a result of his actions. "Are his wife and baby both here?"

"The baby's at Children's Memorial, my wife is over there with their daughter now. Lora's here, the doctor is seeing her now. As soon as they're medically cleared, we'll all be here waiting to hear about Greg's condition."

"I'll let the trauma surgeon know," Caleb promised.

"Thank you," the young man said gratefully.

He and Raine returned to the trauma bay. He made the call up to the OR, leaving a message with the OR circulating nurse about Greg's family. She passed the word on to Eric Sutton, who reassured them he'd come to the waiting room to talk to the family as soon as he was finished.

Satisfied, he hung up the phone. There was a lull in the action. Trauma was either busy or slow, and he found himself looking once again for Raine.

They needed to talk. He just couldn't let her go without a fight. Maybe it was crazy, but the awareness still shimmering between them made him believe in second chances.

He found her in the staff lounge, sipping a soda. She looked surprised to see him.

"I was surprised to see you earlier today. You never mentioned working at the animal shelter while we were going out," he said, being careful to sound casual and not accusatory.

She met his gaze briefly, before glancing away. "No, I didn't. I've only been volunteering at the animal shelter for the past month or so."

The past month. Since their break-up. For some reason, the timing bothered him.

"Your dad is a sweetheart," she continued, staring down into the depths of her soft drink. "He's a great vet, really wonderful with animals. Everyone at the shelter loves him."

Strange, Raine had never struck him as being an animal lover, although now that he knew she was, he wondered what else he hadn't known about her.

And why did it matter now?

"Yeah, my dad has quite the female fan club," he said dryly. "Just ask any of his ex-wives."

She frowned at him and he immediately felt guilty for the lame joke.

"My dad is a great guy," he amended. "He does have a special talent for working with animals."

Raine nodded thoughtfully. And then she suddenly jumped to her feet. "Look, Caleb, I'm sorry things didn't work out between us on a personal level. But at least we know we can work together, right? We helped save Greg's life. Surely that counts for something."

Her words gave him the opportunity he needed.

"Raine, I'm sorry. I shouldn't have accused you of seeing Jake behind my back."

She stared at him with wide blue eyes. "Why were you so ready to believe the worst?" she asked in a low voice.

He swallowed hard, knowing she deserved the truth. "I had a bad experience with being cheated on in the past," he finally admitted. "I walked in and found my fiancée in bed with another man."

"I see." She frowned and broke away from his gaze.

Did she? He doubted it. "Look, Raine, I know now that I overreacted. Jake explained everything."

She brought her gaze, full of reproach, up to his. "So did I, remember? The next day, when I called you?"

He didn't know what to say to that, because what she said was the truth. She had tried to explain, but he hadn't believed her.

"You listened to Jake, but you didn't listen to me," Raine murmured, her blue eyes shadowed with pain. "I guess that sums everything up right there."

Panic gripped him by the throat. "Raine, please. Give me another chance."

She sighed and rubbed her temples. "It's too late, Caleb. There were a lot of other signs that you didn't trust me, but I tried to ignore them. The way you kept asking me where I was going and who I was going to be with. The night with Jake only solidified what I already knew."

"I learned my lesson," he quickly protested. "I promise, this time I'll trust you."

But she was already shaking her head. "It's not that

easy, Caleb. Trust comes from within. You have to believe with your whole heart."

His whole heart? Her words nagged at him. Because he cared about Raine a lot. But had he loved her? He'd thought things were heading in that direction, but now he wasn't so sure.

Those feelings of intense betrayal, when he'd seen her with Jake, had haunted him. Had made him think the worst about her.

He remembered how Raine had tried to explain how thrilled and relieved she'd been to be away from the overbearing scrutiny of her three older brothers. At first she'd teasingly accused him of being just like them.

But then she'd become more resentful.

And he'd accused her of cheating on him.

No wonder she'd wanted a break.

Still, he wanted another chance. Even though there was something different about her. A shadow in her eyes that hadn't been there before. The Raine he'd worked with tonight didn't seem to be the same person she'd been a month earlier.

Because of him?

Caleb's stomach twisted with regret. He hadn't told her about his mother abandoning him and his father, taking off to follow her dream of being a dancer. Or the string of stepmothers and almost stepmothers. Obviously, he should have.

"Raine, I'm sorry. I know I don't deserve another chance, but—" He stopped when their pagers went off simultaneously.

Sixty-nine-year-old male passed out at home, pulse irregular and slow, complaining of new onset chest pain. ETA three minutes.

"How about we focus on being friends?" she said. "Excuse me, but I need to make sure everything is ready for our new patient." Raine brushed past him to head towards the trauma room.

He followed more slowly, watching as Raine and Sarah double-checked the equipment and supplies they had on standby.

They didn't have to wait long. When the doors from the paramedic bay burst open, he was assailed by a strange sense of déjà vu as the paramedic crew wheeled in their new arrival.

Raine's sudden gasp made him frown. And in the next second he understood as he recognized the patient too.

His father.

CHAPTER FOUR

Raine glanced at Caleb, worried about his reaction. She couldn't imagine how it would feel to have your father being wheeled into the trauma bay.

She grabbed the closest ED tech. "Ben, run to the arena and ask Dr. Garrison to come over." She stepped up to put the elderly vet on the heart monitor. Caleb couldn't function as his father's physician. Especially when Dr. Frank's face was sweaty and pale, his eyes closed and his facial muscles drawn, as if he was in extreme pain.

Caleb surprised her by stepping up and taking control. "He's still bradycardic. Raine, start oxygen at two liters per minute. Send a cardiac injury panel and then we'll run a twelve-lead EKG."

"He'll need something for pain, too." The paramedic had placed the oxygen on, so she concentrated on drawing blood, knowing they needed the results stat in order to determine if he should go straight to the cardiac cath lab. But Dr. Frank's pain was her next priority.

"Dr. Garrison can't come," Ben announced when he returned from the arena, a tad short of breath himself. "He's about to deliver a baby."

"A baby?" Raine echoed in shocked amazement. Good grief, could things get any worse? She shot a quick glance at Caleb before giving his father two milligrams of morphine. And then called for the EKG tech.

"I'm fine," Caleb said in a low tone, answering her unspoken question. "We're going to need to call the cardiologist anyway, since I'm sure my father is having an acute myocardial infarct."

"Can't you…just call it…a heart attack?" his father asked in a feebly sarcastic tone.

"Dr. Frank, you need to try to relax," Raine urged, putting a reassuring hand on his arm. "We don't know for sure that you're having a heart attack, but we're going to do all the preliminary tests just in case."

The vet ignored her, his gaze locked on his son. "I should have…told you."

Raine glanced up at Caleb, who'd come up to stand beside his father. She continued to record vital signs as they spoke.

"Should have told me what?" Caleb asked urgently. "Have you had chest pain before?"

"No. Dizzy spells." Caleb's father spoke in short phrases, his breathing still labored. Raine cranked up the oxygen to five liters per minute as his pulse ox reading was only 89 percent. "I got dizzy-and fell off… the ladder."

Caleb's breath hissed out between his teeth. But his tone was surprisingly gentle. "Yes, you should have told me."

"Denial…can be…very powerful." His father's eyes were shadowed with regret.

Raine stepped in with a bright smile, trying to ease the tension between father and son. "Well, thank heavens you're here now. Don't worry, Dr. Frank, we're going to take good care of you."

"You're…a sweet girl…Raine."

Caleb's smile was strained. "Dad, Geoff Lyons is the cardiologist on call, he should be here to see you shortly. How's your chest pain? Any better?"

"Not much," his dad answered.

"Raine, start him on a nitroglycerine drip. If that doesn't help, we'll give him another two milligrams of morphine."

She was already crossing over to the pharmaceutical dispensing machine to fetch a bottle of nitroglycerine and more morphine.

The phone rang and she could hear Caleb crossing over to answer it. She listened as he repeated the critical troponin level of 2.4 and gave his name before hanging up.

His father was more alert than he let on. "Guess I've…earned a trip…to the cath lab."

"Yes." Caleb glanced up in relief when Dr. Geoff Lyons walked in.

"What's going on?" Geoff asked.

Raine gave Dr. Frank more morphine as Caleb and Geoff discussed the results of the EKG and the lab work. She stayed by his side as Dr. Lyons made arrangements for Caleb's dad to be transferred to the cardiac cath lab.

"You'll be fine," Raine told him reassuringly, as she connected him to the transport monitor.

"I'll see you after the procedure, Dad," Caleb added.

"Caleb…take care of Grizz for me," his father whispered.

"I will. I'll run and get him after my shift." Caleb squeezed his father's hand and then stepped back.

"Is there someone else we should call?" Raine asked

him softly, as the cardiac team whisked Caleb's dad away. "Your mom? Brothers or sisters?"

"No." Caleb gave a deep sigh. "My dad isn't married at the moment and he's recently broken up with his current lady friend, Sharon. My mother took off years ago, and she has her own family now."

The way he spoke of his mother, so matter-of-fact, wrenched her heart. He'd never mentioned his mother leaving before. What sort of mother abandoned her son? No wonder Caleb found it hard to believe in women. "I'm sorry," she said helplessly.

"Not your fault." Caleb brushed her sympathy aside as if determined to make her believe he was over it. "We'd better get ready for the next patient."

"The next patient?" She stared at him as if he'd lost his mind. "Caleb, your father is having a heart procedure. I'm sure one of the physicians would be willing to cover for you."

"I'm fine. There's nothing I can do until after his procedure is over anyway." His dark, stormy gray eyes warned her not to say anything more, before he turned and walked away.

Caleb was determined to finish his shift, even though his thoughts kept straying to his father.

He didn't blame his dad for not telling him about the dizzy spells. Rather, he was upset with himself. He should have forced his father to go in to be checked out when he'd fallen off the ladder in the first place.

If he'd have listened to his gut instinct, it was possible he could have prevented the additional damage to his father's heart.

He could feel Raine's concerned gaze following him as they worked on their next patient, an abdominal stabbing sustained during a bar fight. The tip of the blade had just missed the diaphragm, which was lucky as that meant his breathing wasn't impaired, but Caleb was certain either the stomach or the intestines had been hit.

"Raine, we need to explore the depth of the wound," he informed her.

She nodded her understanding and quickly began prepping the area with antimicrobial solution before spreading several sterile drapes around the wound. Once he'd donned his sterile gear, he reached for a scalpel. "Hold the retractor for me, will you? Like this."

She did as he asked, opening the wound so he could see better. The damage wasn't as bad as he'd expected, although the laceration in the small intestine meant the patient would need surgery. He irrigated the wound with sterile saline to help clean it out. "Okay, that's all we can do here. Put a dressing over this, would you? I need to get in touch with the general surgeon on call. This guy needs a small bowel resection."

Once he'd gotten their stab patient transferred to the care of the general surgeon, he checked his watch, wondering how his father was doing. A good hour had passed since he'd been taken up to the cardiac cath lab.

"Caleb? There's a phone call for you." Raine's expression was troubled as she handed him the receiver.

The display on the phone indicated the call was from the OR, not the cath lab. Was this regarding his stab-wound patient? "This is Dr. Stewart."

"Caleb, it's Geoff Lyons. I'm sorry to tell you that your father's condition took a turn for the worse. We had to abort the attempt to place a stent. I called a cardiothoracic surgeon in for assistance. Dr. Summers has taken him to the OR for three-vessel cardiac bypass surgery."

Raine watched the blood drain from Caleb's face and feared the news wasn't good. When he hung up the phone, she crossed over to him. "What's wrong? Your father?"

"In the OR, having cardiac bypass surgery." Caleb's expression was grim. "They couldn't get the stent placed and his condition grew very unstable, so they called in the surgeon."

"I'm sorry," she murmured, feeling helpless. "Do you want me to call Dr. Garrison to cover you? There's only about an hour and a half left of the shift."

"I'll talk to him," Caleb said. She was somewhat surprised he'd given in. Of course, there was a huge difference between having a cardiac cath procedure and full-blown open-heart surgery.

Dr. Joe Garrison agreed to cover and luckily the steady stream of trauma calls seemed to dwindle. At the end of her shift, she transferred her last patient to the ICU and then was free to go.

Raine couldn't bring herself to head home, though. Instead, after she swiped out, she went to the OR waiting room to find Caleb.

He was sitting with his elbows propped on his knees, his head cradled in his hands. He looked so alone, she was glad she'd come.

"Hey," she said, dropping into the seat beside him. "Have you heard anything?"

He lifted his head to look at her, his forehead furrowed with lines of exhaustion. "Not really, other than a quick call to let me know this could take hours yet. Is your shift over already?"

"Yes, and don't worry, it was relatively quiet. Not a problem at all for Dr. Garrison to cover."

Caleb nodded. "I'm glad. I was just thinking about whether or not I should leave for a while to pick up Grizz. I'm sure he'll need to go outside soon."

"I can run and let him out if you like," she offered. "I'd take him home with me, but my apartment doesn't allow dogs."

"Thanks, but I need to get him moved into my house anyway, now that Dad's going to be in the hospital for a while." Caleb rubbed the back of his neck and slowly stood.

She stared at him, wondering about this sudden urge to pick up the dog. Was he looking for an excuse to get away from her?

And, really, could she blame him? He'd asked for a second chance, but she'd refused.

But they could still be friends, couldn't they?

"Do you want some company?" she asked lightly.

He hesitated for a moment, and then nodded. "Sure."

Okay, so maybe Caleb wasn't looking for an excuse to avoid her. She had to stop second-guessing his motives. She stood and followed him to the parking structure where all the ED employees parked. "Do you want me to drive?"

He shook his head. "I'll drive."

She wasn't surprised—her brothers would have said the exact same thing. She didn't understand the macho need to drive, but figured it had something to do with wanting to be in control. She slid into the passenger seat, remembering the last time she'd ridden with Caleb.

On their last date before the Jake fiasco. A romantic dinner and a trip to the theater to see *Phantom of the Opera*. She'd never enjoyed herself more.

Regret twisted like a knife in her heart.

Caleb didn't say anything on the short ride to his father's house. She pushed aside her own tangled emotions, understanding that at this moment, Caleb was deeply worried about his father. And she certainly couldn't blame him.

She was worried too.

"Your dad is strong, Caleb. He's going to pull through this just fine."

He glanced at her and nodded. "I know. It's just…" His voice trailed off.

"What?" she asked.

He let out a heavy sigh. "My dad and I don't see eye-to-eye on a lot of things, but that doesn't mean I don't love him. I just wish I would have told him that before he left to go to the cardiac cath lab. I should have said the words."

Her heart squeezed in her chest. She reached out to lightly touch his arm. "He knows, Caleb. Your dad knows how much you love him."

He didn't respond, but pulled into his father's driveway. She'd been there earlier that day, when she'd driven Dr. Frank home from the animal shelter. He got out of the car and she followed him into the dark house.

"Hi, Grizz." Caleb smiled a bit when the dog greeted them enthusiastically, trying to lick both of them in his excitement to see them.

"Grizz, you're just a big old softie, aren't you?" Raine said, stroking his wiggling body.

"Will you take him out into the back yard for me?"

Caleb asked. "I need to get all his stuff packed into the car as he's coming home with me."

"Sure. Come on, Grizz," she called, walking through the house, flicking on lights as she went. The back door was in the kitchen, and she followed the dog outside, waiting patiently while he took care of business.

He bounded toward her soon afterwards and she stroked his silky fur. "I bet you're already missing Dr. Frank, aren't you?" she murmured. "Don't worry, I'm sure Caleb is going to take good care of you."

She took Grizz back inside the house to find Caleb lugging a forty-pound bag of dog food out to his car.

"All set?" she asked as he closed the trunk.

"Yes." He opened the back passenger door. "Come on, Grizz, you get the whole back seat to yourself."

The ride to Caleb's house didn't take long and when she followed him inside, she was assaulted by memories. Good memories. Painfully good memories. She averted her gaze from the sofa where she and Caleb had very nearly made love.

She wished more than ever she'd made love to Caleb that night. Now it was too late.

She put a hand to her stomach, surprised to note her earlier attack of nausea seemed to have gone away. Determined to hope for the best, she told herself that was a good thing. Maybe the sickness was nothing more than a touch of flu.

Grizz paced around Caleb's house, sniffing at everything with interest. When he'd finished exploring his new surroundings, and apparently deemed them acceptable, he made himself comfortable by flopping on Caleb's sofa.

She heard Caleb sigh, but he didn't make Grizz get

down. Instead, he reached over to scratch the silky fur behind his ears. "I'll be back later, Grizz, okay?"

The dog thumped his tail on the sofa in agreement.

Raine followed Caleb back outside to his car. The ride back to the hospital was quiet.

When he'd parked the car, he turned toward her. "Thanks for coming with me, Raine."

"You're welcome." She tilted her head curiously, wondering if he was wanting to get rid of her. "Ready to head inside to see if there's any news on your dad?"

He took the key from the ignition and flashed a tired smile. "Raine, it's well after midnight. I appreciate everything you've done, but I'm sure you're exhausted. It's fine if you'd rather head home."

Slowly she shook her head. No matter what had transpired between her and Caleb in the past, there was no way in the world she could just walk away. Not now. She opened her passenger side door with determination. "Let's find out how he's doing, okay? Then I'll head home."

Caleb didn't protest when she followed him inside, riding the elevator up to the waiting room. She wanted to believe he was glad to have her around, but suspected he was just too tired to argue.

The desk in the waiting room was empty. Apparently the volunteers who usually manned the area had already gone home for the night.

She stood off to the side, while Caleb picked up the phone to call up to the OR.

"This is Caleb Stewart. Is there any news on my father, Frank Stewart?"

Raine couldn't hear what was said on the other end of the line, but when Caleb nodded and murmured thanks, before hanging up, she couldn't help asking, "Is he still in surgery?"

"Yeah. They're finished with the main portion of the procedure, and they're starting to close him now. They estimate he'll be in the ICU within the hour."

The knotted muscles in her neck eased. "That's good news."

"Yeah, although apparently he ended up having his aortic valve replaced too, in addition to the repairs to his coronary arteries." Caleb scrubbed a hand over his face. "But he's hanging in there, so I'm going to keep hoping for the best."

She watched as he crossed over to take a seat. He glanced up in surprise when she followed. "Raine, I don't expect you to hang out here with me indefinitely."

They may have dated for two months, but he obviously didn't know her very well. Why was he so anxious to believe the worst about her? Just because he'd been cheated on in the past? Was it possible he was incapable of trusting her at all? Maybe. But no matter what had transpired between them, she couldn't have left him alone in that waiting room if her life had depended on it.

She dropped into the seat beside him, curling her legs underneath her. "I'm not leaving, Caleb. I'm staying."

CHAPTER FIVE

CALEB glanced over at Raine sitting in the waiting-room chair, her eyes closed as she'd finally given in to her exhaustion. He stared at her, watching her sleep, trying to figure her out.

After not seeing her for the past month, it was scary how easily they'd ended up here together. He almost reached out to brush a strand of hair away from her eyes, but stopped himself just in time. He didn't want to read too much into her actions, but he couldn't help from wondering if her staying here with him meant she was willing to give him another chance.

And would he mess things up again, if she did?

He let out a heavy sigh, wishing he knew the answer to that one. Raine was beautiful, smart and funny. He'd enjoyed just being with her. But he couldn't blame the demise of their relationship solely on her. He owned a big piece of the problem.

Trust didn't come easy. And he didn't have a clue how to fix the tiny part of him that always held back. The tiny part of him that always doubted.

The tiny part of him that constantly expected and saw the worst.

The door to the waiting room swung open, distracting him from his reverie. An older man dressed in scrubs, a surgical mask dangling around his neck, emerged through the doorway. He recognized him as Dr. Steve Summers, one of the cardiothoracic surgeons who operated out of Trinity Medical Center.

"Raine?" Caleb reached over to gently shake her shoulder to wake her up.

At his touch, she bolted upright and recoiled from him, her eyes wide and frightened as she frantically looked around the room. "What?"

He frowned, bothered by her reaction. Had he interrupted a bad dream? He gestured to the CT surgeon who was approaching. "The doctor is here."

"Caleb Stewart?" the cardiothoracic surgeon asked, as he crossed over to shake his hand. "Steve Summers. I thought your name was familiar. I recognize you from the ED. Your father has been transferred to the ICU. I had to replace his aortic valve along with three of his coronary arteries. His heart took a bad hit and he lost a fair amount of blood, but seems to be holding his own at the moment."

Caleb knew that was a tactful way of saying his father was still in a critical condition. He'd used the same lines with family members himself. "How long do you think he'll need to stay in the ICU?"

"At least a day or two." Steve glanced curiously at Raine, no doubt recognizing her too, but then turned back to Caleb. "If he stays stable over the next couple of hours, I'll take him off the ventilator. The sooner we can get him breathing on his own, the shorter his recovery time should be."

"Can Caleb go up to see him?" Raine asked.

"Sure. Just give the nurses a couple of minutes to get

things settled, and then you can head up." The surgeon flashed a tired smile. "I'm sure he's going to do just fine."

Caleb wished he could be as sure, but he nodded anyway and shook the surgeon's hand gratefully. "Thanks again."

The surgeon returned the handshake before turning to leave. He glanced at Raine. "Do you want to come upstairs to the ICU with me?"

She hesitated, her arms crossed defensively over her chest, her expression uncertain. "I'd be happy to come up if you like, but I don't want to intrude. He's your father. I'm just an acquaintance."

The way she backed off made him question her motives for staying in the first place. Maybe this was her way of telling him she was willing to be there for him, but only up to a point? She had told him they should just try being friends. It was possible she didn't want to come along because they weren't formally dating.

He swallowed the urge to ask her to come along, respecting the distance she apparently wanted to keep. Especially considering Raine had already gone above and beyond, sitting here with him while he'd waited to hear how his father had fared. Besides, it was already two in the morning and he understood she needed to get home. "Are you sure you're okay to drive?" he asked instead.

"Absolutely. I'm awake now." Her lopsided smile tugged at his heart. "Tell your dad I'm thinking about him and that he needs to get better soon, all right?"

"Sure." His fingers itched to touch her, to pull her close, seeking comfort in her warm embrace. But they were colleagues. Maybe even friends. Nothing more. "Take care."

"You too, Caleb," she said softly.

They left the waiting room together, but then parted ways, heading in opposite directions. For a long moment, he watched her heading toward the parking structure, fighting the desperate need to call her back.

Cursing himself for being a fool, he turned away, heading toward the elevator to go up to the critical care unit.

It felt strange to walk into the busy unit as a visitor rather than as a physician. When he approached his father's room, his footsteps slowed.

As a doctor, he'd known what to expect. But seeing his dad so pale, connected to all the machinery, it made his breath lodge in his throat. He took a moment to watch his father's vital signs roll across the screen on the monitor hanging over his bed. The numbers were reassuring, so he softly approached his father's bedside.

The bitter taste of regret filled his mouth. He reached down and took his father's hand in his. "I love you, Dad," he whispered.

His father's eyes fluttered open, his gaze locking on his. Caleb blinked away the dampness of tears and leaned forward, holding his father's gaze. "The surgery is over and you're doing fine, Dad," he assured him, knowing his father couldn't speak with the breathing tube in his throat. "I took Grizz to my house, so you don't need to worry about a thing. Just rest and get better soon, okay?"

His father nodded and then his eyes drifted shut, as if that brief interaction had been all he could manage. Caleb squeezed his father's hand again, and then slowly released it.

Part of him wanted to stay, but there was really no purpose. In fact, he had to get home to take care of Grizz, as he'd promised. His father needed to rest, anyway. There was nothing more he could do here.

Regretfully, he turned away. His dad was a fighter. He was sure his dad would feel better in the morning.

Caleb went home, surprisingly glad when Grizzly dashed over to greet him. He hadn't realized what a difference it made to come home to a pet rather than an empty house.

"Hey, Grizz, were you afraid I wasn't coming back?" He scratched the dog behind the ears. He let the dog outside and then made his way into the bedroom. Grizz followed, tail wagging, glancing around the new environment.

"I bet you miss him, don't you, boy?" Caleb murmured. Grizzly laid his head on the edge of the bed, staring up at him with large soulful brown eyes. "I know. I miss him, too."

It was true, he realized. He did miss his father. But, truth be told, he missed what he and Raine had once had together even more.

Raine had the next day off, so she didn't see either Caleb or Dr. Frank. But she called the ICU and was told Caleb's father was in serious but stable condition. Raine knew if she wanted more details, she'd have to ask Caleb.

Or visit Dr. Frank for herself.

She kept busy at the animal shelter, glad to see the animals were doing much better. Everyone was concerned about Dr. Frank, so she told them enough to satisfy their curiosity without violating his privacy.

The next day, Friday, she was scheduled to work, so she went to the hospital an hour early to sneak up to Dr. Frank's room for a quick visit. Normally, the ICU only allowed immediate family members to come up, but her hospital ID badge worked to open the doors so she was able to walk in.

She found Caleb's father's room easily enough.

"Hi, Raine," Dr. Frank greeted her with a tired smile. "How are you? How are things at the shelter?"

"They're fine. In fact, I brought you pictures. See?" She took several glossy photos out of her purse and spread them out over his bedside table, knowing he'd appreciate them more than a handful of balloons and a sappy card. "Rusty, Annie, Ace and Maggie all miss you."

Dr. Frank's smile widened when he saw the pictures of his favorite dogs at the shelter. There were dozens of animals at the shelter, but since she couldn't take pictures of them all, she'd focused on the dogs who'd been sick, so he could see how much better they were doing. "They're beautiful, Raine. Thanks. I wish I had a picture of Grizzly, too."

"I'm sure Caleb is taking good care of him," she said reassuringly. No matter how much Dr. Frank missed his dog, there was no way she was going to ask Caleb if she could stop by to take a picture of Grizz.

That would be taking their new-found fragile truce a little too far.

"He is. I just miss him," Dr. Frank said in a wistful tone.

"Everyone at the shelter hopes you get better soon. I didn't tell them much, only that you were in the hospital and doing fine."

The older man lifted a narrow shoulder. "I don't mind if they know about my surgery. Seems like they'll figure out something is wrong when I'm not able to work for several weeks."

"Okay, I'll let them know. When are you getting out of here?" Raine asked, changing the subject with a quick glance around his room. "I thought they were transferring you out of the ICU to a regular floor sometime soon."

"That's the plan." Dr. Frank's gaze focused on something past her shoulder so she turned round, in time to see Caleb walking into the room. Her heart lurched a bit in her chest but he wasn't smiling. She hadn't seen him in the past twenty-four hours, and had no idea why he might be upset.

Her stomach churned, the nausea that came and went seemingly at will, returning with a vengeance. Since the nausea hadn't been as bad over the past day or so, she'd convinced herself the sensation had been nothing more than her over-active imagination. Or a touch of flu.

Now she wasn't so sure. Suddenly her stomach hurt so badly she could barely stand upright. She swallowed hard and prayed she wouldn't throw up her breakfast. Fighting for control, she pushed away the desperate fear and worry. Enough playing the denial game. She needed to stop avoiding the possibility. She'd go and buy a stupid pregnancy test so that she knew for sure what was going on.

Everything inside her recoiled at the thought of being pregnant.

"Hi, Dad, you look much better today," Caleb said, crossing over to his father's bedside. He frowned a little when he glanced at Raine. "Are you all right?"

"Fine," she forced herself to answer cheerfully, when she felt anything but. Of course he'd noticed something was wrong. She wished Caleb was a little less observant. "Just hungry. I didn't eat anything for lunch. I'm going to get going now, so I can eat before my shift." She knew she was babbling, but didn't care. She wanted to get out of there, fast. "Take care, Dr. Frank, I'll let everyone at the shelter know you're doing better."

"All right. Thanks for the pictures, Raine." Caleb's dad looked better, but it was obvious he still tired easily. Just her short visit seemed to have worn him out.

She edged toward the door. "Bye, Caleb."

"See you later," he said as she practically ran from the room.

Raine sought refuge in the nearest ladies room, bending over and clutching her stomach until the urge to throw up passed. She didn't have time now, before work, but she was going to have to get a home pregnancy test soon.

Tonight.

And if it was positive, she'd deal with that news the same way she'd dealt with everything else that had happened.

Alone.

Raine was glad she was able to avoid the trauma room for her Friday night shift. The patients seen in the arena certainly needed care, but it wasn't the life-and-death action that the trauma bay held.

But moving to the arena didn't help her escape Caleb.

"You're working tonight?" she asked, when he walked in, hoping her dismay didn't show. The nausea she'd felt earlier hadn't gone away.

Caleb shrugged. "I'll need to take some time off once my dad is discharged from the hospital, so I figured I should work now."

Since his logic made sense, she couldn't argue. "He seems to be doing much better," Raine said.

"Yeah, he is." Caleb raked his fingers through his hair. "I guess they bumped me out of Trauma for tonight. Brock Madison is covering the trauma bay instead."

Probably in deference to what he was going through with his dad. Something she should have figured out for herself, before switching to work in the arena.

Elana had called off sick, so they were a little short-handed, but Raine didn't mind. If she could find a way to keep her emotions under control and her stomach from rebelling, she'd be fine.

Their sickest patient was a woman with congestive heart failure, who'd been taken into the arena when she'd first arrived, but then had quickly needed more care. They would have moved her to the trauma bay, except that they were busy with traumas, which meant they had to manage her here.

"Raine, have you sent the blood gases yet?" Caleb asked.

"Yes." She frowned, glancing at the clock. "The results should be back by now. I'll call the lab."

She made the phone call, gritting her teeth in frustration when the lab claimed they'd never got the specimen. She hung up the phone and turned toward Caleb. "The sample got lost in the tube system. I'll have to redraw it."

"That's fine." He kept his attention focused on the chart.

The night they'd saved Greg Hanson's life they'd been completely in sync. Now that companionable relationship seemed to have vanished. Her stomach lurched again, and she concentrated on drawing the arterial blood gas sample from Mrs. Jones, trying to ignore it.

"Yvonne?" she called out to the middle-aged female tech working on their team. "Will you run this to the lab? I don't want this one to get lost, too."

"Sure." Yvonne willingly took the blood tube from her hands.

"Thanks." She took another sip of her white soda, before logging into the system to document the latest set of vital signs. In the lull of waiting for the lab results, she escaped for a few minutes, seeking refuge in the staff lounge.

Closing her eyes, she tried to focus on staying calm. But the more her nausea plagued her, the more she tensed up. She took several deep breaths, pulled up her legs and rested her forehead on her knees.

She couldn't keep up the pretense much longer. She needed to know if she really was pregnant, and soon. She shouldn't have put it off as long as she already had. She should know by now that denial didn't work.

Hadn't Caleb's dad said something to that effect? About how denial was a powerful thing? After everything she'd gone through, she should know by now that denial was a death-trap. Better to face the things you were afraid of head-on.

Dr. Frank's heart attack had distracted her from her personal problems. Being with Caleb had certainly helped. She missed being with him, more than she'd ever imagined she would. Had she made a mistake in not confiding in him? Would their relationship have survived? Maybe. But even the thought of telling him made her nausea spike. No, it was better that she'd broken things off.

Her fault, not his. And there was no going back. Thinking about what might have been was nothing but foolish fantasy.

Even if Caleb could learn to trust her. Which was doubtful.

Especially now that the damage had been done.

"Raine?" Yvonne poked her head into the staff lounge. "There you are. Dr. Stewart is looking for you."

She pasted a smile on her face, hoping she didn't look as awful as she felt. "Okay, I'm coming."

Caleb glanced up when she approached. "We have her blood gases back and Margaret Jones needs to be transferred up to the medical ICU. You need to make the arrangements." His face was drawn into a slight scowl. "Next time I'd appreciate you telling me who's covering while you're on break."

"I was only gone ten minutes," she snapped. The surge of anger was a welcome respite from soul-wrenching desperation. "But, rest assured, I'll be sure to tell you every time I need to use the restroom so you'll know exactly where I am."

He stared at her for a long moment, before he let out a heavy sigh. "You're right, I was out of line. I'm sorry. Just call up to give report, will you? Our patient in room two, Jerry Applegate, with sutures over his left eye, is also ready to be discharged. I need you to move fast. I'm being asked to clear our patients out as the waiting room is full."

His apology diffused her annoyance. She needed to pull herself together.

She didn't want to lose the collaborative working relationship she and Caleb had managed to maintain in spite of their break-up. Especially not when their friendship seemed a bit tenuous.

She worked quickly to get Mrs. Jones transferred up to the medical ICU. As soon as that transfer was completed, she discharged Jerry Applegate, the man who'd had a few too many beers at the local tavern and had fallen and cut his eye. He'd sobered up the moment Caleb had placed the first suture. She began to ask him about the possibility of alcoholism, but he mumbled something about a retirement party, looking so embarrassed she ended up giving him the teaching materials on the subject rather than her usual spiel before sending him on his way.

The disinfectant used to clean his room wasn't even dry when the triage nurse called.

"We have a female assault victim," the triage nurse informed her. "I'm bringing her back to room two right away."

Raine didn't remember dropping the phone, but soon she realized the buzzing in her ears was actually the phone beeping because it was off the hook. Glancing down, she saw it was lying on its side. She fumbled a bit with the effort of picking up the receiver and placing it back in its cradle.

A female assault victim. Her mind could barely comprehend the news. She took a deep breath and let it out slowly. Surely this wasn't the same circumstances. No, it was more likely a result of some sort of domestic dispute. Like poor Becca. Tragic, yes, but not the same situation at all.

Yet she couldn't seem to make her feet move. She couldn't do this. She couldn't. Her stomach tightened painfully. She needed to find someone else to care for the patient. Anyone. If only Elana hadn't called in sick, her friend would have taken over in a heartbeat.

"Raine?" Yvonne poked her head out from behind the doorway of room two, her eyes wide with compassion and alarm. "I need you. Right away."

Oh, God. A quick glance at the other teams in the arena proved everyone was busy. There was no one to take her place. Four weeks had passed but at this moment it seemed as if it had only been four days.

Dread seeped from her pores as Raine forced herself to walk into the room. A young woman, about her age, was seated on the hospital bed, clutching the edges of a blanket she'd wrapped tightly around herself.

Numbly, Raine took the clipboard Yvonne shoved into her hands and glanced at the paperwork. The girl's name was Helen Shore and she was twenty-five years old. Dragging her gaze back to her patient, she noted the girl looked disheveled, her blonde hair tangled up in knots, her face pale and her mascara smudged beneath her eyes.

Pure instinct and compassion took over. Ignoring her own feelings and the persistent nausea, she stepped forward, keeping her tone low and soothing as she addressed the patient. "Helen, my name is Raine, and I'm a nurse. Can you tell me what happened?"

The girl's eyes filled with tears. "I don't know what happened. I can't remember. *I can't remember!*"

"Shh, it's okay." Raine crossed over to put a supporting arm around the girl's shoulders. She knew, only too well, exactly how Helen felt. The void where your memory should have been threatened to swallow you whole. Her own horrific experience had happened a month ago, but she was suddenly reliving every detail.

She pushed the fears away, trying to keep focused on Helen. The girl was her patient. The poor young woman had come here for help. "Do you have bruises? Do you hurt anywhere?"

Helen nodded, tears making long black streaks on her cheeks. "When I woke up…my clothes were off. And… was hurt. I think—I might have been raped."

CHAPTER SIX

THE room spun dizzily and Raine's knees buckled. She grabbed the edge of the bed, holding herself upright out of sheer stubbornness. But her mind whirled, drawing parallels matching the horrific experience she'd endured with this poor girl's situation.

She swallowed hard and tried to gather her scattered thoughts. She needed to get a grip. This wasn't about her. She needed to focus on the patient. Helen.

"Yvonne, please find Dr. Stewart, will you?" Raine wasn't sure how she managed to sound so calm. "I need him to approve some orders."

"Of course." Yvonne ducked from the room.

Helen tightened her grip on the blanket, her eyes wide and frightened in her face. "Is Dr. Stewart a man? Because I don't want him to examine me unless he's a woman."

The disjointed protest didn't make much sense, but Raine understood exactly what Helen was trying to tell her.

"Dr. Stewart is a man, but he won't examine you," she explained gently. "We have nurses, female nurses, who have special training as sexual assault experts to do that.

Dr. Stewart does need to write the orders, though. We'll need to draw some blood so we can run lab tests, to see if you have any drugs in your system."

"Drugs? I don't do drugs. Oh..." Helen's face paled and her eyes filled with fresh tears. "You mean he gave me something? Is that why I can't remember?"

Rohypnol was the drug they'd found in her bloodstream. But there were various date-rape drugs on the streets. She'd spent hours searching through the information on the internet. Even alcohol could be used to encourage a woman to do something she normally wouldn't do.

There were plenty of men who would take advantage of the opportunity.

Her skin felt cold and clammy, and she tightened her grip on the edge of Helen's bed in an effort to keep her mind grounded in reality. Thankfully the patient was too traumatized to realize there was something wrong with her nurse. Raine tried to speak calmly through the dull roaring in her ears. "We won't know until we get the test results back. When did this happen?"

"Last night, late. We closed the bar. But I didn't wake up until a couple hours ago. I slept all day. I never sleep all day."

Most likely because of the drugs. Especially if they were mixed with something else. "And were you drinking alcohol, too?"

"Yes." Helen dropped her chin to her chest, as if she couldn't bear to make eye contact. "Cosmo martinis."

The potent beverage may have been enough, but Raine didn't think so. Helen's total lack of memory sounded more like a date-rape drug than just alcohol alone. Men used it specifically so that the women they preyed upon couldn't remember anything incriminating.

To hide the extent of their crime.

"We need to contact the police," Raine said softly, knowing Helen wasn't going to like having to retell her story to the authorities. She wanted to say something reassuring, but couldn't think of a thing.

She knew better than most, there was no easy way to get through everything facing Helen from this point forward. Especially if there were long-term ramifications, like becoming pregnant.

Her patient didn't have a chance to respond to the news because at that moment the glass door slid open and Caleb walked in.

"Dr. Stewart, this is Helen Shore," Raine said, maintaining her professionalism with an effort. "We believe she's been sexually assaulted. We need an order for a drug screen and the SANE nurse." She stared at a spot over his left ear, hoping he couldn't tell how she was barely hanging onto her composure.

"Already done," he said. "Yvonne filled me in and the SANE nurse has already arrived. As soon as you're ready for the exam, she'll come in."

Raine froze. Oh, God. No. There was no way she could stay, not for this. She forced herself to meet his gaze. "Will you ask Yvonne to accompany Helen during the exam?"

He flashed a puzzled look, but nodded. "Sure."

Thank heavens. Raine released her death grip on the bed and walked towards the door.

But she didn't quite make it to the opening before her world went black.

Caleb reached out and grabbed Raine, hauling her upright before she hit the floor.

She was out cold, her head lolling against the crook of his arm, her dark red hair and smattering of freckles creating a stark contrast against her pale skin.

"What the—?" He swung her limp body into his arms and carried her to the only open bed they had on their team, room five. There was a minor burn patient from the waiting room slotted to be admitted in there, but he didn't care. At the moment Raine took priority. Gently, he set her on the bed.

Within seconds her eyelids fluttered open and she stared up at him in confusion. "What happened?"

"You tell me," he muttered, his voice grim. He was glad she'd come round so quickly, but couldn't help the sharp flash of concern and annoyance at how she obviously wasn't taking very good care of herself. He hadn't liked the awful way she'd looked awful earlier in his dad's room and now this. "You fainted. When's the last time you had something to eat?"

She winced and avoided his direct gaze. "I…um…ate before my shift."

He didn't believe her. "Take a break. Now." Caleb dragged a hand through his hair. She'd taken ten years off his life when she'd crumpled like a rag doll.

"I'm fine," she protested, pushing up on her elbows to sit upright. She ran a hand over her forehead and he could see the faint sheen of sweat dampening her fingertips. Her pulse was racing and her blood pressure was probably non-existent. "I never faint."

"Could have fooled me," he said, stepping forward to put a hand on her shoulder to keep her in place. "Give yourself a few minutes' rest before going back to work, would you? I'd rather arrange for someone to come in to give you a full physical exam. Please don't take this the wrong way, but you look like hell."

Her eyes widened in horror at the suggestion. "No. I'm fine. I don't want an exam."

"Raine." He stared at her until she met his gaze. "I'm not kidding. Tell me what's going on. What's wrong?"

"Nothing." She avoided his gaze in a way that made him grind his teeth in helpless frustration. Why wouldn't she open up to him? Talk to him? "I swear I just had a physical exam not too long ago. I'm fine."

He stared at her, willing her to open up about what was going on. But she sat up, swinging her legs over the edge of the bed as if to prove she was fine. "I'll be all right in a few minutes. In the meantime, I'll ask Ellen or Tracey to cover for me."

He couldn't force her to stay, but that didn't mean he was particularly happy when she stood on shaky legs. He stayed within reach, watching to make sure she didn't fall again.

It was ridiculous to be hurt by her decision. Raine couldn't have made her feelings any clearer. She didn't want or need his help.

There were no second chances. At least for him.

Biting back a curse, he told himself to let her go. Raine's issues, whatever they entailed, weren't his concern. She was making it clear they didn't have a personal relationship any more. And he had plenty of his own problems to deal with. Like his father, who was almost as stubborn as Raine.

Gingerly, she walked toward the door as if testing the strength in her legs, still looking as if a mild breeze would blow her over.

"Raine," he called, as she crossed the threshold. She glanced at him over her shoulder. "I'm here if you need to talk. Or if you just want someone to listen."

Stark desolation flashed in her eyes, but just as quickly it was gone. "Thanks, but I'm fine. Really. I'll be back in twenty minutes."

This time when she left, he didn't bother trying to stop her.

In Raine's absence, Caleb took control of the patients in their team, including taking on the job of calling the police for the young sexual assault victim.

Their patient care tech, Yvonne, had remained glued to the young woman's side throughout the rape kit exam and even when the police arrived to question her. He didn't complain, even knowing that without Yvonne's help, patients moved slowly through the department.

He kept his distance from Helen Shore, knowing from past experience that most assault patients were far more comfortable with female caregivers. But as he worked, he couldn't get the shattered expression on the young woman's face out of his mind.

Victims of crimes were the most difficult patients to care for. Sexual assaults were right up there next to child abuse, at least in his opinion. Getting angry wasn't exactly helpful to the patients, though, so he schooled his features so that his true disgust and rage toward the assailant didn't show. None of this was the victim's fault.

He could only hope the evidence they obtained would help the police find the bastard who'd hurt her.

When Raine returned, she looked marginally better. Maybe she had finally eaten something. Her face was still lined with exhaustion, though, and he couldn't help wondering why. She looked much worse tonight than she had the night she'd stayed with him in the waiting room. Telling himself that he'd done all he could to open up to her, and that the next move was hers, didn't help. He had little choice but to turn his attention to the matter at hand.

She jumped into the fray without hesitation, quickly picking up on the patient care issues that still needed to be addressed.

"Have we had the drug screen results back yet on Helen Shore?" he asked, when Raine brought him the discharge paperwork on their burn patient.

Her eyes darkened momentarily. "I don't know. I'll check."

He signed the paperwork and then glanced towards Helen's room. The police were still in there, taking her statement. He wasn't sure how much longer they would be, but it didn't really matter since he wasn't about to hurry her out the door.

"Drug screen is positive for flunitrazepam," Raine said, returning to the workstation with a slip of paper in her hand.

Flunitrazepam was the generic name for Rohypnol, the infamous date-rape drug. They wouldn't have the results from the rape kit for several days, but this pretty much sealed poor Helen's fate. There was no doubt in his mind that her rape kit would turn out positive. He sighed and took the results from Raine. "All right. I'll let the patient know."

"I'll go with you." Raine hovered near his elbow as he entered the room. The police officers, one male and one female glanced up at him curiously.

"I have your drug screen results," Caleb said, ignoring the police and focusing on the patient. "Would you rather the officers leave, so I can tell you privately?"

The male police officer looked like he was about to protest, but he needn't have worried, because Helen was already shaking her head.

"No, go ahead," Helen said in a voice barely above a whisper. "They'll need to know either way."

"I'm sorry, but you tested positive for Flunitrazepam, also known as Rohypnol." He handed the drug result to Helen, who barely glanced at it before handing it to the female police officer.

"So there's no mistake," Helen whispered. "He did this on purpose."

"I'm afraid so." Caleb wished there was something he could say or do to make her feel better.

"That's the second case of Rohypnol from the After Dark nightclub in the past few months," the female officer said in disgust. "Could be the same bastard."

Beside him, he heard Raine suck in a harsh breath. And then suddenly she was gone. When he finished in Helen's room, he found her out at the desk working on the computer.

"We have a new admission coming in, new onset abdominal pain," she told him as if nothing was wrong.

"Okay, let me know once you get a set of vitals and a baseline set of labs. Could be his gall-bladder."

"Sure." The forced cheerfulness in her tone bothered him.

But it wasn't until much later, that he realized why. That the shattered look in Helen Shore's eyes reminded him too much of the haunted expression in Raine's.

Raine could barely concentrate as she prepared a summary report for the on-coming shift. Her assault and Helen's may have been by the same person. The idea was staggering. She hoped and prayed the police would find the guy, and soon.

After she finished with report, she gave a small sigh of relief. At last, her interminable shift was over. All she needed to do was to finish up the discharge paperwork on Helen Shore and she could leave.

Taking a deep breath, she entered Helen Shore's room. Yvonne had left the patient's bedside at eleven, since there was currently a hospital ban on over-time. Helen had dressed in her clothes but clutched the blanket around her shoulders, like a lifeline. Raine could relate, and she had no intention of taking it away from her.

"I have your discharge paperwork, Helen." Raine approached her bedside and handed her the slip of paper listing her follow up appointment for the next week. "Do you have any questions before you go?"

Helen slowly shook her head. "No. The other nurse told me she wouldn't have the rest of my test results for a few days. Not that it matters, much," she added bitterly. "I doubt the police will ever find the guy."

"They will." Raine injected confidence in her tone, even though she held the same doubts. She pulled up a chair to sit beside her. "Helen, you need to seek professional help in order to get through this. I know the name of a good therapist, if you don't have one."

"The social worker gave me a list." Helen stared morosely down at her hands. "But what good is talking about it? Doesn't change what happened."

"No, it won't." Raine empathized with the young woman's helpless anger. Especially if it was possible the same guy attacked them both. The After Dark nightclub should be forced to close until this bastard was caught.

Even the police didn't believe it was a coincidence. Detective Carol Blanchard had promised to be in touch if she had any evidence, but so far Raine hadn't heard a thing.

She gathered her scattered thoughts. "There are support groups, however. Other young women like yourself, who've been through the same thing." Raine had attended one of the support group meetings, but hadn't found it particularly helpful. She offered the option though, because everyone coped differently.

And she was hardly the expert in coping strategies. She'd thought she was doing so well.

Only to fall completely apart, tonight.

"I'm afraid to go home," Helen admitted in a low voice. "He knows where I live. What if he comes back?"

Raine understood. She'd experienced the exact same fear. In fact, she hoped to move once her lease was up. And she'd been sleeping on the sofa with Spice, unable to face her bed. "Do you have someone to stay with you?"

"I could ask my sister."

Raine gave a nod of encouragement. "I think that's a good idea. And add a deadbolt lock to your door if you don't have one already. Literature shows that date-rape perpetrators don't go back to the same victims, but it doesn't hurt to be extra-careful."

"I will, thanks."

She leaned over and covered the woman's hand with hers. "Remember, Helen, you're not alone. Try the support group, or talking to a therapist. Unfortunately, date rape is more common than the average person realizes."

Helen lifted her head to meet her gaze. "Sounds like you've had some experience with this," she said.

For a moment Raine longed to blurt out the truth. But she was supposed to be the nurse, helping and supporting the patient, not the other way around. The words stuck in her throat. "I—I've cared for other patient's in similar circumstances," she murmured evasively. "And I can imagine what you're going through. Please take care of yourself, okay?"

"Okay."

Raine walked with her outside to the parking lot where she'd left her car. She stared after Helen for a long moment, before turning to head back inside to swipe out. She couldn't wait to get out of there.

Caleb stood behind her and she caught herself just in time to prevent herself from smacking into him.

"Did you need something?" she asked testily. She wasn't in the mood for a confrontation. Not now. She wanted to go home.

"Yeah. Do you have a minute?"

"Not really. I need to go inside to swipe out." She tried to sidestep him, but Caleb didn't take the hint, turning and following her inside to the nearest time clock where she could swipe her ID badge, formally ending her shift.

She suppressed a sigh and faced him. "Caleb, couldn't we do this some other time? I really don't feel well. I've been sick to my stomach. I think I'm catching some flu bug or something."

"Stop it, Raine. I know the truth."

Her jaw dropped and she stared at him. He knew? How was that possible? No one knew. Except her boss, and Theresa had promised not to say a word.

Had she inadvertently said something when she'd passed out?

"You do?"

"Yes." He crossed his arms over his chest and stared at her. "And I'm not letting you go until you agree to talk to me about it."

CHAPTER SEVEN

RAINE stared at him in shock. To hear him blurt out so bluntly that he knew the truth was staggering. "No. I…can't talk about it. I'm sorry." She turned away, heading for the employee parking lot, wanting nothing more than to go home, to recover from her emotionally draining shift.

But once again Caleb followed her outside. She tried to think of something to say to make him go away. But her mind was blank. And one glimpse at the stubborn set of his features told her he wasn't going to let her go easily.

"You shouldn't drive when you're this upset." He took her arm, steering her towards where his car was parked.

For a moment she tensed beneath his touch, wanting to pull away, but then her shoulders slumped with exhaustion. She simply didn't have the energy to fight. Going along with him was easier than arguing. He opened the passenger door of his car and gestured for her to get inside.

She did, without uttering a single protest.

He slid behind the wheel, glancing at her, but not saying anything. The silence should have been oppressive but, oddly enough, she took comfort in his presence. Maybe because taking care of Helen had brought her suppressed fears to the surface.

He pulled out of the parking lot and headed towards his house, without bothering to ask if she was okay with his decision.

She didn't protest. She was secretly glad he hadn't taken her back to her apartment. Her imagination tended to work overtime there.

"How's your father doing?" she asked when he pulled into the driveway.

He glanced at her. "Better. Still in pain, but overall much better."

"I'm glad," she murmured.

After parking the car, he headed up to his house and unlocked the door. She followed him inside, smiling a bit when Grizzly greeted her enthusiastically.

For a moment she buried her face against his silky fur, hanging onto her self-control by a thin thread. She'd been in Caleb's house often while they'd dated. After her emotionally draining shift, the welcome familiarity of Caleb's house soothed her soul.

She'd missed him. Desperately. They'd shared some very good times, before she'd realized the extent of his inability to trust. And then it was too late. She'd made a terrible mistake.

"Grizz likes you," Caleb said, watching her pet the dog as he made a pot of coffee. "He's not that excited when I come home, more like disappointed that I'm not my father."

She didn't know how to respond, worried she'd burst into tears if she tried. Back when things had started to get more intense between them, she'd wondered what it might be like to share Caleb's home with him. She glanced around, liking the way Caleb's kitchen overlooked the living area, the cathedral ceiling providing a spacious feel.

She took a seat on the butter-soft deep blue leather sofa. Grizzly followed her, sitting on his haunches in front of her and placing his big head on her lap. His soulful eyes stared up at her adoringly, wordlessly begging for attention. She pressed her face to the silky fur on the top of his head.

The sharp stab of regret pierced deep.

Caleb brought in two mugs of steaming coffee. She could smell the enticing scent of the vanilla creamer she loved. With a guilty start, she realized he must have bought it with her in mind, anticipating a night in the not-too-distant future when she might stay over.

And if things had been different, they might have spent the night together. More than once.

Her stomach churned. The nausea surged up with full force. Desperately, she swallowed hard.

There was no point in wishing for something she couldn't have. Caleb hadn't really trusted her before, there was no way that would change now.

And, really, she couldn't blame him.

He settled into the easy chair across from her, as if he didn't dare risk getting too close. She wrapped her hands around the coffee mug, seeking warmth despite the humid summer evening, wondering why he'd brought her here.

His gaze bored into hers. "Raine, I'm sure you'd feel better if you talked about it."

The hot coffee scalded her tongue. She stared into the depths of her mug, not wanting to admit he was right. "I doubt it."

"Raine, what can I say to convince you? You stayed with me when my father was having surgery—at least let me help you now. As a friend."

She sighed, knowing he was right but somehow unable to find the words to tell him what had happened. She was afraid, so very afraid of seeing the same flare of disgust in his eyes.

"Did you meet someone else? Is that it? Is that what you're afraid to tell me? What happened? Did he move too fast for you?"

She blinked. Another guy? Was that really what he thought?

"I know you, Raine," he continued, obviously on a roll. "You're a passionate woman, but you're also sweetly innocent. He's a rat bastard for taking advantage of you. I can imagine exactly how it happened. A goodnight kiss went too far, and he pushed you into a level of intimacy you weren't ready for."

Dear God. He didn't know the truth. *He didn't know*.

Her mind whirling, Raine wasn't sure how to respond. Slowly, she shook her head.

"Come on. I know something happened." He set his coffee mug aside, untouched. "That's why you acted so strangely with our sexual assault patient. Because you were close to experiencing the same thing. Isn't that right? Dammit, tell me." The pure agony in his tone hit hard.

"No. You've got it all wrong," she said, sinking further into the sofa cushions, wishing she could close her eyes and disappear.

He let out a harsh laugh. "Yeah, right. That's why you have that haunted expression in your eyes. Don't protect the bastard."

Suddenly she couldn't take the pretence. Couldn't continue acting as if everything was fine when it was anything but. Unfortunately, the scenario he'd described might be closer to the truth than he realized. Except for one important fact.

"I'm not protecting anyone," she said finally. "I don't even know who he is."

"What do you mean?" Caleb frowned in confusion. "How can you not know?"

"Because I was given Rohypnol." She forced the truth out past the lump in her throat. "You were right, Caleb. Is that what you want to hear? You were right not to trust me. I flirted with a stranger and I paid the price."

Caleb stared at her, his eyes full of horror.

She forced herself to finish. "You want to know what happened? I'll tell you. I was sexually assaulted by a man I can't remember."

Raine's confession stabbed him in the chest, ripping away his ability to breathe. He'd known she was holding something back, but this was worse. So much worse than what he'd imagined. His mind could barely comprehend what she was telling him.

Raine had been assaulted. By a stranger.

Appalled, he jumped to his feet, unable to sit still. "My God. I...didn't know. Why didn't you tell me?" he asked in a strangled tone.

She hunched her shoulders and shivered. He wanted to cross over to her, to put his arms around her and hold her tight, but obviously that was the last thing she'd want.

No wonder he'd seen the same shattered expression in her eyes that had been mirrored in their patient's eyes. He'd suspected some guy had pushed her into something, but he hadn't imagined this. Not that she'd been given Rohypnol and raped. He still could hardly believe it. The confession shimmered in the air between them, forcing him to keep his distance, even though it pained him.

"I couldn't," she whispered. "I haven't told anyone."

She hadn't told anyone? Why in heaven's name not? He paced the length of the great room, jamming his fingers helplessly through his hair. He needed to remain calm when all he wanted was to wrap his hands around the bastard's throat, squeezing until he begged for mercy. He was so angry he could barely see. How on earth had she managed? Especially all alone?

Raine shivered again, the uncontrollable movement capturing his gaze. He swallowed a curse and went into his bedroom. He grabbed the blanket off his bed and carried it into the living room. Wordlessly, he draped it around her slim shoulders, trying not to touch her.

"Thank you," she murmured, pulling the blanket close.

The fury he'd buried threatened to break loose. He didn't know how she could sit there so calmly. He wanted to rant and rave, to throw things. He curled his fingers into fists and he began pacing again, still reeling at the news.

He felt sick, realizing she'd gone through the horror all alone rather than seeking comfort from him. And he understood exactly why.

Because he hadn't believed her when she'd called to apologize after he'd seen her with Jake. And she'd assumed he wouldn't believe her about this as well.

He wanted to smack his head against the wall for being so stupid. For not listening to her when she'd called him the next day. Why had he believed Jake, when he hadn't believed Raine?

Grizz must have realized something was wrong, because the black Lab whined and then abruptly jumped up on the sofa, settling against Raine and placing his large head in her lap. He almost told the dog to get down from the furniture.

But when Raine hugged Grizz close, seemingly grateful for the comfort of the dog's presence, he couldn't bear to yell at Grizz to get down. The dog wasn't a threat to her, not in the way a man might be.

The way he would be? He remembered the way she'd tended to keep distance between them the first few times they'd worked together.

But not afterwards. Not when they'd sat in the waiting room together, waiting for news about his father.

He couldn't stand the thought that she might be afraid of him.

"Raine." He stared at her, hating feeling so helpless. "I don't know what to say."

"You don't have to say anything," she said, her voice muffled by Grizzly's fur. "It's enough that you know the truth."

He clenched his jaw and swung away, so she wouldn't see the simmering anger in his eyes. It wasn't enough to know the truth, not by a long shot. He wouldn't be satisfied until the bastard was caught. Helpless guilt grabbed him by the throat.

If he hadn't let his mistrust get the better of him, maybe he could have handled things differently. He knew now he should have given her the benefit of doubt.

And now it was too late to go back, to fix the mistakes he'd made.

The last thing he wanted right now was to do or say anything that could possibly hurt her. Or scare her.

Control. He needed to maintain control. He couldn't

think about how she must have gone into the hospital, seeking help. Being examined. Talking to the police.

No wonder she'd fainted.

His imagination was worse than knowing the truth. How was she coping when he couldn't keep the awful images out of his mind? Another man's hands on her. Forcing her to have sex. Taking what she hadn't freely given.

Ruthlessly, he shoved the horrible images away.

"I'm sorry," he said finally. "I should have been there with you. You shouldn't have had to go through that alone."

She didn't answer. When he glanced back at her he could only see her face, the rest of her body was buried beneath the blanket and Grizz. Her eyes had closed, her mouth had relaxed and her lips were slightly parted in sleep.

Caleb let out a deep breath and collapsed in the chair opposite. He scrubbed his hands over his face.

He tried to tell himself he must not have handled things too badly if Raine was comfortable enough to fall asleep on his living-room sofa. Either that or he'd underestimated the comfort provided by Grizz.

Hell, he'd convince his dad to give her the dog if only she'd smile again.

Smile. Yeah, right. He didn't know how in the world she'd recover from this. How did any woman put something like this behind them?

Broodingly, he watched her sleep, his gaze caressing the curve of her cheek, the silkiness of her hair. He remembered with aching clarity, their last embrace. Their last kiss.

He grimaced and closed his eyes, drowning in the

bitter-sweet memories. The sexual chemistry between them had sizzled. During their kisses goodnight, it had taken every ounce of willpower he'd possessed to slow things down. Each night the heat had grown more passionate between them. And he couldn't deny that he'd always been the one to pull back, before either of them had got too carried away.

Even though they'd only dated for two months, he'd suspected he was falling for her. And that had caused him to overreact to everything she'd done. He hadn't been able to find a way to stop himself from constantly questioning her.

His selfish fears had pushed her away at the moment she'd probably needed him most.

He opened his eyes and looked at Raine, mourning the loss. His fault. What had happened to Raine was largely his fault. And now there was no going back.

Whatever feelings she might have had toward him were likely gone. What he hadn't destroyed had likely been demolished by her assailant.

Picking up his mug of coffee, he took a sip, grimacing at the cold temperature. His gaze burned with deep regret as he watched her sleep.

Raine opened her eyes, momentarily confused for a moment about where she was. Grizzly let out a deep sigh beside her. She blinked, realizing she was still on Caleb's sofa, suffocatingly warm as a result of being sandwiched between the blanket and the large dog.

She might be sweltering, but she'd also slept the entire night through without waking up. For the first time since the night of the assault.

She'd felt safe with Caleb. And Grizzly.

Feeling better than she had in a long time, she gingerly sat up, surprised to find Caleb asleep in the easy-chair across from her. So both the man and the dog had watched over her. She winced a bit, realizing that the way Caleb's head lay at such an awkward angle he would probably wake up with a severe crick in his neck.

His eyes shot open, startling her.

She licked suddenly dry lips, smoothing a hand self-consciously over her tangled hair. "Good morning."

"Morning." He straightened in the chair, twisting his head from side to side, stretching the tense muscles. "Are you hungry? We didn't eat anything for dinner last night."

Her stomach rumbled and for the second time in as many minutes she was surprised to discover her nausea was absent and her appetite had returned. "Yes, as a matter of fact, I am. Do you want help?"

Caleb shook his head. "No, I'll throw something together. Omelets okay?"

"Sure." The inane conversation helped keep things in perspective. Caleb had always been a nice guy, of course that hadn't changed. But she couldn't lie to herself. She'd caught the fleeting glimpse of appalled horror in his gaze when she'd finally confessed the truth. Luckily, there was no sign of his aversion now.

She untangled her legs from the blanket. "I'll, uh, need to borrow your bathroom for a minute."

"Help yourself. This will take a few minutes, anyway." Caleb seemed to be giving her distance, letting the dog out as she went past him towards the bathroom.

Ten minutes later, feeling slightly more human after washing up a bit, Raine returned to the kitchen. Caleb had changed his clothes too, looking ruggedly handsome in his casual jeans and T-shirt. He was busy pouring the egg mixture into the pan, and then added ham, cheese and mushrooms.

She smoothed a hand over her badly wrinkled scrubs, feeling awkward as Caleb cooked for her. "Are you sure you don't need help with anything?"

"I'm sure. Why don't you sit down at the table? The coffee should be ready in a minute." After a few minutes he pulled plates out of the cupboard, slid two fluffy omelets onto them and carried them over to the table.

For long moments they ate in silence. When the coffee was ready, he poured them each a mug, laced hers with the vanilla-flavored creamer and brought them to the table.

"Thanks," she said, accepting the cup. "I guess I should apologize for falling asleep on you."

"No, you shouldn't." His tone was tense, but his gaze was uncertain as he glanced at her. "I'm glad you felt comfortable enough to sleep here."

She glanced away, hating the awkwardness that loomed between them.

"Besides, did you really think Grizz was going to let you leave without a fight?" Caleb asked lightly. "He was in doggy heaven, sleeping on the sofa beside you."

A smile tugged at the corner of her mouth, especially when Grizzly's head perked up at his name. "I didn't mind. He was wonderful company."

Caleb took a sip of his coffee, eyeing her over the rim. "You honestly haven't told anyone else? Not even your brothers?"

Her smile faded. She shook her head. "Especially not my brothers."

Caleb frowned. "Elana?"

"No. She and Brock have been so happy, planning the nursery for the new baby, that I couldn't find a way to tell her." She forced herself to meet his gaze. "I've been too embarrassed. Too ashamed to tell anyone."

"You have nothing to be ashamed of, Raine," he said with a frown.

Too bad she didn't really believe him. "I've been seeing a counselor and talking to her has helped," she said instead.

He nodded encouragingly. "That's good."

She set her fork down, not really in the mood to talk about this any more. "Thanks for breakfast, Caleb, but I really should get going."

Caleb didn't pick up on her hint. "Do the police have any leads on this guy?"

"Not that I know of," she admitted.

"They must have something to go on," he pressed. "Surely you remember some of the men who were there that night."

Her stomach cramped and she put a hand over it, as the nausea returned. Like it always did when she thought about how she'd acted that night at Jamie's bachelorette party, dancing and flirting with the various players and fans of the rugby team who had come in to celebrate their win, buying rounds of drinks for their group.

One of whom could have drugged her. Assaulted her.

Had he fathered a child, too?

CHAPTER EIGHT

"RAINE?" She glanced up when Caleb called her name, staring at him blankly when he leaned forward, his gaze full of concern. "You're awfully pale. Are you all right?"

"Fine," she forced herself to answer, willing the nausea away. Telling Caleb the truth had felt good last night, but now she was beginning to regret giving in. Why did he feel the need to keep talking about what had happened? There was no reason to keep harping on it. She wasn't ready to give him every excruciating detail.

As Helen had said, talking about it didn't change what had happened.

And if he knew everything, he'd realize he might have been right to accuse her of wanting other men. Hadn't she attended the bachelorette party that night, flirting like crazy, in an effort to prove she was over Caleb?

Grizz came over to lick her fingers, as if he could sense her distress, and she stroked his silky ebony fur, trying to summon a smile. "If you don't mind, I'd rather not talk about that night. It's been really hard, but I'm trying to move past what happened to me."

Instantly, Caleb's face paled, his gaze stricken. "I'm sorry. I should have realized…"

His self-recrimination wasn't necessary. Being treated differently was part of the reason she'd chosen not to say anything to anyone. She lifted her chin. "I don't want your pity, Caleb. I've been trying to move forward in my life. To focus on all the positive things I have to be grateful for, rather than dwelling on the negative."

He frowned a little and rubbed the back of his neck. "Pity is not at all what I'm feeling right now. I admire you. I think you're amazing, Raine. Truly."

His sincere, earnest expression eased some of the tension in her stomach. "I'm not. Obviously, taking care of Helen proves I still have a long ways to go. But each day gets a little better. At least, it had been, until last night."

If anything, he paled more. "Because you told me? Telling me made it worse for you?"

"No," she hastened to reassure him. "Because of Helen. I *fainted*, for heaven's sake. I thought I was handling trauma fairly well, even though taking care of Becca had been really hard. We saved Greg Hanson, which helped immensely. I thought I'd gotten over the worst, but then Helen came in and I lost it."

"You handled the stress all far better than anyone could expect." He frowned a little. "I knew you'd taken a temporary position in the minor care area. This was the reason?"

"Yeah. I couldn't take off work for more than a week and still pay my rent, so I asked Theresa, my boss, to put me in Minor Care. Just happened that one of the nurses was out on a medical leave so it was easy to cover her hours."

"I thought you were avoiding me," he admitted.

She lifted her shoulder in a half-shrug. "I was avoiding everyone, not just you."

He stared at her for several long seconds, the last few bites of his meal forgotten. "I feel so damned helpless," he said in a low, agonized tone. "Is there something I can do? Anything?"

She started to shake her head, but then stopped. She looked at Caleb, seated across the table from her, keeping his distance from the moment he'd discovered the truth, as if she were some sort of leper. They didn't have the same relationship they'd once had, but certainly over these past few days they'd re-established their friendship. Hadn't they?

"Actually, I could use a hug." The moment the words were out of her mouth, she wished she could call them back as they made her sound pathetic. Hadn't she just told him she didn't want his pity?

"Really?" The flare of cautious hope in his eyes caught her off guard. He quickly rose to his feet and crossed over to her, holding out his hand in a silent invitation.

Was she crazy? Maybe. Reaching out, she put her hand in his and allowed him to draw her to her feet. And then he slowly, carefully, as if she might break, drew her into his arms.

Enticed by his solid warmth and gentle strength, she wrapped her arms around his waist and buried her face against his chest, breathing deeply, as if she could never get enough of his heady, comforting scent. She'd missed this so much! More than she would have thought possible.

Maybe she'd made a mistake by not telling him. She'd avoided it because she'd known that the person he'd once been attracted to was gone for ever. She'd never be that free-spirited girl again. But she might have misjudged him. Caleb would have stood by her as a friend.

She tightened her grip, silently telling him how much she appreciated this. And when his mouth lightly brushed against the top of her head, she sucked in a quick breath, stunned by a flash of desire.

For a moment she closed her eyes, wishing desperately for the chance to go back, to make a better decision.

His broad hand lightly stroked her back, and she knew his intention was probably to offer comfort, but her skin tingled with awareness. She was tempted to reach up to kiss him. Ironically, she was happy to know she could still feel desire, this deep yearning for physical closeness. That what had happened to her, as awful as it was, hadn't stolen everything.

She still wanted Caleb. The attraction she'd felt for him the moment they'd met was still there.

But would he ever trust her with his whole heart?

She closed her eyes against the prick of tears. No, she didn't think Caleb was really capable of trusting her with his whole heart and soul. And crying wasn't going to change that. Enough of the poor-me syndrome. She had a lot to be thankful for. Negative energy wasn't productive.

Taking a deep breath, she let it out slowly. A tiny part of her wanted to stay in his arms like this for ever, but regretfully she pressed a quick kiss against the fabric of his shirt before loosening her grip on his waist. He immediately let go, and her moment of euphoria deflated when she realized the desire she'd experienced was clearly one-sided.

"Thanks," she murmured, determined not to show him how much she'd been affected by his embrace. "I needed that."

"Any time," he said, in a low husky tone.

Surprised, she glanced up at his dark gray eyes, realizing he sincerely meant it. Was it possible he may still have some desire for her? Even after what had happened? She was afraid to hope. "I…uh, should get going. I'm scheduled to work today."

She sensed he wanted to argue, but in the end he simply nodded. "Okay, give me a few minutes to clean up in here, I don't want to leave everything out with Grizzly around."

"I'll help." She stacked their plates and carried them over to the kitchen sink. And as they worked companionably side by side in the kitchen, she caught a glimpse of the future she might have had with Caleb.

If only she'd swallowed her pride and returned his calls instead of going to the bachelorette party in an effort to forget about him.

"Are you ready to go?" Caleb asked, glancing over at Raine. He wished he could come up with some valid or believable reason to encourage her to stay.

Rather than just the fact that he didn't want her to leave.

Holding her in his arms had been amazing. Humbling. He'd known she'd only wanted comfort from a friend and nothing more, so he'd garnered every ounce of willpower to keep his embrace non-sexual and non-threatening, despite his deeper desire for more.

One step at a time. He was still hurt that Raine hadn't come to him sooner, that she'd chosen to ignore his phone calls rather than to confide in him. But she was here now. Had spent the night on his sofa, with Grizz. Which meant she trusted him at least a little.

Didn't she?

"Sure. I'm ready if you are."

He wasn't ready at all, but he searched the kitchen counter until he found his keys. When he turned back to face Raine, he found she'd dropped to her knees to give Grizz a big hug. The dampness around her eyes wrenched his heart.

He couldn't stand the thought that she'd endured all this alone.

The atmosphere in the car during the ride back to the hospital was quietly subdued. He wanted to offer to give her another hug, but worried about coming on too strong. Logically, he knew it was best to let Raine set the pace for what she wanted or was comfortable with. He could only imagine what she'd gone through.

So he didn't reach for her, even though he desperately wanted to.

"Thanks for the ride," she said softly, when he'd pulled up to her car in the parking lot. "And thanks for letting me borrow Grizzly last night. It's the first night I've slept peacefully since…" Her voice trailed off as she fumbled for the doorhandle.

Oh, man, now he didn't really want her to leave, if last night was the first night she'd slept well since the assault. But she seemed intent on getting out of the car quickly, so he jumped out and came around to open the door for her, trying to think of a polite way to convince her to stay. "I'm sure Grizz would be thrilled if you'd come spend another night on my sofa."

Her lopsided smile tugged on his heart, but she gave a small shake of her head, declining his offer. "Thanks again." She lifted up on tiptoe and brushed a light kiss on his cheek, surprising him speechless. He wanted badly to crush her close, but kept his arms at his sides so he wouldn't scare her. "Bye, Caleb."

He could barely force the words from his throat. "Bye, Raine. I'll be at work tonight too, so I'll see you later."

He stood, staring after her as she climbed into her car and started the engine. And when she backed out and drove away, it was all he could do not to follow her home.

She'd kissed him. Asked for a hug.

Was he a complete fool for thinking her actions were a sign she was willing to give him another chance?

Raine drove home, feeling better than she had in a long time. The cramping nausea that had plagued her endlessly seemed to have vanished.

Maybe her life was finally getting back on track. Telling Caleb, as difficult as it had been, had helped. At least around him she didn't have to pretend any more.

When she passed a drugstore, her previous doubts resurfaced. Quickly making a U-turn, she headed back to the store to purchase a home pregnancy test. Enough procrastinating.

It was time to know the truth, one way or the other.

Despite her extreme self-consciousness, no one looked at her with blatant curiosity when she purchased a two-in-one home pregnancy kit. The company had been smart enough to provide two tests in one box, providing a back-up in case she did something wrong the first time.

Clutching the bag tightly to her chest, she walked up to her second-story apartment and greeted Spice, who sniffed the remnants of Grizzly's scent on her scrubs with feline disdain.

"Don't worry," she said, scratching the cat behind the ears. "You're still my favorite."

Spice walked away, with her tail high in the air, seemingly looking at her with reproach.

Raine took the pregnancy test with her into the bathroom. She took a shower and then sat down to read the directions on the test kit. The process was easy enough and didn't require that she wait until the morning. Without giving herself a chance to change her mind, she carefully followed the instructions. The brief period of waiting seemed to take three hours instead of three minutes.

Gathering her strength and mentally preparing for the worst, she took a deep breath and went over to look at the test strip.

The words *Not Pregnant* practically jumped out at her. She blinked and leaned closer, looking again to make sure she wasn't simply imagining things.

Not Pregnant.

She wasn't pregnant. Her knees went weak and she dropped onto the seat of the commode, her mind grappling with the news. This was good. She should be relieved she wasn't pregnant.

So why the strange sense of emptiness underlying the relief?

She'd always hoped to have children one day, but not yet. And not like this. But, still, she couldn't quite push aside the feeling.

She shook off her conflicting thoughts. Now she knew. Whatever was bothering her wasn't a baby. She put a hand over her stomach, which still didn't feel totally normal, but certainly not as upset as it had been earlier. Was it possible she'd tested herself too early? She turned back to pick up the box, reading the instructions again. Sure enough, the company did recommend taking the test again after a week, just to be sure.

Another week? She wasn't sure she could stand to wait that long. Hopefully she'd get her period before then.

She put the pregnancy kit up in the medicine cabinet. She could test herself again, but stress was the likely culprit making her feel sick. The fact that most of her nausea had faded after talking to Caleb only reinforced the possibility.

Her counselor had been right. Keeping everything that had happened to her bottled up inside wasn't healthy.

Caleb had sounded surprised that she hadn't told her three older brothers. She loved her brothers dearly, but they'd been completely against her moving to the big city from their small town of Cedar Bluff. They loved her, but if she told them what happened, she feared they would have gone straight into over-protection mode. They would have insisted on moving her back home and never letting her out of their sight again. And she also knew they might have been tempted to confront every rugby fan them-selves—taking the law into their own hands.

She shivered, a cold trail of dread seeping down her spine. No, she couldn't tell them. Not yet.

Not until the police had caught the guy.

Maybe not ever.

For a moment she glanced helplessly around her apart-ment. Was she crazy to just sit back, waiting for the police to get a lead? Sure, they had Helen's case loosely linked to hers, but that news alone didn't mean they had a suspect. Should she be taking some sort of action? Would seeing a face trigger some latent memory?

She was scheduled to work tonight, unless she could find someone to cover for her. Caleb was scheduled to work, too. A part of her wanted nothing more than to take him up on his offer to spend the night again on his sofa.

But she couldn't lean on him too much. She needed to be strong. And maybe that meant taking action, rather than sitting around, doing nothing.

Caleb went to work early, to visit his dad and in hope of seeing Raine.

He'd been tempted to call her several times that day. Only the memories of how he'd over-reacted before when they'd been dating held him back.

She didn't need him constantly hovering. But doing nothing, and not seeing her at all, was killing him.

When he went up to his father's room on the regular floor, he was disappointed to find Raine wasn't there. But at least his father looked much better.

"Hi, Dad. How are you?"

"Doc says I'm hanging in there. They made me get up and walk in the hallway." His father grimaced as he rearranged the photographs of the animals at the shelter on his bedside table. Caleb had to admit Raine's simple gift was genius.

"I'm glad to hear that. You need to move around if you want to go home." He glanced at the glossy pictures, realizing how in some ways Raine had known his father better than he had. "Tell me about the animals at the shelter."

That was all the encouragement his father needed. He went into great detail on the dogs he'd recently cared for, ending with a particularly engaging Irish setter. "This is Rusty, he's Raine's favorite."

Raine's favorite? She'd seemed quite taken with Grizz last night. Caleb leaned forward to get a better look. "He's cute."

"The color of his coat matches her hair," his father explained with a smile. "Her apartment doesn't allow dogs, or I know she would have already adopted him."

The idea of Raine longing for the companionship of a dog made his gut tighten. She deserved to have a dog as a pet. Look how quickly she'd bonded with Grizzly. He almost said as much to his father, but then realized that if his dad knew how Raine had spent the night, he'd only have more questions. Questions he didn't have the right to answer.

It was Raine's story to tell, not his. And the fact that she hadn't told anyone but him was enough for him to keep quiet.

"Seems like you and Raine are pretty close," Caleb said.

His father shrugged. "Not really. We don't talk about our personal lives very much. But, yeah, I enjoy working with her."

"She, uh, hasn't stopped in to visit at all today, has she?" Caleb asked casually.

His father's gaze sharpened. "No. why? Is there something going on between the two of you?"

"Not in the way you're thinking," Caleb said wryly. "We work together in the ED, and I was curious, that's all."

"Hrmph." His father scowled at him. "What's wrong with you, son? Are you blind? Can't you see what a great catch Raine is?"

It was on the tip of Caleb's tongue to remind his father he didn't jump into relationships the way he did, but he bit back the retort. Because, truthfully, he had jumped into a relationship with Raine. Faster than he had with anyone else.

And the moment he'd seen her with Jake he'd assumed the worst.

"I'm not blind," he assured his father dryly. "Raine is beautiful and kind. She's also a great nurse."

His father rolled his eyes. "Now you're going to tell me you're just friends."

"We are. Don't push," he warned, when his father looked as if he might argue. "Besides, I have to go. It's almost time for my shift."

"Go on, then. Save lives." His father waved him off.

Caleb walked toward the door, but then turned back. "Dad?" He waited for his father to meet his gaze. "I love you. Take care of yourself, understand?"

His father looked surprised, but then he nodded. "Thanks, Caleb," he said in a gruff tone. "I will. And I love you, too."

Caleb headed down to the emergency eepartment, glancing around for Raine and frowning when he didn't find her. Had she decided to go back into the minor care area, the small exam rooms that were literally located just outside the main emergency department? After several minutes of looking, he sought help from the charge nurse on duty.

"Which area is Raine Hart working in tonight?" he asked.

"She's not here," the charge nurse informed him. "She called and asked Diane to work for her. Diane is assigned to the trauma bay."

For a moment he could only stare at her in shock, his

breath lodged painfully in his chest. Raine wasn't working tonight? Why? Because she was avoiding him? Or because she was too upset?

Dammit, he never should have left her alone.

CHAPTER NINE

CONCENTRATING on patient care helped distract him for a while, but every time there was a lull between patients, his mind would turn to Raine. He tried to call her cellphone on his break, but she didn't answer, which only made things worse. By the time he'd reached the end of his shift, he was crazy with fear and worry.

Caleb went home to take care of Grizz and then paced the kitchen, inwardly debating what to do. He glanced at the clock, realizing it was past eleven-thirty at night, but at the moment he didn't care. He let Grizzly back in and then drove straight over to Raine's apartment complex.

She lived in an eight-unit building, on the second floor, in the upper right hand corner. He frowned when he saw the windows of her apartment were dark.

Because she was sleeping? Or because she wasn't home?

He pulled up to the curb, parked his car and got out. There was a long surface parking lot behind the building, and he ambled back to look for her car.

It wasn't there.

So she wasn't home. The knot in his gut tightened painfully, and the old familiar doubts came flooding to the surface. Where was she? Who was she with? What was she doing?

He knew that Raine wouldn't be with another man, not now. Not so soon after the assault. She'd had to gather her courage to ask him for a hug, for heaven's sake. But the edgy panic plagued him anyway. He thrust his fingers through his hair, wishing he could tune out his wayward thoughts.

He'd avoided serious relationships during medical school, concentrating on his studies. After watching the parade of women come and go in his father's life, he hadn't thought he'd been missing much. Until he'd become a resident and met fellow resident Tabitha Nash.

He remembered all too clearly how betrayed he'd felt when he'd walked into their bedroom to see his naked fiancée in the arms of another man. In their bed.

He'd immediately moved out, and had guarded his heart much more fiercely from that point on. Which was why he'd been so willing to believe the worst about Raine when he'd seen her with Jake.

He walked back to his car, climbed behind the wheel and tried to convince himself to go home. Raine was an adult and if she needed him, she knew how to get in touch with him.

But he couldn't make himself turn the key in the ignition.

When he'd met Raine, he'd told himself to go slow. She was four years younger and more naïve than some of the women he'd dated, probably because she hadn't been used to life in the big city. Regardless, her bubbly enthusiasm for life along with the strong pull of sexual attraction had been difficult to resist.

All too soon he'd found himself falling for her. And when they hadn't been together, he'd constantly questioned where she was and who she was with. Even though he'd known he'd been coming on too strong, he hadn't seemed able to stop.

After he'd realized she hadn't cheated on him with Jake, he'd wanted a second chance. Kept thinking that maybe, after some time had passed, they'd be able to get over their issues. But now he wasn't so sure that was even an option. Even after knowing what had happened, as much as he knew Raine's attack hadn't been her fault, he still didn't like to think about how she'd flirted with a stranger, however innocently. Her laughter had always drawn male attention…

He ground the palms of his hands into his eye sockets. He needed to get a grip. None of this was Raine's fault. None of it! He should go home. Sitting out here in front of Raine's building was making him feel like a stalker. Especially when, for all he knew, Raine could have driven home to see her brothers. Maybe she'd finally decided to tell them what happened.

Go home, Stewart. Stop being an idiot.

Bright headlights approached, momentarily blinding him as he was about to put the car into gear. When the oncoming car slowed and the blinker came on, his pulse kicked up.

Raine. Sure enough, the blue car turning into the parking lot was Raine's. She was home.

Relieved, he shut off the car and climbed out, loping around to the parking lot behind the building.

"Raine?" he called, catching her as she was about to go inside.

She whirled around, putting her hand over her heart. "Caleb?" she said, when she realized who he was. "What are you doing here? You scared me to death."

"I'm sorry." He stood, feeling awkward. "I was worried when you didn't come in for your shift. I wanted to come over to make sure you were okay."

She hitched her purse strap higher on her shoulder. "I'm fine."

He frowned when she realized she was dressed in a sleek pair of black slacks and a bright purple blouse. They weren't suggestive in the least, considering she had the blouse buttoned to her chin, but he couldn't imagine she'd dressed up to go and see her brothers. "Where were you?" the question came out harsher than he'd intended.

She arched a brow and let out a disgusted sigh. "You haven't changed much, have you?"

He'd tried not to sound accusatory. Obviously he hadn't tried hard enough. "I'm sorry, I know what you do in your free time isn't any of my business. I swear I'm only asking because I'm concerned about you."

She stared at him for several long seconds, toying with the strap on her purse. "If you must know, I went to the After Dark nightclub."

He sucked in a harsh breath. "What? Alone? Why for God's sake?"

"Shh," she hissed, glancing around. "You'll wake up the entire neighborhood. And you can relax, it's not as bad as it sounds. I didn't go inside."

Calming down wasn't an option, but he tried to lower his voice even though his tone was still tense. "What do you mean, you didn't go inside?"

Her expression turned grim. "I'm so tired of feeling like

a victim, so I decided to take control. To see if I could help find the guy. I went to the nightclub but stayed in my car, watching the various people coming and going, trying to see if any of the faces jogged my memory. But it didn't work." Her face reflected her disgust. "Unfortunately, I didn't recognize a single soul."

Caleb bit his tongue so hard he tasted blood. He would not yell at Raine. Would not chastise her for going to the nightclub alone. Even if she had stayed in her car, there was a chance that the guy who'd assaulted her might recognize her and either try for round two or silence her for ever.

He bit down harder, until pain pierced his anger. Finally, he took a deep breath. Everything was fine. Getting her upset wouldn't help matters. He lowered his voice, trying to reassure her. "Raine, I wish you'd told me. I'd have been happy to go with you."

"You were working, but I'll remember that if I decide to go again, which I sincerely doubt, since the entire attempt was pretty useless." She shook out her keys, choosing one from the ring to unlock the door. "Do you want to come in for a few minutes or not?"

Her half-hearted invitation caught him off guard but there was no way in the world he was going to turn her down. "Ah…sure."

She unlocked the door and held it open so he could follow her inside. He'd only been to her apartment a few times as they'd spent more time at his house while they'd been dating. When she opened the apartment door and flipped on the lights, his gaze landed on the sofa, half-buried beneath a blanket and pillow.

She slept on the couch in her own home? Because the

bastard had brought her back here? He stumbled, useless anger radiating down his spine. He blocked off the anger, knowing it wouldn't help.

"Uh, make yourself comfortable," she said, her cheeks flushed as she swept away the bedding to make room on the sofa. "Do you want something to drink?"

Whiskey. Straight up. He tried to smile. "Whatever you're having is fine with me."

Her flush deepened. "I don't have beer or wine or anything. I drink a lot of bottled water these days." Her tone was apologetic.

"Water is fine." A soft mewling sound surprised him and he glanced down. "Is that a cat?"

Raine smiled, the first real smile since she'd come home. "Yes. This is Spice." She bent down to pick up the cat who'd strolled into the room, snuggling the feline for a moment. "I've had her about a month now, since I started volunteering at the shelter. But I have to warn you, I think she's jealous of Grizzly."

He crossed over, trying to be friendly with the calico cat, but she hissed at him, raising her hackles, so he backed off. "My dad mentioned you had a soft spot for Rusty, the Irish setter, at the shelter, but that your lease here didn't allow dogs. I'm glad you were able to get a cat."

Raine put the cat on the floor and shooed her away. "Yes, Rusty is adorable. He was brought in as a stray, severely malnourished." Her blue eyes clouded with anger. "We suspect he was abused by a man, since he's wary of the male workers at the shelter. He bonded with me right away, though, as I happened to be there when he was brought in. He's a wonderful dog. I have to say it took me a while to get him calmed down enough to let your father examine him."

His heart squeezed in his chest. Rusty was abused? No wonder Raine had bonded with the dog. The two had been kindred souls, needing each other. Once again, a feeling of helplessness nearly overwhelmed him. There was really nothing he could do to help her. Nothing.

Except to ignore his own issues to be there for her if she needed him.

"I'm glad he has you, then."

She nodded and went into the small kitchenette to get two bottles of water out of the fridge. She came back into the living room and took a seat on the sofa next to him. He was surprised and glad she'd chosen to sit next to him, rather than taking the chair halfway across the room.

Glancing around the apartment, he was struck once again by the fact that she'd taken to sleeping on the sofa. "Would you consider moving?" he asked, thinking she might be able to put the event behind her more easily if she wasn't here in this apartment with the constant reminders. Plus, if she was open to moving, maybe they could find a place that would allow dogs.

"Not right now. Unfortunately my lease goes through to the end of the year." She twisted the cap off her water and took a long drink.

He could hear the regret in her tone and wanted to offer to pay off her lease just so she could move out. But the Raine he knew valued her independence. He decided it wouldn't hurt to ask around, see if anyone was interested in moving closer to the hospital and potentially taking over her lease. She couldn't fault him for that, could she?

"How is your father doing?" Raine asked, changing the subject.

"He's fine. I went up to see him before my shift. He

misses you and the work at the shelter a lot, I think." Caleb stared at his water bottle for a moment. "I didn't appreciate just how much his volunteer work means to him."

Raine's smile was wistful. "Your father loves animals, but he's also pretty social with the other volunteers. I get the sense being alone is hard for him."

"Yeah. He definitely doesn't want to be alone." He dragged his gaze up to meet hers. "I probably should have explained to you a long time ago about how my mom took off when I was five years old, rather than springing that news on you when my dad was heading off to the cath lab."

"I'm sorry, Caleb. That must have been horrible for you."

He shrugged off her sympathy. "We survived, but my dad started dating again shortly afterwards, bringing home a series of stepmother candidates to meet me."

She winced. "I'm sure that didn't go over very well."

"Maybe it would have been all right if my dad had found someone great, but instead he seemed to make one mistake after another." He downed half his water and set it aside. "My dad went through four marriages and four divorces. Hell, you'd think he'd learn but. no, he keeps finding new women and jumping right back into the next relationship. I've finally convinced him to stop marrying them at least."

"I see," Raine said slowly. She didn't look as if she completely agreed with him. "But, Caleb, surely you realize that your father's mistakes aren't your own."

"I made a similar error in judgment," he said slowly. "Remember I told you that my fiancée cheated on me? We were both residents, working a lot of shifts, often on opposite schedules, but I trusted her. Until I came home early one night to find her in bed with another guy." He tried to soften the bitterness in his tone. "Good thing I found out before I married her."

Her frown deepened. "Not all women cheat, Caleb."

He nodded. "I know. Logically, I know that I can't assume the worst. But my gut doesn't listen to my head."

"So you've been overcompensating ever since," she said softly.

"Yes." He let out a heavy sigh. "I'm sorry I didn't believe you. I tried to call you to apologize but you wouldn't take my calls."

She glanced away. "I know. I wish I had. But we can't go back. Even if we had tried again, I doubt our relationship would have survived. Especially not after what I did."

"Raine, please. Don't say that. You didn't *do* anything. The assault was not your fault." He wished he could reach out and pull her into his arms, but he was afraid of scaring her.

"My counselor says the same thing, but saying that doesn't change how I feel." She finally brought her gaze up to meet his.

"I figured you didn't take my calls because you were still angry with me."

She stared at him for a few seconds. "I was angry with you, Caleb," she said finally. "I went to the bachelorette party in the first place to get over you. But afterwards, you need to understand, the real reason I didn't take your calls was because I'd changed. I'm not the same person I was when you first asked me out. I'll never be that person ever again."

Raine finished her water as a heavy silence fell between them. She wished, more than anything, she could ask

Caleb to hold her. Despite how they'd broken off their relationship a month ago, she missed him. Missed being with him. When he'd hugged her that morning, she'd felt normal. The way she'd been before the night that had changed her for ever. As if maybe she really was healing.

"Does the attack still give you nightmares?" he asked in a low voice.

"Not exactly." She picked at the label around her empty bottle and then set it aside. "I don't remember anything from that night. Unfortunately, my imagination keeps trying to fill in the blanks."

Caleb's jaw tightened. "I hope to hell they find the bastard."

"Me too." She tried to think of a way to change the subject. Understanding Caleb's past helped clarify his actions. She could clearly see why he'd questioned her all the time about where she was going and who she was going to be with. But even if she had known all this back then, she didn't think she would have done anything differently. She still would have taken a break from their relationship. She still would have attended the bachelorette party with the rest of the girls.

And the outcome would have been the same.

They'd both made mistakes. Unfortunately, hers were insurmountable.

"Raine, you'll get through this," Caleb said finally, breaking the silence. "Maybe it will take time, but you're strong and I know you'll get through this."

He was completely missing the point. "I know I'll get through it, Caleb. It's already been over a month. I've done a pretty good job so far of moving on with my life. I volunteer at the animal shelter and I've returned to work. I know I'll get through this."

"So where does that leave us?" he asked with a frown.

Her heart tripped in her chest. If only it were that easy to salvage what they'd once had. "What do you want me to say?" she asked helplessly. "I just told you I'm not the same person I was before. I'm not the person you were attracted to. And even if I were, what's changed, Caleb? You didn't trust me before. Didn't believe me when I told you Jake had too much to drink that night. What's changed now?"

"I don't know," he said bluntly, and she had to give him points for being honest. "I can promise to try to work through my trust issues. But you won't know if I have or not unless you give me a second chance."

A second chance? Did she dare? "I'm a different person now," she reminded him.

"Maybe you are, but that doesn't mean I've stopped caring about you."

He cared about her? Her heart squeezed in her chest. Was she crazy to even think of trying to renew a relationship with Caleb? Was she even capable of such a thing? She'd enjoyed being held by him, but that was a long way away from actually dating. And there was a part of her that couldn't believe he'd be able to put aside his trust issues that easily. Would it bother him that she'd been with another man, however involuntarily?

She feared that innate distrust would eventually rip them apart.

Yet she trusted Caleb physically. Being with him felt a little like coming home. "I care about you too, Caleb." She took a deep breath and tried to smile. "If you're serious about wanting a second chance, then I'm willing to try, too."

His eyes widened, as if he hadn't expected her to agree.

"Really? I promise I won't rush you. We'll take things slow and easy."

She hesitated, wondering if he was going to have more trouble with this than she was. Caleb's imagination could easily run amuck, just like hers had. "I won't break, Caleb. I was the one who asked you for a hug this morning, remember?"

"I remember."

She set her empty water bottle aside and inched closer. "And you told me I could ask for a hug any time, right?"

His expression turned wary. "Yes. But I don't want to rush you, Raine. Don't feel like you have to do anything you're not ready for."

"I won't," she assured him, reaching out to take his hand in hers, feeling reassured when his fingers curled protectively around hers. "I'm ready for another hug, Caleb. Would you hold me?"

CHAPTER TEN

"Of course. I aim to please," he said lightly, but there was the slightest hesitation before his strong arms wrapped around her, drawing her close.

Raine sighed and burrowed her face into the hollow of his shoulder. She took a deep breath, filling her senses with his warm, familiar, musky scent.

She closed her eyes against the sting of unexpected tears. This was what she'd wanted ever since leaving his house earlier that morning. This was what she'd been missing.

Caleb lightly stroked a hand down her back, and even though she knew he only meant to soothe her, a flicker of awareness rippled along her nerves. He paused when she trembled, and then slowly repeated the caress. This time she bit back a moan as a wave of desire stabbed deep.

"Are you all right?" Caleb asked, his voice a deep rumble in her ear.

"I'm fine," she whispered, trying to hide how much he was affecting her. "This is nice."

There was another moment of silence and she inwardly winced, knowing nice was the least appropriate word to describe how she was feeling. She'd asked for a hug because she cared about Caleb. But responding to him with awareness and desire only confirmed her feelings for him hadn't lessened during the time they'd spent apart.

But did Caleb feel the same way? Somehow she doubted it. Because deep down she knew that if Caleb had ever really loved her, he would have believed in her.

And despite how he'd asked for a second chance, he was treating her like a victim. Someone to protect. Not a partner. If their relationship had stumbled before, she couldn't imagine how they'd manage to overcome everything that had happened.

Were they crazy to even try? Could they really find a way to overcome their problems?

"I'm glad you're not afraid," Caleb murmured. "It's nice to know you can relax around me."

Relax? With her body shimmering with awareness? Was he kidding? She couldn't help but smile. She lifted her head and met his gaze. "I'm not afraid of being close to you like this."

His gaze locked on hers, and his eyes darkened with the first inkling of desire. She went still, afraid to move. Slowly, ever so slowly, he bent his head until his mouth lightly brushed against hers.

Caleb's kiss was whisper soft and so brief she almost cried out in protest when he pulled away. But then he repeated the caress, gently molding his mouth to hers, giving her plenty of time to push him off.

She didn't.

When his arms tightened around her and he shifted his position slightly to pull her closer against him, she experienced a secret thrill. He kissed her again and again, but didn't deepen the kiss until she opened her mouth and tasted him.

With a low groan, he invaded her mouth, kissing her deeply, the way she remembered.

But after a few minutes of heaven he pulled away, tucking her head back into the hollow of his shoulder, his chest rising and falling rapidly beneath her ear. "Sorry," he muttered.

Sorry? She frowned. "For what?"

"I promised we'd go slow," he said in a low rough voice full of self-disgust. "A few more minutes of kissing you like that and I would have forgotten my promise."

She frowned. "I'm a woman, not a victim," she said, her tone sharp.

He pressed a chaste kiss to the top of her head. "I know, but there's no rush, Raine. Just holding you in my arms is more than enough for now."

She closed her eyes on a wave of helpless frustration. This wouldn't be enough for her. Maybe Caleb needed more time to grapple with what had happened.

He continued his soft caress, stroking his hand down her back and soon her irritation faded. She snuggled against him, relishing the closeness.

Maybe this was Caleb's way of starting over. Like from the very beginning. And if so, he was right.

There was no rush.

Raine realized she must have fallen asleep because her world tilted as Caleb lifted her off the sofa and carried her into the bedroom. She hadn't been in her bed since that night, but she didn't protest—unwilling to ruin the moment with bad memories.

When he slid in beside her, she relaxed, unable to deny the wide bed was much more comfortable than the cramped sofa, despite their bulky clothes. Using his chest as a pillow, she closed her eyes and tried to relax, regretting more than ever that they hadn't made love during the two months they'd been together. If they had, maybe she'd have that memory to sustain her now.

Hours later, she woke up again when Caleb shifted beneath her. This time she felt the mattress give, and she blinked the sleep from her eyes, watching as he sat on the edge of the bed running his fingers through his tousled hair. Her stomach tightened with anxiety. "Are you leaving?"

He twisted toward her, as if surprised to find her awake. He flashed a crooked smile and leaned over to brush a kiss over her mouth. "I don't want to go, but I almost forgot about Grizz. I let him out after work, but that was hours ago. I need to get home to take care of him."

She'd forgotten about Grizz too, but maybe he was just using the dog as an excuse. Sleeping in Caleb's arms had been wonderful, but suddenly it seemed as if the passionate kiss they'd shared had never happened. She tried to smile. "Too bad you can't bring him over here."

He must have sensed the wistfulness of her voice, because he rolled back toward her, stretching out beside her. "Raine, I wouldn't leave at all if it wasn't for the dog. I promised my dad I'd take care of him. I don't think Grizz has ever been alone all night before."

"I know. I'm sorry. Of course you have to go." She was ashamed of her selfishness. Hadn't they agreed there was no rush? Why was she clinging to him, afraid to let him go? "Thanks for staying, Caleb. I appreciate it more than you know."

"Raine," he murmured on a low groan as he gathered her close. "I don't want to leave. But I have to." He kissed her, deeply, his muscles tense, his need evident.

She drowned in the sensation as he gave her a glimpse of what their renewed relationship might hold. But then, all too soon, he broke away, moving as if to get up out of her bed. "You're making this difficult for me. I really have to go," he said in a gravel-rough tone.

She forced herself to let him go. "Give Grizzly a hug for me, okay?"

He stopped, and then turned back to her, propping his hand beneath his head so he could look down at her. "You could come with me. If you don't have other, more pressing plans, we could spend the day together."

She didn't have any plans, much less pressing ones. And spending the day with Caleb held definite appeal. But she didn't want to sound too pathetically eager. "You're not scheduled to work?"

"No. Are you?"

She shook her head. She wasn't needed at the animal shelter today either. What better way to start over than to spend a Sunday together? "All right, if you're sure."

For an answer, he kissed her again. She couldn't help pulling him close to deepen the kiss. "I'm sure," he said, breaking off from the kiss. "And we'd better leave soon, because I'm very close to not caring if Grizz relieves his bladder in my house."

She laughed, feeling light-hearted for the first time in weeks. She gave him a playful push. "All right, let's go."

Caleb scrubbed the exhaustion from his face as he waited for Raine to finish in the bathroom.

Holding Raine in his arms had been worth sacrificing his sleep. He didn't regret a moment of their night together. Kissing her, holding her, had been a test of his willpower.

Maybe his body was hard and achy this morning, but he didn't care. Somehow he'd managed to ignore his needs and give Raine the security she deserved. Her peace of mind was far more important than his discomfort.

Long into the night, he'd been unable to keep his imagination from dwelling on what she'd been through. He'd only brought her into the bedroom after she'd almost fallen right off the sofa. He'd hoped he could help her get over her aversion to sleeping in her bed.

Unfortunately he'd been tortured by images of how the bastard had brought her here, taking Raine against her will. He was surprised his suppressed anger and tense muscles hadn't woken her up.

Grimly, he told himself that focusing on what had happened wasn't going to help rekindle their relationship. He needed to get over it. And soon.

The way Raine had responded to his kiss proved she was on the road to recovery. He refused to hamper her healing in any way. If she could get past what had happened, surely he could do the same.

"Okay, I'm ready," she said, hurrying back into the living room where he waited. She poured fresh water into a bowl for Spice and then gave the cat a gentle pat. "See you later, sweetie."

"We could bring Spice if you want. Maybe Grizzly will grow on her," he said, eyeing the cat doubtfully.

Raine brightened, but then reconsidered with a shake of her head. "That's a good idea, but maybe some other time."

He hid his relief. Considering the way the cat had hissed at him, he couldn't imagine Spice would be all too thrilled to meet Grizz, but he'd wanted the decision to be hers.

When they got to his house, he couldn't help feeling guilty when he found Grizz stretched out in front of the door, obviously waiting for him. The dog jumped excitedly, his tail wagging furiously when Raine came in behind him.

"Come on, Grizz, go outside first," he muttered, shooing the dog out back.

The dog took care of business and then came back to the door, looking eager to come back in. Raine opened the door for Grizz as he put out food and water for him.

"I need to call the hospital, see how my dad is doing," Caleb said, glancing at the clock. "And I'd planned to visit today, too, if you don't mind."

"Of course I don't mind," Raine said, looking affronted.

He flipped open his cellphone to call Cardiology. It took a few minutes before he was connected with his father's nurse.

After Caleb explained who he was, the nurse sounded relieved to hear from him. "Your father is not having a good day. He's refusing to get out of bed and has been crabby with the nurses. His surgeon has been in to see him, though, and medically he's doing fine. Emotionally, not so well."

He didn't like the sound of that. "Okay, let him know I'm coming to visit. And tell him I'm bringing company. Hopefully that will cheer him up."

"I will."

He closed his phone and glanced at Raine. "Dad's

crabby today, refusing to get up and overall being a pain to the staff. I hope it's not a sign he's taking a turn for the worse."

Raine frowned at the news. "I hope not, too." She glanced down at Grizzly, who'd finished inhaling his food and had come over to nudge her hand with his head, seeking some attention. "Hey, I have an idea. Maybe we can take Grizzly in to visit."

Caleb stared at her. Had she lost her mind? "Since when are dogs allowed to visit patients? Especially on a surgical floor? And I think he's a little too big to sneak in."

"No, really, this could work." Raine took out her own cellphone and dialed a number. He soon realized she was talking to someone in the safety and security department. "Hi, Bryan? This is Raine Hart. How are you? It's nice to talk to you, too. Hey, I'd like to invoke the pet visitation policy. There's a patient, Frank Stewart, on the third-floor cardiac surgery unit who's depressed today. He's a veterinarian, volunteering his time at the animal shelter, and I'd like to schedule a visit with his black Lab, Grizzly."

Caleb listened in astonishment. A pet visitation policy? He'd never heard of such a thing. But apparently Raine knew all about it and, more, she knew how to arrange the visit.

"Great. We'll be there in two hours, then. Thanks very much." Raine's expression was full of triumph as she snapped her phone shut. "It's all set. We need to stop by Security and the nurses will arrange for your dad to be brought down in a wheelchair to the family center. There's a private conference room we can use."

"Amazing," Caleb murmured. And he wasn't just talking about how she'd picked exactly the right way to cheer up his dad. Raine was a truly amazing woman in all the ways that mattered. "All right. Hopefully this will help to cheer him up." Because if this didn't work, he was afraid nothing would.

Caleb couldn't believe no one stopped them as he and Raine walked into the front door of the hospital, holding Grizzly's leash. Following the rules, they crossed over to the security offices, located down the hall from the main lobby.

"Hi, Bryan," Raine greeted the tall, rather young-looking security guard with a hug. For a moment he wondered if there had once been more between Raine and the handsome officer. A sharp pang of jealousy stabbed him in the region of his heart. "Good to see you. How's Melissa? And the baby?"

"They're great," Bryan said.

Belatedly, Caleb noticed the security officer's wedding ring. Cursing himself for being an idiot, he reached down to pat Grizz. Damn, he'd done it again. Jumped to a stupid conclusion without giving her the benefit of the doubt.

"I think your patient is already down here, waiting for you." Bryan led the way down toward the family center conference room.

Sure enough, the door of the conference room stood ajar and he could see his father, slumped in a wheelchair with his eyes closed, looking almost as bad as he had that first night in the ICU. Alarmed, he pushed the door open and rushed in. "Dad? Are you all right?"

"Huh?" His father straightened in his seat, prising his eyes open. And then his entire face lit up, brighter than a Christmas tree, when he saw the dog. "Grizzly! Come here, boy."

Caleb let go of the leash, relaxing when his father bent over to pet the dog, who immediately tried to crawl up into his father's lap, not that the ninety-pound dog would fit.

"Grizz, it's so good to see you," his father crooned, lavishing the dog with attention. "Did you miss me? Huh? Do you miss me, boy?"

Caleb was very glad Raine had arranged the visit. When she came up to slip her arm around his waist, leaning lightly against him, he realized why his father kept trying to find someone to share his life with. Because it was nice to share everything, good times and bad, with someone.

He'd only been in kindergarten when his mother had taken off, but he was ashamed to realize he hadn't really looked at the situation from his father's point of view in the years since. His father had been abandoned by his wife. And he'd had a small son to care for while trying to run a veterinary practice. Could he blame his dad for wanting someone to share his daily life with? For wanting help in raising a son?

Was it his father's fault he'd picked the wrong women? His father deserved better. He suddenly he couldn't stand the thought of his father being alone.

"Have you thought about patching things up with Shirley?" he asked abruptly.

"Shirley?" His father's face went blank for a moment, and then the corner of his father's mouth quirked upward. "You mean Sharon?"

Oops. Damn. "Yeah, that's it. Sharon."

Raine scowled. "Wait a minute—Sharon? What about Marlene Fitzgerald? From the shelter?"

"Marlene?" His father's cheeks turned a dull shade of

red and suddenly every iota of his father's attention was focused on Grizz. "We're just friends," he muttered.

"Just friends?" Raine's brows hiked upward. "Really? Because she looked devastated when she heard you'd had emergency open heart surgery."

She had? Caleb was exasperated to discover Raine knew more about his father's recent love life than he did.

"She came to visit, but I sent her away." His father frowned. "A woman wants a man who'll take care of her, not an invalid like me."

Caleb hid a wince, because he could certainly understand. Starting a relationship so soon after open heart surgery probably wasn't a good plan.

"That's not true," Raine protested, going over to kneel beside his father's wheelchair. Grizz licked her cheek, but she didn't take her imploring gaze off his father. "A woman wants a man to be her partner. And the whole point of a partnership is taking turns helping each other."

Caleb stared at her as the full impact of her words slowly sank into his brain.

He'd been an idiot. Like his father, Raine didn't want to be an invalid. She'd said as much, hadn't she? She didn't want him to take care of her, the way he'd been trying to do since he'd discovered she'd been assaulted.

His gut clenched in warning. He'd asked for a second chance, but he knew that a big part of his reasoning had been because he'd wanted to help Raine through her ordeal. To support her.

But obviously that wasn't at all what she wanted from him.

CHAPTER ELEVEN

A COLD chill trickled down his spine. Could he be a true partner for Raine? Could he put aside his doubts for good? God knew, he wanted to.

Just minutes earlier he'd watched her hug Bryan, the young security guard, and instantly the old familiar doubts had crept in.

He wanted a second chance with her—but if he blew it this time, he knew there wouldn't be another.

"Maybe you're right," his father said, giving Raine a half hopeful, half uncertain look. "But I can barely get around. I'll wait to talk to Marlene until after I get back on my feet."

"I think you should talk to her sooner rather than later," Raine mildly disagreed, scratching Grizzly behind the ears. "Unless you think for some reason she won't get along with Grizz?"

"The dogs at the shelter seem to like her well enough, and she's not afraid of them. I'm sure Grizz will like her, too."

"Well, that's good, because you certainly wouldn't want to call on a woman who doesn't get along with your dog," Raine lightly teased.

"Sharon was afraid of Grizz," his father said. "I should have known that was a bad sign. I think Grizz could tell, too because he growled at her. And he never growls at anyone."

Raine laughed, a light-hearted sound that reminded Caleb of the wonderful times they'd spent together. She'd told him she wasn't the same woman she'd been before, but he didn't agree. The old Raine was still there, and given enough time and healing she'd return. "Definitely not a good sign. Spice hissed at Caleb, too," she confided.

He put a lid on his troublesome thoughts. "Guess that means I don't have much of a chance, huh?" he asked in a light tone.

Raine glanced over her shoulder at him and raised a brow. "I don't know. I'll think about it."

His father glanced between them with a knowing smile, looking a hundred times better than when they'd first arrived. "What plans do the two of you have for today?"

"Nothing special," Raine said with a shrug.

"Why not go to the state fair?" his father persisted. "It opened on Friday and goes all week."

"The fair? I haven't been on the Ferris wheel in ages," Raine murmured. But her eyes brightened with interest, and Caleb knew his father had presented the perfect solution.

"I haven't been to the fair lately either, but I'm up for it if you are," he said, hoping she'd agree.

Her smile widened. "I'd love to."

"Have fun," his father said, shifting in his seat. He glanced longingly at the dog. "Do you think the nurses would notice if Grizz stayed with me in my room?"

"I think they might become a tad suspicious, especially

when he needs to go outside," he said wryly. "How much longer will you need to stay in the hospital?"

"They're talking about sending me home in a day or two, depending on how well I can walk," his father admitted.

"Well, I guess you'd better get walking, then." He made a mental note to talk to Steven Summers for himself. "I'll be happy to move in for a while to help once you're home."

"Thanks." The older man leaned over to give the dog one last hug. "See you soon, Grizzly," he murmured.

Caleb felt bad leaving his father at the hospital, but they needed to take Grizzly home. "Good idea, bringing Grizz in for a visit," he said to Raine as they walked with Grizzly outside.

"He really perked up, didn't he? And I bet Marlene would be willing to help your father, too, if he'd only give her a chance."

"Maybe he will." Caleb didn't want his father to be alone, but he also didn't want his father to rush into anything.

He wanted his father to take his time, to find the right woman to partner with.

And as he glanced at Raine he knew it was time to take his own advice. Raine wasn't Tabitha. She was a hundred times better than Tabitha. If he couldn't trust Raine, he couldn't trust anyone.

Thrilled with the idea of going to the state fair, Raine could hardly maintain her patience as Caleb took care of Grizz. She hadn't been to the fair since going with her older brothers, years ago.

When Caleb was finally ready to go, she nearly skipped

with anticipation. The sounds and scents of the fair reminded her of happier times.

"There's the Ferris wheel," she said, clutching Caleb's arm with excitement.

"Do you want something to eat first? Or after the ride?" he asked.

"Eat first, but I don't want any of that weird fried food on a stick," she said, grimacing at the people in front of them who were eating deep-fried Oreo cookies on a stick. "I'm sorry, but that looks disgusting."

"Okay, nothing on a stick," he agreed good-naturedly.

They settled on burgers, and then wandered down the midway. She remembered the Ferris wheel as being huge, but now that she was an adult the ride wasn't nearly as impressive.

But Caleb had already bought their tickets, so she stood in line beside him. When it was their turn, she felt like a giddy teenager, sliding into the seat next to him.

Caleb put his arm around her and she leaned against him contentedly as they began their slow ascent. When they reached the top, she gazed down at the fairgrounds, amazed at how far she could see.

"Look at all the people," she said in a low whisper, suddenly struck by how much more crowded everything looked from up here.

"Check out the lines of people streaming in through the entrances," Caleb pointed out. "We must have arrived well before the rush."

She leaned a little closer to Caleb, abruptly glad to be up in the Ferris wheel, far away from the crowd. She'd never been enochlophobic before, but she was feeling apprehensive about going back down amidst the masses of people.

"You're not afraid of heights, are you?" Caleb asked, as if sensing her fear.

"No, not at all." And she wasn't afraid of crowds either. She was determined not to let anything ruin her day.

"Good." He leaned down and pressed a soft kiss against her mouth.

The ride was over too soon. When their car came to the bottom of the Ferris wheel and stopped, she stepped off with reluctance.

She led the way back down the midway, but people were pressing against her, and she must have muttered "Excuse me" a dozen times in her attempt to get past.

When a particularly large man shoved her backward, a rush of panic exploded. *"Let me through!"*

"Raine?" She could hear Caleb calling her name, but couldn't see him. And suddenly she wasn't standing in the midway of the state fairgrounds any more.

The music of the After Dark nightclub was deafening. Her feet ached from dancing, but suddenly she just wanted to go home. But where was Jamie? And the rest of her friends?

Sandwiched between two guys, she tried to brush past, but their large frames held her captive. Yet despite the close contact, she wasn't alarmed.

"Hey, you're not leaving already, are you?" the one guy asked, taking hold of her arm. "I thought we were celebrating? I just bought you a drink."

She'd recognized two of the rugby followers they'd danced with earlier. The one guy talked a lot, but the other one just looked at her. "Just a soft drink, right?" she'd clarified, before accepting the glass.

"Yeah, just a soft drink."

The brief memory faded away. That had been the last thing she remembered before waking up the next day, feeling extremely hungover. Her body had ached in places it shouldn't have but it hadn't been until she'd found the white stain on her sheets that the sick realization had dawned.

She'd been drugged and raped.

"Raine!" Caleb's worried face filled her field of vision, his hands lightly clutching her shoulders. "What happened? Are you all right?"

She tried to nod but realized her face was wet with tears so she shook her head. "I need to get out of here," she whispered. "Can we leave now? Please?"

Caleb's expression turned grim and he nodded, tucking her close. "Excuse us," he said loudly, using his arm as a battering ram as he barreled through the crowd. "Move aside, please."

It seemed like an eternity but they eventually broke free of the worst of the mass of people. "What happened?" he asked in a low, urgent tone. "Did you see someone who looked familiar?"

She shook her head, unable to speak. He worried that she'd seen someone from that night, and she had, but only in her repressed memories. Caleb must have understood, because he didn't push for anything more but simply tucked her under his arm and led the way out of the fairgrounds to the street where they'd parked their car.

Safe in the passenger seat, she slowly relaxed. "Thanks," she murmured.

His gaze was full of concern. "I'm sorry. I didn't realize the crowds would get to you."

"Neither did I," she admitted. "And it wasn't just the

crowd, it was being in that crush that brought back memories of that night."

Caleb started the car and pulled into traffic. "Do you think you could recognize him?" Caleb asked.

"Maybe." But she wasn't completely certain. For one thing, there had been two guys and she was sure only one of them had taken her home. But which one she had no idea. They'd claimed to be friends of one of the rugby players, but which player? "The nightclub was really crowded, and it was hard to move, just like it was on the midway. Two guys bought me a soda, but unfortunately, that's the last thing I remember."

"It's okay. They'll catch him," Caleb said with a confidence she was far from feeling. When he reached out to take her hand, she grasped it gratefully. She was relieved when he let the topic go without pressing for more details.

"Sorry we didn't get to see much of the fair," she said, feeling slightly foolish now that the initial panic had faded.

"It doesn't matter, Raine. I was only interested in spending the day with you." His sincere tone made her believe he truly didn't mind. "I'm sure Grizz is lonely. I'll cook you dinner at my place instead."

"Really?" she couldn't remember him ever offering to cook for her when they'd dated before. She had to admit she was impressed with his willingness to start over. "Are you sure you don't mind?"

"Of course I don't mind. We'll have to stop at the grocery store, though, to pick up a few things."

"Okay." When they stopped at the grocery store, located not far from Caleb's house, they bought more than just a *few things*. Caleb started with thick ribeye steaks and fresh mixings for a salad, but somehow their entire cart was soon full of other goodies before they made their way to the checkout.

She'd never grocery shopped with a man before, other than with her brothers, but in her experience with the men in her family she knew the food they'd purchased today would be lucky to last a half a week. Less, if she stayed with him.

Not that he'd invited her to stay, she reminded herself. This was their second chance, and there was no rush.

Pushing the longing aside, she focused on spending the rest of the day with Caleb, without being affected by the shadows of the past.

Caleb tried to remain nonchalant after Raine's meltdown at the state fair, but he couldn't help sending her worried glances when she wasn't looking.

The frank fear etched on her face would remain seared into his memory for a long time.

He was stunned she'd remembered something from the attack. He'd wanted to press for more information about that night, but had forced himself to back off, grimly realizing the details he'd wanted to hear would only hurt her.

And he didn't want to hurt Raine, ever again.

He watched her play fetch with Grizzly out in the back yard; the dog had been ecstatic to see them when they'd returned home. Being with Raine seemed so right. As if she belonged here. Although in his scenario she'd be playing with her own dog, Rusty, instead of Grizz. Not that he wouldn't have minded keeping Grizz either. But clearly his dad needed Grizzly more than he did.

As he put the groceries away, he wondered how to

broach the subject of her staying here with him overnight. The thought of letting her go home to face the night alone made him feel sick to his stomach. No matter how he tried, he couldn't get over feeling protective of her.

But he'd do his best to be a partner, like she wanted.

He made a quick call to his father's surgeon, verifying that indeed his father would likely be discharged on either Monday or Tuesday. He then made arrangements to be off work for a few days so that he'd have time to help his father make the transition home.

After that, he made two salads, cutting up the ingredients and putting everything in the fridge for later. He went outside, to find that Raine had dropped into one of his wide-backed Adirondack chairs, exhausted after her romp with Grizzly.

"Let me know when you're hungry, and I'll throw the steaks on the grill," he said, taking a seat in the chair next to hers.

"I'm ready whenever. I'm glad we came back, I think poor Grizz has been lonely."

"Yeah, I'm sure he'll be much happier when my father is finally discharged from the hospital." He reached over to scratch Grizz behind the ears. "I talked to Dr. Summers and he told me to plan on my father coming home tomorrow or Tuesday."

"That's wonderful news. I'm sure it will take a while, but your father will feel much better now that he's had the surgery."

"I hope so." He stood and walked over to light the charcoal sitting in the bottom of the grill. "Guess dad won't be eating steaks for a while," he mused.

She let out a quick laugh. "Nope, guess not. Good thing we're having them tonight, then, isn't it?"

He tried to make sure the atmosphere between them stayed relaxed and companionable as he grilled the steaks, sautéing some fresh mushrooms on the side. He brought out the salads and two TV trays so they could eat outside. He thought about offering to open a bottle of Merlot but, remembering Raine's preference for water, decided against it.

Certainly he didn't need any alcohol. Raine's presence was intoxicating enough.

As dusk began to fall, the mosquitoes came out, so reluctantly they carried everything inside.

Together, they cleaned up the mess Caleb had left in the kitchen. Working as a team, the chore didn't take long.

"Caleb, do you mind if I ask you a question?" Raine asked, after they'd finished.

"Of course not." He draped the damp dishtowel over the counter to dry.

"Do you want me? Intimately? The way you did before?" she asked, her cheeks stained bright red. "Or are you turned off because I was raped?"

What? He wanted to kick himself for making her doubt his feelings. Instantly he crossed over to her, clasping her shoulders and trying to encourage her to meet his gaze. "No, Raine, I'm not turned off by what happened. Why would you think that?"

"Because each time you kissed me last night, you were the one to pull away."

He couldn't deny it. But when he'd pulled back, it had been because he'd been close to forgetting what she'd been through. "Only because I promised I wouldn't rush you into doing anything you weren't ready for."

She bit her lower lip. "And what if I can't know what I'm ready for if we don't try?"

He stared at her. Was she really saying what he thought she was saying? "Raine, just a few hours ago you freaked out at the fair. I think that shows you still have a way to go before fully recovering from the assault." And he'd never forgive himself if he frightened her.

She must have read his mind. "You won't frighten me, Caleb. I freaked out at the fair because of the strangers surrounding me. But I didn't feel the least bit frightened last night. In fact, I felt safe and normal for the first time in weeks. You helped me realize that I've gotten over the worst of what happened." She frowned. "But I know that just because I'm getting over what happened, it doesn't mean you have."

Her insight struck a chord, because she was right. How long had he known about her assault? Three days? Not nearly enough time to come to grips with what she'd been through. But that was his problem to wrestle with, not hers. And he did want her, too much for his peace of mind. "Raine, please don't worry about me."

"I won't worry about you if you agree to stop worrying about me. Deal?"

"Deal," he said, his voice clogging in his throat when she stepped closer, wrapping her arms around his waist.

"Kiss me," she whispered.

He couldn't have denied her request to save his soul. He kissed her, lightly at first, but when she responded by melting against him, he deepened the kiss, sweeping his tongue into her mouth.

Last night he'd made the mistake of treating Raine like a victim, and he vowed not to make that same mistake again. He loosened his iron-clad grip on his control, showing her how much he wanted her.

Grizz barked, interrupting their kiss. Caleb struggled to calm his racing heart as he glared at the dog. "What is your problem? Get your own girl."

The dog looked at him, perplexed. Raine giggled. "Maybe he needs to go outside."

Muttering something not very complimentary about the dog, he peeled himself away from Raine long enough to let the dog out. Grizz did his business and then bounded back inside.

He turned back toward Raine. "I'd like you to stay with me tonight. No pressure, we can just sleep if that's all you want."

She tilted her head, regarding him solemnly. "And what if I want more than just to sleep?"

His groin tightened, betraying the depth of his need. Forgetting what she'd been through was easier if he concentrated on her. "Your decision, Raine. Always your decision. We can stop any time."

"Then I decide yes." Her simple words stole his breath. Her faith in him was humbling.

He was damned if he'd let her down.

He barely remembered leading her to his bedroom. One moment they were standing in the kitchen, the next she was in his arms, kissing him like she'd never stop.

He'd planned to take this slowly, to give her plenty of time to change her mind, but when she tugged at his clothes, he could barely suppress a low groan.

Taking control of the situation the best he could, he shucked off his jeans and shirt, keeping his boxers on, and then helped her strip down to her bra and panties. From there he lifted her up and set her gently on the bed.

She gazed up at him as he stretched out beside her.

"Slow and easy, Raine," he murmured. "There's no rush, remember?"

"I want you, Caleb," she whispered, stroking her hand down his chest, dangerously close to the waistband of his boxers.

He swallowed hard, and bent to press a trail of kisses down the side of her neck to the enticing V between her breasts, as he stroked his hand down over the curve of her belly, and then lower to the moist juncture of her thighs. "I want you, too. Let me show you how much."

She gasped and arched when he pressed against her mound. "Make love to me," she begged.

"Absolutely," he promised huskily, determined to make this experience a night she'd never forget.

One that would forever replace the dark shadows of the past.

CHAPTER TWELVE

RAINE clung to Caleb's shoulders, her senses reeling from his sweetly arousing touch. They weren't even naked and her body hummed with tension. She knew Caleb was going slow, worried about scaring her—but right now nothing existed but this moment. The two of them together, at last.

His caresses grew more intimate, sending shivers of pleasure rippling down her back. He peeled away her bra and underwear. She lightly raked her nails down his back and the way his muscles tensed and the low groan that rumbled in his throat gave her a secret thrill of satisfaction.

Caleb wanted her. Truly wanted her. And knowing he wanted her was the best aphrodisiac in the world.

When he continued to caress her, driving her to the edge, she sensed what he intended and pulled away. "No, Caleb. Not just me. Both of us together."

He stared at her, his eyes glittering with desire. "Are you sure?"

"Yes, I'm sure." She reached out to stroke his hard length beneath his boxers and he let out a low groan. "You're overdressed," she chided.

He drew back and fumbled for a condom. After stripping off his boxers, he sheathed himself and then rose above her. For a split second she froze, but then he kissed her and she relaxed, knowing this was exactly what she wanted.

As if sensing her moment of unease, he flipped onto his back, tugging her over so that she straddled him. His smoky gray eyes were nearly black with need. "Your choice, Raine," he huskily reminded her.

She stroked his chest and lifted up, until he was right where she wanted him to be. And when she gingerly pressed against him, he let out another low groan.

Beads of sweat popped out on his forehead but he didn't move, refusing to take control. She wasn't very experienced, had only one lover in college, but she lifted her hips and slid down, until he filled her. Even then he didn't move so she repeated the movement, lifting up and down, finding the rhythm and enjoying being the one in control.

He grasped her hips, deepening his thrusts, and she gave a murmur of encouragement. The tension built to the point where she didn't think she could hold back another moment.

And then abruptly, she peaked, spasming with pleasure so intense she cried out at the same moment she felt Caleb pulsating inside her.

Together, at last.

She was asleep when Grizzly nudged her hand. She opened one eye and peered at the clock, noting the sun had just barely begun to peek over the horizon. It was early. Too early. She closed her eyes, trying to ignore him.

Grizz nudged her again, insistently, and she let out a

tired sigh, knowing the poor dog probably needed to go outside. Carefully, so as not to wake Caleb, who was sprawled across the center of the bed, she slid out from beneath his arm. Grabbing her jeans and one of his sweat-shirts, she hastily dressed before tiptoeing from his bedroom.

She softly closed the door behind her, so he could sleep a little longer, and then met Grizzly at the back door, where he waited rather impatiently.

"Go on, you big oaf," she said fondly, opening the door.

She made herself a pot of coffee, figuring Caleb wouldn't mind. When the coffee finished brewing, she added her favorite vanilla-flavored creamer, and then carried the mug outside.

Curled up in Caleb's Adirondack chair, she watched Grizz sniff the grass and basked in the glorious night they'd shared.

Being intimate with Caleb had been amazing. He had been tender and kind, treating her as a precious treasure yet making it clear how much he wanted her.

Maybe they could make this work. Surely he'd trust her now.

She sipped her coffee and forced herself to face the truth.

She was falling in love with Caleb.

Love. There was a part of her that was amazed, con-sidering everything she'd been through, at how she could actually fall in love with Caleb. Somehow it was easier now to relinquish her heart.

Yet on the heels of her happiness came a warning chill. What if Caleb didn't feel the same way? Sure, he cared about her, he'd told her that much, but love? In order to love someone you had to trust them completely. Implicitly.

Was Caleb capable of loving her the way she loved him?

Curling her fingers around the steaming mug, she tried to suppress her dire thoughts. He'd promised to work on his trust issues. She wasn't foolish enough to believe it would happen overnight. As long as he was making the effort, she could be patient.

Grizzly sniffed his way around the yard, happily marking every bush and tree with his scent, making her smile. From the very beginning she'd always felt at home with Caleb. There'd been this sense of rightness in being with him.

"Raine?" he bellowed so loudly she started, sloshing coffee onto the front of his sweatshirt. She uncurled herself from the chair, even as Grizzly bounded toward the door.

"I'm out here," she called.

He threw open the door, his gaze landing on her with something akin to wary disbelief. "I couldn't find you."

"Grizzly needed to go out and I didn't want to wake you." She tried to make light of the situation, but his brief yet very real panic couldn't be ignored.

He'd thought she'd left. Like his mother had abandoned him all those years ago. No wonder he found it so difficult to trust.

And in that moment she realized he'd never really gotten over that feeling of being abandoned. Not really. And though she believed he'd try, she honestly didn't know if he ever would.

Raine began the process of cooking eggs and bacon for breakfast, sensing Caleb was annoyed with himself.

Determined to remain positive, she chatted as if nothing had happened. Caleb needed time and there was no rush. So she put forth her best effort, telling Caleb about some of the other animals at the shelter.

"Which reminds me, I probably need to get home soon," she said lightly. "Spice is going to be very unhappy with me."

"No, Spice is going to be unhappy with me," Caleb corrected. "Especially when you go home smelling like Grizz."

She shrugged. "I love my cat, but someday Spice is going to have to learn to co-exist with a dog, because I really want a dog of my own, too."

Caleb's smile was fleeting, but then he stared broodingly at his plate. "I hope you're not leaving because I acted like an idiot," he said finally.

"No, but tell me, how did you think I'd gotten home without a car? The distance between your place and mine is a pretty long walk."

He shrugged, his expression tense. "I wasn't thinking, it was a knee-jerk reaction."

Like the night he'd come in and found a semi-intoxicated Jake draped all over her, trying to kiss her.

She pushed her plate away. "Caleb, I could tell you I'd never betray you like that, but I'm pretty sure that nothing I can say will convince you. This is something you have to figure out on your own."

He gave a terse nod and rose to his feet. He stacked their dirty plates and then carried them into the kitchen. "I want to change, so maybe I'll take lessons from you."

"Not me," she protested. Her cellphone chirped and she frowned, pulling the instrument from the pocket of her jeans. She recognized her youngest brother's number on the screen. "Hello?"

"Raine?" Michael's familiar voice boomed in her ear. "Is that you?"

"Mikey! It's good to hear from you," she said, sincerely pleased to hear from the youngest of her three brothers. "What's up?"

"Where are you?" he demanded. "I'm at your apartment, and your car is here, but you're not answering the door."

Oh, boy. Her eyes widened in alarm. He was at her apartment? What on earth for? She ignored his over-protective tone. "Yes, Mikey, you're right. I'm not there. I can be there in a few minutes—though, if you need me. Is something wrong?"

"Nothing's wrong, but I'm in town for two days of training and figured I could bunk with my baby sister. I left you a message on your answering machine—didn't you get it?"

He had? She hadn't listened to her messages lately. "Er, no, I didn't."

"So I came to your apartment, and found your car was here, but you're not. You told me you worked second shift, right? I figured I needed to get here before you headed off to work."

She sighed and glanced at Caleb, who was listening to her one-sided conversation with a frown. "I don't work today, and it's fine if you want to stay with me for a few days."

"Where are you?" he demanded.

She refused to respond to her brother's Neanderthal tactics. "I'll be home in about fifteen to twenty minutes. You can either wait for me or go find something to do for a while."

"I'll wait," he said, and she could just imagine the scowl on her handsome brother's face.

"Fine. See you in a bit." She snapped her phone shut.

"Let me guess, one of your brothers?" Caleb asked wryly.

"Yes." She supposed it was a good sign that he didn't assume it was some former boyfriend. "He's at my apartment, waiting for me."

"Then I guess we'd better get going." Caleb let Grizzly outside and then led the way out to his car. "Are you going to tell him?"

"About us? I think he's going to figure it out when you bring me home," she said with a weary sigh. She wasn't in the mood for her brother's macho protectiveness, she really wasn't.

"No, not about us. About the assault."

She couldn't temper the flash of annoyance. "No. Why would I do that?"

"Because he's family, and he obviously cares about you. He should know," Caleb persisted.

After they'd spent the night making love, he went right back to the assault? Disappointment stabbed deep. Hadn't they moved beyond that? "No, he doesn't need to know. And if I were you, I'd worry about yourself, because Michael is not going to be pleased to meet you." At the moment she wasn't so pleased with Caleb either.

He sent her an exasperated glance. "It'll be fine."

"If you say so," she muttered darkly, crossing her arms over her chest.

When Caleb pulled up in front of her eight-unit apartment building, she saw her brother pacing on the sidewalk, talking and gesturing wildly into his phone. Great. No doubt he was telling Ian and Slade all about her spending the night with a man.

Good grief, she didn't need this.

She pasted a smile on her face when she climbed out of Caleb's car. Caleb came round to stand beside her and when Michael saw them, he abruptly ended his conversation and came striding toward her. "Hi, Raine. Who's this?"

"Caleb, this is my brother, Michael. Mikey, this is my friend Caleb Stewart. He's one of the ED physicians on staff at Trinity Medical Center."

"So what? Am I supposed to be impressed he's some sort of doctor?" Michael demanded, glaring at Caleb. "After he's spent the night sleeping with my baby sister?"

She rolled her eyes. "Knock it off. I'm twenty-six years old and you're acting like an idiot. What I do with my personal time is none of your business."

Her brother's gaze narrowed in warning. She'd known he'd react like this, as if she were some sixteen-year-old who couldn't make her own decisions.

"Michael, it's nice to meet you." Caleb stepped forward to offer his hand and she had to give him credit for trying to make peace. Her brother reluctantly shook it. "Raine talks about her three older brothers all the time. I know she cares about you very much."

Her brother's gaze softened a little. "I'm glad to hear that, because you need to know that if you hurt her, the three of us will hold you responsible."

She quickly interrupted to prevent the conversation from going anywhere close to the assault. "I can take care of myself, Mikey. And even if I can't, the mistakes I make are my own. Now, play nice with Caleb, or I won't introduce you to my boyfriends ever again."

"Sure, no problem." Michael rocked back on his heels and gave her a cheeky grin. "But just so you know, I already spilled the beans to Ian and Slade."

She knew it! She scowled at him. "Great. Thanks a lot. I should make you sleep in a hotel." She turned toward Caleb. "See what I mean? I tried to explain what it was like living with them, but you thought I was exaggerating."

The corner of Caleb's mouth quirked upward. "Nah, I knew you weren't exaggerating. I don't have a sister, but if I did, I think I'd probably feel the same way they do." He lifted one shoulder in an apologetic shrug.

"That's right, you would." Michael clapped him on the back, as they finally saw eye to eye on something.

She suppressed another sigh. "Well, grab your gear, then, and come on up. What time does your training start?"

"Noon." Michael glanced at Caleb in surprise when he fell into step beside them. "I hope you don't mind if I bunk here for the next two nights," he said, as if realizing three was, indeed, a crowd. "I haven't seen you in a while and figured this would be a good chance to catch up."

Which was his way of telling her that she'd better not plan on having Caleb stay over while he was there. As if she would.

"It's fine," she assured him. "Caleb's dad is actually scheduled to come home from the hospital either later today or tomorrow anyway."

"The hospital?" Michael's eyebrows rose. "I'm sorry to hear that. I hope he's okay?"

"He had triple bypass surgery and a valve replacement a few days ago, but he's doing much better," Caleb told him.

"I'm glad," Michael said.

"Mikey's a volunteer firefighter and a paramedic back home in Cedar Bluff," she explained for Caleb's benefit.

"I'm impressed. Fighting fires is a tough job."

"Well, I do more paramedic work than anything else," her brother said modestly. "Thankfully there aren't a lot of fires in Cedar Bluff. We have to do a lot more training, though, since we don't get as many chances to work in real fire situations. Which is why I'm here in Milwaukee."

Raine led the way inside her apartment, greeting Spice who lightly ran over to meet the newcomers. Spice veered away from Caleb, but meowed softly and brushed up against Michael's leg.

"She's a cutie. Probably smells Leo, the male tomcat we have down at the station," Michael said, bending down to stroke the cat. "Leo is quite the Romeo."

"Just like you, huh?" Raine said dryly. For all his protectiveness of her, her youngest brother was legendary with women. "Does anyone want coffee?" she called out, heading into the kitchen.

"I do," her brother announced. "Give me a minute to borrow your bathroom."

When her brother disappeared behind the bathroom door, she glanced at Caleb. "Are you all right?" she asked, considering he hadn't said much since meeting her brother.

He threw her an exasperated look. "Raine, your brother doesn't scare me. None of your brothers scare me. Don't worry about it. Although I do see what you mean about what it must have been like living with them. They don't recognize any personal boundaries, do they?"

"Not really." She filled the coffee-maker with water and started the pot brewing. "My parents died when I was just a sophomore in high school. The three of them were really pretty wonderful, moving back home to raise me."

Caleb's gaze was full of sympathy. "That must have been hard on you."

"It was hard on all of us. Mikey was a senior in high school himself, but Ian and Slade put their own college plans on hold to come home to help keep the family together. Truly, I owe them a lot. Which is why I pretty much got used to them sticking their nose into my personal business." She tried to lighten the sudden seriousness of the conversation. "Can you believe they went so far as to read my diary? Nothing was sacred. Absolutely nothing."

Caleb's lips twitched. "Will you let me read it?"

"No." She glowered at him. "Don't even think about it."

"Raine!" her brother bellowed from the bathroom.

She ground her teeth together, tempted once again to tell Michael to go find a hotel. "Now what's the problem?" she asked.

"My problem?" Her brother stomped out of her bathroom, a deep scowl creasing his forehead, and it took her a moment to realize he had her pregnancy test kit clutched in his hand. "Here's my problem. Are you pregnant?"

CHAPTER THIRTEEN

RAINE'S eyes widened in horror as her brother, the human bulldozer, revealed her most painful, shameful secret. She glanced frantically at Caleb in time to watch all the color drain from his face as he stared with utter disbelief at the pregnancy test kit.

And in that one awful, terrible moment she knew. No matter what he'd said earlier, he didn't trust her. Would likely never trust her.

Which meant he'd never love her the way she loved him.

There was a moment of dead silence before she moved, snatching the kit out of her brother's hand, wishing she dared to smack him with it. "No, I'm not pregnant." The stomach cramps she'd experienced earlier that morning convinced her that her period wasn't far off. "Keep your nose out of my business."

"Raine, you having a baby is my business. Our business. The child would be our niece or nephew. Of course, we'd help you raise the baby if some jerk took off and abandoned you." Michael glared at Caleb.

Caleb opened his mouth to speak and she sent him a

dark look, warning him not to say a word, either in his own defense about the child not being his or about the assault. "Leave Caleb alone, Mikey. I mean it. You're my brother and I love you, but that does not give you the right to intrude into my personal life."

Her brother raised his hands innocently, as if realizing he might have pushed too far. "Hey, I'm just saying—we'll stand by you."

She let out a sigh, knowing that at least that much was right. Her brother had always been there for her. And if she had gotten pregnant, her brothers would support her.

Unlike Caleb, whose face was suddenly completely devoid of all expression.

Obviously, she and Caleb needed to talk. Yet at the same time she couldn't help feeling irritated at his reaction. Why did she always have to explain herself? Couldn't he ever just once give her the benefit of doubt? What good would any explanation be if he refused to believe in her?

She'd known earlier that Caleb's lack of trust wasn't something she could help him overcome.

This was only irrefutable proof that he'd need to fix his problems on his own.

An awkward silence fell and she dreaded the conversation she and Caleb needed to have. "Mikey, give us a few minutes alone, would you?" she asked softly.

"Uh, yeah. Sure." Michael glanced between the two of them, with a shrug. "Actually, I was looking for a razor so I could shave." He scrubbed a hand over his jaw. "Can I borrow one of yours?"

"Help yourself," she said, knowing he would anyway. After her brother left them alone, she turned to Caleb. "I'm sorry. I tried to tell you my brothers were over-protective."

"You thought you were pregnant?" His tone was accusing.

She lifted her chin. "I guess attempting a second chance wasn't a good idea after all."

A flash of disbelief glittered in his eyes. "What sort of second chance did we have if you weren't honest with me? You never said a word about possibly being pregnant."

She stared at him, wondering if he was using this as an excuse to quit on the relationship before it even started. "I told you about the sexual assault. Didn't it occur to you that pregnancy might be a consequence? Besides, what difference does it make now? I used the test, I'm not pregnant."

He blew out a breath and turned away, avoiding her gaze. "Why didn't you say anything to me about it? You told me everything else, didn't you?"

She shook her head, tears stinging her eyes. This was his issue, not hers. "And if I say yes, I've told you everything else, will you believe me?"

When he didn't immediately answer, she swallowed hard. "I'm sorry, Caleb, but this isn't going to work." Trying to ignore the way her heart was aching, she walked over to her apartment door and opened it. "Thanks for driving me home. I'm sure I'll see you around at work."

Caleb stared at her for a long moment, and then walked past her. "Yeah. See you around," he muttered as he left the apartment.

Fighting tears, she slowly closed the apartment door behind him and then leaned heavily against it. Her stomach clenched and the familiar nausea that she now knew was a result of stress returned with a vengeance.

Caleb hadn't believed in her before the assault and he clearly didn't now. Even after the closeness they'd shared.

This time she knew their relationship was over.

Caleb left Raine's apartment and walked outside, reeling from their argument.

He couldn't believe she'd never told him her fears about being pregnant as a result of the assault. Of course he'd considered the possibility but hadn't pushed for the details. When she hadn't mentioned it, he'd assumed it wasn't a problem.

What else hadn't she told him?

Earlier that morning, he'd been angry when he'd thought she'd taken off without a word. He could readily admit that he'd overreacted, automatically thinking the worst.

When he'd found her outside, sitting on the deck with Grizzly, he'd felt like a fool. Especially when she'd given him a look full of reproach. He'd known then he needed to stop reading the worst into everything she said or did.

But this was different. They'd grown closer together over these past few days. They'd spent the night making love. Why would she keep secrets from him at this point in their relationship?

It was clear that if her brother hadn't found the test kit and bluntly confronted her with it, she wouldn't have mentioned the possibility at all.

He was so lost in thought he didn't realize he'd walked several blocks past his car until he came upon a stop sign for a major road. Muttering a curse, he spun on his heel and stalked back to where he'd left his car.

As he opened the door, about to slide in, he couldn't

help glancing up at Raine's apartment window. Of course she wasn't standing there, watching him. He climbed in behind the wheel and slammed the door behind him.

He hoped, for her sake, she did tell her brother what had happened. Raine had been through a terrible ordeal. She needed all the support she could get.

His cellphone rang, interrupting his thoughts. He glanced at the number, surprised to realize it was the hospital. His dad? His heart rate spiked in alarm as he quickly answered. "Hello?"

"Caleb? Can you pick me up?" After yesterday's visit, his father sounded surprisingly upbeat. "Doc says I'm ready to be discharged."

"Really? Sure, of course I'll pick you up. I can be there in a few minutes."

"Are you bringing Raine with you?"

His father's innocent question sent a shaft of pain through his heart. Raine would have loved to come with him to pick up his father. For a moment the reality of what had just happened upstairs in her apartment hit hard.

Their relationship was over. For good.

But this wasn't the time to tell his father the news. Not yet. "No, her brother is in town right now, visiting with her." He tried not to let his father hear the desolation in his tone. "But I'll let her know you're coming home. She'll be thrilled."

"Okay." His father readily accepted the excuse. "And don't forget we have to pick up Grizz on the way home."

"I won't forget. See you soon, Dad."

Caleb started the car and headed straight over to the hospital, grateful for something else to think about rather than the mess he'd made of his personal life.

Because there was no denying how lonely his house would feel now that both Raine and Grizzly were gone.

Caleb had been fully prepared to stay with his father during the first week after his hospitalization to help care for him at home. But surprisingly his father seemed to have taken Raine's advice to heart.

"Caleb, this is Marlene Fitzgerald, one of the volunteers at the animal shelter," his father said, introducing him to a spry, silver-haired woman standing next to him. She looked to be similar in age to his father, which by itself was unusual, since his father's women in the past had all been much younger. "Marlene, this is my son, Caleb. He's a doctor on staff here in the emergency department at Trinity Medical Center. He chose the path of taking care of people rather than animals."

Caleb stepped forward to take the older woman's hand. "Hi, Marlene. It's nice to meet you."

"Same here, Caleb." Marlene smiled, blushing a bit. "I hope you don't mind if I temporarily move in to help care for your father for a few days."

Temporarily move in? He arched a brow at his father. "Uh, no. Of course not. But I can help too, Dad. You've had major surgery, and I've arranged to take some time off work."

"There's no need for you to take off work for me," his father said gruffly. "I appreciate your efforts, but Marlene offered to help and I think together we'll be able to manage just fine."

"If you're sure…" Caleb gave in, as it appeared his father had planned everything out. "I'd still like to stop by each day to see how things are going."

"I'll take you up on that offer. Can't pass up the opportunity to get a house call," his father joked.

Caleb carried his father's belongings as Marlene pushed his wheelchair down to the hospital lobby. He went round to bring up the car and, as promised, stopped by his house on the way home to pick up Grizzly.

Marlene didn't seem to mind the dog, greeting Grizz with enthusiasm. She clearly loved animals as much as his father did.

He wanted to believe Marlene and his father were meant to be together, but the old suspicions wouldn't go away. Marlene seemed perfect now, but his father's relationships never seemed to last.

After dropping Marlene and his father off at home, taking time to ensure his dad was settled comfortably in his favorite recliner, with Grizz at his feet, Caleb headed home.

Greeted by nothing more than the echo of his own voice, he called the hospital to notify them he was available to work if needed after all. They promised to call if something opened up or if someone called in sick. Dejected, he stared out at his back yard, wondering what to do with the extra time on his hands.

If Raine was here, he would have been thrilled to have more time off work. But now he would rather have something to do to keep his mind off her.

Raine had been right about one thing. His trust issues were his own problem to fix. Keeping secrets wasn't the way to inspire trust, yet even before that he'd known he'd made mistakes.

Mistakes he wasn't sure how to fix.

Was he doomed to the same fate as his father? To have nothing but one failed relationship after another?

As much as he didn't want to go down that same path, he was at a loss as to how to break the pattern.

Raine sank down onto her sofa, overwhelmingly relieved when Mikey finally took off to attend his training session. She wanted, needed time alone to pull her battered emotions together.

She couldn't help replaying that moment her brother had asked if she was pregnant over and over in her mind. Her stomach clenched painfully. Even though she knew that Caleb hadn't fully trusted her before then, the shattered expression in his eyes still haunted her.

Did Caleb have a right to be upset? Should she have told him her fears?

Maybe.

She and Caleb had been doomed, right from the beginning. She'd been right to break things off before the assault.

The past would always stand between them.

Spice jumped up on the sofa beside her and she drew the cat into her arms, cuddling her soft fur. If only people were more like animals, full of unconditional love.

Her brothers loved her unconditionally. Was it unfair to expect the same from Caleb?

She didn't think so. Her parents had died too young, but she'd always known how much they'd loved and cared for each other. She wanted and deserved the same sort of love.

Since sitting around and wallowing in self-pity wasn't an option, she decided to spend the rest of her afternoon at the animal shelter. With Dr. Frank gone, they were probably short-handed. And she'd rather be busy to keep her mind off of Caleb.

She took a quick shower, shocked to discover her instincts were right. She'd gotten her period.

She'd begun blowdrying her hair when her phone rang. For one heart-stopping moment she wondered if the caller was Caleb. Was he calling to apologize and beg her to come back?

And why was she even tempted by the possibility when nothing had changed?

She dashed over to the phone, slowing down with a sharp stab of disappointment when the number displayed an unknown caller on her caller ID.

Letting the call go to her answering-machine, she headed back towards the bathroom to finish up. But stopped dead in her tracks when a familiar voice came over the speaker.

"Raine, this is Detective Carol Blanchard with the Milwaukee Police Department. Please call me as soon as you get this message. We need your help in identifying a suspect we have in custody. We believe he could possibly be the man who raped you."

They had a suspect? Raine dropped the brush she was holding, unable to believe it. Her fingers trembled so badly she had difficulty dialing Detective Blanchard's phone number. She told herself not to get her hopes up too high, but she held her breath, waiting for the detective to answer.

"Detective Blanchard."

"Detective, this is Raine Hart returning your phone call."

"Raine, I'm so glad you called me back so quickly. I know you don't remember the man who assaulted you, but we wanted to have you come down to the station to look at a line-up anyway. Our hope is that you can maybe pick out the guy who was at the nightclub the night of your assault."

"A line-up?" Her mouth went desert dry and her heart thudded painfully in her chest. "Uh, sure. If you think it might help."

"We do think this would help," Detective Blanchard assured her. "The DNA testing is going to take time, and we'd like to at least place this suspect at the scene of the crime. Could you be here in an hour?"

An hour? So soon? She swallowed a momentary flash of panic. "Of course. No problem."

"Great, we'll see you in an hour, then."

Raine hung up the phone, feeling jittery. She hurried to finish in the bathroom, wishing more than anything that Caleb was here with her. If they hadn't argued, he would have gone with her for moral support.

She pushed away the useless thoughts. But as she used the hairdryer, she couldn't help worrying.

What if she couldn't pick this guy out as one of the men who were at the After Dark nightclub that night?

And if she couldn't identify him, would he go free?

CHAPTER FOURTEEN

As RAINE walked up the concrete steps leading into the police station she saw a familiar figure walking down the stairs in the opposite direction. The woman walked with her shoulders hunched and her head down to avoid direct eye contact with anyone.

But Raine still recognized her. Helen Shore. Her sexual assault patient from the ED.

The knot in her stomach tightened. Had Helen successfully picked the suspect out of the line-up? Or was the fate of this man going to rest solely on her shoulders?

Her footsteps slowed as a tidal wave of doubt swept in. What if she picked the wrong man? Or, worse, what if she picked the suspect they had, but he was actually innocent?

The DNA evidence would eventually exonerate him if that were the case, but not for several weeks yet.

She took a deep breath, and walked into the police station. Detective Blanchard was waiting for her.

"Hi, Raine. How are you doing?" The detective's expression radiated true concern.

The tenseness in her stomach eased a bit. "Pretty good, all things considered."

Detective Blanchard's gaze was sharply assessing.

"You look good," she said slowly. "Like you've really re-covered. I'm glad. Well, are you ready?"

No, she wasn't ready. But she nodded. "Yes, but what happens if I can't pick this guy out of the line-up? Does he walk away?"

"Come with me, and I'll explain how this works." The detective led the way into a small room, with a one-way mirror lining the wall. "This suspect isn't going to walk away, no matter what happens here today. I don't want you to feel pressure to make the so-called right identification. We have enough evidence to hold this guy for a while. So don't worry about him being back on the street, because that's not going to happen. Just relax and do your best."

"Okay." She placed a hand over her heart, willing her pulse to slow down, and swallowed hard. "I'm ready."

Detective Blanchard hit a button on the intercom. "We're ready—bring the suspects in."

Raine watched as six men walked into the brightly lit anteroom in single file, each going to their assigned numbers. They all stood staring straight ahead, their hands down at their sides. A tingle of apprehension slithered down her spine, even though she knew they couldn't see her. She clasped her arms over her chest, wishing more than anything that Caleb was here to hold her.

She took her time, looking at each of the men. When she reached suspect number five, the tingle turned into a full-fledged shiver.

He was the silent one who'd been there that night. She was sure of it. But, still, she forced herself to look at suspect number six, too. And then Detective Blanchard gave the order for the men to turn to the right and then to the left, so she could get a thorough look at their profiles.

Her gaze went back to suspect number five. She was absolutely certain he was one of the two guys who'd been next to her that night. She remembered the way he'd watched her so intently without saying much, letting his buddy do all the talking for him.

"Number five," she said, looking at Detective Blanchard. "I recognize suspect number five as being in the nightclub that night. He and another man bought me a drink, and I don't remember anything after that."

"Are you sure?" Detective Blanchard asked, her gaze impassive.

For a moment her heart sank. Had she picked the wrong man? She turned back and looked at them again, but she knew number five was the man who'd been there. "Yes, I'm sure." Her voice rang out with confidence. "Number five."

A smile broke out on Detective Blanchard's face. She reached over to touch the intercom button. "Thanks, we're finished here." The men filed out of the room.

The detective turned toward her. "Good job, Raine. Number five is the suspect we arrested. His name is Colin Ward and your positive ID will help us when we present our case to the grand jury."

Overwhelming relief washed over her. Colin Ward? Sounded like such an average name. "What happened?" she asked curiously. "How did you end up arresting him?"

"We set up a sting operation at the After Dark nightclub with one of our young, very attractive female officers. We also had a cop working undercover behind the bar and we caught him spiking her drink with Rohypnol. The bartender quickly swapped it out but she played along, as if she was drunk. Colin Ward insisted on helping her out to her car, and once he'd stashed her in the passenger seat and slid behind the wheel with her keys, we nailed him."

"I can't believe he did it again," she whispered.

"He's a predator, no question about it. And when the DNA match is confirmed, and we're very sure it will be, this guy will go to jail for a long time."

She was glad, fiercely glad, that he'd been caught. How many others had he raped? She knew only too often that many women didn't come forward after something like that. Especially when they couldn't remember what had really happened.

She wanted to ask if Helen Shore had been able to identify him, too, but she held back, unwilling to break her patient's confidentiality. Helen's ability to ID him wouldn't matter as she herself had been able to pick him out without a problem.

Detective Blanchard walked her back outside, telling her she'd be in touch when and if the case went to trial. The detective thought that if the DNA evidence was positive, Colin Ward would cop a plea.

Raine nodded, hardly listening. No matter what happened from here, her nightmare was over. She'd thought she'd feel better once the guy was caught, and she did, except there was a part of her that still felt empty.

Because she didn't have Caleb.

She walked to her car and slid behind the wheel. She was tempted, very tempted, to call Caleb. He was the only one who'd understand how she felt. And in spite of their most recent break-up, she knew he'd want to know. She went so far as to pull out her cellphone, bringing up his number, but then hesitated.

No. She flipped her phone closed. She needed to figure out how to move forward with her life without him.

Because even if she called him now, and they managed to mend their rift from this morning, how long would the peace last?

Only until the next time she did something stupid. Or until the next time she grew tired of his inability to trust her.

She loved him, but they didn't have a chance at a future. Better to figure out a way to get over him, once and for all.

Caleb's father called two days after he'd been discharged, asking if Caleb could come over for a while because Marlene had to go and help her daughter, who needed an urgent babysitter for her sick child. He readily agreed, heading over right away.

Grizzly met him at the door, waving his tail excitedly. "Hi, Grizz, how are you? Taking good care of Dad, hmm?"

"Caleb? Is that you?" his father called from the kitchen.

"Yes, I'm here." Caleb made his way through the house into the kitchen. "Has Marlene left already?" he asked.

"Yeah, her daughter had to be at work by nine, so she went over first thing."

"I hope she doesn't bring germs back to you," Caleb said, pulling up a chair and sitting down beside his dad. "You need to stay as healthy as possible."

"Marlene said the same thing. She's just as worried as you are. I'm sure I'll be fine," his father said. "I'm surprised you didn't bring Raine with you. How is she?"

Caleb had dodged questions about Raine in the past few days, but he couldn't keep lying to his dad. He blew out a heavy breath. "She's fine, as far as I know. But we're not seeing each other any more."

"What?" His father glared at him. "Why not? What happened? Raine was perfect for you, Caleb. A keeper!"

He couldn't suppress a flash of annoyance. "And how would you know a keeper, Dad? You're hardly the expert. None of the women you picked stuck around long enough to be a keeper. What's the longest relationship you had since Mom left? Three years?"

His father's eyes widened and his frankly wounded expression hit Caleb like a punch to the gut.

His breath hissed out between his teeth. What was wrong with him? This wasn't his father's fault. "I'm sorry. I shouldn't have said that."

His father stared at him for a moment. "No, don't apologize. I never realized you felt that way."

Caleb winced. "I should have just kept my mouth shut," he muttered.

"No, I think you need to understand, Caleb. The reason I had trouble holding relationships together after your mother left was largely my own fault."

Caleb couldn't help but agree to a certain extent, because his father had obviously picked some losers. "No, it wasn't your fault, Dad. The women you were with made lousy choices."

"Listen, Caleb. I didn't love them. I couldn't love them, because I was still in love with your mother."

Caleb stared at his father in shock. "You loved her? Even after she left us?"

His father's smile was sad. "Son, you don't always control who you love. Your mother got pregnant with you and we tried to make a marriage work. But she was young and a very talented dancer. She talked constantly about pursuing a dancing career. When she told me she was moving to New York, alone, I wasn't entirely surprised."

He'd heard the story of his mother getting a part in the

Broadway play so the fact that she'd left them to dance wasn't a surprise. But his father's easy acceptance of her leaving was. "She left us both for her own selfish reasons and that's okay?"

"She was young," his father defended. "And I knew she wasn't ready to settle down. But I loved her. Even after she left, I didn't stop loving her."

"So why the string of women?" he asked.

His father flushed. "I felt bad for you, Caleb. I wanted you to have a mother. And I can't deny I was looking for some companionship, too."

Caleb scrubbed a hand over his face. "I understand. I can't blame you."

"You're missing the point. I couldn't give the women in my life the love they deserved. And they obviously knew that. So that's why those relationships ended. Carmen put up with me the longest, until she realized I wouldn't return her love. I think there was a part of me that kept holding back, hoping your mother would return once she'd gotten her dancing out of her system."

Caleb frowned. "She's married to someone else now. Heck, she has a new family of her own." He couldn't quite hide his bitterness. He'd reached out to his mother once, after high school, but she hadn't been very interested in the family she'd left behind.

"I know." His father didn't look surprised. "But it still took my heart a long time to give up hope. But don't blame the women who've come and gone over the years, Caleb. The blame is mine."

Caleb sat there, dumbfounded by the turn in the conversation. He sensed his father was telling the truth. For so long he had blamed the women in his father's life for not being trustworthy. And he'd blamed his father for his poor choices.

But it had never occurred to him how his father had ended up sabotaging his own relationships because he'd still loved his son's mother.

Had he let his own bitterness after the incident with Tabitha do the same? Ruin his chance at a decent relationship?

"If you love Raine with your whole heart and soul, you need to fight for her," his father urged in a low voice. "Don't let her go, Caleb."

Was it really that easy? He loved Raine. With his whole heart and soul. And he knew, honestly knew, she wouldn't intentionally hurt him.

His dad was right. Raine was a keeper.

He jumped to his feet. "Dad, I have to go." Then he realized he couldn't leave and abruptly sat back down. "Sorry, I almost forgot. I can't go right now. I'll wait for Marlene to come back."

"Tell you what. Throw something together for me to eat for lunch, and then you can go." His father idly rubbed his chest. "I promise I'll do my physical therapy exercises."

"Really?" Caleb glanced at his father doubtfully, desire warring with duty. "Are you sure?"

"I'm sure." His father put a hand on Grizzly's head. "Grizz and I will be just fine. I'll call you if I need something."

"Okay." Caleb grinned, clapping his dad on the back. "Thanks. For everything."

He was going to win Raine back, although he knew it wouldn't be an easy task.

He needed help. And he wasn't afraid to use every possible resource at his disposal.

Raine glanced up in surprise when her doorbell buzzer went off. Mikey? If so, her brother was early.

"Yes?"

"Raine? It's Caleb. I'd like to talk to you if you have a minute."

Caleb? Her heart squeezed in her chest and hope, ever foolish, surged. "Uh, sure. Come on up."

"Actually, I need you to come down."

She frowned. Why did she need to come down?

Admittedly curious, she grabbed her keys and headed out of the apartment, taking the stairs down to the lobby level. When she went outside, she was surprised to see Caleb standing there with Rusty, the sweet Irish setter from the animal shelter.

"Rusty!" she exclaimed, going down into a crouch to greet the dog. He waved his tail excitedly, lavishing her with doggie kisses that she laughingly avoided as much as possible. "It's so good to see him. I'm surprised he's letting you near him without growling," she said. "He's normally afraid of men."

"I know. It took me a few days to win him over, but I did. He's not afraid of me. I'm taking that as a sign we were meant to be together."

"You adopted him?" She was glad Rusty was going to a good home, but she couldn't hide the wistfulness in her tone.

"I'd like to. But that depends on you."

She frowned, slowly rising to her feet. "What do you mean?"

"Rusty has learned to trust me, and I'm hoping you will, too, when I ask for you to give me another chance."

Hope lunged in her heart, but she held back. "I don't know if that's a good idea," she began.

"Wait, please hear me out," he interrupted. "You were right, my problems weren't about you. They were about me. I needed to learn to trust myself. To let myself love you. It's a long story, but my dad made me realize what an idiot I've been."

His dad? The kernel of hope grew bigger.

"I love you, Raine. More than I can say. Every time I pushed you away, it was because I was holding back, protecting myself from being hurt. But I've been hurting since I walked away from you. And even if you send me away right now, I'm still going to love you."

She wanted to believe him, she really did. "I love you, too, Caleb. But sometimes love isn't enough. I don't think I can live with a man who constantly doubts me."

Contrary to her words, his face brightened. "But that's just it. I trust both of us. All I'm asking right now is for a chance to prove it to you."

Rusty nudged her hand, asking for attention. "You're not fighting fair," she murmured, glancing between the dog and the man she loved, who managed to gang up on her.

"I'm fighting for my life, Raine," he said, taking her comment seriously. "But I understand I've hurt you, even though I didn't mean to. So if you need time, that's fine, you can take all the time you need. But know that no matter what happens, I'll be waiting for you."

His willingness to back off surprised her. And she realized she couldn't let him take all the blame. "Not everything was your fault, Caleb. I didn't always confide in you. Living with three older brothers taught me that I couldn't talk about everything that bothered me because they would make such a big deal out of every little thing. So I learned to suppress a lot of what I was thinking and feeling. I'm sure my tendency to hide my deepest feelings didn't help your ability to trust me."

"Sweet of you to try to take the blame, Raine, but it's not your fault by a long shot. But if you're willing to give me a second chance, I won't argue."

Wasn't this the third chance? Maybe, but who was counting? Not her. Not any more. She was lucky enough to have people in her life who loved her unconditionally. Wasn't it time she did the same? Didn't Caleb deserve her unconditional love?

"I am willing," she said softly.

"You are?" He looked afraid to hope.

"Yes. Because I love you, too. I've been miserable without you. If you really think we can make this work, I'm more than willing to try again."

"Thank God," he murmured, reaching over to pull her into a warm embrace. "Things will be different this time, Raine. You'll see."

"I know." She lifted her eyes to his and he bent to capture her mouth in a searing kiss. Instantly she melted against him, longing for more.

"Wanna come to my place?" Caleb asked huskily, when she finally came up for air. "You could help Rusty get acquainted in his new home."

"Sure, I'll come over for a bit. But don't worry, he's going to love his new home," she assured him, giving the dog's silky ears a good rub.

"I don't want to rush you, Raine," Caleb said in a low

voice. "But my home can be your home too. Rusty and I will be waiting for you whenever you're ready."

She went still. "Really? Just like that?"

He nodded, no sign of hesitation. "Just like that."

Wow. She wasn't sure what to say. "I should probably tell you that the police caught the guy who assaulted me."

"They did?" Caleb looked surprised. "That's good news, Raine. I'm happy for you."

"I had to pick him out of a line-up," she confessed. "I wanted you with me so badly, but it all worked out. He's going to stay in jail without bail until the DNA results are in."

"I'm sorry I wasn't there for you," Caleb said, pulling her close for another hug. "I hope one day you'll be able to put all this behind you."

"I will," she said confidently. She couldn't help wondering if her relationship with Caleb hadn't somehow grown stronger through everything that had happened. If she hadn't changed, would the two of them be standing there right now? She doubted it. "I can face anything with you beside me."

Caleb gave her another one-armed hug, the other hand firmly on Rusty's leash. "I feel the same way, Raine. As if I can conquer anything with you at my side. I love you so much."

"I love you, too." Her smile shimmered straight from her heart as she tugged Rusty's leash from his hand. "Take us home, Caleb."

His eyes lit up with hope and promise. "Yes. Let's go home."

A NURSE
TO TAME
THE PLAYBOY

BY
MAGGIE KINGSLEY

*For my father, who was always my severest critic,
and who I very much hope would have enjoyed this book.*

DID YOU PURCHASE THIS BOOK WITHOUT A COVER?

If you did, you should be aware it is **stolen property** as it was reported
unsold and destroyed by a retailer. Neither the author nor the publisher
has received any payment for this book.

First published in Great Britain 2010
Harlequin Mills & Boon Limited,
Eton House, 18-24 Paradise Road, Richmond, Surrey TW9 1SR

© Maggie Kingsley 2010

ISBN: 978 0 263 87915 5

Harlequin Mills & Boon policy is to use papers that are natural,
renewable and recyclable products and made from wood grown in
sustainable forests. The logging and manufacturing process conform
to the legal environmental regulations of the country of origin.

Printed and bound in Spain
by Litografia Rosés, S.A., Barcelona

Maggie Kingsley says she can't remember a time when she didn't want to be a writer, but she put her dream on hold and decided to 'be sensible' and become a teacher instead. Five years at the chalk face was enough to convince her she wasn't cut out for it, and she 'escaped' to work for a major charity. Unfortunately—or fortunately!—a back injury ended her career, and when she and her family moved to a remote cottage in the north of Scotland it was her family who nagged her into attempting to make her dream a reality. Combining a love of romantic fiction with a knowledge of medicine gleaned from the many professionals in her family, Maggie says she can't now imagine ever being able to have so much fun legally doing anything else!

Recent titles by the same author:

A BABY FOR EVE
A WIFE WORTH WAITING FOR
THE CONSULTANT'S ITALIAN KNIGHT
A CONSULTANT CLAIMS HIS BRIDE

CHAPTER ONE

Monday, 10:05 p.m.

IT WAS a truism known to every woman over the age of twenty-five, Brontë O'Brian thought wryly as she gazed down through the large observation window at the man standing below her in the forecourt of ED7 ambulance station. There were two types of men in the world. There were the dependable men, the reliable men, the men who—if you had any sense—you settled down with, and then there were men like Elijah Munroe.

'He's quite something, isn't he?' Marcie Gallagher, one of the callers from the Emergency Medical Dispatch Centre, observed wistfully as she joined her.

'So I've heard,' Brontë replied.

And not just heard. She knew exactly how tall Elijah Munroe was—six feet two—how his thick black hair flopped so endearingly over his forehead, how his startlingly blue eyes could melt ice, and how his smile always started at one corner of his mouth, then spread slowly across his face, until every woman—be she nineteen or ninety—was lost.

'Unfortunately, Eli doesn't do long term,' Marcie continued, and Brontë nodded.

She knew that, too. She knew that for a couple of months every woman Elijah dated walked around on air, completely convinced he was The One, until one morning with a smile—always with that smile—he was gone.

'I'm surprised one of his ex-girlfriends hasn't skewered him with a surgical instrument,' she observed, and Marcie shrugged.

'What reason could you give? It's not like he promises he'll stay. He's always upfront about not being into commitment.'

'Very clever.'

'Honest, surely?' Marcie protested.

No, clever, Brontë thought firmly, as she noticed that Elijah Munroe had been joined by the head of ED7 ambulance station, George Leslie. Very clever indeed to always be able to get exactly what he wanted by appearing to be upfront and on the level, but then she'd never thought Elijah was a stupid man.

'Only a leopard who never changes his spots,' she muttered under her breath, but Marcie heard her.

'You know him?' she said, curiosity instantly plain on her lovely face, and Brontë shook her head quickly.

Which wasn't a lie. Not a complete lie. Elijah having dated three of her ex-flatmates before just as quickly dumping them hardly qualified as knowing him, especially as the one time they'd met in Wendy's hallway he'd walked straight past her without a word. A fact which still rankled considerably more than it should have done.

'We're all eaten up with curiosity, wondering who he's been dating for the past couple of months,' Marcie continued. 'Normally we find out within twenty-four hours, but he's been remarkably coy about his current girlfriend.'

Coy wasn't a word Brontë would have used to describe Elijah Munroe. Rat fink, low-life, scumbag… Those were the words she would have used but she had no intention of telling Marcie Gallagher that.

'It's quarter past ten,' she said instead. 'I'd better get down to the bay.'

'Can you find your own way there?' Marcie asked. 'I'd take you myself, but…'

'You need to get back to EMDC for the start of your shift.' Brontë smiled. 'No problem.'

And Elijah Munroe wouldn't be a problem either, she told herself as Marcie Gallagher hurried away. So what if she was going to be shadowing him around the Edinburgh streets for the next seven nights, watching his every move? She was thirty-five years old, knew exactly how he operated, how many hearts he'd broken, and that knowledge gave her power.

Oh, who was she kidding? she thought as she turned back to the observation window in time to see Elijah smile at something George Leslie had said and felt her heart give a tiny wobble. Knowing his reputation didn't make her any less susceptible to his charm, and he had charm by the bucket load.

'Which means it's just as well Elijah Munroe only ever dates pretty women,' she told her reflection in the glass. 'Pretty women with model-girl figures, and impossibly long legs, and you don't fit the bill on any of those counts.'

For which she was truly grateful. Or at least she should try to be, she thought with a sigh as she squared her shoulders and walked towards the staircase which would lead her down to the very last man on earth she had ever wanted to work with.

'Why me?'

Elijah Munroe's tone was calm, neutral, and if George Leslie hadn't been his boss for five years he might have been deceived, but George wasn't deceived.

'I don't suppose you'd settle for, "Why not you?"' he said with a broad, avuncular smile, then sighed as Elijah gave him a hard stare. 'No, I didn't think you would. Eli, we both know Frank's going to be off sick for at least a fortnight. I've no one to team you up with, and I can't send out an ambulance unless it's two-manned, so unless you'd rather sit on your butt in the office…'

'I'm stuck with the number cruncher,' Eli finished for him. 'You do realise sending her out on the road with me is probably illegal? Okay, so she's only going to drive, but what if I discover I need help—that I've been sent on a two-man job?'

'Miss O'Brian is a fully qualified nurse. In fact, she was a charge nurse in A and E at the Waverley General until a year ago,' George Leslie declared triumphantly, and Eli frowned.

ED7 ambulance station might be situated in the heart of Edinburgh's old town, which meant most of the patients he collected ended up in the Pentland Infirmary, but he'd occasionally had to go to the Waverley and he couldn't remember any nurse called O'Brian.

'George—'

'Eli, if the ambulance service have decided she's not just qualified enough to drive, but also to assist you if required, that's good enough for me, and it should be good enough for you.'

'Yes, but—'

'Seven nights,' George Leslie said in his best placating tone. 'Seven night shifts when she'll drive you around—'

'Noting down all she considers to be ED7's inefficiencies—'

'Which is why it's vital you keep her sweet,' George Leslie declared, then his lips twitched. 'And I know how easy it is for you to keep women sweet.'

'Anyone ever tell you you'd make an excellent pimp?' Eli said drily, and his boss's smile widened.

'Oh, come on, Eli, it's common knowledge you've a way with the ladies.'

'And right now I'm on the wagon. And before you ask,' Eli continued as his boss's eyebrows rose, 'it's not because I've contracted a sexually communicable disease. I've just decided to take a break from dating for three months.'

'Eli, I'm not asking you to get inside Miss O'Brian's knickers,' George protested. 'Just to be as pleasant and as winning as I know you can be with women. Look, there's a lot riding on this government report,' he continued swiftly as Eli opened his mouth clearly intending to argue. 'There's talk of amalgamating stations, job cuts—'

'But we're already pared right back to the bone,' Eli declared angrily, and his boss nodded.

'Exactly, but in the current economic situation the authorities are looking for ways to save money, and if they can shut down a station they will.'

'But—'

George Leslie put out his hand warningly.

'Miss O'Brian's just arrived,' he said in an undertone. 'I'll leave you to introduce yourself, but you be nice to her, okay? There's a hell of a lot riding on her report.'

Which was great, just great, Eli thought as his boss hurried away. He didn't want to be 'nice', he didn't want to be the poster boy for the station. All he wanted was for this number cruncher to go away and annoy the hell out of someone else but, dutifully, he pasted a smile to his face and turned to face the woman he was going to be sharing his ambulance with for the next seven nights.

At least she wasn't a looker, he decided as he watched her walk towards him. Having managed to stick to his 'no dating' decision for the past two months, it would have been plum awkward if she'd turned out to be a looker, but she was…ordinary. Mid-thirties, he guessed, which was younger than he'd been expecting, scarcely five feet tall, with short brown hair styled into a pixie cut, a pair of clear grey eyes, and her figure… He tilted his head slightly, but it was impossible to tell whether she was buxom or slender when she was wearing the regulation green paramedic cargo trousers, and bulky high-visibility jacket which concealed pretty much everything.

'Thirty-six, twenty-six, and none of your business.'

His head jerked up. 'Sorry?'

'My measurements,' she replied. 'You were clearly scoping me out, so I thought I'd save you the trouble.'

Not ordinary after all, he thought, seeing a very definite hint of challenge in her grey eyes. Sassy. He liked sassy. Sassy was always a challenge and, where women were concerned, he liked a challenge.

No, he didn't, he reminded himself. No dating, no involvement for one more month. He'd made the three-month pledge, he intended to stick to it, and yet, despite himself, a lifetime of pleasing women kicked automatically into place, and he upped his smile a notch.

'You haven't,' he observed. 'Saved me the trouble, that is,' he added as her eyebrows rose questioningly. 'There's still the unanswered question of, "none of your business."'

'Interesting approach,' she said coolly. 'Do the staff at this station always assess the physical attributes of government assessors?'

'Only the pretty ones,' he replied, upping his smile to maximum, but to his surprise she didn't blush, or look even remotely confused, as most women did when he complimented them.

Instead, she held up three fingers and promptly counted them off.

'Number one, I'm not pretty. Number two, charm offensives don't work on me so save your breath and, number three, I'm here to assess the efficiency of this station so your personal opinion of my looks is completely irrelevant.'

Uh-huh, he thought, wincing slightly. So, Miss O'Brian was no pushover. That would teach him to make assumptions, and it was something he wouldn't do again.

'I think we should restart this conversation,' he said, holding out his hand and rearranging his smile into what he hoped was a suitably contrite one. 'I'm Elijah Munroe. My friends call me Eli, and I'm very pleased to meet you.'

'I'm Miss O'Brian, and I'll let you know in due course whether I can reciprocate the pleasure,' she replied, shaking his hand briefly, then releasing it just as fast.

Snippy, as well as sassy. Well, two could play that game, he decided.

'No problem,' he observed smoothly, 'but though I fully understand your desire to keep our relationship strictly professional, I feel I should point out that calling you by your full name could prove a little time-consuming in an emergency.'

And that is round three to me, sweetheart, he thought with satisfaction, seeing a faint wash of colour appear on her cheeks.

'Fair point,' she conceded, and then, with clear and obvious reluctance, she said, 'My name is Brontë. Brontë O'Brian.'

A faint bell rang somewhere in the deepest recesses of his mind, but he couldn't for the life of him quite grasp it.

'Brontë. Brontë…' he repeated with a frown. 'Could we possibly have met before? Your Christian name… It sounds strangely familiar.'

Damn, damn, and damn, Brontë thought irritably. Why couldn't her parents have called her something completely forgettable, like Mary, or Jane? If they'd given her an 'ordinary' first name she would have remained as forgettable as she'd obviously been that night in Wendy's hallway, and she most certainly didn't want to jog his memory.

'It probably sounds familiar because of the Brontë sisters,' she said quickly. 'As in Charlotte—'

'Emily, and Anne,' he finished for her, then grinned as she blinked. 'And there was you thinking the only books I would read would be ones with big, colourful pictures, and three words across the bottom of every page.'

It was so exactly what she'd been thinking that she could feel her cheeks darkening still further, but no way was she going to let him get away with it.

'Of course I didn't,' she lied. 'I just didn't take you for a fan of Victorian literature.'

'Ah, but you see that's where a lot of people make a mistake,' he observed. 'Taking me solely at face value.'

And it was a mistake she wouldn't make again, she decided. He might still be smiling at her, but all trace of warmth had gone from his blue eyes, and a shiver ran down her back which had nothing to do with the icy November wind blowing across the open forecourt.

'Which of these vehicles is our ambulance?' she asked, deliberately changing the subject, but, when he pointed to the one they were standing beside, her mouth fell open. 'But that's…'

'Ancient—clapped out—dilapidated.' He nodded. 'Yup.'

'But…' She shook her head. 'I don't understand. The ambulance I passed my LGV C1 driving test on… It was state of the art, with a hydraulic lift—'

'We had seven of those,' he interrupted. 'Unfortunately, five are currently off the road because the hydraulic tail-lifts keep jamming and, believe me, the last thing you want on a wet and windy night in Edinburgh is your patient stuck halfway in, and halfway out, of your ambulance.'

'Right,' she said faintly, and saw his lips twist into a cynical smile.

'Welcome to the realities of the ambulance service, Brontë.'

Welcome indeed, she thought, but she point-blank refused to believe all those ambulances could have been faulty. She'd read the documentation, the glowing reports. Not once had the hydraulic system failed on the ambulance she had been given to prepare her for her driving test, which meant either ED7 had received five faulty vehicles—which she didn't think was likely—or the crews were running them into the ground.

'Top left, breast pocket.'

'Sorry?' she said in confusion, and he pointed at her chest.

'Your notebook—the notebook you're just itching to get out to report this station for trashing their ambulances—it's in your top left, breast pocket. Your pen is, too.'

Damn, he was smart. Too smart.

'Can I take a look round your cab?' she said tightly. 'As I'm going to be driving you, I'd like to see if the layout is any different to what I passed my test on.'

'Be my guest,' he said, but, as she put one foot inside the driver's door, she saw him frown. 'You'll need to change those boots.'

'Why?' she protested, following his gaze down to her feet. 'I'm wearing regulation, as supplied, boots.'

'And they're rubbish. None of us wear government-issue boots. These boots,' he continued, pointing at his own feet, 'have stepped in stuff you wouldn't even want to think about, had drunks vomit all over them, been run over by trolleys and, on one memorable occasion, my driver accidentally reversed over my feet, and the boots—and my feet—survived. Take a tip. Buy yourself some boots from Harper & Stolins in Cockburn Street. Their Safari brand is the best.'

'I'll bear that in mind,' she replied, but she wouldn't.

What she *would* do, however, was make a note of the fact that none of the paramedics at ED7 were obeying health and safety rules if they were all refusing to wear the boots they had been issued with.

'Your notebook and pen are still in the same pocket,' he said with a grin which annoyed the hell out of her. 'Want to note that down, too, while it's fresh in your mind?'

What she wanted to say was, *And how would you like my pen shoved straight up your nose?* but she doubted that would be professional. Instead, she clambered into the driving seat of his ambulance, and glanced at the instrument panel.

'I see you have an MDT—a mobile display terminal— to give you details of each job you're sent on?'

'Yup,' he replied, getting into the passenger seat beside her. 'It's a useful bit of kit, when it's working, but it crashes a lot, which is why this baby—' he patted the radio on the dashboard fondly '—is much more important. Just remember to switch it off when you've finished making or receiving a call because it's an open transmitter which means everything you say is broadcast not only to EMDC but also to every ambulance on the station which can be…interesting.'

It could get a lot more interesting if he didn't back off, and back off soon, she thought grimly.

'All your calls come from the Emergency Medical Dispatch Centre at Oxgangs, don't they?' she said, trying and failing to keep the edge out of her voice.

He nodded. 'Seven years ago the powers that be decided to close all the operations rooms, and replace them with one centralised, coordinating organisation.'

'Which makes sense,' she said. 'Why scatter your controllers about Edinburgh when they can all be in one central place, ensuring the ambulance resources are deployed effectively and efficiently while also maintaining the highest standards of patient care.'

'Well done,' he said, his lips curving into what even the most charitable would have described as a patronising smile. 'That must be word for word from the press cuttings.'

'Which doesn't make it any the less true,' she retorted, and saw his patronising smile deepen.

'Unless, of course, you happened to be one of the unfortunate callers they decided were surplus to requirement,' he observed, and she gritted her teeth until they hurt.

So much for her being worried she would fall for his charm. The only thing worrying her at the moment was how long she was going to be able to remain in his company without slapping him.

'What's our call sign?' she asked, determinedly changing the conversation.

'A38.' He smiled. 'My age, actually.'

'Really?' she said sweetly. 'I would have said you were much younger.' *Like around twelve, given the way you're behaving.* 'According to government guidelines, you should reach a code red patient in eight minutes, an amber patient in fourteen minutes and a code green in just under an hour. How often—on average—would you say you hit that target?'

'How on earth should I know?' he retorted, then bit his lip as though he had suddenly remembered something. 'Look, can we talk frankly? I mean, not as an employee of the ambulance service and an employee of a government body,' he continued, 'but as two ordinary people?'

She was pretty sure there was an unexploded bomb in

his question. In fact, she was one hundred per cent certain there was but, having got off to such a bad start, the next seven nights were going to seem like an eternity if they didn't at least try to come to some sort of understanding.

'Okay,' she said.

He let out a huff of air.

'I don't want you in my cab. I don't mean you, as in you personally,' he added as she frowned. 'I don't want *any* time-and-motion expert sitting beside me, noting down a load of old hogwash. There are things wrong with the ambulance service—we all know that—but what it needs can't be fixed by number crunching. We need more money, more personnel, and more awareness from a small—but unfortunately rather active—sector of the public that we're not a glorified taxi service for minor ailments.'

'And what makes you think I'm going to be noting down nothing but a load of old hogwash?' she asked, and heard him give a hollow laugh.

'Because it's what you bureaucratic time-and-motion people *do*, what you're paid for, to compare people and how they perform in given situations, and then find fault with them.'

She opened her mouth to reply, then closed it again, and stared at him indecisively. How honest could she be with him? She supposed he'd been honest with her, so maybe it was time for her to be honest with him. At least up to a point.

'Would it reassure you to know this is the first time I've been sent out on an assessment?' she said. 'I've done all of the training, of course, but you're my first case, so the one thing I can promise is I won't be comparing you to anyone.'

He met her gaze in silence for a full five seconds and then, to her dismay, he suddenly burst out laughing.

'Dear heavens, if it's not bad enough to be stuck with a number cruncher, I have to get stuck with a *rookie* number cruncher!'

'Now, just a minute,' she protested, two spots of angry colour appearing on her cheeks, 'you were the one who said we should be honest with each other, and now you're laughing at me, and it's *not* funny.'

He let out a snort, swallowed deeply, and said in a voice that shook only slightly, 'You're right. Not funny. Definitely not funny.'

'*Thank you,*' she said with feeling, and he nodded, then his lips twitched.

'Actually—when you think about it—you've got to admit it is a *little* bit funny.'

She met his eyes with outrage, and it was her undoing. If the laughter in his eyes had been smug, and patronising, she really would have slapped him, but there was such genuine warmth and amusement in his gaze that a tiny choke of laughter broke from her.

'Did you just laugh?' he said, tilting his head quizzically at her. 'Could I possibly have just heard the smallest chuckle from you?'

Brontë's choke of laughter became a peal. 'Okay, all right,' she conceded, 'it *is* funny, but it's not my fault you're my first victim. Someone has to be, but I promise I won't bring out any manacles or chains.'

'Actually, I think I might rather like that.'

His voice was liquid and warm and, as her eyes met his, she saw something deep and dark flicker there, and a hundred alarm bells went off in her head.

No, Brontë, *no*, she told herself as her heart rate accelerated. Just a moment ago you wanted to hit him, and now he's most definitely flirting with you, and any woman who responds to an invitation to flirt with Elijah Munroe has to be one sandwich short of a picnic.

'Shouldn't…' She moistened her lips and started again. 'Shouldn't we be hitting the road? Our shift started at ten-thirty, and—' she glanced desperately at her watch '—it's already ten-forty.'

'We can certainly go out,' he agreed. 'But, strange as it might seem, we don't normally go looking for patients. Normally we wait for them to phone us, but if you want to go kerb crawling with me…'

Oh, *hell*, she thought, feeling a deep wash of colour stain her cheeks. Of course they had to wait for calls, she knew that, but did he have to keep on looking at her with those sun-kissed, Mediterranean-blue eyes of his? They flustered her, unsettled her, and the last thing she needed to feel in Elijah Munroe's company was flustered so, when the radio on the dashboard crackled into life, she grabbed the receiver gratefully.

'ED7 here,' she declared, only to glance across at Eli, bewildered, when she heard a snicker of feminine laughter in reply. 'What did I do wrong?'

'This station is ED7,' he said gently. 'We're A38, remember?'

Great start, Brontë, she thought, biting her lip. Really tremendous, professional start. Not.

'Sorry,' she muttered. 'A38 here.'

'Pregnant woman,' the disembodied voice declared. 'Laura Thomson, experiencing contractions every twenty minutes. Number 12, Queen Anne's Gate.'

Brontë had the ambulance swinging out of the forecourt and onto the dark city street before the dispatcher had even finished the call.

'Should I hit the siren?' she asked, and Eli shook his head.

'No need. We'll be there in under five minutes despite the roads being frosty but, with contractions so close, I wonder why she's waited so long to call us?'

Brontë wondered the same thing when they arrived at the house to discover the tearful mother-to-be's contractions were coming considerably closer than every twenty minutes.

'I've been trying to get hold of my husband,' Laura Thomson explained. 'He's working nights at the super-market to earn us some extra money, and this is our first baby, and he's my birthing partner.'

'I'm afraid he's going to miss out on that unless he arrives in the next five minutes,' Eli replied ruefully as the young woman doubled up with a sharp cry of pain. 'In fact, I'd be happier if you were in Maternity right now.'

'But my husband won't know where I am,' the young woman protested. 'He'll come home, and I won't be here, and he'll be so worried.'

Brontë could see the concern on Eli's face, and she felt it, too. A quick examination had revealed Laura Thomson's cervix to be well dilated and, if they didn't go, there was a very strong possibility she was going to have her baby in the ambulance.

Quickly, she picked up a discarded envelope from the table, scrawled, 'Gone to the Pentland Maternity' on it, then placed the envelope on the mantelpiece.

'He'll see that, Laura,' she declared, and the woman nodded, then doubled up again with another cry of pain.

'Okay, no debate, no argument, we go *now*,' Eli declared, and before Brontë, or Laura Thomson, had realised what he was going to do he had swept Laura up into his arms as though she weighed no more than a bag of flour. 'Drive fast, Brontë,' he added over his shoulder as he strode out the door, 'drive *very* fast!'

She didn't get the chance to. She had barely turned the corner at the bottom of Queen Anne's Gate when Eli yelled for her to stop.

'This baby isn't waiting,' he said after she'd parked, then raced round to the back of the ambulance and climbed in. 'How much maternity experience do you have?'

'Not much,' Brontë admitted. 'We didn't tend to get mums-to-be arriving in A and E.'

'Well, welcome to the stork club,' he replied. 'The baby's head is already crowning, and the contractions are coming every minute.'

'I want…my husband,' Laura Thomson gasped. 'I want him here *immediately*.'

'Just concentrate on your breathing,' Eli urged. 'Believe me, you can do this on your own.'

'I know,' Laura exclaimed, turning bright red as she bore down again. 'I just want him here so I can *kill* him because, believe me, if this is what giving birth is like, this baby is never going to have any brothers and sisters!'

A small muscle twitched near the corner of Eli's mouth.

'Okay, when your son or daughter is born, you have my full permission to kill your husband,' he replied, carefully using his hand to control the rate of escape of the baby's head, 'but right now work with the contractions, don't try to fight against them.'

'That's…easy…for you to say,' Laura said with difficulty. 'And…I…can…tell…you…this. If there is such a thing as reincarnation…' She gritted her teeth and groaned. 'Next time I'm coming back as a man!'

'You and me both, Laura,' Brontë declared, seeing Eli slip the baby's umbilical cord over its head, then gently ease one of its shoulders free, 'but if you could just give one more push I think your son or daughter will be here.'

Laura screwed up her face, turned almost scarlet again and, with a cry that was halfway between a groan and a scream, she bore down hard, and with a slide and a rush the baby shot out into Eli's hands.

'Is it all right?' Laura asked, panic plain in her voice as she tried to lever herself upright. 'Is my baby all right?'

'You have a beautiful baby girl, Laura,' Eli replied, wincing slightly as the baby let out a deafening wail. 'With a singularly good pair of lungs. Are there two arteries present in the cord?' he added under his breath, and Brontë nodded as she clamped it.

'What about the placenta?' she murmured back.

'Hospital. Let's get them both to the hospital,' he replied, wrapping the baby in one of the ambulance's blankets. 'Giving birth in the back of an ambulance isn't ideal, and I'll be a lot happier when both mum and baby are in Maternity.'

Brontë couldn't have agreed more and, by the time they had delivered Laura and her daughter to Maternity, the young mother seemed to have completely forgotten her pledge to kill her husband if her beaming smile when he arrived, looking distinctly harassed, was anything to go by.

'That's one we won tonight,' Eli observed when he and Brontë had returned to the ambulance.

She smiled, and nodded, but his good humour didn't last. Not when they then had several call-outs for patients who could quite easily have gone to their GPs in the morning instead of calling 999. She knew what Eli was thinking as she watched his face grow grimmer and grimmer. That as a government assessor she must be noting down all of these nonemergency calls, would be putting them in her report as proof positive that ED7's services could be cut and, though part of her wanted to reassure him, she knew she couldn't. Assessing, and criticising, was supposed to be what she was here for, but she felt for him, and the depth of her sympathy surprised her.

'Coffee,' Eli announced tightly when he and Brontë strode through the A and E waiting room of the Pentland Infirmary after they'd delivered a city banker who confessed in the ambulance to having twisted his ankle two weeks before, but had been 'too busy' to go to his GP. 'I need a coffee, and I need it now.'

'Sounds good to me,' Brontë agreed, but, as she began walking towards the hospital canteen, she suddenly realised Eli was heading towards the hospital exit. 'I thought you said you wanted a coffee?' she protested when she caught up with him.

'Not here,' he said. 'The coffee they serve here would rot your stomach. Tony's serves the best coffee in Edinburgh, and it's where all the ambulance crews go.'

'But—'

'Look, just drive, will you?' he exclaimed. 'Buccleuch Street, top of The Meadows, you can't miss it.'

Just drive, will you. Well, that was well and truly putting her in her place, she thought angrily, and for a second she debated pointing out that she was a government assessor, not a taxi driver, but she didn't. Instead, she silently drove to Buccleuch Street, but, when she pulled the ambulance up outside a small building with a blinking neon sign which proclaimed it to be Tony's Twenty-four Hours Café, she kept the engine running.

'Eli, what if we get a call?' she said as he jumped down from the cab.

'Hit the horn, and I'll come running. Black coffee, café au lait, latte or cappuccino?'

'Cappuccino, no sugar, lots of chocolate sprinkles, but—'

'Do you want anything to eat?' Eli interrupted.

'No, but—'

'You'll be sorry later,' he continued. 'Tony's makes the best take-away snacks, and meals, in Edinburgh.'

He probably did, she thought, as Eli disappeared into the café. Just as she was equally certain Eli would instantly come running if she had to hit the horn, but did he have to make life so difficult for himself? Of course he was legally entitled to a break, and he could take it wherever he chose, but biting her head off was not a smart move. One word from her and he could be out of a job.

And you're going to say that one word? a little voice whispered in the back of her head, and she blew out a huff of impatience. Of course she wouldn't. She'd felt as frustrated as he had by some of the calls, and from what she'd seen he possessed excellent medical skills. He just also very clearly detested bureaucracy and, to him, she was the living embodiment of that bureaucracy. If only he would meet her halfway. If only he would accept she was finding this as difficult as he was. And if only he hadn't brought a hamburger back along with their two coffees, she thought with dismay when Eli opened the ambulance door and the pungent aroma of fried onions filled the air.

'You're not actually going to eat that, are you?' she said, wrinkling her nose as he got into the passenger seat, and the smell of onions became even stronger.

'You have something against hamburgers?' he replied, taking a bite out of his and swallowing with clear relish.

'Not at the proper time,' she declared, 'but at half past three in the morning…?'

'Well, the way I figure it,' he observed, 'if we worked a nine-to-five job like regular people, this would be lunchtime.'

'Right,' she said without conviction. She took a sip of her coffee, then another. 'Actually, this is very good.'

'Told you Tony's made the best coffee in Edinburgh,' he said, stretching out his long legs and leaning his head back against the headrest. 'And nothing beats a good dose of caffeine on a night when you seem to have picked up so many patients who aren't even code greens.'

She shot him a sideways glance. All too clearly she remembered the instructions she had been given. Don't ever become personally involved with a station you have been sent out to assess. Remain coldly objective, and clinical, at all times.

Oh, blow the instructions, she decided.

'Look, Eli, I can completely understand your frustration with some of the people we've picked up tonight,' she declared, 'but the trouble is, though the vast majority of the population realise, and accept, they should only call 999 in an emergency, there's a very small number who seem to think if they arrive in A and E by ambulance they'll be seen a lot faster even if there's nothing very much wrong with them.'

'Yeah, well, one visit to A and E would soon disabuse them of that,' he replied. 'In my day, if there was any indication that a patient was simply trying to queue jump, we made them wait even longer.'

'You used to work in A and E?' she said, considerably surprised.

Eli finished the last of his hamburger, crumpled the paper which had been surrounding it into a ball and dropped it into the glove compartment.

'Ten years at the Southern General in Glasgow for my sins. I was charge nurse until I packed it in.'

'Why?' she asked curiously. 'Why did you give it up?'

He took a large gulp of his coffee, and shrugged.

'Too much paperwork, too much time spent chasing big-shot consultants who couldn't be bothered to come down to A and E to see a patient.' He glanced across at her, his blue eyes dark in the street lamp's glow. 'I hear you were a charge nurse in A and E at the Waverley before you became a number cruncher. What made you give it up?'

'Much the same reasons,' she said evasively, and his gaze became appraising.

'Nope. There was something else.'

She shifted uncomfortably in her seat. He was right, there was, but she had no intention of confirming it. Her private life was her own.

'Would you settle for, it's none of your business?' she said.

'Not fair,' he protested. 'I gave you a straight answer.'

'No one ever tell you life isn't fair?' she countered, wishing he would just drop the subject. 'Look, my reasons are my own, okay?'

He gazed at her over the rim of his polystyrene coffee cup.

'I'll find out,' he observed. 'I always do.'

'Omnipotent now, are you?' she said, not bothering to hide her irritation, and he grinned.

'Nah. Just good at wheedling stuff out of people. In fact…'

'In fact, what?' she asked as he came to a sudden halt and stared at her as though he wasn't actually seeing her, but something a million miles away. 'Eli—'

'Of *course*!' he exclaimed, slapping the heel of his hand against his forehead with triumph. '*Now* I remember why your name sounded so familiar. Wendy Littleton, sister in Obs and Gynae at the Pentland. She and I dated a couple of years back, and she shared a flat with someone called Brontë. Don't tell me it was you?'

She sighed inwardly. She supposed she could try to deny it, but how many Brontës were there likely to be in Edinburgh, and what did it matter anyway?

'Yes, that was me,' she said with resignation.

'Talk about a small world,' he declared. 'Wendy Littleton. Gorgeous black hair, and big brown eyes, as I recall.'

'Actually, her hair was brown, and her eyes were blue,' Brontë replied drily.

'Oh. Right,' he muttered. 'But you and I never actually met, though, did we?'

Should she be nice, or should she make him squirm? No contest, she decided.

'Yes, we've met,' she replied. 'Just the once, but I obviously didn't make much of an impression. Neither did Wendy, come to think of it,' she continued, 'considering you dumped her.'

'I didn't dum—'

'Dumped—walked out on—call it whatever you like,' she declared. 'The bottom line is she was so miserable after you left she emigrated to Australia. She actually got married a couple of months ago.'

'Well, that's good news,' he said with clear relief but, having started, Brontë wasn't about to stop.

'Not for me, it wasn't,' she said. 'Wendy's father owned the flat we lived in so when she emigrated he sold it to give her some stake money which left me homeless.'

'Oh.'

'Yes, oh.' She nodded. 'Luckily, I managed to get a room in a flat with one of the Sisters in Men's Surgical at the Pentland. Anna Browning. Name ring any bells?'

To her surprise a dark tide of colour crept up the back of his neck.

'Yes,' he said awkwardly. 'Look, Brontë—'

'Unfortunately, Anna went back to Wales after you dumped her,' Brontë continued determinedly, 'so I had to go flat hunting again. Which was how I met Sue Davey of Paediatrics. She was the one with the gorgeous black hair, and big brown eyes.'

'Okay—all right—so you've roomed with some of my ex-girlfriends!' Eli exclaimed with obvious annoyance. 'Dating is hardly a crime, is it?'

No, but making women fall in love with you, and then leaving them, sure is, she wanted to retort, but before she got a chance to say anything their radio bleeped and Eli reached for the receiver.

'A38,' he all but barked.

'Hey, Eli, don't shoot the messenger,' a female voice protested. 'Code amber. Twenty-six-year-old female, Rose

Gordon, apparently unable to walk or talk properly. Number 56, Bank Street. Her family's with her.'

'Possible CVA?' Brontë said, quickly emptying the remains of her coffee into the gutter, and putting the ambulance in gear.

'Maybe, maybe not,' Eli declared, clearly still irritated. 'While those symptoms would certainly suggest a stroke, it's better not to go in with any preconceived idea because we could miss something. Luckily, her family are with her so hopefully we'll be able to get more information.'

They did. Though Mr and Mrs Gordon were clearly very upset, they weren't hysterical.

'She's never been like this before,' Mrs Gordon said, looking quickly across at her husband for confirmation. 'She can't walk, or talk, and—' a small sob escaped from her as she glanced back to her daughter who was slumped motionless in a seat '—she seems so confused. It's almost as though she's drunk, but Rose never drinks.'

'Any underlying medical condition we should know about?' Eli asked, kneeling down beside the young woman to take her pulse.

'Rose is a type 1 diabetic,' Mr Gordon replied, his face white and drawn, 'but she tests herself regularly, never misses an insulin dose, so I don't think it can be linked to that.'

Brontë exchanged glances with Eli. Actually, there was a very good chance it could be. Rose Gordon's face was pale and clammy, her eyes unfocused, and when a type 1 diabetic's sugar level became very low they could all too quickly develop hypoglycaemia which made them appear confused, and agitated, and unable to speak or stand properly.

'Has she been working under a lot of pressure recently?' Brontë asked as she handed Eli one of their medi-bags. 'Changed her routine at all?'

Mrs Gordon shook her head. 'She's a schoolteacher—has been for the past four years—and the pressure's just the same as it always was. As for her routine… I can't think of anything she's doing she hasn't done before.'

'She's going to the gym now before she comes home,' a small voice observed. 'She said it was good for anger management.'

Eli and Brontë turned to see a young boy of about eight hovering by the door, his eyes wide and fearful, and Mrs Gordon reached out and put a comforting arm around his shoulders.

'This is Rose's brother, Tom,' she said. 'Rose will be all right, sweetheart. These nice people will make her all right.'

She sounded as though she was trying to convince herself as much as her young son, but Brontë's mind was already working overtime and, judging by the speed with which she saw Eli take a blood sample from Rose Gordon, his was, too. Exercise could all too easily affect blood sugar. Particularly if the diabetic hadn't eaten enough beforehand to ensure their blood sugar stayed high.

'1.6 mmols,' Eli murmured, handing the sample to Brontë, and she sucked in her breath sharply.

The normal range for a diabetic was between 4.5 and 12.0 mmols so this was dangerously low, and swiftly she handed him some glucagon.

'What's wrong—what's the matter with Rose?' Mrs Gordon asked, panic plain in her voice, as Eli searched for a vein in her daughter's arm.

'She's hypoglycaemic,' Brontë explained. 'My guess is she's forgotten to take a snack before going to the gym and all the energy she's expended has really leached the sugar from her body. Don't worry,' she continued, seeing the concern on the woman's face, 'she'll be fine. Give her fifteen minutes, and she'll be as good as new.'

That the Gordons didn't believe her was plain, but, within fifteen minutes, Rose was standing upright, albeit a little unsteadily, and able to apologise profusely to everyone. Eli gave her some sugar jelly to raise her blood sugar still further and, when Rose's blood sugar reading reached 4.6 mmols, he asked Mrs Gordon to make her some pasta.

'Rose needs carbohydrate,' he explained. 'What I've administered given her a quick boost, but what she needs now is something to give her slow-burning energy.'

Quickly, Mrs Gordon bustled away to the kitchen, and, after reassuring Rose's father that Rose was unlikely to become hypoglycaemic again if she kept her food intake high before she took any exercise, Brontë followed Eli out to the ambulance with a smile.

'It's nice when you can get someone back to normal in such a short time, isn't it?' she said.

'One of the pluses of the job, that's for sure,' Eli replied.

He didn't look as though it was a plus. In fact, as the night wore on, he became more and more morose and, when they eventually returned to ED7, just as dawn was breaking over Edinburgh, Brontë decided enough was enough.

'Look, Eli,' she said after he had handed in his report and she walked with him across the ambulance forecourt towards the street, 'I may be new to this job, but I worked in A and E for seven years. I know all about the people who could quite easily have gone to their GP instead of the hospital and, believe me, I'm not going to be marking either you, or ED7, down because so many of tonight's calls weren't even code greens.'

'I'm not thinking about the people we picked up tonight,' he said impatiently.

'Then what's with the moodiness?' she demanded. 'I know you don't like number crunchers—'

'It's got nothing to do with your job,' he interrupted. 'It's…' He shook his head. 'Personal.'

Personal? She stopped dead on the pavement outside the station, and gulped. He wanted to talk to her about something *personal*? She didn't think she was ready for 'personal,' not when his deep blue eyes were fixed on her, making her feel warm and tingly all over, but he was waiting for her to answer so she nodded.

'Okay,' she said. 'Spill it.'

'What you were saying earlier about your flatmates… I think you should know I'm taking a break from dating.'

Of all the things she had been expecting him to say, that wasn't it, and she stared at him, bewildered.

'And you're telling me this because…?' she said in confusion, and for a moment he looked a little shame-faced, then a slightly crooked smile appeared on his lips.

'I just thought you should know, in case you were concerned I might hit on you, or were hoping…well…you know.'

She straightened up to her full five feet.

'I was hoping *what*?' she said dangerously.

'Oh, come on, Brontë,' he declared, 'it's common knowledge I like women, and they like me.'

She opened her mouth, closed it again, then shook her head in outraged disbelief. 'So you're saying I... You think that I... Sheesh, when they were handing out modesty, you sure were right at the back of the queue, weren't you?'

'Brontë—'

'Believe it or not, *Mr* Munroe,' she continued furiously. 'Whatever charms you supposedly possess leave me completely cold, and if you had attempted—as you so poetically phrased it—to hit on me, you would have required the immediate services of a dentist. You are not my type. You never were, never will be. And even if you *were* my type,' she could not stop herself from adding, 'I'm taking a break from dating myself.'

'Why?'

Damn, but she'd said too much as she always did when she was angry, but she had no intention of revealing any more, and she swung her tote bag high on her shoulder, only narrowly missing his chin.

'I,' she said, her voice as cold as ice, 'am going home to get some sleep, and you... As far as I'm concerned, you can go take a running jump off Arthur's Seat as long as you're back here this evening to do your job.'

'Brontë, listen—'

She didn't. She turned on her heel, and strode off down the street, because she knew if she didn't she would hit him.

The nerve of the man. The sheer unmitigated gall. Implying she might be interested in him, suggesting she might have difficulty keeping her hands off him.

He's right, though, isn't he? a little voice laughed in her head, and she swore under her breath. No, he wasn't. He was smug, and arrogant, and opinionated.

But he has gorgeous eyes, hasn't he?

He did. He had the kind of eyes to die for, and thick black hair which just screamed out to be touched, and as for his broad shoulders…

Hell, but having to work along side Elijah was like being on a diet in a cake shop. You knew he was bad for you, you knew you would deeply regret it, and yet, despite all of that, you were still tempted.

Which didn't mean she was going to give in to temptation. She only had to work with him for another six nights, and not even she could make a fool of herself in that amount of time. And she had no intention of making a fool of herself. She'd done it far too often in the past, and to even consider it with a man who had a reputation like Elijah Munroe's…

'No way, not ever,' she said out loud to the empty Edinburgh street.

CHAPTER TWO

Tuesday, 10:07 p.m.

'I DON'T care how you do it, or who you have to upset, but I am *not* going out with Brontë O'Brian again!'

'Eli, we went through all this yesterday,' George Leslie protested. 'There *is* no one else I can put her with, and if I pull out one of the other guys just to accommodate you, there will be hell to pay.'

'Why can't she work days?' Eli argued. 'She could work days with Luke. He's a trauma magnet, can't leave the station without falling over multiple pile-ups, and I'm sure that would keep Ms O'Brian's employers happy.'

'I suggested she work days when I first heard she was coming,' his boss replied, 'but her employers were insistent she did nights.'

'And we all know what that means,' Eli said irritably. 'They think the worthy Edinburgh folk will be all tucked up tight in their beds at night, so we'll have minimal call-outs, and they can use that as an excuse to make some of us redundant.'

'That's my guess.' George nodded.

'Charlie Woods,' Eli said. 'He owes me a favour. I'm sure he'd be prepared to swap—'

'Except his wife is due to give birth any day now,' George interrupted. 'Eli, can't you just live with it? Ye gods, you've already done one night, you only have another six to go.'

'You don't know what she's like,' Eli declared. 'She's pig-headed, opinionated, always thinks she's right—'

'Sounds a bit like you.' George grinned.

'I am *nothing* like her,' Eli snapped. 'George, I want out. There has to be a way for you to get me out of this, or I swear…'

'You'll do what?' his boss demanded with clear exasperation. 'Walk out on me? Throw your career down the toilet? For heaven's sake, man, I am not asking you to bond with her, be her best friend forever. All I'm asking is for you to be civil, pleasant, and do the job you're paid for.'

'But—'

'And can I point out it's not just your job on the line if we get a lousy report,' George continued, his normally placid face bright red. 'It's everyone's job, so get a grip of yourself, a smile on your face, and be *nice*.'

Which was easy for George to say, Eli thought as his boss strode away. He didn't have to work with the damn woman. He didn't have to sit beside an interfering know-it-all who was constantly sticking her nose in where it wasn't wanted, and making snide comments about his dating habits.

And that's what this is all about, isn't it? a small voice whispered in his head. *It's got nothing to do with her as a person. It's because of what she said about her flatmates, implying you were some sort of low-life.*

With a muttered oath he kicked out at one of his ambulance wheels angrily. Hell's teeth, but what right did she have to judge his dating habits? It wasn't as though he had ever deceived anyone. It wasn't as though he had ever lied. He had always been upfront, made it clear he wouldn't be sticking around forever, so what was her problem?

She still had it, he thought, as he heard the sound of slow footsteps crossing the forecourt, and turned to see Brontë walking towards him, her face set and tight. Well, I'm not any happier with the situation than you are, sweetheart, he thought, except...

George was right. No matter what his private feelings were, it wasn't just his neck on the line here. If Brontë O'Brian gave ED7 a damning report, a lot of heads would roll. Heads belonging to people he knew. People who had families, commitments, mortgages, so somehow he had to placate this woman, get her onside, and he squared his chin.

'Brontë, can we talk?' he said when she drew level with him.

'It's a free country,' she replied.

Which wasn't exactly the most encouraging of answers and he gritted his teeth. He didn't 'do' apologies—had never in his life felt the need to apologise for anything he'd done—but he was going to apologise now if it killed him.

'About this morning... What I said...' He gritted his teeth even harder. 'I probably seemed a bit arrogant to you, a bit of a prat.'

'Can't argue with that,' she said, and he clenched his fists until the knuckles gleamed white.

She was enjoying this. He would bet money she was enjoying it, and if it hadn't been for George he would have told her to take a hike.

'What I said this morning,' he continued determinedly, 'I shouldn't have said it.'

'No, you shouldn't.'

'Look, I'm apologising here,' he exclaimed, 'so couldn't you at least give me a break, and meet me halfway?'

She tilted her head thoughtfully to one side.

'You've said you were arrogant, and you've said you were a prat,' she observed, 'but I'm not hearing any apology.'

'Okay, all right,' he snapped. 'I'm *sorry*. I was wrong, okay? I shouldn't have said what I did, and I'm *sorry*.'

For a second she said nothing, then, to his surprise, the corners of her mouth tilted slightly upwards.

'Why do I get the feeling you'd rather have your fingernails pulled out one by one than apologise to anyone about anything?' she said.

A reluctant answering smile was drawn from him. Damn, she was smart, though not for the world would he ever have said so.

'Can we call a truce and start again?' he said. 'I promise I won't open my big mouth if—'

'I don't refer to your ex-girlfriends,' she finished for him, and he nodded.

'So, do we have a deal?' he asked, holding out his hand.

Oh, shoot, she thought, as she took his hand and felt a jolt of electricity run right up her arm. She'd come into work tonight still angry with him, still furious, and yet now she was all too aware that a lean, muscular, highly desirable man was holding her hand, and it felt so good, much too good. How had he done that? How had he managed to turn her emotions upside down in an instant?

Practice, Brontë. Years and years of practice, so watch

your step, or you'll end up like all the other girls he's dumped.

'You're frowning at me,' Eli continued, irritation replacing the smile on his face. 'Does that mean you're planning on making me apologise some more, or…?'

'We have a deal,' she agreed, releasing his hand quickly. 'Except…'

His dark eyebrows snapped together. 'Except what?'

'Can I ask you something?' she replied. 'You don't have to answer if you don't want to,' she added quickly as his eyebrows lowered still further, 'but do you ever plan on settling down with just one woman?'

'Heck, no,' he replied. 'I've never been married, or engaged, and I don't intend to be. No ties, no responsibilities, that's my idea of perfection.'

'Sounds to me like someone hurt you pretty badly at some point,' she observed, and he rolled his eyes impatiently.

'Why does there have to be some deep-seated psychological reason for the fact I don't want to be tied down, trapped?'

'There doesn't, I suppose,' she replied, 'but I'm just curious as to what makes a serial dater like you tick.'

One corner of his mouth turned up. 'Sex.'

'And that's it?' she protested.

He grinned. 'Pretty much.'

It was her turn to roll her eyes. 'You're impossible.'

'Look, what you call "serial dating," I call *fun*,' he declared. 'If more people would only realise—accept—nothing lasts, and you should just enjoy the moment, the happier everyone would be.'

Her grey eyes searched his face curiously. 'And are you happy?'

Of all the dumb questions she could have asked, that had to be the dumbest, he decided.

'Of course I'm happy,' he declared. 'I have a job I love, a nice flat, a good circle of friends—why wouldn't I be happy?'

'I'm pleased for you. No, I *mean it*,' she added as he raised a right eyebrow, clearly challenging her remark. 'To be content with your life, to want nothing more, feel you need nothing more… You're very lucky.'

It wasn't luck, he thought, as they both heard their MDT bleep, and Brontë hurried to read the message. It was being realistic, seeing the world for what it was. And he hadn't been lying when he'd said he was happy. Of course he was happy. Okay, so his three months' self-imposed celibacy was beginning to irk big time, and his flat felt empty, lonely, with just himself rattling around it, but the celibacy had been essential after what happened with Zoe. That was a mistake he most definitely didn't want to make again.

'Middle-aged man collapsed in supermarket,' Brontë announced. 'Seems to be unconscious, no family with him, but the supermarket first-aider is in attendance.'

'Could be anything,' Eli replied. 'Heart attack, drunk, or faker.'

The first-aider clearly didn't think the middle-aged man was faking. She was flapping around in panic when they arrived, and her relief at seeing them was palpable.

'He was standing at the checkout, and just keeled over,' she declared. 'I've put him in the recovery position, but I'm not qualified to do anything else. The first-aid course I went on—it only lasted four weekends—and—'

'You've done exactly the right thing,' Eli interrupted, smiling widely at her. 'We'll take over now.'

Brontë shook her head as the young first-aider turned bright red and walked away in a clear daze.

'Not fair. That poor girl was in a big enough spin before, but now you've got her practically hyperventilating.'

'Can I help it if I'm charming?' Eli protested, his blue eyes dancing, and Brontë only just restrained herself from sticking out her tongue at him.

Except he was probably right, she thought as she watched him begin the standard Glasgow coma scale assessment tests to check the man's overall physical condition. Being charming was undoubtedly as natural to Eli as breathing. So, unfortunately, was the fact he was as unreliable as the weather forecast.

But you like him.

Oh, I could, she thought, as she stared at his long, slender fingers, and, unbidden, and unwanted, an image came into her mind of those fingers touching her, caressing her. I could so easily like him very much indeed, but never in a million years would she allow herself to get involved with him. At least with the other men she'd dated she'd been completely unaware of what lay ahead, but with Eli Munroe she knew only too well.

'I'm not sure about this one,' Eli observed, sitting back on his heels. 'What do you think, Ms O'Brian?'

His expression was solemn but his eyes, Brontë noticed, were gleaming, and she knew why. He might only have performed two of the GCS tests on their patient so far but the man having achieved the lowest possible result both on the ability to open and close his eyes on command, and on responding verbally to questions, indicated he must be nearly at death's door but he had to be the healthiest-looking sick person she had ever seen.

'I'd recommend the reflexes test next, Mr Munroe,' she replied, and a suspicion of a smile appeared on Eli's lips.

Gently, he lifted the man's hand, positioned in directly over the man's nose, then let it drop. Magically, it didn't hit the man on his nose as it should have done if he really was unconscious, but landed neatly at his side, and Eli let out a deep, heartfelt sigh.

'I'm afraid it looks a lot more serious than I thought,' he declared, and Brontë had to bite down hard on her lip to quell the chuckle she could feel bubbling inside her.

She'd come across cases like this before in A and E. Sometimes the patients were mentally ill, or drunk, but most often they faked unconsciousness to get themselves out of a sticky situation and, judging by the amount of alcohol the man had in his shopping trolley, she strongly suspected he was trying to get away without paying for it.

'Eye socket test?' she suggested, and Eli winked across at her.

If the man truly was deeply unconscious he would scarcely react, but if he wasn't... Pushing hard against the upper part of his eye socket with your finger wouldn't damage his sight but, by heavens, he would certainly feel it.

He did. At the first push, the man's eyes flew open, and he sat up angrily, only to put his hand to his head with an unconvincing groan when he saw Brontë and Eli.

'I don't know what happened,' he murmured in a faltering voice. 'One minute I was about to pay for my groceries, and the next... I just came over all queer.'

'It can happen,' Eli agreed as he solicitously helped the man to his feet, 'which is why I think you should go straight home to bed. Forget all about your shopping, you can do it tomorrow.'

'But—'

'No, please, don't thank us,' Eli continued, steering the man towards the supermarket door. 'It's all in a day's— or should I say night's—work for us.'

That the man wanted to do anything *but* thank them was clear, but that he also didn't want to take on six feet two of muscular male was also apparent and, with a face like thunder, he walked out of the supermarket door and disappeared into the night.

'You know, it never ceases to amaze me how far some people will go to fake illness,' Brontë declared as she followed Eli back to their ambulance. 'I mean, if it was me, the last thing I'd want is someone performing a whole battery of tests on me if I knew I was perfectly okay.'

'Yeah, well, when you've been in this game as long as I have, nothing seems strange any more,' Eli replied. 'I'm just surprised *you're* surprised after seven years of A and E.'

She glanced across at him sharply. 'If this is your not very subtle way of wanting to know why I left, forget it.'

'Can't blame a bloke for trying,' he said with a broad smile, and she shook her head at him.

'You know, I don't think you actually *do* dump all your ex-girlfriends,' she observed. 'I think they dump you because you keep on asking the same old questions, and eventually they can't stand it any more.'

'Oh, very witty, very droll,' he said drily. 'And will you stop saying I dump women. I do *not* dump women. We just mutually decide when it's over.'

'Yeah, right,' she said, not even bothering to try to look

as though she believed him. 'Do you want to know my theory as to why you're taking a three-month dating sabbatical?'

'Do I have a choice?'

'I think you got careless,' Brontë declared, ignoring the irritation in his voice. 'I think your last girlfriend got too close, and started bringing home wedding magazines, and stopping outside jewellers' windows to point out engagement rings, and that freaked you good and proper, and now you're trying to figure out where you went wrong.'

Eli's lips twitched into not quite a smile.

'That's not a bad guess.'

'And have you figured out where you went wrong?' she asked, and his smile became rueful.

'Not exactly. How long have you given up dating for?'

'Permanently.'

'Permanently?' he exclaimed. 'Hell, but someone sure did a number on you, didn't they?'

She was saved from answering by the bleep of their radio, but when she lifted the receiver, the caller sounded uncharacteristically nervous.

'I have a message for Eli,' the anonymous voice announced. 'Could you tell him Peg would like to see him asap.'

Brontë sighed with resignation as she switched off the receiver.

'Don't tell me,' she said, turning to Eli. 'Peg is yet another of your ex-girlfriends.'

He cleared his throat.

'Actually, she's a heroin addict. Turns tricks for a living. Male—female—doesn't matter to her so long as the punter will pay enough to fund her habit.'

Brontë blinked.

'And how do you know her?' she asked without thinking, then flushed scarlet when she realised how that might sound. 'Sorry—forget it—none of my business.'

'No, it's not,' he agreed. 'But Peg…' He chewed his lip, then seemed to come to a decision. 'She caught pneumonia two winters back. My partner, Frank, and I saw her lying in the street so we picked her up and took her to hospital. Ever since then…' Eli shrugged. 'She seems to feel she owes me something, so if a youngster tries to tag along with her, and her friends, she let's me know, and sometimes I'm able to help, to turn them around before it's too late.'

And I feel like the lowest form of pond life, Brontë thought as she stared at him awkwardly. She wished she hadn't jumped to conclusions. She wished even more she could figure out the man sitting next to her. One minute he was a completely shameless flirt, a serial dumper of women, then he unexpectedly turned into the Good Samaritan. It didn't make any sense. *He* didn't make any sense.

'Do you want to go and see her now?' she asked hesitantly.

'It's not a logged case, Brontë,' he replied. 'We're only supposed to answer logged calls, not personal ones.'

'And I didn't hear that,' she said. 'Where does Peg live?'

'Are you serious?' he said, and Brontë huffed impatiently.

'Just give me the address, Eli.'

'She…' He rubbed his chin awkwardly. 'She doesn't exactly "live" anywhere. She—and her friends—camp out most nights by Greyfriars Church.'

Greyfriars Church. It was hardly the most hospitable of places in the daytime but, on a freezing-cold November night, Brontë couldn't think of a more miserable place to be, and her opinion didn't change when they reached the church and she saw the black, locked gates.

'Where's your friend?' she asked as she and Eli got out of the ambulance.

'Inside.'

'*Inside?*' she repeated as he retrieved a medi-bag. 'You mean, she sleeps amongst the tombstones?'

'Yup.' Eli nodded, then his teeth gleamed white in the darkness. 'Not afraid of ghosts, I hope?'

Only my own, Brontë thought, but she didn't say it.

'I've always liked that statue of Greyfriars Bobby,' she said instead, pointing at the life-size figure of the little dog on a plinth in front of the church. 'My parents used to bring my brother, sister and I to see it when we were small, and tell us how Bobby came back every night for fourteen years to sleep on his owner's grave until he eventually died.'

'Yeah, well, putting up a statue to anyone—be it a person or a dog—is a lot easier than trying to help real, living people.'

Eli's voice sounded uncharacteristically hard, and bitter, and she glanced across at him curiously, but he wasn't looking at her. His eyes were scanning the grave-yard, and then he nodded.

'There she is,' he said.

Following the direction of his gaze, Brontë saw a slim form flitting amongst the tombstones.

'How do we get in?' she asked. 'Do we have to climb over the railings, or…?'

'I know another way in.'

He did, and Brontë very soon wished he hadn't. It wasn't just the way the church seemed so much bigger and more ominous in the dark, nor the way the tombstones leant towards her like grasping, clutching fingers. It wasn't even the mort-safe coverings which had been installed over some of the graves by her Edinburgh forebears to prevent grave-robbers. It was the smell.

Sharp, acrid, and overpowering, it didn't matter how much she tried to hold her breath she couldn't escape the smell of unwashed bodies, and stale alcohol. It's just a smell, she told herself. Smells can't harm you, they can't hurt you, but, unbidden and unwanted, she felt her heart beginning to beat faster, could feel the all too familiar wave of panic rising within her, and she wrapped her arms around herself tightly.

'Must be well below zero tonight,' Eli observed, clearly misunderstanding her gesture.

She nodded.

'How many…' She swallowed hard. 'How many people sleep here every night?'

'It depends,' Eli replied. 'Sometimes ten—sometimes twenty.'

'How do they survive?' she exclaimed. 'How can they keep alive on nights like this? I would have thought—' She came to a sudden halt. Something warm, wet, and slimy was seeping through her left boot, encircling her toes, and she let out a small yelp. 'Oh, *yuck*! What have I just stood in?'

'Do you really want me to tell you?' Eli asked, and she shook her head quickly.

She didn't, especially as she already had a very strong suspicion what it was.

'Take my advice—'

'Buy some boots from Harper & Stolins in Cockburn Street,' she finished for him. 'I know, you said.'

'Yes, but this time *listen*,' he declared. 'We don't refuse to wear the regulation boots because we're picky. We don't wear them because they're rubbish, so get yourself a decent pair.'

She would, she thought, as she flexed her wet toes and grimaced. She would go to the shop at the end of this shift, but not until she'd had a very long, and very hot, shower.

'Okay, wait here,' Eli ordered. 'Peg and her friends… they know me, but you're a stranger, so it's best if I explain who you are.'

He was gone before she could argue, could tell him she didn't want to wait in this place on her own. Figures were emerging from behind the tombstones now, some of them coughing, all of them staggering, and though they looked merely curious, puzzled, she didn't know how long that would last, nor did she want to find out.

Anxiously, she searched the moonlit cemetery for Eli, but he was nowhere to be seen. Perhaps the newcomer had taken off, which would mean they could leave, too. She fervently hoped so. It was so cold here, so very cold. Dark, too, despite the moon. Dark and creepy, and she almost jumped out of her skin when she felt a hand clasp her shoulder.

'I didn't mean to frighten you,' Eli murmured, as she swore under her breath.

'Yeah, well, next time *warn* me, okay?' she said, trying to calm her thudding heart. 'What's the situation?'

'According to Peg, the newcomer's just a boy. He left his home in Aberdeenshire about a year ago—won't say why, but Peg reckons something bad happened. He got robbed of what little savings he had on his first night in Edinburgh, and with no money he couldn't pay for anywhere to live, and with no home address he couldn't get any benefits, so he's been living rough ever since.'

'What does Peg want us to do?'

'When did "I" become "us"?' Eli asked, and she could hear the smile in his voice.

'When I broke every rule in the EMDC manual by allowing this visit,' she replied, 'so quit stalling.'

'Basically she wants us to get him out of here. She thinks he has a bad cold, which is not good news. Pneumonia, or a severe chest infection, would mean we could take him to the Pentland which would get him off the streets for a while, but a cold…' He sighed. 'Peg's gone to ask if he'll let me examine him.'

The boy must have agreed because, out of the gloom, Brontë could see a white hand beckoning to them, and quickly she followed Eli as he picked his way through the tombstones, keeping as close to him as she could, so she almost collided into his back when he came to a sudden halt by one of the bigger mausoleums.

'Is this him?' she whispered, only to instantly feel stupid because, of course, it had to be, and yet…

She had expected to see a young man but the person sitting hunched on the ground in front of them, dressed in threadbare trainers, thin denim trousers, and a tattered wine-coloured jacket, didn't even look old enough to have left school. How on earth had he survived if he'd been sleeping rough for a year?

'What's your name, son?' Eli murmured as he crouched down in front of the boy, seemingly heedless of the broken glass, and discarded syringes, glinting in the moonlight.

With an effort, the boy raised his head. His skin was stretched tightly across his cheekbones, and there were dark shadows under his eyes, but though those eyes looked tired and scared, Brontë didn't think he was taking drugs. At least, not yet.

'I'm…John,' the boy replied. 'John Smith.'

Yeah, right, Brontë thought, and I'm Mary, Queen of Scots.

'I understand you have a bad cold,' Eli continued, 'and you've agreed to let me examine you?'

A defeated shrug was the only reply, and Eli took a stethoscope out of the bag Brontë was holding out to him.

'How old are you, John?' Brontë asked, and the boy's eyes slid warily away.

'Eighteen,' he said. 'I'm eighteen.'

'Fourteen more like,' she could not help but reply, and the boy rounded on her angrily.

'Look, I didn't ask you to come,' he said. 'You came of your own accord, so I don't need the third degree!'

Eli shook his head warningly at Brontë, then turned back to John.

'Fair enough,' he said softly, 'no third degree.'

Quickly, he sounded the young man's thin chest, and took his pulse while Brontë stood silently by. So, too, she noticed, did Peg. Not close enough to see what Eli was doing, but close enough to help if she was needed. Which meant she was on guard, Brontë realised. On guard because everyone there would know Eli was carrying drugs, and nervously she moved closer to him.

'How is his chest?' she asked when Eli had finished his examination.

'He has a cold, nothing serious,' he replied.

She could hear the disappointment in his voice. She felt it herself, and quickly she hunkered down beside him and the boy.

'John, listen to me,' she began. 'Why don't you go home? I'll buy you the train ticket—'

'*No!*' the young boy broke in vehemently. 'I'm not going home!'

'But how are you managing for food?' Brontë demanded. 'You've no money, no means of getting any.'

'People…when they get takeaways…they don't always eat it all,' the boy replied. 'They throw away some of it, so I get by. I just…'

'Just what?' Brontë prompted, and the boy raised his dark eyes to hers.

'I'm so scared all the time. Scared someone will come along and set fire to me when I'm sleeping. It happens,' he continued, hearing Brontë's sharp intake of breath. 'One of the older homeless guys… He told me it happened to one of his mates, so I don't sleep. I just keep on walking, and walking, and I get so tired, so very tired.'

'Okay, John, listen to me,' Eli declared. 'You have to sleep and the safest place is businesses with flat roofs. No one will be able to see you up there, and they usually have a raised part to stop you rolling off, so as long as you're not stoned or drunk you'll be safe.'

The boy nodded. 'Flat roofs. Anywhere else?'

'A bathroom with a keypad is the best of all,' Eli replied. 'A lot of big businesses, and shops, have them. Get yourself as clean as you can, and hang about until you've found out what the code is. Watch for a night to check cleaning crews don't work outside the normal business hours and it will be yours for ages if you leave it clean without a trace of you having been there.'

'Right.' The boy's eyes met Eli's. 'Thanks.'

Slowly, Eli straightened up and Brontë could see his breath on the cold night air, the sparkle of frost on the roofs. If it was so cold now, how much colder was it going to get as the night progressed?

'Eli…' He wasn't listening to her, he was already walking away, and she hurried after him, stumbling slightly on the uneven ground. 'Eli, wait!'

He did and, when he turned to face her, his face was harsh, angry.

'How old would you say Peg was?' he asked.

Brontë frowned. She hadn't paid much attention.

'Fifty-five…sixty?' She hazarded.

'She's thirty-two.'

Brontë glanced back over her shoulder to where Peg was still standing beside John. Even in the dark she could see most of the woman's teeth were gone, her hair was lank, and stringy, and she had the running nose, extreme restlessness, and dilated pupils of someone who desperately needed another 'fix.'

'John—or whatever his name really is—will be like that in a year if we don't get him out,' Eli continued. 'So many of the people here…' He waved his hand at the men and women clustered together. 'It's too late for them. No matter what help we throw at them, or what services are provided, it's too late, but there's still hope for John and if we can save one…'

'I have some money on me,' Brontë began, digging deep into her pocket. 'It's not much—about twenty pounds—'

'Which will get him into a homeless shelter, and feed him for three—maybe four—days, and then what?' Eli interrupted. 'He needs long-term help. He needs to be in hospital for a few days so social services can assess him, put a plan in place.' His eyes met hers. 'How willing are you to break yet another of the EMDC manual rules?'

'Right now, I'd happily break the lot of them,' she answered, 'but, Eli, if all he has is a cold we'll get our heads in our hands if we turn up at the Pentland with him.'

'Not if you know the right person to go to.'

'And you do?' she asked and, when his mouth curved into a wide grin, she shook her head. 'Stupid question. Of course you do. What's her name?'

'Dr Helen Carter. She works Tuesdays and Thursdays in A and E at the Pentland, and she'll help.'

Dr Carter did. Within minutes of their arrival, she had John whisked up to a ward, and had called the social services.

'I'm not guaranteeing anything, Eli,' she declared, 'but with some luck, and a little bit of help from the Almighty, perhaps we can set that young lad back on track.'

'Helen, I love you.' Eli beamed, and Dr Carter shook her head and laughed.

'Away with you. I'm old enough to be your mother.'

Which didn't, Brontë noticed, stop Helen Carter blushing when Eli kissed her cheek, but she said nothing as she followed him out of A and E because she was too busy thinking.

He'd warned her not to judge him by his outward appearance, and he'd been right. Who *was* this man, what made him tick, and what else was going on in his head he didn't allow the rest of the world to see? Yes, he was a serial womaniser, but he also cared very deeply, not only about the people they collected who were very ill, but also about those who were down on their luck. It was as though there were two completely separate Eli Munroes, and no matter how hard she tried she just couldn't reconcile the two of them.

'The callers at Oxgangs,' she said as they got into the ambulance, 'do they know who Peg is?'

He shook his head. 'They think the same as you did, that she's an ex-girlfriend. Only Frank—the guy I'm normally partnered with—knows.'

But *why*? she wanted to ask. Why didn't he tell people, why keep something like this—an act of great kindness—hidden?

'Eli—'

'I haven't thanked you yet, and I should have done,' he interrupted as she put the ambulance in gear.

'What for?' Brontë asked.

'Breaking the rules.'

'I couldn't do anything else,' Brontë replied as she eased the ambulance out onto the main road before picking up speed.

'Yes, you could,' he said softly. 'A lot of people… when they see down-and-outs begging on the streets, sleeping in cardboard boxes… They think, failures, losers, not my problem.'

'I guess I'm all too aware it doesn't take much to put any one of us in the same position,' Brontë murmured. 'You just need to lose your job, and with no pay cheque you can't pay your mortgage payments, or the rent on your flat, and once you've got nowhere to live…'

'It's welcome to dead-end alley.' Eli sighed. 'With all too often no way back, no way out.'

Brontë glanced across at him, and took a deep breath.

'What you were saying to John about safe places for him to sleep,' she began. 'It seemed—not that it's any of my business, or anything—but it almost sounded like you'd had, you know, personal experience of living rough.'

Eli's face tightened. 'You're right. It's none of your business.'

'Okay.' She nodded. 'Sorry.'

For a moment he said nothing, then his face relaxed slightly, and one corner of his mouth reluctantly turned up.

'You're a very dangerous woman, Brontë O'Brian.'

'Me—dangerous?' she echoed, confused. 'How?'

'Anyone else would have probed, and cajoled, and tried to get an answer out of me, and I would have bitten their head off, but you simply shrug, and say, "Okay," which almost makes me want to explain.'

'And that would be a bad thing?' she said, and heard him sigh.

'A very bad thing.'

She wanted to ask him why, but what right did she have to ask him anything? They weren't friends, she scarcely knew him, and—and it was a very big *and*—she doubted whether he would give her an answer anyway. So she drove silently past the National Library of Scotland, over the South Bridge, turned right into the Cowgate where a gang of youths seemed to be fooling about, and then suddenly her whole world went black, and she hit the brakes in complete panic.

'Don't break, *don't* break!' Eli yelled. 'Just keep your steering wheel straight.'

She did as he ordered even though all of her instincts were telling her to push the brake pedal straight to the floor, and suddenly she could see again. Without her re-alising it, Eli had switched on the windscreen wipers and, though the windscreen was smeared and dark, at least she could see through it, and she pulled the ambulance to a halt and leant her head on the steering wheel.

'What the *hell* happened?' She gasped as her thudding heart slowed to a gallop.

'Beer bottle. Those kids we were passing, one of them must have thrown it at the windscreen.'

'But that's…*insane*!' she exclaimed. 'Didn't they realise…didn't they think… I could have swerved straight into them!'

'Doubt if it even crossed their minds,' Eli replied, pulling a duster out of the glove compartment.

How could he be so indifferent? How could he simply sit there as though it was an every-night occasion? Unless…

She swallowed shakily. 'Does…does this happen a lot?'

'Depends upon what you mean by a lot,' he replied. 'If there's nothing interesting on TV, gangs of young lads tend to congregate around the streets, and then they get bored.' He frowned. 'It's pretty unusual, though, to get a full bottle of beer thrown at us. Normally they're empty.'

'And is that supposed to make me feel *better*?' she said, her voice rising in pitch.

'At least they didn't deliberately run out in front of you,' he observed. 'Scared the hell out of me the first time it happened. Apparently, you earn extra kudos from your mates if you can run across the road in front of an ambu-lance when it's on a code red, with its siren flashing.'

'Fascinating,' she said, desperately trying to smile, and

failing miserably, and then her heart leapt back into her mouth when Eli suddenly swore. 'What is it—what's wrong?'

'They're still there—the gang,' he said grimly. 'And they are about to get a very large piece of my mind.'

He was going to get out of the ambulance and confront them, and she could see the young men in her mirror, laughing, jeering, bottles clutched in their hands, and, before she could stop herself, she grabbed hold of Eli's arm.

'Don't!'

'Brontë, I'm just going to talk to them,' he said, trying to shrug off her hand which only made her hold on even tighter.

'You are *not* going out there!' she all but screamed at him. 'You're staying where you are, you hear me?'

'Brontë, calm down,' he said, worry replacing the ir- ritation in his eyes. 'Look, I won't go out if you don't want to me to.'

'You promise?' she said convulsively, and gently he prised her fingers from his arm.

'They've gone now, anyway,' he said, 'and I want you to take some deep breaths. Lots and lots of deep breaths.'

She could hear it in his voice. The same tone she'd always used when she was dealing with panicking kids in A and E, and it mortified her beyond belief. Somehow she had to get a grip of herself, or she was going to have a full- blown panic attack right in front of him.

'I'm fine now—I'm okay now,' she said as calmly as she could, and he shook his head.

'Coffee,' he said. 'You need coffee, and I'll drive.'

She wanted to protest, to tell him she was perfectly

capable of driving, but she knew one glance at her shaking hands would tell him she was lying, but getting out of the ambulance… She didn't know if her legs would take her that far, and he clearly read her mind.

'When I get out, you slide over the gear-stick into the passenger seat.'

'But—'

He'd already gone, and awkwardly she did as he'd ordered, forcing her legs to work, and forcing herself not to shout at Eli to get back into the safety of the ambulance when he paused to clean the windscreen. Neither did she ask where they were going, because she knew where it would be and, when he pulled the ambulance up outside Tony's, she was sufficiently in control of herself to manage a crooked smile.

'Sorry about that,' she said, wishing her voice didn't still sound so shaky. 'I just…the bottle… I hadn't expected it, you see.'

'Do you want your usual?'

She nodded, but when he'd gone into Tony's she shut her eyes tight. Her usual. After just two days he'd called her coffee her 'usual,' as though she was beginning to belong to this station, but she didn't, and it wasn't just because she'd be leaving in a few days. She didn't belong anywhere near medical services, not any more.

'I got you a doughnut as well as a coffee,' Eli said when he returned. 'I figured you probably needed some carbs and sugar.'

'Thanks,' she said, then noticed the chocolate biscuit in his hand. 'No hamburger for you tonight?'

'I didn't want to run the risk of you throwing up,' he replied, and she gripped her polystyrene cup of coffee tightly.

'I'm okay now,' she insisted. 'Stop fussing, will you?'

He did. In fact, he said nothing at all for a good five minutes, but she was all too aware he was watching her from the corner of his eye and, when she'd finished the doughnut, and half emptied her cup of coffee, he turned towards her.

'Okay, are you going to tell me what that was all about?'

Pretending not to understand him wasn't an option, but neither did she want to tell him the truth.

'I admit I lost it a bit when that bottle hit the window,' she conceded, 'but, come on, Eli, any normal person would have reacted the same way. If your world suddenly goes black, and you can't see anything, and you're driving…'

'Good attempt, Brontë, but no sale,' he said. 'I thought you looked peaky in Greyfriars but I put that down to the cold. I know you got a terrible fright when the bottle hit the windscreen, but what I want to know is why you freaked out when I wanted to get out of the ambulance and confront those yobs.'

'There were a lot of them,' she protested. 'I was afraid you might get hurt.'

He sighed, and pushed his black hair back from his forehead.

'Brontë, I am not being nosy, I'm not being intrusive, but you've got to look at this from my point of view. You're riding with me, so don't you think I have a right to know if some situations are going to make you panic?'

He was right, he did have a right to know, but she didn't want to talk about it, talking about it only brought it all back.

'Eli…'

'It's got something to do with why you left A and E, hasn't it?'

She stared at the windscreen. She could still see some stray streaks of beer he'd missed, and there were little bits of lint on the windscreen from the duster he'd used, and she didn't want to say anything but she knew she had to.

'I was on duty one Saturday night,' she began, her voice jerky, low. 'We had the usual crowd in. People who had drunk too much, drug addicts who had collapsed in the street, ordinary members of the public who had hurt themselves and who looked as though they'd rather be anywhere but there, but they needed help.'

'A typical Saturday night, in other words.' He nodded.

'Pretty much,' she murmured. 'And then…' She took a steadying breath, trying only to remember the facts, and not how she had felt, but it didn't work, it never did. 'This gang came in. They were all drunk, and one of them… He'd gashed his hand pretty badly, and I was dressing it, and he was screaming I was a bitch, deliberately hurting him.'

'And?' Eli prompted gently when she came to a halt.

'His friends… They began crowding into the cubicle. They were pushing me, jostling me, pulling at my clothes, and then one of them…' She gripped her coffee tightly. 'One of them pulled a knife on me.'

'Nasty,' Elijah murmured, his eyes never leaving her face. 'He hurt you.'

It was a statement, not a question, and she tried to smile and failed.

'He punctured my lung. I was off work for four months, and when I went back… The first gang of drunks we had in… I froze, couldn't go anywhere near them, so that was it. Nursing career down the toilet, but with rent to pay and bills coming in I needed a job, so when I saw this one advertised I thought I'd apply, and I got it.'

'Did you have counselling after the attack?'

A bitter laugh came from her. '"Face your fear, and then you'll conquer it." That's what the shrink said, and I know he's right, but what do you do when you can't actually face the fear, when every part of you is shrieking, Run, just run.'

Eli cleared his throat.

'Brontë, you do realise that, when you're out with me, the odds are virtually one hundred per cent that we'll encounter drunks.'

'But I won't be treating them,' she pointed out. 'I won't have to touch them. I'm not denying that being near someone drunk makes me uneasy, but as long as it's not a crowd, a gang, and I don't have to touch them, I can cope.' She met his gaze. 'What are you going to do?'

Her grey eyes were unhappy, but he could see resignation in them, too, and, for a second he didn't understand her, and then it hit him. He could get her fired. That was what she was thinking, and, by heavens, *he could*. All he had to do was take her back to the station, explain how she'd freaked out, and she'd be out of his hair for good.

Except he wouldn't do it. If he told George what had happened, she'd have no job, no money coming in, and she looked so damn small sitting next to him, small and beaten, and he hated seeing her look beaten. She'd been born to be sassy, snippy, and if he shafted her now, after all she'd been through, what kind of man would that make him?

'Well, when you've finished your coffee, you and I are going to go kerb crawling until we get a call,' he said.

'But I thought…'

'Take a tip from one who knows,' he said lightly, 'don't think. Thinking is a very bad idea. Now, finish your coffee.'

She pulled a handkerchief out of her pocket, blew her nose vigorously, and then she smiled at him.

A big, wide smile that completely altered her face, making it soft, and luminous, almost pretty, and he found himself smiling back. Found himself noticing, too, that, under the lamplight, her hair wasn't a dull brown after all, but had little strands of gold in it, and her eyes weren't simply grey but actually a pale silver but, as he continued to stare at her, he suddenly realised something else. He wanted to reach out, gather her into his arms and tell her he'd make everything all right, and that was *insane*.

What on earth was happening to him? he wondered, clasping his hands together tightly to prevent them from carrying out the thought. He didn't 'do' protective, any more than he 'did' apologies, and just because she was sitting there looking so tiny, her lips parted in a wide smile…

Feeling protective of a woman was right up there alongside involvement, commitment, on the list of things he'd spent a lifetime avoiding.

'Eli?'

Uncertainty was slowly replacing the gratitude in her eyes, and he shook his head to clear it.

'Well, I owe you one for Peg, don't I?' he said, and saw her smile disappear, and hurt replace it.

'I wouldn't have told anyone about her,' she said, her voice low, subdued.

He knew she wouldn't, and he felt like a heel for saying what he had, but somehow he had to distance himself from this woman because he could feel an abyss opening up in front of him. A yawning abyss which would be oh-so easy to fall into and, when a caller's voice echoed over the airwaves, he grabbed the receiver like a lifeline.

CHAPTER THREE

Thursday, 12:06 a.m.

SOMETHING was badly wrong, Brontë decided as she drove down St John's Street, then turned left. At first, when she'd come on duty this evening, she'd thought it was just her, that she was bound to feel a little awkward, a little uncomfortable, after her panic attack yesterday, but it was more than that, much more.

'Take a sharp right at the junction. It's the quickest way to Chambers Street, but watch the corner. The roads themselves are okay, but the pavements and street corners are pretty icy tonight.'

She smiled her thanks across at Eli, but he wasn't looking at her and that, she realised, was the problem in a nutshell. Whenever she'd glanced in his direction this evening he hadn't met her gaze, and yet whenever she looked away she knew his eyes were upon her.

He thinks you're a fruit cake, her mind whispered. *He's had second thoughts about what happened yesterday, and he's decided you're a fruit cake.*

Which was so unfair. It wasn't as though she'd lost it at any point tonight. They'd been sent out to attend a woman who had been having a bad asthma attack, a child who had scalded himself, and an elderly gentleman with a severe chest infection, and she'd behaved completely professionally the whole time, but he had clearly decided she was trouble, and his tiptoeing around her was getting to her big time.

'I don't see anyone lying in the street,' she said, scanning the road ahead of them, 'but Dispatch definitely said Chambers Street. Could they have been given the wrong address?'

'Maybe.'

Well, that was short and sweet, she thought irritably. Last night, he'd been so kind, so solicitous, and she'd managed the rest of the shift without incident, but tonight it was like sitting beside a stranger. A polite, distant stranger who only ever spoke in monosyllables.

'Could that be him?' she declared, seeing a sudden movement beside one of the buildings. 'He's not lying in the road, but he's walking oddly, like he's injured.'

'Or drunk,' Eli murmured. 'Dispatch said the caller couldn't stay at the scene which usually means a drunk. If someone has suffered a heart attack, or an epileptic fit, passers-by tend to stay with them, but a drunk… No one wants to get involved.'

'Drunk, or not, I think he's hurt his leg,' Brontë replied as she drew the ambulance to a halt at the kerbside. 'See how he's dragging it?'

Eli said nothing. He simply retrieved a medi-bag, but, when he opened the cab door, he hesitated momentarily.

'There's no need for you to come with me,' he observed. 'I can deal with this.'

He might well be able to, she decided, but if she

couldn't cope with one drunk she was in considerably worse shape than she thought.

'I'm coming,' she said firmly, and he muttered something under his breath which she very much doubted was, 'Terrific,' and she exhaled sharply.

Why didn't he just come right out and tell her that riding with him wasn't going to work? It was so clearly what he was thinking, and she'd far rather he simply said it instead of skirting round her like she was some sort of ticking time bomb.

'Eli—'

'He's gone over,' Eli interrupted as a thud echoed round the empty street.

The man had. He was now flat on his back on the pavement, and he'd taken a dustbin with him, sending its contents spilling out onto the icy pavement.

'The street cleaners are going to love this when they come on duty tomorrow.' She smiled, but no returning smile greeted her words.

In fact, she might just as well have been talking to the dustbin, she thought with annoyance, as Eli walked away and she gingerly quickened her pace over the frosty pavement to catch up with him.

'Drunk for sure,' Eli observed when they reached the man, 'but you were right about the leg. My guess is he's fallen on some broken glass.'

It would have been Brontë's guess, too, as Eli pulled some scissors, swabs and antiseptic out of his bag. She could see a jagged tear in the man's trouser leg through which blood was slowly seeping, and she could also see some tiny shards of glass.

'Looks like a stitch job to me,' she said.

Eli nodded. 'And I doubt he's kept his tetanus shots up to date so we'd better take him to A and E after I've cleaned that gash.'

He was going to need more than just the gash cleaned, Brontë thought ruefully when the man suddenly rolled over and was violently sick down the front of his jacket. A complete bath would be more in order, but that obviously wasn't uppermost in Eli's mind.

'Look, you really don't have to stay with me,' he said. 'Why don't you go back to the cab?'

She counted to ten, but it didn't help. Okay, so the alcohol fumes emanating from the man would have been enough to knock most people over at ten paces, but she was coping, and she deeply resented the implication that he thought she wasn't.

'I'll stay,' she said.

'There's no need,' Eli insisted, as he began bagging up the soiled swabs he had used. 'I can get him into the ambulance by myself.'

'Oh, really?' she retorted, unable to curb her sarcasm. 'So you're going to lift a twenty-stone man all by yourself on a pavement that's like glass? I don't think so.'

Quickly, she bent down and put her hands under the man's shoulders, exhaling through her nose to keep her breathing to a minimum. One drunk, she told herself, as she felt the familiar quickening of her heart. It's one drunk. One virtually comatose drunk, and you can handle that. You have to for your own self-respect.

'Brontë, you don't have to do this,' Eli said gently, his eyes concerned, and she swore under her breath.

'I'd do it a lot faster if you helped,' she snapped. 'Or are you just going to stand there and watch?'

She saw his jaw clench, but she sure as heck wasn't going to apologise. There was a fine line between watching out for her, and constantly treating her like a stick of dynamite, and he had well and truly crossed that line.

'Drive fast,' Eli said once they got the man safely into the back of the ambulance, and he climbed in beside him. 'If he throws up again, we'll be stuck with a two-hour lay-off at the station until the cleaners can disinfect the ambulance.'

She nodded, and, within ten minutes, the man had been delivered into the arms of an A and E staff nurse at the Pentland who looked anything but pleased by the new arrival.

'Apparently that's the fourth drunk one of our ambulances has brought in tonight,' Eli explained. 'Which means ED7's name is now well and truly mud amongst the nursing staff.'

'Some nights in A and E are like that,' Brontë replied as she drove out of the ambulance bay in front of the hospital. 'We used to get cycles at the Waverley. One night it would be a rash of heart attacks, the next a whole host of broken legs. One summer—' she chuckled as she remembered '—it was wall-to-wall food poisoning. We ended up using everything from kidney dishes to buckets for people to be sick in.'

Eli didn't laugh. He didn't do anything but stare fixedly out of the window, and she gritted her teeth.

'I can't believe it will soon be Christmas,' she said, deliberately changing the subject. 'Just twenty-eight shopping days left, according to the newspapers.'

'Yes.'

'Do you spend Christmas with your family, or on your own?' she continued determinedly.

'On my own.'

Look, work with me here, she thought, crunching the gears as she turned the corner at the bottom of the road. I'm trying to make conversation, but I'm getting nothing back in return. She risked a quick glance at him but all she could see was his stiff, rigid back. Dammit, even his body language suggested, Stay back—keep away.

'It's almost twenty to three,' she said. 'What say we take an early break, head for Tony's?'

Eli cleared his throat.

'Actually, I was wondering whether we shouldn't perhaps go back to the station tonight for our coffee. I mean, you haven't met any of the other paramedics, or talked to them,' he continued, not meeting her gaze, 'so I was wondering whether we should give Tony's a miss this evening.'

Which she might have bought if he hadn't already told her that all of the ambulance crews took their coffee breaks at Tony's. He just didn't want to be alone in the cab with her, she thought grimly. Well, enough was enough, and she was going to tell him so.

Swiftly, she turned into College Street, brought the ambulance to a halt, and switched off the engine.

'What's wrong?' Eli asked.

'You—me,' she said. 'We need to talk.'

His lips quirked unexpectedly.

'Isn't that normally my line?'

'Yeah, well, you know what they say about the old ones being the best ones,' she declared. 'We need to talk about what happened yesterday.'

His smile disappeared in an instant and she saw wariness creep into his eyes.

'What's there to talk about?' he said.

'Eli, me driving you… It is not going to work if you keep watching me as though you're terrified I'm suddenly going to strip off all my clothes, put my knickers on my head and run manically through The Meadows. And if you dare to say, "That I would like to see,"' she warned as one corner of his lips curved, 'I *swear* I will hit you.'

'Okay, I won't say it,' he replied. 'I might think it….'

'*Eli!*'

'Okay, okay. Is that what you think I've been doing?' he continued. 'Worrying, about you?'

'Oh, come on,' she protested. 'This is the first time you've actually looked me in the eye all night, and you're skirting round me like I'm an unexploded keg of gunpowder which is going to blow at any moment. What else am I supposed to think?'

She was right, he thought as he stared back at her. Those strange feelings he'd experienced yesterday… He'd simply been worried. Understandably worried. After all, it wouldn't only be her neck on the line if she had a complete panic attack while they were out on the road, it would be his, too, because he was covering up for her.

And what about you noticing what a lovely smile she has, and her eyes aren't really grey but quicksilver? a nagging voice asked at the back of his mind.

Sexual deprivation, he told himself firmly. He'd been celibate for the past two months and, for a guy who had always enjoyed a regular sex life, that was bound to take its toll. In fact, it was a miracle it hadn't happened before, and, once Brontë had completed her report, and left the station, and he started dating again, everything would fall into its proper perspective.

'Eli?'

She looked both irritated, and annoyed, and relief flooded through him. He wasn't losing it. He wasn't falling into any abyss. His feelings had been *normal*, and he smiled.

'You're right. Memo to self—quit worrying, kid gloves off, and we go back to the way we were. You chewing my head off, and me refusing to take it.'

'Since when did I chew your head off?' she demanded, and he grinned.

'Virtually from your first hello.'

'Well, you deserved it,' she said. 'All that flattery… Maybe it works on other women, but it sure as heck doesn't work on me.'

'No, it doesn't, does it?' he said, his blue eyes suddenly thoughtful. 'I wonder why that is?'

Because I know what you are, she was tempted to retort, but she didn't, not least because it wasn't true. The more she got to know him, the less she was able to puzzle him out. Like his kindness to Peg, a kindness he wanted no one to discover. His kindness to her last night when he must have thought she was half demented. Even the way he could be bothered to worry about her tonight—though the worrying had become deeply irritating—was completely unexpected.

'I told you before you weren't my type,' she said lightly, 'which probably explains why your charm offensives don't work on me. Plus,' she added, feeling impelled to embroider the lie, 'I've always preferred blonds to brunettes.'

His eyebrows rose with interest.

'So the guy who did a number on you, the one who made you decide to give up dating permanently, was blond, was he?'

Damn, that would teach her to embellish.

'Stop fishing,' she declared, considerably flustered. 'I told you before it was none of your business, and it isn't.'

'I told you why I gave up dating for three months,' he pointed out, 'so I reckon it's only fair you tell me your reason.'

'You didn't tell me,' she countered. 'I figured it out myself, so that doesn't count, and, anyway, did nobody ever tell you life—'

'Isn't fair?' He smiled. 'Yup, you did, and that's no answer, so tell me.'

Right now, she realised with dismay, she would probably have told him anything because he was smiling at her. Not the normal smile she'd seen so many times since she'd started working with him, but the smile the women he'd dated always remembered so wistfully, and she could see exactly what they meant. That smile was a doozy. It was a smile which said, Tell me everything. A smile that said, I really want to know all about you, and she took an uneven, shaky breath. Oh, criminy, but even when he was faking interest—and she knew he was faking it—the combination of his deep blue eyes and that smile was dynamite.

'Silence isn't an option, Brontë,' he continued as she stared at him, horribly aware she probably looked slack-jawed. 'I want an answer.'

Damn, but she couldn't even remember what the question was.

'Eli…'

'A38, could you give us your current position, please?'

'Typical,' Eli complained as Brontë grabbed the receiver with relief. 'Just when I thought I might finally be getting an answer. But that doesn't mean you're off the hook, O'Brian,' he added with a grin. 'I don't give up easily.'

He obviously didn't, Brontë thought, but right now it wasn't his persistence which concerned her. She was too busy desperately trying to get her brain back into gear.

'A38, here,' she said into the receiver, and was pleased to hear her voice sounded, if not normal, at least relatively calm. 'We're in College Street.'

'Then we have a cat A for you,' the caller replied. 'Number 49, Holyrood Gate. Roland Finlay. Fifty-five years old, fallen out of bed, possible "suspended."'

'What's a "suspended"?' Brontë asked as she started the ignition.

'Someone who is either dead, or has had a heart attack,' Eli explained. 'Hit the siren, and go.'

Brontë did. She reversed swiftly out of College Street, then headed east, their blue siren flashing and wailing as she went.

'Up the siren's strength to max,' Eli advised, 'and if you meet any traffic drive straight down the middle of the road. Now is the not the time for any "After you, Claude" driving, now is the time for speed, and if other vehicles don't get out of your way they take the consequences.'

Which sounded scary. In fact, when she'd been taking her LGV C1 driving lessons, she'd been worried she might freeze completely if she ever had to drive at breakneck speed through the Edinburgh streets but, to her amaze-

ment, she discovered it was actually downright exhila-
rating.

'You're enjoying this, aren't you?' Eli chuckled as she
let out a small whoop of triumph after she'd squeezed
between two cars with scarcely a millimetre to spare, then
shot straight through some red traffic lights without even
breaking.

'Yup.' She beamed.

'Maybe you should retrain to be a paramedic.'

'Yeah, right,' she said drily. 'Except somehow I doubt
there'd be much call for a paramedic who can only treat
kids and little old ladies.'

'You'll get over your fear,' he said softly. 'Trust me, it
will happen.'

Trust him? If anyone had suggested to her two days ago
that she should trust Elijah Munroe she would have
laughed in their face. Everything she had been told, everything she'd seen of the way he treated women, made the
idea of 'trust' a ludicrous one, and yet… Maybe he was
right. Not about retraining to become a paramedic—she
wasn't at all convinced the work would suit her—but, if
she could conquer her fear, maybe she could go back to
doing the work she had always loved, and the thought
made her smile.

'What's funny?' he asked.

'Nothing—not important,' she replied, then added,
'We're in Holyrood Gate. Any idea where number 49 might
be?'

'I can see number 19,' Eli said, peering out of the
window, 'but that's 24, and that's 26. Jeez, was it an ar-
chitect on drugs who allotted these numbers?'

Brontë drove to the very top of the street, with Eli

scanning every block they passed but, when she turned at the top of the road to retrace their steps, he pounded his fist angrily on the dashboard.

'Why don't people put bigger number signs on their homes?' he exclaimed. 'Forget the trendy, dump the discreet, because when it's an emergency like this people like us need to know where the heck you are!'

Brontë said nothing, feeling perhaps now was not the right time to tell him her own flat number was every bit as small as the ones they had passed.

'Number 16, number 11,' she murmured as she drove slowly back down the street, 'number 9... Could it be inside that block there—the one with 45 on the wall?'

'It could be.' Eli nodded. 'But what's the bet 49 is on the third floor, and there's no elevator? Every paramedic's worst nightmare when it's a "suspended."'

'Right now, my nightmare is finding somewhere to park,' Brontë said, with frustration. 'It's bumper-to-bumper cars out there.'

'Then park in the middle of the road.'

'But we'll block the street.'

'And someone might be dying, so *park*.'

She did and, after they'd pulled their med-bags, and a carry-chair, out of the ambulance, they hit the ground running. Or at least they would have done if Mr Finlay's home had been on the ground floor but, as Eli had predicted, number 49 was the third-floor flat, and there was no elevator.

'I'm going to have to start taking some exercise,' Brontë declared breathlessly as she followed Eli round the landing on the second floor and saw to her annoyance that he didn't look even slightly winded.

'Running naked through The Meadows would give you some,' he replied, throwing her a grin over his shoulder.

'You're not going to let me forget that, are you?' she said, easing the defibrillator she was carrying onto her other shoulder.

'Nope. And I still haven't discovered why you've given up dating, but I will.'

She shook her head, but inwardly she was smiling. It was so good to have him talking to her again, so good not to feel awkward and uncomfortable in his presence. Okay, so his special smiles might make her feel considerably flustered, but she would rather deal with them than the wary silence she'd had to endure all night.

'I heard the siren,' a middle-aged woman declared when she opened the door of number 49 before they'd even knocked. 'It's my husband. He's not breathing. Please help him. Please, *please*, help him.'

Swiftly, Brontë followed Eli and Mrs Finlay through to the bedroom and saw Mr Finlay lying in a crumpled heap beside the bed.

'I don't know what happened,' Mrs Finlay continued, panic plain in her face. 'I was watching the late-night movie on TV, and heard this loud thud. I think he was perhaps going to the toilet, but I don't know, I honestly don't know.'

Eli was already connecting Mr Finlay to the heart monitor and within seconds it was obvious the man was in PEA—pulseless electrical activity. Mr Finlay's heart wasn't moving any blood around his body, and unless they could get his heart moving again he would be dead within minutes.

'Do you want me to do the chest compressions, or to set up the Ambu bag?' Brontë asked.

'Ambu bag,' Eli replied.

The chest compressions he was applying would push some oxygen to Mr Finlay's essential organs, but he needed those lungs full of oxygen, and fast. He also needed life-saving drugs, and she could see Eli searching for a suitable vein in Mr Finlay's arm after she'd affixed the Ambu bag and, instinctively, she glanced at her watch. Their window of opportunity for bringing Mr Finlay back was narrowing by the minute.

'ET?' she suggested, and Eli nodded.

A vein would have been much faster, but inserting an endotracheal tube into Mr Finlay's throat, and giving him the drugs that way, was better than nothing but just as Eli had successfully inserted the tube, the heart monitor suddenly let out a shrill warning.

'What does that mean?' Mrs Finlay asked frantically. 'That noise…those lines and numbers on the screen… What do they mean?'

That her husband had gone into VF—ventricular fibrillation—when the heart went into total chaotic activity, and things had just got a hundred times worse, Brontë thought, but she didn't say it, and neither did Eli.

'It's just a small blip, Mrs Finlay, nothing for you to be concerned about,' he said instead with a reassuring smile as he instantly resumed CPR. 'We just need to give your husband's heart rhythm a little boost, that's all.'

'But—'

'Could you do something for us, Mrs Finlay?' Eli continued quickly. 'Obviously, we're going to need to take your husband to hospital, so could you collect some blankets for us to keep him warm? Oh, and some flasks full of boiling water would be very helpful, too,' he added as Mrs Finlay turned to go.

Brontë knew they had plenty of blankets in the ambulance, and they most certainly didn't need any flasks of boiling water, but she also knew what Eli was doing. He was trying to get Mrs Finlay away from the scene rather than allowing her to watch them attempting to resuscitate her husband. It was something she'd never had to do in A and E. In A and E, a patient's family was always kept firmly outside, away from any medical procedures which could be upsetting, but here, on the front line, the ambulance services didn't have that luxury.

'How high do you want the power?' she said, once Mrs Finlay had gone.

'Two hundred joules,' Eli replied.

There was no tension in his voice, no indication at all of the seriousness of the situation, and Brontë could not help but admire his skill and professionalism as she swiftly rubbed the defibrillator paddles with electrical conducting gel, ensuring the gel completely covered the surface of the paddles, so Mr Finlay's skin wouldn't be badly burned. Calm, and unflappable, as well as unexpectedly kind and thoughtful, he was exactly the kind of nurse she would have wanted working beside her at the Waverley.

Exactly the kind of man you'd want in your life, too, if he wasn't so completely unreliable with women, a small voice whispered in her head, and she squashed the thought immediately.

'Clear!' Eli said, taking the paddles from her and placing them on either side of Mr Finlay's thin chest, and immediately Brontë sat back on her heels so she would not be subjected to a two hundred joules shock herself.

Mr Finlay's back arched slightly on the floor as the

electricity coursed through him, and Eli and Brontë stared at the heart monitor. No change.

'Three hundred joules,' Eli ordered.

Swiftly Brontë changed the voltage on the defibrillator.

'Three hundred joules,' she confirmed.

'Clear!' Eli exclaimed, and again Brontë sat back, but though Mr Finlay's body arched again, the heart monitor didn't change.

'Three hundred and sixty joules,' Eli said, 'and get me the epinephrine.'

Brontë nodded. Epinephrine could help the heart be more receptive to jolts of electricity and, if Mr Finlay's heart wasn't being kick-started into a regular rhythm by the three hundred and sixty joules alone, it was the only thing they had left to try.

Anxiously, she watched the heart monitor as Eli administered the three hundred and sixty joules, but there was no alteration, not even the slightest suspicion of one, and she handed him the epinephrine. Quickly, he injected it, applied the paddles again, and from then on he swung into a grim routine. Drug…shock…drug…shock, with the only sound being that of kettles being boiled in the kitchen.

How long had they been doing this? Brontë wondered as she felt the minutes tick by. How long could they continue doing it before they would have to concede Mr Finlay was not going to come back?

'I don't give up easily, Brontë,' Eli muttered as though he'd read her mind. 'Paddles again.'

Obediently, Brontë handed them to him and, as Eli placed them on either side of Mr Finlay's chest, and the electric shock ran through him, the heart monitor's erratic recordings suddenly changed. Miraculously, they had a pattern. It was much too slow, much too deep, but at least it was regular.

'Pulse?' Eli demanded.

'Weak and slow, but there,' Brontë replied.

'Okay, we go,' Eli declared, and she nodded.

They might have got Mr Finlay back, but his heart could return to VF at any minute. He needed A and E, but first they would have to negotiate three flights of stairs, and Mr Finlay was a big man. A very big man.

'How strong is your back?' Brontë asked as Eli stood, and Mrs Finlay appeared carrying an armful of blankets, and two flasks.

'I was going to ask you the same thing,' Eli replied wryly. 'Thank heavens for the carry-chair. Trying to get him down those stairs on a stretcher would have been a nightmare.'

It wasn't much easier with the carry-chair, Brontë decided. By the time they'd reached the ground floor she was breathless, and sweaty, and her arms and shoulders felt as though they had been pulled out of their sockets.

'Blue this one in, Brontë,' Eli ordered, as he climbed in beside Mr Finlay and his wife at the back of the ambulance. 'Up the siren to max, and step on it!'

She did, but it wasn't an easy ride. According to their sat nav, the quickest way to the hospital was via some of Edinburgh's back roads, but those streets also contained a hazard she hadn't been prepared for.

'I'm sorry—so sorry,' she shouted over her shoulder as she heard Eli swear when the ambulance lurched jerkily to one side yet again. 'If I could avoid these wretched speed bumps, I would, but I can't.'

'And if I had my way I'd strap every Edinburgh councillor to a trolley, then put him in an ambulance and drive them over these damn things for ten minutes, and you can bet your life they'd have them all dug up before I could say Elijah Munroe!' he exclaimed.

Brontë could not help but agree with him, and nor could she restrain her sigh of relief when she saw the lights of the Pentland Infirmary shining through the dark in front of them. Their journey might only have taken ten minutes, but it had seemed like a lifetime.

'I hope Mr Finlay makes it,' she observed after the nurses and doctors had taken over from them, and whisked Mr Finlay and his wife away.

'We did our best,' Eli replied with a tired smile, 'and it's all we can do. Which reminds me,' he added. 'When we were coming down the stairs, I noticed—'

'I didn't always bend my knees,' she finished for him. 'Yes, I know. I'm out of practice lifting people.'

'It's not that,' he said. 'It's your boots.'

'I bought a new pair,' she protested. 'I went to Harper & Stolins this afternoon…' She glanced at her watch. 'Actually, yesterday afternoon now, and I bought a pair.'

'Those are not Safari boots,' he said firmly. 'You may well have bought them from Harper & Stolins but they are not Safari.'

'The Safari ones were too heavy,' she replied. 'The Wayfarer ones were lighter, more fashionable—'

'There's a reason for them being heavier,' he interrupted with great and obvious patience. 'It's to ensure you keep your toes.'

'Okay, all right.' She grimaced. 'So I bought the wrong boots, but must you always be so…so…'

'Right about everything?' he suggested with a smile.

'Smug,' she countered. 'Smug was the word I was searching for. I'll go back this afternoon and buy a pair of Safaris.'

'What time this afternoon?'

She had to think. Working nights was really throwing her awareness of time completely.

'I'll probably be sleeping until about two,' she replied, 'then I need to do some washing, and buy some food.... As tonight's late-night shopping, I'll probably go about eight o'clock.'

'Then I'll meet you outside Harper & Stolins at eight o'clock to make sure you get the right boots this time. And before you argue with me,' he added as she opened her mouth to do just that, 'I'm damned if I am going to have to live for the rest of my life with the knowledge that, because I didn't supervise you, you lost all your toes.'

'But—'

'Eight o'clock, Brontë.'

She gave in. 'Okay, I'll meet you outside the shop. Happy now?'

He was until they got back into the ambulance, and then she heard him groan.

'What's up?' she asked.

'That last call-out. It was a failure.'

'Mr Finlay?' She faltered. 'You mean… He's died?'

'I don't know,' Eli replied. 'It's one of the downsides of being a paramedic. Unless we specifically make enquiries, we never get to find out what's happened to the people we pick up.'

'Then what are you talking about?' she protested. 'We arrived at Holyrood Gate to find Mr Finlay wasn't breathing, you got his heart beating again, we've delivered him to A and E, so you've given him the best possible chance of survival. No way is that a failure.'

'It is if you look at the dashboard,' Eli declared. 'I hit the timer when we got the call-out, and hit it again when we arrived in Holyrood Gate, and I've only just checked it. Look at the reading, Brontë.'

She did, but it didn't help.

'I'm sorry, but I'm still not with you,' she said.

'Brontë, it was a cat-A, high-priority call. If you remember, an ambulance crew should arrive at a cat-A call-out in eight minutes. It doesn't matter what happens to the patient *after* we get there, just so long as we get there in eight minutes, and we took nine minutes.'

She gazed at him in disbelief. 'Then, you're saying…'

'If we had arrived at Holyrood Gate in eight minutes to discover Mr Finlay had been dead for two days, it would be counted as a success. If we arrived, as we did, in nine minutes, providing him with life-saving treatment, it's a failure.'

'But that's…' She thought about it, but thinking didn't make it any better. *'Nuts.'*

'Yup,' he agreed, wearily rubbing his hands over his face, 'and it's not just nuts. It also costs the station dearly because the more eight-minute targets we miss, the less money the government will give us to buy new vehicles, and employ more staff. Mr Finlay's call-out was a financial disaster for ED7.'

All the elation Brontë had felt in getting Mr Finlay safely to the Pentland drained away in an instant. She knew she couldn't possibly have got to Holyrood Gate any faster. No one could unless they'd had wings, and as she stared unhappily at Eli, she realised he suddenly looked every one of his thirty-eight years.

'How do you stand this?' she asked. 'The stupid rules, the petty restrictions?'

'Because…' He drew in a deep breath, then shook his head awkwardly. 'Hell, but this is going to sound so pretentious. I might hate the bureaucracy, the reducing of patients to numbers instead of people with feelings, hopes and dreams, but… Every once in a while I make a difference. Every once in a while my being there can pull someone through who wouldn't otherwise survive, and on those occasions…'

'It's the best job in the world,' she said, and he smiled, a weary, sad smile.

'That's about it.'

It was how she'd used to feel in A and E, she remembered. The rush of adrenaline when they'd been able to resuscitate someone, the buzz in the department when everything went well. Yes, there were downsides. The consultants who could be rude and overbearing, the times when they couldn't save someone, but she missed it, she missed it so much.

'Coffee,' she said firmly. 'I think we both need coffee, and I want the biggest, stickiest, sugar-covered doughnut Tony's can supply.'

'Not a hamburger?' Eli said, his blue eyes crinkling, and she knew the effort it had taken him to make that small joke, and gave him a mock hard stare.

'A doughnut, Mr Munroe.'

'Then hit the road, O'Brian,' he replied, 'and don't spare the horses.'

She didn't. She reached the café in record time but,

when Eli had gone to get their food and drinks, she stared morosely out of the ambulance.

How in the world had she ever believed she could do this job? It had been a mistake even to have applied for it. She should have looked into the details more fully, paid more attention to what her duties would be, but she had been so desperate for a job, any job.

And you wanted something which would keep you connected, however tenuously, to nursing, her mind whispered, and she sighed.

Not once since she'd started working at the station had she ever taken out her notebook because it was the patients who interested her, they always had. Nursing was where her heart lay and, though Eli seemed to think she could retrain to be a paramedic, unless she could get over her fear of crowds it just wasn't an option, and that left her…

Nowhere, she thought with an even deeper sigh. Absolutely nowhere.

'One-a cappuccino, one-a doughnut,' Eli announced with a flourish as he opened the cab door.

'You're a lifesaver,' she replied, forcing a smile to her lips, but he wasn't fooled for a second.

'Let it go, Brontë,' he said gently. 'Take a tip from one who knows. The petty restrictions, the rules and regulations, let them go and concentrate on the fact we got Mr Finlay to hospital because, if you don't, it eats away at you, makes you cynical, bitter.'

'I know,' she murmured, 'but…' She shook her head. 'I don't think I'm cut out for this job.'

'I don't think you are either,' he agreed, and she glowered at him.

'Couldn't you at least *pretend* to think I might be?' she

exclaimed. 'Sheesh, but you really know how to dent a woman's self-esteem, don't you?'

'Would you rather I'd lied?' he asked, and she bit her lip.

'No, but you could have glossed it up a bit,' she pointed out. 'You could have said, "Well, Brontë, I think you're really good at this job, but I just know you'd be even better doing something else."'

He grinned. 'Yeah, but the big question is, would you have bought it if I'd said that?'

She wouldn't, but it was singularly depressing to know this was the second job she'd failed at within the space of a year.

'If you decide this isn't right for you,' he continued as she took a morose bite out of her doughnut, 'how about retraining to become a paediatrics nurse, or something in surgical?'

'I could, except…' She grimaced slightly. 'I don't mind kids, but nursing them all the time… And as for surgical… There wouldn't be the same buzz I used to get from A and E.'

'Brontë—'

'Anyway, it's not your problem, is it?' she said brightly. 'So let's talk about something else.'

She was right, he realised, it wasn't his problem so why did he feel so concerned? What she did, where she went after the end of this week, was surely her own business, and it shouldn't matter to him what decision she made, and yet, to his acute annoyance, he discovered it did.

Protective. Hell but he had that feeling again, and it didn't make any sense. He had never once felt protective of any his ex-girlfriends, so why in the world was he feeling it now about a woman he barely knew?

Because she's had such a rotten time this past year, he told himself. She's been stabbed, she suffers from panic attacks, and she's going to be out of a job because she sure as heck can't do an assessor's one. Only a complete louse wouldn't feel sorry for her.

Except feeling sorry isn't the same as feeling protective.

'Why are you glowering at me?'

'Glowering?' he repeated blankly, and saw Brontë shake her head.

'You're glowering at me, like I've rained on your parade or something, so what have I done wrong now?'

No way was he going to tell her his thoughts, and so he said the first thing that came into his head.

'Why Brontë?'

'Why Brontë, what?' she asked, taking a sip of her coffee.

'No, I meant how did you get your Christian name?'

'Oh, that's easy,' she replied. 'My parents both lecture in, and are fanatical fans of, English nineteenth-century literature, so I got stuck with Brontë. Actually, in the greater scheme of things, I was lucky. My big brother got landed with Byron, and my little sister with Rossetti.'

'And are your brother and sister medics like you?'

'Oh, heavens, no.' She laughed. 'Byron is an investment banker, and Rossetti's a criminal lawyer.'

His eyebrows rose. 'Serious high-flyers.'

'Yup, I'm the dummkopf of the family,' she replied, and saw a flash of unexpected irritation cross his face.

'Why do you think you're the dummkopf?' he demanded.

'Because I am in comparison to them,' she replied.

'Look, it's no big deal,' she continued, as he opened his mouth, clearly intending to interrupt, 'we can't all be high-flyers and I don't have a problem with it. Do you have any brothers or sisters?'

'No.'

An oddly shuttered look had suddenly appeared on his face. A look which suggested she had inadvertently strayed into an area he considered very much off limits, and she wished she hadn't asked, except it was hardly a controversial question, and yet it appeared it was.

'Good coffee,' she said awkwardly. 'Good doughnut, too.'

'Maybe I'll tempt you into trying one of Tony's hamburgers one night,' he said, clearly deeply relieved to be talking about something else. 'Better yet, maybe you'll tell me about the blond who did such a number on you that you've given up dating permanently.'

She rolled her eyes.

'Don't you *ever* give up?' she exclaimed.

'Nope.'

Which would teach her the folly of embellishing a lie, she thought ruefully. There wasn't a blond, never had been unless she counted the fair-haired medical student she'd dated for a few weeks when she was training to be a nurse, but how to explain what she didn't fully understand herself. That as far as men were concerned she seemed to have an invisible sticker on her forehead saying, *This one's a mug*. Eli knowing she was a fruit cake when it came to encountering drunken gangs was one thing, her admitting to him she was also the world's biggest all-time loser in the game of love was something else entirely.

'Next question, please,' she said firmly.

'Quit stalling, O'Brian,' he pressed. 'Tell me.'

She wouldn't have told him anything, but he was smiling that smile at her again. The 'tell me all your troubles' smile, the 'you can trust me' smile, and she gazed heavenwards with frustration.

'Look, if I tell you, will you quit harassing me?' she demanded, and when he nodded, she took a deep breath. 'It's got nothing to do with any blond. I just have such lousy taste in men I thought, Why keep on getting hurt, why not just concede defeat, and give up on dating completely.'

A frown appeared in his blue eyes. 'You mean, you attract men who hurt you physically?'

'No, I don't mean that,' she said irritably.

'Then you attract psychos, weirdos?'

'You mean like the loony tune I'm currently sitting next to?' she said in exasperation. 'No, I don't mean that either. It's just…every man I've ever dated… It always starts off okay, and then…' She shrugged. 'I guess I don't see the warning signs quickly enough that the men I get involved with aren't right for me.'

'Why?'

'I don't *know*. Look, you asked me,' she continued quickly as Eli opened his mouth clearly intending to push it, 'and I've answered your question. *End of discussion*.'

Not for Eli it wasn't, she realised as he waved the remains of his hamburger pointedly at her.

'Okay, as I see it,' he declared, 'you're making two fundamental mistakes here. First, you're choosing the wrong men to date.'

'Well, duh,' she replied. 'I wonder why I didn't think of that. *Of course* I'm choosing the wrong men to date, but I don't deliberately set out to fall in love with men who will break my heart. I just seem to end up with them.'

'And that's your second mistake,' Eli observed. 'You're looking for *lurve*, for the happy-ever-after ending, and there's no such thing.'

She blinked. 'You don't believe there's any such thing as love?'

'Of course there isn't,' he replied, taking a large gulp of his coffee. 'All that hearts and flowers stuff, the mushy sentimental ballads and films… It all boils down to sex.'

'But—'

'Brontë, the quicker you wake up and face reality, the less chance you'll have of being hurt,' he insisted. 'Forget about love, forget about happy-ever-afters. Relationships between men and women all come down to one thing. What the sex is like. If the sex is mediocre, you cut your losses. If the sex is okay, you stick around for a bit because okay sex is better than no sex at all, and if the sex is phenomenal you enjoy it while you can, and then move on. It's what grown-up, realistic men and women do.'

'No, you're wrong, so wrong,' she argued back. 'There *is* love in this world. Yes, there's a lot of suffering, a lot of pain, but I truly believe there are people out there caring for one another, loving one another. If I didn't believe that— if I just accepted, as you seem to, that everyone just looks after themselves—what kind of world would we have?'

Eli shook his head impatiently.

'You're confusing two completely different issues here,' he declared. 'I'm not saying you walk on by if someone's in trouble, or ignore another human being's suffering. There are a lot of things I care passionately about. Injustice, inequality, bigotry—'

'But not love?' she interrupted.

'No, not love,' he said firmly, and she sighed in defeat.

'Could any two people possibly be more incompatible?' she observed. 'More poles apart in what they think, believe?'

'Doubt it,' he replied.

There didn't seem anything left to say, and, as Brontë stared down at the remains of her doughnut, it somehow didn't seem nearly as appealing as it had earlier.

'I think I've had enough of this,' she said, putting what was left of her doughnut back into its paper bag.

'I'm actually not very hungry tonight either,' Eli murmured, gazing down at his hamburger without enthusiasm.

'Back to the station, to wait for a call-out?' she suggested.

'Best thing,' he agreed. 'Except you'd better get rid of that icing sugar on your cheek first. No, the other cheek,' he continued impatiently as she put her hand up to her left cheek. 'Here, let me.'

She didn't get the chance to tell him she wasn't an idiot, that she could manage perfectly well on her own, thank you very much. He had already begun brushing the icing sugar from her cheek. Brushing it matter-of-factly at first, and then the pressure of his fingers suddenly changed. His touch became feather-light, almost caressing, and she forgot to breathe, forgot to do anything, but stare back at him. He hadn't moved closer to her, she could swear he hadn't, and yet he seemed so much nearer, the cabin so much smaller, and, when his fingers slid slowly down her cheek, and cupped her chin, she swallowed hard.

'Eli….'

She couldn't say anything else, and he didn't say anything at all. He just held her chin in his hand, his blue eyes fixed on her, so dark, so very dark in the light from the street lamp, and she could hear his breathing, could hear her own erratic breath in the silence, could feel a slow spiralling heat growing deep within her, and slowly she reached up and covered his hand with her own.

His fingers were warm, much warmer than hers, and she shivered involuntarily, saw his lips part, knew her own had, too, and she felt herself leaning towards him, saw he was leaning towards her in return, and then, suddenly, without warning, he wasn't holding her chin any more, and she was looking shakily out of the window, not sure whether it had been her, or him, who had moved first, or if they had moved in unison, but it was definitely Eli who spoke first, and his voice, when he did, sounded strained, husky.

'We'd better get back to the station.'

She nodded, or at least she thought she nodded, and with her heart still jumping erratically in her chest, she switched on the ignition and hoped to heaven he couldn't see just how much her hands were trembling as she drove away.

CHAPTER FOUR

Thursday, 7:55 p.m.

SHE should have arranged to meet Eli earlier, Brontë
thought as she stamped her feet, and blew on her fingers
to try to restore some heat to them, as an icy wind swirled
around Cockburn Street. Better yet, she should have told
him at the end of their shift this morning that she'd
suddenly remembered something absolutely vital she had
to do, and couldn't meet him at all.

Not that they'd exactly been talking when they'd
finished work, she remembered ruefully. He'd seemed as
anxious to get away as she had, which meant this shopping
trip was going to be awkward, and uncomfortable, and she
should have stayed home.

'Oh, stop it, Brontë,' she muttered to herself. 'It's not
like this is a date. You've both agreed you're completely
incompatible, and him coming on this shopping trip is
more a colleague-to-colleague advisory type thing.'

*Which doesn't explain why you've washed your hair,
and put on your favourite knee-length brown leather
boots, and equally favourite racing green coat with the
faux-fur-trimmed hood.*

Well, my hair needed a wash, she defensively told her reflection in the large window of Harper & Stolins, and as for my clothes… Only an idiot wouldn't have wrapped up warmly when it definitely felt like snow.

Yeah, right, Brontë, a little voice laughed as she tried in vain to smooth down her fringe which was most definitely sticking up. *So it's got nothing to do with what happened earlier this morning, then?*

Oh, my word, but that had been something else, Brontë thought, feeling a flutter of heat in her stomach as she remembered. When he'd touched her cheek, when their eyes had met, and time had seemed to disappear… She'd been so certain he was going to kiss her, had so wanted him to kiss her, and she closed her eyes, to relive the memory, and let out a tiny yelp when a hand clasped her shoulder.

'Will you stop *doing* that?' She gasped, clutching at her chest as she whirled round to see Eli standing behind her.

'I thought it was just dark cemeteries which spooked you,' he protested, 'not well-lit streets in Edinburgh.'

Everything about you spooks me, she wanted to reply, but she didn't.

'Yeah, well, wear shoes with heavier soles next time,' she said instead.

In fact, change absolutely everything you're wearing, she thought as her gaze took in his appearance. Eli dressed in his paramedic cargo trousers, and high-visibility jacket, might be enough to set most feminine hearts aflutter, but Eli wearing a pair of hip-hugging denims, a blue-and-white open-necked shirt and an old black leather jacket was guaranteed to give every woman a cardiac arrest. A fact that was all too obvious from the number of women who were giving him second glances as they walked by.

'So,' he said, 'are you ready for the big boots expedition?'

Was it her imagination or did he seem just a little bit uncomfortable, a little unsure, almost as though he wished he was anywhere but here?

'Look, you don't have to do this,' she said quickly. 'I promise faithfully I'll buy the correct boots this time, so you don't need to babysit me.'

'Hey, it's no problem,' he insisted. 'And I have to safeguard your toes, remember?'

She laughed, and he did, too, and if his laughter sounded slightly strained to her ears, she decided it was probably just because he was as cold as she was.

'Okay,' she said, 'let's get on with it, shall we?'

Getting on with it, however, looked as though it might take considerably longer than she'd anticipated. They were certainly whisked instantly through to the seating area when they entered Harper & Stolins, and there were assistants aplenty, but unfortunately each and every one of them appeared to want to talk to Eli. Of course, that was probably because all of them were women, Brontë thought wryly, but feeling like a spare parcel abandoned at a sorting office was not how she had envisaged spending her boot-buying expedition.

'Any chance of some service here?' she said eventually to one of the girls who was hovering on the outskirts of Eli's fan club.

'Sorry,' the girl declared, looking as though she actually meant it, 'but Eli's a very popular customer.'

'So I see.' Brontë sighed. 'I'm looking for a pair of Safari boots, size five.'

The girl was back within minutes, clutching a pair, and

it was only when Brontë put them on she realised the folly of wearing a skirt when you were trying on safety boots.

'What's wrong?' Eli asked as he joined her beside the mirror, and saw her rueful expression.

'Not exactly flattering, are they?' she replied, looking down at her feet. 'In fact, I look like I'm auditioning for clown of the year.'

'They're not supposed to be flattering,' Eli observed. 'They're supposed to keep your toes in one piece.'

'I know, but…' She sighed as she lifted one foot. 'I should have worn trousers.'

'Not for me you shouldn't. It's nice to see you have legs.'

And he was staring at them. Staring at them in a quite blatant way, and she suddenly felt completely exposed, which was crazy because she walked around Edinburgh in skirts all the time, and had never once felt vulnerable.

'Of course I have legs,' she replied in a rush, horribly aware her cheeks were darkening. 'Everyone has legs. Unless they've lost them due to some accident, or were born that way, of course, in which case they won't but, generally, normally, most people have legs.'

And I'm babbling, she thought, babbling like an idiot, but I wish I'd worn trousers because he's still staring at my legs and my knees are too chunky, and my calves aren't exactly model-girl slim, and Eli likes girls with impossibly long legs, not that I give a damn about that, but…

'Everyone might have legs,' he said, 'but not everyone has great ones like you.'

He thought she had good legs. No, correct that. He thought she had *great* legs, and he was still looking at them, making her feel even more self-conscious.

'Do we have a sale?' the assistant asked, glancing from Brontë to Eli, then back again.

'I think so, yes,' Brontë replied. 'I mean they fit, and they're Safaris, so...'

She wished Eli would say something, anything, and what was worse was two of the assistants were nudging each other, and giggling, and she didn't know why they were giggling.

'These boots are the right ones, aren't they, Eli?' she continued pointedly. 'The ones you wanted me to buy?'

He blinked, then nodded. 'Absolutely. Definitely.'

'Well, that's my footwear sorted out for tonight,' she said far too brightly as she sat down, feeling considerably flustered. 'Problem solved, mission accomplished.'

'So, what now?' he asked as she slipped into her knee-length boots, and headed for the till, clutching the Safaris.

'Now?' she repeated. 'Well, I guess once I've paid for the boots I go home, and you go and do whatever you were planning on doing before we clock on in a couple of hours.'

'You mean I don't even get to share a celebratory dinner with you?' he protested after she'd settled up with the cashier, and he followed her out onto the street. 'I've come all the way here from my warm and cosy flat in Lauriston Place to give you the benefit of my not-inconsiderable advice, and now it's snowing, and I don't even get something to eat?'

He wanted to prolong this nondate? He wanted to go somewhere else with her? She would have thought he would have been anxious to get away, to do something else, see someone else, and yet he clearly wasn't.

Go home, Brontë. Thank him for his kindness, and go home where it's safe.

Except he was right about the snow. Little flakes were beginning to whirl about in the wind, and settle on the pavement, and he hadn't needed to come and help her, even if she hadn't really needed any help. All she'd needed was to concede defeat, forget about fashion and style, and accept she had to wear a pair of boots which made her feet look like a penguin's.

'Dinner would be nice,' she admitted. 'But I live on the south side of Edinburgh so I wouldn't have a clue where to go round here.'

'The Black Bull in the High Street,' he announced. 'It's my favourite restaurant. They might not make coffee quite as good as Tony's, but they do make a mean Hungarian stroganoff and poached salmon to die for.'

And he was obviously as equally well known in the Black Bull as he was in Harper & Stolins, Brontë thought drily, when a beaming waitress ushered them towards a table by the roaring log fire, and an equally attentive waitress quickly took their orders. A stroganoff for Eli, and poached salmon for her.

'Do you know every single woman in Edinburgh?' Brontë asked as she shrugged off her coat, and held her hands out to the fire. 'And I'm emphasising the word *single* here.'

'Can I help it if I'm a popular guy?' Eli answered, and, despite herself, Brontë laughed.

'It's nice here,' she said, her eyes taking in the old oak panelling, the wheelback chairs, chintz curtains, and pictures of Old Edinburgh. 'Very cosy, and atmospheric. Though I'm surprised you like it. I'd have pegged you as more a minimalist, modern sort of a guy.'

'Now, what did I tell you about the dangers of taking

me at face value?' he teased and, when she laughed again, he nodded approvingly. 'You don't do that often enough. Laugh, I mean. I wonder why that is?'

'Maybe I just take things more seriously than you do,' she replied. 'Or, maybe this past year has forced me to be more serious.'

To her surprise, Eli reached out, and covered one of her hands with his.

'Try not to remember it,' he said gently. 'Try not to look back, but look forward instead.'

Which was easy for him to say, Brontë thought wistfully as she stared down at his strong, capable fingers. He knew exactly what his future was, whereas she didn't even know what she would be doing next week.

'By the way, I think I've figured out why you're having such problems with men,' Eli continued, releasing her hand as the waitress placed their orders in front of them.

'I thought we'd already worked that one out,' she protested, trying not to mind that his hand was no longer covering hers. 'It's because I'm a lousy picker, and I believe in love which, according to you, doesn't exist.'

'Well, those are certainly issues, but I think they're part of a much bigger problem. How old is your brother?'

'Byron?' she said, bewildered by his unexpected change in conversation. 'He's thirty-six.'

'And your sister, Rossetti?'

'She's twenty-eight, but...' She frowned at him. 'Sorry, but I thought you were going to explain why I have such bad luck with men, but now you're talking about my family, so is there a reason behind your questions, or are you just going off at a tangent?'

He sighed pointedly. 'Could you just bear with me here

for one minute, Brontë. This is important. How old are you?'

'Thirty-five, but I don't see—'

'You've got middle-child syndrome.'

'I've got what?' she said, starting to laugh, but he looked so perfectly serious she stopped. 'Okay, enlighten me. What's middle-child syndrome?'

He took a bite of his stroganoff, then sat back in his seat.

'The first child in a family is always the most antici-pated and exciting for the parent so it's put on a pedestal, applauded for everything it does, and made a big fuss of. That's your brother, Byron. The baby of the family basks in the sentimentality of being the last child, so it's basi-cally spoiled rotten. That's your sister, Rossetti.'

'And me?' she said, curious in spite of herself as she ate some of her poached salmon and found it to be every bit as good as he'd promised.

'Well, you… You were just there. Never getting the same praise as your brother and sister because having been through the toddler stages with Byron, your parents just expected you to learn how to do the same things he had, and Rossetti would be completely indulged because they knew she was going to be their last child. You were stuck in the middle, overlooked a lot of the time, so you grew up to suffer from severe low self-esteem.'

'I suspect your psychology is a bit skewed,' she observed uncomfortably, and he shook his head as he took a sip of water.

'Nope, it's pretty well documented.'

'But I don't feel inferior to my brother and sister.'

'*I'm the dummkopf of the family.* That's what you said,'

he declared, 'and it bothered me—it bothered me a lot—
that you should think being a nurse made you inferior to
them.'

She wanted to tell Eli he was wrong, that she didn't feel
at all inferior to Byron or Rossetti, but she suddenly
realised she couldn't. It was hard not to feel inferior when
her brother would telephone to say he was heading off to
Hong Kong, or New York, or Tokyo, and it had been even
harder to feel genuinely happy for Rossetti when their
parents had bought her a plushy, three-bedroom flat while
she was still living in rented accommodation.

'Okay, so maybe I do feel a little inferior to them,' she
conceded, realising Eli was waiting for an answer. 'In
fact, if I'm going to be completely honest, there were
times, when I was growing up, and Byron won yet another
collection of school prizes, and Rossetti appeared never
to do anything wrong in my parents' eyes, I did wish I
belonged to another family.'

'Knew it!' Eli exclaimed triumphantly.

'But…' Brontë continued determinedly. 'Every child
feels inferior to its siblings at one time or another. I bet you
did, too. I bet there were times when you thought, "Oh, to
have been born into a different household, to some other
family."'

'In my case, I would have been happy to have belonged
to any family,' he murmured.

His face had that shuttered look again, she noticed. The
look it always assumed when she strayed too far into something he clearly considered very personal, and she ate some
more of her salmon, then slowly put down her knife and
fork.

'Sounds like you had a rough childhood.'

'Water under the bridge now,' he said dismissively, but she sensed it wasn't, not for him.

'Eli—'

'Anyway, we're talking about you,' he interrupted, 'not me.'

So back off, Brontë. That's what he was saying. *Back off, keep out and don't probe.*

'Okay, if I accept you're right about me suffering from middle-child syndrome—which I don't,' she declared, seeing him roll his eyes as she picked up her knife and fork again, 'I fail to see how being a middle child explains my lousy track record with men.'

'It's obvious,' he said, attacking his stroganoff impatiently. 'If you're a middle child, with low self-esteem, that, in turn, makes you an easy target for fundamentally weak men who will walk all over you. You should be looking for a man who is self-confident, a man who is easy in his own skin.'

Like you, her heart whispered, and unconsciously she shook her head.

'Which is fine, in principle,' she argued back, 'but, surprising though it may be to you, even in the twenty-first century women don't tend to do the choosing, and if we see an example of the alpha male you seem to be describing there's precious few women who would go up to such a man, and ask *him* out.'

'But—'

'Eli, alpha men gravitate towards alpha women,' she continued, 'so they are not going to be asking someone like me out.'

A flash of anger appeared in his blue eyes.

'What do you mean, "someone like you"?' he said irritably. 'What's wrong with you?'

'Look at me, Eli.'

'I *am* looking,' he protested.

'No, not like that,' she replied with exasperation. 'Look at me the way a man looks at a woman he's scoping out.'

'Yeah, right,' he said wryly, 'and like I want all my teeth knocked out.'

'I'll give you a pass on this one, I promise,' she insisted, 'just look at me.'

Obediently, he put down his knife and fork, steepled his fingers together and leant forward.

'Okay, I'm looking.'

And, dear heavens, he was, she thought, feeling a flood of heat surge across her cheeks as his gaze swept over her figure, then up to her face, lingering for an instant on her lips, and then returned to her eyes. That look would have melted a polar ice cap, and as for her... Thank heavens she was sitting so close to the fire, because if she hadn't been she didn't know how on earth she would have explained why she not only felt ablaze, but also looked it.

'Okay, tell me what you see?' she managed to ask.

No way on this earth was he going to tell her what he saw, he thought as he moved uncomfortably in his seat, all too aware of a painful tightness in his groin. No way was he going to say he saw a woman who wasn't even pretty, far less beautiful. A woman whose gold-flecked brown hair was currently sticking out at a wild angle, and whose nose was chapped and red at the tip because of the cold weather they'd been having. A woman who, for some insane, inexplicable reason he still wanted to lean forward and kiss.

She'd think he was crazy. *He* thought he was crazy, and he had done so ever since last night when, if she hadn't moved away—or maybe he did first, he honestly couldn't remember now—he would have kissed her for sure, and that would have been bad, seriously bad.

'I see…' He cleared his throat. 'I see a young woman with a very winning personality.'

'Oh, wonderful.' Brontë groaned. 'That's exactly what every woman wants to hear. *Not*. Why don't you just offer me a paper bag to wear over my head the next time I go out?'

'Look, I phrased that wrongly,' he said quickly. 'What I meant—'

'It's okay, it's all right,' she said dismissively. 'I asked for your opinion, and you've given it. I know I'm not an alpha woman.' She thought about it, and frowned. 'Actually, I'm probably not even a gamma woman if there is such a thing, because I bet your first thought when you saw me on Monday night was, Ordinary, boring.'

It had been, he remembered. It had been exactly what he'd thought, and he'd been so wrong, so very wrong, just as he had been wrong to prolong their meeting after she'd bought her boots. Having almost made a complete fool of himself in Harpers & Stolins, by staring at her legs—and she had very good legs, he remembered, forcing himself not to look down and check them out again—he should simply have waved her farewell, and gone home, instead of urging her to spend more time in his company.

So why did you?

Because I wanted to prove to myself that last night— this morning—had been a temporary aberration, he thought ruefully. I wanted to see her outside of the station environment, so I'd realise she's just another woman, not in any way different or special, but the trouble is she *is* different and I don't know why.

'You're taking too long to answer, Eli,' she pointed out, and he felt a tide of heat creep up the back of his neck.

'Of course I didn't think you were boring,' he lied, and she shook her head.

'Yes, you did, and that's what I am. Brontë O'Brian. Memorable only because of my name, so thanks for your advice about dating only superconfident alpha men but, trust me, it ain't going to happen.'

'What about dating men who are all screwed up?' he said before he could stop himself, and Brontë laughed.

'Men like you, you mean?' she replied.

The minute the words were out of her mouth, she wished them back. What she'd said… It sounded almost—hell, it sounded *exactly*—as though she was hitting on him, and she hadn't intended to do that, and she opened her mouth to say something flippant, light, but the words died in her throat.

He had reached out and taken one of her hands in his, and was staring down at it, his face a little wry.

'I certainly feel completely screwed up at the moment,' he murmured.

'Do you?' she said faintly, and he nodded.

'You see, the trouble is…' He met her gaze. 'I just can't figure you out at all.'

'I thought…' Oh, my heavens, but he was stroking the palm of her hand with his thumb, and she was having difficulty thinking, far less speaking. 'I thought we'd established I was easy to read. That I'm suffering from middle-child syndrome, and I'm ordinary and boring.'

'You're definitely suffering from middle-child syndrome, but you're anything but ordinary and boring. You're…' A rueful smile appeared in his blue eyes. 'You're one of a kind, Brontë O'Brian.'

One of a kind. Did that mean what she thought—hoped—it meant? Did it mean he found her desirable, not ordinary and boring at all, but actually desirable? She knew she should say something, but she didn't know what to say, didn't want to mess it up, and she cleared her throat, only to pause.

A log had shifted in the grate beside her, sending a shower of snapping, crackling sparks spiralling up into the chimney, but it wasn't that which had caught her attention. It was the muffled, feminine laughter behind her and, as she glanced over her shoulder and saw the knowing smile on the face of one of the waitresses, she realised something she should have seen before. Something she must have been blind not to have been aware of, and a twist of pain tore through her.

Eli was flirting with her. Not because it meant anything, not because he was interested in her, but simply because he could, and she, like a poor sap, was falling for it, falling for his charm, just as all the other women in his life had. He was playing with her, and she had never played games when it came to relationships. For her it had always been all or nothing, and with Eli she knew as surely as she knew anything that if she didn't stop this right now it would simply lead to a broken heart, and she couldn't go that way, just couldn't.

Blindly, she pulled her hand out of his, and reached for her coat.

'I…I have to go,' she said through a throat so tight it hurt.

'But why?' he protested, confusion plain on his face. 'You haven't finished your meal—'

'I need… I have to go home to get changed,' she said,

frantically searching under the table for her carrier bag from Harper & Stolins, desperate to get away from him.

'But, we're not on duty until ten-thirty,' Eli declared. 'We've another hour—'

'I need to shower as well,' Brontë said, looking everywhere but at him. 'I…I need to shower, and change, and get ready for tonight.'

She was already heading for the restaurant door and, without even counting them, Eli pressed some notes into the waitress's hand, and hurried after her.

'Brontë, what's wrong?' he demanded when he caught up with her in the street.

'Nothing…absolutely nothing,' she said with forced brightness. 'Thank you for the help with the boots, and the lovely meal. I'll see you tonight.'

'But, Brontë—'

Don't come after me, she prayed, as she walked quickly away from him down the High Street, the sound of her feet muffled by the now lying snow. *Please, please, don't come after me,* her heart cried as she dashed a hand across her cheeks, despising herself for her weakness and stupidity.

To her relief he didn't. To her relief, no familiar voice called her name, no firm hand grasped her shoulder, but it didn't help. She might be able to lose herself amongst the other late-night shoppers who were thronging the street, but she couldn't shut out the mocking little voice in her head.

The little voice that whispered, *Fool, Brontë. You are such a fool.*

Eli rotated his shoulders wearily as Brontë drove carefully down Johnstone Terrace towards Stables Road. An RTC,

Dispatch had said, and it wasn't the first such accident they'd been called out to tonight. In fact, from the minute they'd clocked on at ten-thirty, they'd scarcely had a moment's rest, not even for their customary coffee break. The now deeply lying snow, coupled with inexperienced city drivers unused to driving in such conditions, had meant accident after accident, and ED7's resources had been stretched to breaking point.

'The police are here,' Brontë observed as a flashing light suddenly appeared in the dark in front of them. 'Must be a serious one.'

It looked it, even from a distance and, when they got nearer, it looked even worse. The car had clearly skidded right across the road, but then it had hit a wall, and brought part of the wall down on top of it.

'I'm afraid the driver looks in a pretty bad way,' one of the policemen declared when Brontë and Eli walked towards him. 'According to her ID, her name is Katie Lee, aged twenty.'

And she hadn't been wearing a seat belt, Eli thought as he stared at the car. He could see the distinctive ringed crack on the windscreen which meant the young woman had 'bullseyed' it when her car had hit the wall, and there were tiny spots of blood and bits of hair embedded in the glass. Why didn't people learn—why did they never seem to learn?

'Dear heavens, the whole front of the bonnet is completely crushed,' Brontë whispered.

He could hear the shock in her voice, the appalled horror, but then she would only ever have seen people who had been brought in to A and E by ambulance, and not the situations they had come out of, as he always did.

'Watch out for broken glass, and bits of metal,' he replied, 'and if you see any oil, let me know. We don't want to be inside something that might go up like a fireball.'

'Right,' she said faintly. She glanced up at him. 'I'm okay, honestly I am. It's just…'

'The first bad RTC is always a bit of a shock.' He nodded. 'I threw up after my first one.'

She managed a smile but, when he smiled back, she looked away quickly and he bit his lip.

She'd scarcely said a word to him all night, and it wasn't simply because they'd been run off their feet. She was clearly edgy and uncomfortable in his company, and it was all his fault.

Why in the world had he virtually asked her whether she would consider dating him, he wondered, as he leant into the driver's seat to take the young woman's pulse, and heard the mobile phone lying on the car floor begin to ring. He still didn't know why he'd said it. The words had just come out, completely without warning, so thank heavens Brontë had taken the initiative, and ended the conversation. If she'd said, 'Okay, Eli, where do you want to go on this date?' he would have been in severe trouble because he'd made his no-dating pledge, and it still had a month to run.

Oh, get outta here, Eli, his mind laughed. *That isn't what's freaking you out. What's freaking you out is that for the first time in your life you feel all at sea with a woman, and it's scaring you half to death.*

'Katie…Katie, can you hear me?' Brontë said as she leant in through the broken window of the passenger door.

'My legs…my legs hurt so much, and my chest…' The

young woman groaned as she tried to take a breath. 'It's like there's a big, heavy weight on it.'

'Pulse weak, BP falling,' Eli muttered as he swiftly wrapped a cervical collar round the young woman's neck to support it before they could attempt to take her out of the car. 'Looks like compound fractures tib and fib and possible pelvis fracture to me.'

It would have been Brontë's initial assessment, too, plus she strongly suspected severe internal injuries.

'Pethidine?' she suggested, and Eli nodded.

'Haemaccel drip, too,' he added. 'Is the heart monitor good to go?'

'Just about,' Brontë murmured. 'Okay, it's on.'

They both stared at the screen, then exchanged glances. The young woman's heart rate was erratic, extremely erratic, and the last thing they wanted, or needed, was her to go into VF within the small confines of the car, or, even worse, to go asystole. Asystole hearts couldn't be shocked. All they could do, if that occurred, was perform CPR, and affix an Ambu bag to try to keep the oxygen flowing to the young woman's brain, but casualties who presented at A and E with asystole rarely survived.

'Is there no way we can switch that off?' Brontë exclaimed as the young woman's mobile phone began to ring again, and she saw a message flash up on the display screen.

A message which read, 'Katie, can you call me? It's Mum.'

'Try to ignore it,' Eli replied.

Brontë gritted her teeth, and tried her best, but it was hard. Hard to see that message constantly flashing, and to know that unless they got Katie to A and E quickly she might never be able to reply. Hard, too, she thought as she glanced over at Eli's lowered head as he swiftly inserted a drip, to persuade herself that the man working so closely beside her meant nothing to her, that he was simply a colleague, but she was going to do it. She was going to distance herself from him no matter what it took. She had to for her own self-preservation.

'How are we going to get her out of the car?' she said when she'd finished attaching an Ambu bag. 'So much of it is crushed. Should we call for the fire brigade?'

Eli frowned, then, as Katie Lee groaned, he clearly came to a decision.

'We can't afford to wait. Her BP's going through the floor, and I think she's bleeding internally.'

'But…'

'We get her out, Brontë.'

And they did, by the simple expedient of Eli taking most of the weight of the roof of the car upon himself as well as Katie's legs and torso.

'Your shoulders are going to be black and blue tomorrow,' Brontë observed, seeing Eli wince when he straightened up after they had safely carried Katie into the ambulance.

'Nothing I can't live with,' he replied dismissively. 'And getting her to A and E is much more important than me getting a couple of bruises.'

He meant that, she knew he did. Even in the short time she'd been working with him she'd seen he would always go that extra mile for the people who needed his professional skills, and yet he wouldn't go one step for the women in his life. Was it simply because he truly didn't believe in love, or was there something else? She wished she knew. She wished even more that she didn't care about the answer because not caring would have been much, much safer.

'I'll be glad when this shift is over,' she said after she and Eli had taken the young woman to the Pentland. 'I'm shattered.'

'Me, too,' he replied. 'And yet, in a weird and horrible way, having to deal with all these accidents, fighting to keep people alive until we can get them to A and E… It's the sort of night we paramedics long for. Which—when you think about it—means we're either adrenaline junkies or must have hearts of stone.'

'I think it simply means if you've been trained to do difficult, complex procedures, the last thing you want is to be constantly presented with trivial ones,' Brontë said thoughtfully. 'I bet a plumber feels exactly the same. I bet he thinks, Wish I was out there fitting a challenging, state-of-the-art power shower system instead of unblocking yet another bog-standard sink.'

Eli stared at her in open-mouthed astonishment for a second, his eyes red-rimmed and shadowed with exhaustion, and then, to her surprise, he burst out laughing.

'Only you could think of that!' he exclaimed.

'But it's *true*,' Brontë insisted, and he laughed again.

'I know it is, but only you would say it out loud which is why I think I like…'

'Like what?' she asked, and saw him shake his head uncomfortably.

'Nothing. Not important.'

'But—'

'Isn't that Dr Carter?' he interrupted. 'Maybe she'll have some news for us about John.'

Helen Carter did, but it wasn't good.

'I'm really sorry, Eli,' she said unhappily. 'But it was Mr Duncan who did the rounds on Men's Medical this morning, and he created a bit of a stink about young John.'

'In other words, he kicked him out,' Eli declared with barely suppressed anger. 'He took one look at the boy's chart, refused to listen to any of the background information, and discharged him.'

'I think the words, "This is not a bed-and-breakfast establishment for down-and-outs" was used.' Dr Carter sighed. 'I did put a note on John's file, saying "exceptional circumstances"—'

'I'm sure you did, Helen,' Eli interrupted grimly, 'but Duncan's one of the old-school consultants, never does anything unless it's by the book. He just doesn't seem able to see that if we help people when they first present they'll need less medical attention in the future.'

'You did your best, Eli,' Dr Carter replied, her round face concerned.

'Yeah, well, it wasn't good enough this time, was it?'

And before Helen Carter could say anything else, he had walked away, and, with a quick glance of apology at Dr Carter, Brontë hurried after him.

'Eli, it wasn't your fault,' she said when she caught up with him in the street.

'And is that supposed to make me feel better?' he retorted. 'Peg *trusted* me, Brontë, and I failed her and the boy. Especially the boy.'

'At least you tried—'

'And a fat lot of use that did!' he snapped.

'Eli—'

'Just drive,' he said. 'I don't care where you go, but get

me away from here because, if you don't, I swear I'll go back in there and find Duncan, and if I do…'

He didn't need to finish his sentence. Brontë waited only until he had snapped on his seat belt and she was off, driving down the Canongate, onwards past Abbey Mount, but, when she turned into Montrose Terrace, she heard him unclip his seat belt.

'I can't sit here,' he muttered. 'Stop the ambulance, Brontë. I need… I have to walk.'

Obediently, she drew up at the kerbside but, when he got out, and began walking up and down the pavement, his hands tight, balled fists at his side, she knew she couldn't simply sit there in the ambulance, watching him. No matter what he was, or what he had done, her heart bled for him. He had tried so hard to help John, had really cared about what happened to the boy, and she couldn't let him walk up and down the snow-covered pavement alone.

'Are you okay?' she asked tentatively as she approached him.

'What kind of damn fool question is that?' Eli exclaimed, then closed his eyes and, when he opened them, she could see regret there. 'I'm sorry, so sorry.' He gave an uneven laugh. 'Do you realise I've apologised to you more in the past four days than I have to anyone else in my whole life?'

'Maybe that's because you've never met anyone quite as irritating as me before,' she said, hoping to at least provoke a smile, but she didn't. 'Do you want to go and look for John? We could try Greyfriars. He might have gone back to Peg.'

'Didn't you hear what she said when we took him away

on Tuesday?' he said morosely. 'She said, "I don't want to see you back here again, young feller."'

'Yes, but she meant it kindly,' Brontë replied, hating to see him looking so defeated. 'She meant she hoped he was going on to a better life.'

'He won't see it as such. He'll see it as an order not to go back to Greyfriars. He could be anywhere, Brontë, and trying to find him…' He shook his head. 'There are so many homeless people in Edinburgh.'

'Perhaps he'll go home,' Brontë said without much hope, but feeling she had to try to give Eli some. 'Or if he doesn't go home, maybe someone from one of the charities might pick him up, and he'll be okay.'

'Brontë, just what planet are you living on?' Eli exclaimed angrily. 'He's more likely to become a crackhead, or a rent boy, than be *okay*.'

'I know—'

'You *don't*,' he replied, almost shouting at her now. 'You have no idea what it's like to be out on these streets, alone, and friendless. No comprehension of the temptations, the quick-fix drugs that are offered to you which you're only too happy to accept because they allow you an escape for just a little while. Well, I *do*.'

'Eli—'

'Yeah, you were right about me,' he continued, his mouth twisting in a bitter parody of a smile as she stared up at him. 'I was out on these streets for a year, so I know *exactly* what's it like.'

His face was harsh and white in the lamplight, and she didn't know what to do, what to say, so she did the only thing she could think of. She put her hand on his arm in what she hoped was a comforting gesture and, for a second, she thought it might have helped. For a second, she thought he was actually going to cover her fingers with his own, then he pulled his arm free with a muttered oath.

'Eli, don't give up hope,' she insisted, thinking he was going to walk away from her. 'Every time we go out we can keep an eye out for him, and maybe we'll get lucky, maybe we'll find him.'

He could see sympathy and pity in her eyes and something inside him broke. He didn't want her sympathy, or her pity. He didn't want to feel the urge to put his arms around her, and the desire to have her hold him back. He was Elijah Munroe, who had never in his life needed anyone, and he wasn't about to start now. Somehow she was managing to get past his defences, and he had to stop it, end it, and he lashed out at her with the only weapon he had left.

'What—no questions about my time on the streets?' he jeered. 'Aren't you just longing for me to tell you all the gory, grisly details?'

She flinched, almost as though he had hit her, and he saw her eyes cloud with hurt.

'I thought…' He saw her shake her head. 'I hoped you might know me better than that. I would never intrude on something that's very personal to you.'

'Oh, of course, I forgot.' He nodded. 'Saint Brontë. Always the sympathetic, always the understanding. Little Miss Perfect.'

What little colour she had drained from her face.

'I'm not perfect—not by a long shot,' she said, and he could hear the tremble in her voice. 'I screw up just like everyone else, make mistakes as we all do—'

'You wanted to know whether I had any brothers or sisters?' he interrupted, hating to see the pain and bewilderment in her face, but it was preferable to sympathy and pity. 'I could have twelve for all I know because my mother dumped me in an orphanage when I was four. "I'll be gone for five minutes," she said, and then she disappeared, and I never saw her again.'

He waited for her to dish out the sympathy he knew he couldn't bear, because then he would be able to lash out at her again, but she didn't give him sympathy.

Instead, she said, 'Do you know why she left you?'

'Got fed up with me, I suppose,' he replied dismissively. 'Got fed up with having a whining brat hanging about her skirt all day, spoiling her life, and by all accounts I wasn't a very loveable child.'

Brontë didn't know whether he had been or not. All she knew was there was a world of hurt inside this man, a world of pain and self-hatred, and, though what he had said to her had been cruel, she had to swallow hard to subdue the tears she could feel clogging her throat.

'And your father?' she said hesitantly.

'I don't remember any man in the house, so I'm guessing I was a bastard.' He smiled. A tight smile that made her wince. 'Which is what you always believed I was, so you were right yet again, Miss O'Brian. Someone give the lady a prize.'

'How did you end up on the street?' she asked, longing to put her arms around him, to comfort him, but his rigid face told her that would be a very big mistake.

'I got fostered out a few times from the orphanage, but each family sent me back.' He shrugged. 'Too much trouble. Always getting into fights, always running away.'

'Because you were unhappy,' she protested. 'And what person—be they adult or child—wouldn't lose their temper, and keep running away, if they were suddenly uprooted from what they'd known all their lives and continually placed somewhere alien, strange?'

'Yeah, well, by the time I was fourteen I'd had enough of being passed around as the parcel nobody wanted, so I ran away. I lived for a year on the streets in Edinburgh until one of the priests from a night shelter found me sleeping beside their dustbins. At first I thought he was pervert, after my youthful body,' Eli continued with an ironic laugh, 'and the poor bloke ended up with a black eye, and a broken nose.'

Brontë didn't laugh—she couldn't—and she knew he wasn't laughing either, not inside. She could picture him oh-so clearly in her mind; how frightened he must have been, how desperate.

'He took you in?' she said, trying to keep her voice as even as possible, but knowing she wasn't succeeding.

Eli nodded. 'He taught me how to read and write, gave me books, paper and pens, and then he started taking me out on his pastoral visits, and I met all these people. People who were ill. People who were dying.'

'And that's when you decided you wanted to become a nurse.'

'Yes.'

She stared down the dark and empty street for a few seconds, then back at him.

'Eli, there are ways of tracking down your mother. Societies who specialise in finding missing people. You could—'

'And why the hell should I want to find her?' he interrupted, his face dark and angry. 'She didn't want me. If she'd wanted me she would never have dumped me.'

'Maybe she had a good reason,' she said uncertainly. 'Maybe she didn't want to give you up, but she didn't have enough money to take care of you, or maybe she was very ill, and knew she couldn't cope.'

His lip curled.

'Saint Brontë, always the understanding, always the forgiving. Doesn't it ever get tiring living up on that damned pedestal of yours? No wonder men walk all over you, use you like a doormat, because that's exactly what you are!'

She stared up at him, her face ashen in the moonlight, and, as a clock tolled the hour in the distance, he saw her swallow, then hesitantly pull the ambulance ignition keys from her pocket and hold them out to him.

'It's half past six,' she said. 'Our shift's over so, I think… As I live just round the corner… Would you mind very much driving the ambulance back to the station for me?'

'Not a problem,' he said dismissively, and she backed up a step.

'It's just…I think…I would like to go home now,' she said.

'You do that,' he replied.

But, as he watched her trudge away through the snow, her shoulders hunched against the biting wind, he had to clench his hands together to stop himself from running after her. To stop himself from getting down on his knees and begging her to forgive him for the awful, unforgivable things he'd said.

It's better this way, he told himself when she turned the corner and he couldn't see her any more. Much better, he insisted, closing his eyes tightly against the snow which was beginning to fall again, and if he didn't feel that way at the moment he eventually would. Time, as he had discovered, could make you accept almost anything.

CHAPTER FIVE

Friday, 10:14 p.m.

'OKAY, I want to know what happened, and I want it in words of one syllable,' George Leslie declared, his normally amenable face tight and angry.

'I'd be more than happy to give you an answer if I knew what you were talking about.' Eli smiled as he rubbed down the windscreen of his ambulance, then tossed the chamois leather into the glove compartment.

'Ms O'Brian.'

Eli's smile disappeared in an instant. 'What about her?'

'Don't play the innocent with me,' his boss retorted. 'Three more shifts—that's all you had to keep a lid on your blasted temper for. Three shifts to be pleasant, and civil, but, no, you had to go and screw it up.'

'She's been complaining about me, has she?' Eli observed, his face an unreadable mask, and George Leslie grimaced reluctantly.

'She phoned me this afternoon to ask if she could be assigned to another ambulance because she felt she had upset you. Complete nonsense, of course,' George continued with a pointed glare at Eli. 'I know perfectly well if there was any upsetting going on you were at the root of it.'

'She thinks she's upset me?' Eli said incredulously, and his boss nodded.

'Frankly, I didn't believe a word of it either, but—'

'Who are you teaming her with?' Eli interrupted, and George Leslie threw his hands up with irritation.

'As I told Ms O'Brian, I can't team her with anyone else unless I do some massive alterations of people's shifts which will go down like a lead balloon with the other paramedics, and for three shifts it's just not worth the hassle, so she's stuck with you.'

'I see.'

'I don't think you do,' George Leslie observed. 'Eli, I want whatever has caused this friction sorted. She seems a pleasant enough person, not at all like a normal number cruncher—'

'She isn't.'

'—so can you *please* try not to rub her up the wrong way?'

'George—' Eli began, only to clamp his mouth shut.

The bay door had opened, and Brontë had stepped hesitantly onto the forecourt. George had seen her, too, and his eyebrows snapped down.

'I don't want to have this conversation with you again, Eli,' he declared in a hissed undertone. 'Understand?'

Eli didn't as his boss walked away. He didn't understand why Brontë hadn't simply told George he was impossible to work with. He fervently wished she had as he watched her square her shoulders as though preparing for his next onslaught. He had said such terrible things to her at the end of their last shift, things which still made him feel guilty, and he didn't want to feel guilty. He wanted his easy, uncomplicated, carefree life back again, not the woman who was so unsettling it.

'Cold night again,' Brontë declared hesitantly as she drew level with him. 'Minus twelve, according to the forecast, and there must be about six inches of snow on the roads now.'

'Yes,' he replied.

Heavens, but she looked so tired. He could see dark shadows under her eyes as though she hadn't slept well. He had slept badly, too, tossing and turning, unable to forget the look on her face before she'd turned and walked away from him.

'Hopefully we won't be as busy as we were last night,' she observed.

'Hopefully not.'

'Eli—'

'Brontë—'

They'd spoken in unison and, though he knew it was wrong, he took the coward's way out.

'You first,' he said, and saw her bite her lip, then take a deep breath.

'I saw you talking to George,' she said. 'I did try to get him to change the roster—to assign me to someone else— honestly I did, but he said it would be too difficult. I'm sorry.'

She looked it, too, he thought with mounting irritation. She looked as though she wanted to be anywhere but here, talking to anyone but him, and his guilt morphed into a much more convenient anger.

'Why the hell didn't you just tell George the truth?' he

demanded. 'That I was rude and obnoxious to you last night, and you can't stand working with me?'

She looked confused.

'But that wouldn't have been the truth,' she said. 'I overstepped the mark—intruded into your private life—and you had every right to chew me out.'

He stared at her in disbelief. Surely she couldn't truly believe that? She must be being sarcastic, but there was nothing in her grey eyes except genuine regret, and he swore in exasperation.

'Dammit, Brontë. Must you always be so understand-ing, so accommodating, so…so damn *nice*? After what I said to you this morning… You should be calling me a low-life scumbag, and slapping my face!'

To his surprise, a hint of a smile appeared on her lips.

'I didn't know you were into S and M, as well as serial dating.'

'S and M…?' His mouth opened and closed sound-lessly for a second, then he gazed heavenwards with frus-tration. 'Brontë, you are *impossible*.'

'Probably.' She nodded. 'You know, I'm really clocking up the labels since I started working with you. I always knew I was boring and ordinary—'

'You are not!'

'And now you've added middle-child syndrome, low self-esteem, doormat and impossible to my labels.'

'The doormat crack,' he said uncomfortably. 'That was totally out of order.'

'It would have been if I don't have a horrible suspicion you're right,' she replied ruefully. 'So, in a way, you did me a favour, and this morning I made a pledge. No more nice-girl Brontë. It's kick-ass Brontë from now on.'

'I'm glad to hear it,' he said, meaning it, 'but that doesn't absolve me from guilt. I was the jerk last night. Me, not you. *Me*.'

'But—'

'I was angry,' he interrupted. 'I know that's no excuse, but I was angry with Duncan for being so stupid. Angry with society for turning its back on youngsters like John, and…' He met her gaze. 'I was angry with you for somehow getting me to talk about myself, my past. I don't do that, you see. Not ever.'

'Maybe you should,' she said gently, her large grey eyes soft.

'The past is past,' he replied dismissively. 'It does no good to resurrect it, dwell on it, because nothing can be changed, altered.'

'No,' she agreed. 'But sometimes the past needs to be faced, to be come to terms with, so it can't hurt you any more, and you can move on.'

'Like you getting over your lousy track record with men, and conquering your low self-esteem?' he suggested with a glimmer of a smile, and she smiled back.

'Exactly,' she said, then she tilted her head speculatively to one side, and he saw a glint of laughter appear in her eyes.

'What?' he asked warily.

'I'm just wondering whether you still wanted me to slap you?'

'Depends on how big a punch you pack,' he replied.

She laughed, and he tried to laugh, too, but all he could wonder was, How had she done that? One minute he had been so angry with her, and then the next… And he wanted to stay angry with her, because being angry was safe. Being angry meant she couldn't affect him, and being angry with her was infinitely preferable to the undeniable relief he had felt when he'd seen her smile.

Responsible, protective, his mind whispered, and he tried to crush down the nagging little voice, tried to make it go away, but it wouldn't go away, and when he heard the bleep of their MDT he beat Brontë into the ambulance by a long country mile.

'What have we got?' she asked as she joined him.

'LOL, 22 Jeffrey Street, Violet Young,' he replied. 'Neighbour can see her lying in the hallway, apparently unconscious, but can't get in because the front door is locked.'

'Well, I don't think that's even remotely funny,' Brontë muttered as she drove out of the bay.

'Sorry?' Eli replied in confusion, then the penny dropped and he laughed, properly this time. 'LOL doesn't mean "laughing out loud," as it does in chatspeak, Brontë. It means "little old lady."'

'Then why didn't the display say that?' she protested, and he smiled.

'Yeah, and like A and E doesn't have a language all of its own?'

He was right, it did, Brontë thought, trying not to smile back too fulsomely, but it didn't work, and she groaned inwardly.

What had happened to the pledge she'd made so sincerely this morning? The pledge the new kick-ass Brontë had made to be pleasant and yet detached, friendly and yet slightly aloof. All that resolve had disappeared in an instant under the spell of a pair of deep blue eyes and a killer smile.

Distance, she told herself. What she desperately

needed was to maintain some distance, but how did you distance yourself from a man when your wayward heart kept letting you down? When you discovered the more you found out about him, the more you wanted to hold him, not because he was handsome, not because he could be so charming, but because of the pain and hurt you now knew he kept so carefully hidden from the world. She was a lost cause, and she knew it, but of one thing she was certain. He was never going to find out how she felt. Not ever.

'Lot of houses,' she said, deliberately changing the subject as she turned into Jeffrey Street, and saw the row of buildings stretching far ahead of her. 'Let's hope the numbers run concurrently.'

They did but, even if they hadn't, the neighbour who had called 999 was out on the snow-covered pavement and waved them down.

'I'm so glad you're here,' she declared the instant Eli and Brontë got out of the ambulance. 'Mrs Young... I thought she was just staying indoors today because of the snow, but her daughter phoned me half an hour ago. Said she couldn't get a reply when she dialled her mother's number, so I went round and...'

'She didn't answer when you rang the doorbell?' Eli said, and the neighbour shook her head.

'I looked through the letter box, and she's just lying there, in the hall, and...she's not moving.'

That the neighbour was deeply upset was clear, and Eli smiled at her encouragingly.

'Why don't you go back indoors now?' he suggested. 'We'll take it from here.'

The woman looked from Eli to Brontë, then back again.

'Are you sure? I don't want to leave my kids alone for too long, even though they're in bed, but if I can help…?'

'You've done more than enough already,' Eli insisted, and relief appeared instantly on the woman's face.

It was a relief Brontë would have felt herself if she'd been in the woman's shoes. There was just something about Eli that inspired confidence. Something which suggested if anyone could make things right he could. He was such an enigma, such a conundrum. Consummate professional, Good Samaritan and serial womaniser. Which of them was 'the real' Elijah Munroe? Maybe they all were. She wished she knew.

No, you don't, her head reminded her. *You're going to keep your distance, remember?* But, as she watched Eli crouch down to look through Mrs Young's letter box, she knew her pledge was a forlorn one.

'Can you see her?' she asked, and he nodded.

'She's at the very end of the hallway, and from the odd way she's lying, I'm thinking possible broken arm or leg, though it could be a CVA. The hall light's on which would suggest she collapsed—or fell—sometime this evening rather than earlier in the day.'

'Which is good news, isn't it?' Brontë replied, but Eli wasn't listening to her. He was running his hands over the door frame, and she stared at him incredulously. 'You're not thinking of trying to break down that door, are you?'

'Somewhat horrifyingly, you don't have to be superman to do it,' he murmured. 'That's just a normal front door key lock, and if you get the pressure dead centre, they break pretty easily.'

'They do?' Brontë gulped, thinking of the exact same lock she had on the front door of her own flat.

'A deadlock is much better any day of the week,' he observed, 'and if you add a bolt to the deadlock, you're even safer. To be completely secure you could put a bar across your front door, though that would mean if you collapsed behind it we wouldn't be able to get in to resuscitate you, but I guess you'd be a safe corpse.'

'Right,' Brontë replied, making a mental note to phone a joiner the minute she finished this shift.

That mental note became a certainty when she saw Eli stand back, take a deep breath, then hit the door squarely with his foot and the lock gave way instantly.

'I'm impressed,' she declared, then shook her head. 'No, I'm not. I'm horrified you can do that so easily.'

'It helps if you take a size eleven.' He grinned, then swore when, out of nowhere, an Alsatian dog suddenly appeared at the end of the hallway, its teeth bared in a deep growl. 'Oh, wonderful. Why didn't the neighbour tell us she had a dog?'

'What do we do now?' Brontë whispered, only to wonder why she was whispering because it wasn't as though the dog would understand what she was saying.

'We'll need to phone the cops. Get them to send out one of their dog handlers.'

'But Mrs Young…' Brontë protested. 'The longer we wait…'

'I know, but do you really want to take on Fang there?' Eli demanded, and Brontë stared at the dog.

She'd grown up with dogs. There had always been at least two at home when she, and Byron and Rossetti, had been growing up, and, though none of them had been quite as big as the Alsatian standing in the hallway, the dog's eyes looked more frightened than angry.

'Good dog,' she said softly, taking a step into the house. '*Nice* dog.'

'Are you *crazy*?' Eli hissed, catching hold of her arm, and the dog's growl became a snarl.

'I know what I'm doing,' Brontë said out of the corner of her mouth. Or, at least she hoped she did as she saw the dog crouch, and the hackles on its back rise. 'Let go of me, Eli.'

'But, Brontë…'

'*Lovely* doggy, we're not going to hurt you, or your mistress,' she continued, keeping her eyes fixed on the dog as she advanced another step. 'I know you're frightened, and we're strangers in your home, but we're here to help.'

The dog sat down. Its lip was still curled back over its teeth, and it hadn't taken its eyes off her for a second, but at least it no longer looked to be in 'I'm going to spring and rip out your throat' mode, and the snarling had lessened to a low, warning growl.

Faintly she could hear Eli muttering, and guessed he was telephoning the police to ask them to send out a dog handler. Or for someone to sweep up her remains, she thought wryly as she walked forward another step, watching the dog the whole time.

'*Nice* dog, *friendly* dog,' she crooned. 'Everything's going to be fine, just fine.'

She risked a quick glance at Mrs Young. She thought the elderly lady's chest was rising and falling slowly, and for a second she thought she saw her eyes flicker open, but she couldn't be sure. She could also see a dark blue plastic toy shaped like a bone, and an idea came into her head. It wasn't much of an idea, but it was better than nothing, and nothing was what she had at the moment.

Slowly, she bent down, and picked up the toy.

'Want to play fetch?' she asked.

The dog's tail thumped once against the floor, then stopped. It was clearly torn between a favourite game, and guarding its mistress, but the door to the sitting room was open, and if she could just lure the dog in that direction…

'Brontë…'

'Shut up, Eli,' she said, hoping her tone sounded more like an endearment than an order to the watching dog. 'Want to play fetch?' she repeated, waving the toy bone backwards and forwards slowly and saw the dog's head follow her movements.

It was now or never, she realised, and, taking a deep breath, she shouted, *'Fetch,'* then threw the toy as hard as she could into the sitting room. The Alsatian was off like a flash, following it, but Brontë was faster. The minute the dog was in the sitting room, she pulled the door shut, then leant against it, breathing hard, keeping her fingers tight round the handle.

'Was that the police you were phoning?' she asked as Eli brushed past her towards Mrs Young.

'They'll be here in three minutes,' he answered.

His voice was tight, cold, but she ignored that.

'I hope they make it faster,' she said instead, as a cacophony of growls, and scraping paws, began to fill the air, and the sitting room door juddered beneath her fingers. 'My parents used to have a dog who could turn any door handle with its teeth.'

Eli didn't reply. He was already setting up their heart monitor, and, though she wanted to go and help, the thought of one very angry dog suddenly bursting out of the sitting room was not an appealing one.

'How is Mrs Young?' she asked.

'Heart rate not too bad given her age, pulse a little weak, and my guess is her right leg is broken,' he answered.

And Eli clearly needed help, not her standing with her fingers clamped tightly round the sitting room door handle, so it was with a huge sigh of relief that Brontë greeted the burly, uniformed figure who suddenly appeared at the front door.

'I hear you have a dog problem?' The man grinned.

'You could say that,' Brontë admitted as the sound of barking and snarling intensified from inside the sitting room. 'Could you hold on to this door for me, and not open it until my colleague and I have taken the dog's owner to the Pentland?'

'No problem,' the dog handler replied, and, as soon as his hand had replaced hers on the door handle, Brontë hurried to Eli's side.

'What do you want me to do?'

'Get an Ambu bag on her, and then we go,' he declared. 'She's very, very cold, which means she's been lying here for quite some time.'

'She has a name, young man,' Mrs Young murmured faintly, and Eli smiled down at her.

'So, you're awake, are you, Mrs Young?'

'No, I just talk when I'm unconscious,' she muttered. 'Of course I'm awake. I just don't seem to be able to *stay* awake.'

Brontë's eyes met Eli's. Hypothermia. There was a very strong possibility that Mrs Young was suffering from hypothermia as well as a broken leg.

'I'm afraid we're going to have to take you to the

hospital, Mrs Young,' she said gently and saw a flicker of alarm cross the old lady's face.

'But what about Bubbles? You'll have to phone my daughter, tell her to come and take care of him because I can't leave Bubbles on his own.'

The Alsatian who was currently trying to tear down the sitting room door was called *Bubbles*? Brontë glanced across at Eli to share the joke but, oddly enough, he didn't seem to find it nearly as amusing as she did.

'My colleague is just going to put this Ambu bag on you, Mrs Young,' he declared, 'and then it's off to the hospital for you. And, yes, I'll get someone to phone your daughter about Bubbles,' he added as the old lady began to protest, 'so stop worrying about him and start thinking about yourself.'

A small smile appeared on Mrs Young's lips, and she transferred her gaze to Brontë.

'Is he always this bossy, dear?' she said, and Brontë nodded.

'I'm afraid so,' she relied. 'In fact, he's notorious for it so, if I were you, I'd just give in gracefully.'

Mrs Young did and, once the Ambu bag was in place, they lifted her into a carry-chair, and quickly out to the ambulance.

'I'd say she's going to be okay, wouldn't you?' Brontë said to Eli after they'd delivered Mrs Young into the waiting arms of the A and E staff. 'I know she's elderly, and if you break a leg at that stage in your life it can really knock you for six, but her heart rate was strong, and she seems a spunky, never-say-die lady.'

'I'd bet money on her being back home within the month,' Eli replied as they walked through the waiting room to the exit.

'Her daughter seemed nice, too,' Brontë continued. 'And I'm so pleased she's going to look after Bubbles. I know you didn't take to it,' she added, seeing Eli's jaw tighten, 'but it was only trying to protect its mistress.'

Eli said nothing.

'I know it looked a bit scary,' Brontë continued, 'but you have to look at it from its point of view. Its mistress wasn't moving, and we were strangers in its home.' Eli's silence was now positively deafening, and Brontë blew out a huff of impatience. 'Okay, you're clearly itching to chew my head off, so why don't you just do it, and get it over with?'

Eli waited until they were safely out on the street, and then he rounded on her.

'What you did—with that dog,' he said through clenched teeth, 'was either the bravest thing I've ever seen, or the stupidest.'

'And my guess is you're favouring the stupidest,' she said with a smile, but he didn't smile back.

'I said we should wait for the dog handler,' he declared, 'but did you listen to me, obey me? No, of course you didn't—'

'Eli, I know dogs—'

'You know every dog in the world?' he flared. 'Whoa, but that must make you pretty unique.'

'I didn't mean I know every dog,' she protested, 'but I weighed up the situation, took a calculated risk—'

'One which almost had me flat out on the floor beside Mrs Young with a heart attack!'

He wasn't joking. She could tell from his taut face, and angry eyes, he wasn't joking, and she bit her lip.

'Look, I'm sorry if you were worried, but I was

watching the dog's eyes, and I thought it seemed more frightened than anything else.'

'You thought—you *thought*!' He muttered something unprintable under his breath. 'Brontë, you had no way of knowing what that dog might do. It could have bitten you very badly, torn your hand off—'

'But it didn't,' she insisted. 'I'm not a fool—'

'Do you really want me to comment on that?'

'—and if it had looked completely out of control I would have waited for the dog handler. I *would*,' she insisted as he shook his head at her, 'but with dogs it's generally their eyes you go by. Their eyes, and their body language.'

'And that's the biggest load of rubbish I've ever heard,' he retorted. '*All* dogs are unpredictable. *All* dogs can turn into killing machines, and the bigger they are, the more damage they can inflict. I remember once, when I was living on the streets…' He closed his eyes, then opened them again. 'Let's just say I don't even want to think about what happened to the poor bloke, far less talk about it.'

She stared silently at him for a second, and when she spoke her voice was low, contrite. 'I'm sorry…I didn't realise…. Were you really that worried about me?'

It took him all his self-control not to reach out, grab her by the shoulders and shake her. Worried? His heart had practically stopped when she'd walked towards that dog, looking so small, so vulnerable, but he didn't say that.

'If you put your hand on my chest you'll feel my heart still going like a train,' he said instead.

A tinge of colour appeared on her cheeks, and she laughed a little shakily.

'I'll take your word for it,' she said, then cleared her

throat. 'I really am sorry. I promise I won't ever do something like that again.'

'Is that a solemn "cross your heart and hope to die" promise?' he demanded, and when she hesitated, as though having to consider his question, his eyebrows snapped together. *'Brontë!'*

'Just kidding,' she said with a smile. 'It's a promise.'

He fervently hoped it was as they went back to their ambulance. He didn't ever want to go through another ten minutes like that ever again.

Protective, responsible, the irritating little voice in his head whispered again, and he tried to shut it up, to tell the annoying voice he would have felt the same concern for anyone, but the little voice simply laughed and, as it did, the answer suddenly came to him. An answer that was so blindingly obvious in its simplicity he wondered why he hadn't thought of it before.

Why in the world was he angsting like this? he wondered as Brontë drove away from the hospital. He was attracted to her, and he was pretty sure she was attracted to him, so all he needed to do was ask her out. His no-dating pledge only had three weeks left to run anyway, so what did it matter if he cut it short? He would simply ask her out, they'd go out on a few dates, become lovers and then, once he'd got her out of his system, he'd move on as he always did, with the problem solved, the angsting over.

'What's funny?'

'Funny?' he repeated, glancing across at Brontë in confusion.

'You're smiling,' she observed, 'so I just thought… If you've got a good joke I could sure do with hearing it.'

The joke was on him, he thought, because the solution had been there all the time, staring him right in the face, and yet for some unaccountable reason he hadn't been able to see it. He could see it now. He was back on familiar territory now, and it felt good.

'Brontë, I was wondering,' he began, only to groan when their MDT bleeped into life.

'"Code amber. RTC. Male aged thirty-two,"' Brontë read. '"Junction of College Street and Nicolson Street. Two cars involved. One casualty with whiplash. Other driver uninjured. Police in attendance."' She frowned. 'Sounds like a possible shunt to me, if only one person is hurt.'

'My guess is it's a payment point,' Eli replied, wishing the casualty to the farthest side of the moon as Brontë turned onto the North Bridge.

'A what?' she asked.

'In RTCs almost half of those supposedly suffering from whiplash are actually people who are attempting to get the insurance money out of the other driver,' Eli explained. 'And the "payment point" is the part of the neck they keep pointing to, and declaring they're in agony.'

'We didn't call them "payment points" in A and E at the Waverley,' Brontë declared. 'We called them PITAs.'

'And I don't need my nursing diploma to guess what that acronym stands for.' Eli laughed. 'And it just about sums these jokers up. They waste our time, the police's time, and put the other driver through hell, and all for money.'

'Isn't that why RTAs are now called RTCs?' Brontë observed as she headed for Nicolson Street. 'Because some smart lawyers figured out if the police described a car crash as an accident, their clients would be off the hook?'

'Yup.' Eli nodded. 'So now we have road traffic collisions, but we still get the payment-point brigade.'

The policeman who was waiting beside the two cars when they arrived clearly thought Eli's diagnosis was the correct one.

'He's kicking up a real racket—swears he's in total agony,' he declared, 'but the idiot keeps forgetting which part of his neck is supposed to be hurt. It's the poor woman in the other car I feel sorry for. Her car got the worst of it, and she can't stop shaking.'

She couldn't, and it took Brontë a good fifteen minutes to calm the woman down, and persuade her there was nothing she could do here, and she really should phone for a taxi and go home.

'How's our whiplash patient?' she asked when she was eventually able to join Eli by the other car.

Eli rolled his eyes heavenwards. 'What do you think?'

'The Pentland?' she said, and he nodded.

'I know it goes against the grain to transport someone we believe is faking it to hospital,' he replied, 'but there's always the possibility—no matter how remote—that an X-ray will reveal an injury I've missed.'

Eli was right, but Brontë couldn't help but think, as she drove towards the hospital, that it was hard to feel sympathetic towards a 'casualty' who, despite constantly protesting he was in the most appalling pain, still managed to make a dozen phone calls on his mobile phone.

That journey—and their patient—pretty well set the tone for the next few hours. The sensible Edinburgh citizens might have decided after last night's road chaos to stay home and keep safe, but there were still enough of the young, and the just plain cavalier, out on the streets, to keep Eli and Brontë busy until well after four o'clock.

'And it's snowing again,' Brontë said irritably as she drove down the Canongate, and had to switch on her windscreen wipers to clean her screen. 'Which no doubt means even more idiots will decide it might be a "fun" idea to take to the roads, and see how far they get before they skid and hit something.'

'Or someone.'

She knew who he was thinking of, and she glanced across at him quickly.

'I've been looking for him, Eli,' she said. 'When I've been driving along… Every time I pass a group of kids, or some homeless people, I've been looking for John.'

'Me, too,' Eli replied. 'It's been so cold these past couple of nights, Brontë, so very, very cold. I keep hoping he's got a room in one of the shelters, but there's so little accommodation available.'

'Do you think Peg will be all right?' she asked tentatively, and saw him force a smile.

'Peg's a pretty tough cookie. If anyone can survive, she can, but there are so many homeless people out there. When I see elderly people like Mrs Young, I think of the long lives they've had, the happy memories they must be able to look back on, but young addicts, young alcoholics…' Eli shook his head. 'All I can think is, How did you get lost, how did you lose your way? Other kids your age will have a life, a family, friends, but you… Your life is going to be so short. So very, very short.'

'My brother, Byron, has this theory,' she observed. 'He says people make their own choices in life.'

'That's true to a certain extent,' Eli replied, 'but what power did we—as a society—give these young people to enable them to make any kind of choice?'

'Eli—'

'Sorry—sorry,' he interrupted with a rueful smile. 'It's one of my pet hobby horses, and I shouldn't inflict it on you.'

'You're not inflict—'

'Coffee. I need a coffee,' he insisted, 'so let's head for Tony's.'

He saw her hesitate, then take a deep breath.

'Actually, I've been thinking about what you said before—about me not having met or spoken to any of the other paramedics at the station,' she said in a rush. 'You made a very good point, so I think we should take our break at the station tonight.'

Damn, but that was the last thing he needed, to be surrounded by his colleagues, when what he wanted was some privacy so he could ask her out.

'Good idea, in principle,' he observed lightly, 'but Friday nights… They're always busy, everyone flat out, so there's little likelihood there will be anybody for you to talk to.'

'Oh.'

She didn't look happy, but he wasn't about to waver, and so he smiled what he hoped was his best encouraging smile.

'Tony's?' he said, and thought he heard her sigh with resignation as she nodded, but he couldn't be sure.

Brontë was sure. Brontë didn't want to go anywhere near Tony's tonight. She wanted to be safe amongst a crowd. She wanted other people to distract her, not to be sitting alone in an ambulance with Eli, but she would rather have stuck a fork in her eye than admit that to him.

Be pleasant, and yet detached, she reminded herself when she pulled up outside Tony's. That's all you have to be. Pleasant, detached, and slightly aloof. How hard could that be?

Damned hard, she thought as he got out of the ambulance, then turned to look at her with the smile which always made all rational conversation disappear instantly from her brain.

'Cappuccino and doughnut?' he said.

She thought about it. 'A cappuccino, for sure, but tonight I want a hamburger. A big, juicy hamburger, with lots of onions.'

His eyebrows rose, but he didn't say anything until he returned to the ambulance with their orders.

'Never thought I'd see you eat one of those,' he observed, as she bit into the hamburger, then closed her eyes, clearly relishing the taste.

'Yeah, well, you're corrupting me.'

'Am I?'

It could have been a completely innocuous observation. It could have been the kind of joking thing a friend would have said, but it wasn't, and she knew it wasn't. His voice was suddenly low, velvety, within the silence of the ambulance, and the atmosphere had changed—she could feel it, sense it, but this time she knew what he was doing; this time she was prepared, and she opened her eyes, and met his gaze full on.

'Only for hamburgers,' she said.

'Really?'

His voice was teasing, liquid, and she felt her heart pick up speed.

'Really,' she replied firmly, wishing he would just let it go, would stop, but he didn't.

Instead, he looked at her over the rim of his coffee, his eyes dark and oh-so blue. 'Care to make a wager on that?'

She took another mouthful of hamburger, and swallowed it with difficulty, all too aware her heart rate had now gone into overdrive.

'Nope,' she replied. 'Not interested, not a betting woman.'

'Then maybe I can offer you something you *will* be interested in,' he said softly.

This wasn't merely flirting, she realised as her eyes met his, and what she saw there made her stomach lurch and her pulses race. This was something more, and, though part of her wanted to tell him to stop, to say nothing else, the other part—the weak, traitorous part—wanted to hear what he was going to say, and it was that part which won.

'I'm listening,' she said.

He put down his coffee.

'Brontë, I know you think I'm smug, and arrogant—'

'And a bit of a prat at times,' she interrupted. 'Don't forget the "bit of a prat."'

'It's engraved on my heart,' he said lightly, though she could see she had rattled him. 'But the thing is… You're a very special woman, Brontë.'

He was going to ask her out. He was going to ask her out, and, though she knew exactly what she should say in reply, knowing it didn't mean she was necessarily going to do it.

'Go on,' she said, taking a slow sip of her coffee more to buy herself some time than from any real thirst.

'Without being vain,' he continued, 'I think you like

me, too, so I was wondering whether you'd like to come out to dinner with me before our shift tomorrow?'

She stared down at her coffee, then up at him.

'To dinner?' she repeated slowly. 'Now, are we just talking dinner here, or are we talking something more?'

He smiled his killer smile.

'Oh, come on, Brontë, we're both adults, and I think you and I could really have some fun together.'

Some fun together. Not a proper relationship, not the possibility of that relationship ever leading to something more permanent, but just some 'fun', and her heart constricted with pain and disappointment as she stared at his handsome face. Pain and disappointment which were very quickly overtaken by anger. A blazing furious anger with herself for yet again being so naive to hope he might have offered more, and an equally furious anger with him for believing she had so little self-worth she would even consider settling for what he usually offered the women in his life.

Carefully, she put her coffee down on the dashboard in case she was tempted to do something rash with it.

'And how long would this "fun" last?' she asked, keeping her voice neutral with difficulty.

He blinked. 'Sorry?'

'I'm just wondering, you see,' she observed, 'whether I'd get the usual two months with you, or whether I might get real lucky and be allowed a little bit longer.'

His dark eyebrows snapped together.

'I don't think that comment was necessary,' he replied icily, and she forced herself to shrug.

'I would have said I was just being realistic,' she replied, 'because, you see, what you call "fun," results in a hell of a lot of heartbreak for a lot of women, so it's a road I'm rather reluctant to travel down.'

'I have never in my whole life broken any woman's heart!' he exclaimed. 'I've always been upfront, never promised I'd stick around for ever.'

Why could he not see it? she wondered. Why did he keep on denying what was so obvious to her?

'Eli, are you blind, or stupid, or both?' she demanded. 'Can't you see—don't you understand—that it doesn't matter how upfront you think you're being? I doubt if there's a woman alive who, when you've asked her out, hasn't thought, This is for keeps, this is going to last. No matter what you say, no matter how hard you try to persuade them you're only dating them for "fun," they think, Me. He's going to settle down with me because I can change him.'

'I don't believe that,' he retorted, and she shook her head at him.

'That's because, for all your talk, you know *nothing* about women. You just take and take, and give nothing of yourself. Dating—sex—it's all a no-risk game to you, isn't it? Don't let anyone close, don't let anyone into your mind, and heart.'

'And you're such an expert on dating, are you?' he snapped, and hot, furious colour stained her cheeks.

'At least I *tried*!' she exclaimed. 'At least when I went into a relationship, I went into it wholeheartedly not thinking I'll just have some "fun," then dump the guy. Okay, so maybe my relationships didn't work out, and I ended up getting my face pushed in the mud, and my heart trampled in the dirt—'

'A bit difficult to have those two things done to you at

once,' he interrupted sarcastically, and she moved beyond anger into incensed.

'Must you make a joke out of *everything*?'

'Look, listen—'

'No, *you* listen,' she broke in, her grey eyes blazing. 'Relationships, love—everything's one big game to you, and do you want to know why? It's because—deep down—you're a coward. You play at everything, never letting anyone get close to the real you, hiding behind this…this supercool image when, in reality, you're just a coward. I know your mother hurt you very badly—'

'Leave my mother out of this.'

His voice was low, dangerous, but she'd started and she couldn't stop.

'And maybe her leaving you resulted in you having trust issues—'

'You're saying I've set out to make every woman pay for what my mother did?' he exclaimed in disbelief, and she exhaled with exasperation.

'Of course I'm not saying that,' she replied. 'What I'm saying is I think you're scared to get too close to anyone in case you get hurt again.'

He shook his head impatiently.

'That is the biggest load of psychobabble I've ever heard.'

'It makes just as much sense as you telling me I have lousy taste in men because I have middle-child syndrome,' she countered, and he crushed the paper bag which contained his uneaten hamburger between his fingers.

'I've had enough of this conversation.'

'You were the one who started it,' she pointed out, and he rounded on her.

'Then I'm the one who's finishing it!'

'Fine.' She nodded. 'Throw a hissy fit, sit there in a snit, because you don't like the truth when you hear it, but you can do it on your own.'

'Where the hell are you going?' he demanded as she opened the driver's door, and got out.

'Back to the station where the air is less toxic.'

'Don't be ridiculous,' he declared. 'You can't walk back through The Meadows at half past four in the morning. Heaven knows what weirdos you're likely to meet at this hour.'

'I'll take my chances.'

'You're being stupid.'

She knew she was as she slammed the door, and walked away. Crossing The Meadows on her own at half past four in the morning was not a smart idea. Crossing The Meadows when the snow was falling in ever-increasing, large, whirling flakes was even crazier. Even if no one approached her she would still have all those streets to walk unless she could find a taxi, but she had to get away from him. She had to get away because she knew if she didn't she was going to burst into tears, and no way was she going to give him the satisfaction of knowing she cared so much, and so stupidly longed to be the one woman who might change him.

'Brontë, wait a minute!'

She heard the sound of his door closing, then a muttered oath which meant he'd tripped over something. Serve him right, she decided grimly, not slowing her stride by an inch. If he thought shouting at her some more would get him anywhere, he was dumber than a rock.

'Brontë.'

He had caught up with her, but, when he clasped her

shoulder and tried to turn her to face him, she shrugged him off.

'Go away, Eli. Just…just go away!'

'But I want to talk to you,' he insisted, coming round in front of her, barring her way.

'Then you're going to be sadly disappointed,' she retorted, trying her hardest to sound indifferent, but unfortunately a wayward tear slid down her cheek.

'Oh, jeez, *don't*,' he said, staring at her in complete horror. 'Brontë, please, don't cry.'

'I'm not,' she replied, her voice betraying her. 'I just… I've simply got something in my eye.'

And desperately she wiped her nose with the back of her hand, and it was that small action which cut him to the bone. That completely uncalculated, almost childlike, defiant little action which stirred and touched something deep inside him, something he couldn't pinpoint or define.

'You're getting wet,' he said, reaching out and gently brushing the snowflakes from her hair and eyelashes. 'Please come back to the ambulance before you catch your death of cold.'

'Old wives' tale,' she replied, her voice thick. 'Germs cause colds, not getting wet.'

'Do you always have to have the last word?' he demanded, putting his hands on her shoulders in case she was thinking of walking away.

It was all he meant to do, just to keep her there, to stop her from doing anything rash, but, as he gazed down into her tear-filled eyes, she suddenly sniffed, and wiped her nose again, and those two actions were his undoing. Before he could think, before he could even rationalise what he was about to do, he bent his head and kissed her.

He meant it only to be a light kiss, a gentle kiss, but, as her lips opened under his, and he tasted her sweetness, her softness, and heard her give a small, shuddering sigh, that light kiss wasn't enough. Before he could stop himself, he had wrapped his arms around her, bringing her closer, closer, intensifying the kiss, deepening it, until all he was aware of was the fire and heat within him, and the need never to let her go.

And Brontë felt it, too, the same fire, the same heat, the same need, and she wound her arms round his neck, tasting him, his warmth, wanting so much to touch him, to feel his skin, but their bulky high-visibility jackets prevented that touch.

I want him, she thought, as she threaded her fingers through his hair to bring him closer, returning his kisses with a depth to match his own. I have always wanted him right from the first moment I saw him in Wendy's hallway when he walked right past me, but I can't let this continue because he'll leave me. He'll leave me just as he's left every other woman he's kissed, and it was that certainty which gave her the strength to jerk herself out of his arms, and back away from him.

'Don't, Eli, *don't*,' she said, her voice breaking on a sob. 'Don't flirt with me, play with me, lead me to believe you really care, because I can't stand it.'

'Brontë—'

'I'm not like you,' she said blindly. 'I can't live the way you do—being with one person one month, then another the next—and if I let myself get too close to you, you'll break my heart, and I don't think I'll ever be able to put the pieces back together again.'

'I would never break your heart,' he protested, his

breathing harsh and erratic in the silence, and he reached for her again, only to see her back away still further.

'You might not mean to, you might not intend to, but you *will*.'

'Brontë—'

'Answer me one question,' she interrupted. 'How long would I get with you before you move on to someone else?'

He thrust his hands through his wet hair, his face impatient.

'How can I answer that?' he exclaimed. 'We'd just take it one day at a time, like every other couple do.'

'But we wouldn't be like every other couple, would we?' she cried. 'Because you've already told me you never want to settle down with just one woman, and I…' She took a long, juddering breath. 'I'm thirty-five years old, Eli, and I don't want what you call "fun." I want someone who will be there for me, someone who will care for me, someone…' Her voice broke again. 'Someone who will *love* me, and that's not you, is it?'

She saw indecision, and uncertainty, war with one another on his face, and then he shook his head.

'I'm sorry,' he murmured.

'So am I,' she said but, as she turned to go, he put his hand out to stop her.

'I won't let you walk back through The Meadows alone. If…' He bit his lip. 'If you can't bear to sit beside me in the ambulance I'll walk back to the station instead.'

'You could get mugged just as easily as me,' she pointed out, and he forced a smile.

'I'm bigger than you, tougher.'

'Are you?' she said, then shook her head. 'We'll go

back together, but I want you to promise me something. I want you to promise there'll be no more flirting, or flattery, and definitely no more kisses, because I can't take any more of this. I really can't.'

He didn't say anything. He simply nodded and, as she walked back to the ambulance, not looking at him, not saying anything, all she could think was it didn't matter if he kept his promise because it was too late. She was already in love with him, and her heart was already breaking.

CHAPTER SIX

Sunday, 12:15 a.m.

SHE'D always hated Saturday nights at the Waverley, Brontë remembered as she drove over the North Bridge. Saturday nights in A and E meant drunks, and RTCs, chaos and mayhem. They meant exactly the same thing for the ambulance service. From the minute they'd clocked on she and Eli had been working flat out and for that, at least, Brontë was grateful. Working flat out meant they hardly had time to talk to each other. Working flat out meant no awkward silences, or uncomfortable pauses.

Oh, who was she kidding? she thought, as she risked a quick glance at Eli. She'd expected tonight to be difficult, but what she hadn't expected was for Eli to be so angry. Not an obvious anger, not a blatant anger, but a simmering, bubbling, undercurrent of anger she could feel, almost taste, and normally she would have moved into what her brother, Byron, called her 'make everyone happy' mode. She would have talked and talked until she was sick to death of the sound of her own voice, but tonight she didn't.

Tonight she was tired, and weary. Tired from tossing

and turning sleeplessly, and weary from alternatively telling herself she'd made the right decision, and then berating herself for being an idiot not to have simply grabbed those two months from Eli and enjoyed them while she could.

'Left, you should have taken a left there for Bread Street,' Eli declared as she turned right at the junction.

'Are you sure?' she replied. 'I thought it would be faster if I cut along the Grassmarket?'

'It's not.'

'Right,' she muttered, and began to reverse back up the street.

'What on earth are you doing?' Eli exclaimed.

'Going back,' she protested. 'You said, turn left—'

'That doesn't mean I expected you to reverse back up a one-way street!'

Damn, but she hadn't even seen the one-way warning sign, and swiftly she drove back down the road, crunching the gears so badly even she winced.

'Sorry,' she mumbled.

'You do realise this detour means not only is our patient still waiting, we also can't possibly hit our target arrival time?'

'I *said* I was sorry,' she retorted. 'I made a mistake, okay, and I'm *sorry*.'

Just tonight and tomorrow night, she told herself as she drove on and heard Eli mutter something which didn't sound like, 'Apology accepted.' I've only got to get through tonight, and tomorrow night, and then I'll never have to see him again, but how was she going to get through those two shifts when she doubted if she could stand even another hour in his company?

'Watch the corners,' Eli declared as she took one too fast. 'There's at least a foot of snow out there now, and it's fallen on ice.'

'Look, would you prefer to drive instead of me?' she snapped.

'Perhaps I should, if you're going to be silly,' he replied tersely, and she gripped the steering wheel until her knuckles showed white to stop herself from decking him.

Silly. He thought she was silly. Well, maybe she was, to have fallen in love with a man who quite patently didn't give a damn about her unless it was to add another notch to his bedpost. If anyone had the right to be angry, it was her. His heart wasn't broken. He would go on and find someone else fast enough, whereas she… She swallowed painfully as she cut across town, then came down Bread Street. Don't think, she told herself, don't remember the touch of his lips, his hands, because that's a fool's game.

'You've just gone straight past the house,' Eli declared. 'It's number 22, Bread Street.'

She knew it was. The caller had said, 'Harry Wallace, twenty-nine years old, in an apparently catatonic state, his mother with him, number 22, Bread Street,' and yet she'd gone right past the house without even noticing.

Pull yourself together, her mind whispered as she turned the ambulance too fast and swore as she felt the wheels spin slightly on the compacted snow. *This patient needs you, so pull yourself together.*

And Eli stared grimly out of the window, and was tempted to ask Brontë what her problem was, except he already knew the answer. According to her, he was the problem, and that accusation only made him all the angrier.

If she had simply turned down his dinner invitation this morning, he could have lived with it. Okay, he would have been irritated, annoyed, because women didn't normally turn down the chance to become involved with him, but she hadn't simply turned him down. She'd said she wouldn't go out with him because he had broken too many hearts which was nonsense. Okay, so Zoe had created the mother and father of all scenes when he'd left her, but that was because he'd made a mistake, not because he'd left a trail of heartbroken women in his wake.

'Will I take the defibrillator, just in case?' Brontë asked as she pulled the ambulance to a halt, and opened her door.

'You should know by now we always take everything,' he replied acidly.

She opened her mouth, then clamped her lips shut, and he had to bite down hard on the angry words that sprang to his lips, too, as she retrieved the defibrillator, then stomped up the path to the house. The sooner she was out of his life, the better. The sooner she left the station, the quicker he would forget her, and her troubling accusations.

And her kiss? his heart whispered. *Will you forget that, too?*

It was just a kiss, he told himself. No different from any other woman's kiss, but no matter how often he had told himself that since this morning he knew it wasn't true. It had been a kiss like no other kiss. A kiss that had made him feel as though he had somehow—oddly—finally come home, and he didn't want to feel like that, or even think it.

'I'm so glad you're here,' Mrs Wallace said when she answered Brontë's knock. 'My son…Harry…he suffers from bipolar depression. I don't know whether he's been deliberately not taking his medication, forgotten to take it, or if this is something new, but I came round when I couldn't get an answer to any of my phone calls, and…' She spread her arms helplessly. 'He's just sitting there.'

Harry Wallace was, and though both Eli and Brontë attempted to get some response from him, Harry either wouldn't, or couldn't, communicate.

'Is this the only medication your son is taking, Mrs Wallace?' Eli asked, lifting a bottle of pills from the mantelpiece, then putting it back down again.

'I'm afraid I don't know,' Harry's mother replied. 'He was diagnosed with bipolar almost ten years ago, and he's been on so many different pills since then. His bathroom cabinet's full of bottles, some with just a few pills in them, some completely full.'

'Show me,' Eli said and, as he followed Mrs Wallace out of the room, Brontë chewed her lip.

Discovering what pills Harry Wallace had in his bathroom wouldn't be hugely helpful. Knowing what he was currently taking, however, would, and, quickly, she crossed to the mantelpiece, and lifted the bottle of pills. As she'd hoped, they had a GP's name on them and she pulled her mobile phone out of her pocket.

That the GP was not happy about being called at one o'clock in the morning was plain, but he eventually gave her a list of Harry Wallace's current medications, and she had just finished writing the names down on a scrap of paper when Eli and Mrs Wallace returned to the sitting room.

Who are you talking to? Eli mouthed at her, and she turned the piece of paper over, scribbled the word GP on it, and held it up to him. To her complete bewilderment he began making slicing motions across his throat, clearly wanting her to end the call, but she had no intention of being so rude, not when she'd just asked the GP whether he could come to Bread Street.

'Brontë, *end the call.*'

She could hear the barely suppressed anger in Eli's voice, and she gritted her teeth. It was one thing to be angry with her over something personal, but when he brought that personal antagonism into their professional lives…

'Thanks for your help, Dr Simpson,' she said into her mobile phone, flipped it shut and turned to face Eli. 'Harry's GP is coming, and I have a list of the medications he should be taking.'

Eli took the piece of paper she was holding out to him, then smiled reassuringly at Mrs Wallace.

'As we're not sure whether Harry has simply missed a dose, perhaps inadvertently taken more than he should, or the medication is no longer controlling his bipolar, I think it would be best if we take him to hospital, and let the experts examine him.'

'But, Eli, Dr Simpson is on his way here,' Brontë declared pointedly, but she might just as well have been talking to the wall because he was already helping Harry Wallace to his feet.

'If you'd like to come with us, Mrs Wallace,' Eli said, 'you're more than welcome.'

But I'm clearly not, Brontë thought, as Mrs Wallace reached for her coat and Eli ushered Harry out into the hall without even a backward glance at her.

What in the world was he doing? Okay, so he was clearly still angry with her about what had happened in

The Meadows last night, but Dr Simpson was going to arrive and find Harry Wallace's house in darkness. Well, it wasn't good enough, she decided, and she was going to tell Eli that in no uncertain terms after Harry had been safely admitted to the Pentland.

It took longer than she'd thought. Harry Wallace seemed to be quite well known to the staff of A and E, and to Men's Medical, and it was more than forty minutes before they could finally get away, but the waiting didn't decrease Brontë's anger. If anything, it fuelled it because Eli seemed to be simmering, too, and when she drove away from the hospital, she didn't drive far. Just round the corner, then she pulled the ambulance to a halt.

'Okay, I want an explanation, and it had better be a good one!' she exclaimed. 'It's one thing to be angry with me personally, but when it affects a patient's treatment—'

'Brontë—'

'You're obviously in a major strop because I got a list of the medications Harry Wallace is currently taking,' she interrupted, not even bothering to hide her fury. 'All right, so I thought of phoning his GP, and you didn't, but what the heck does that matter? I know you're the accredited paramedic, and I'm not, but surely a good idea is still a good idea?'

'Brontë—'

'And I persuaded Dr Simpson to come round to the house,' she continued, on a roll now. 'Dr Simpson, who, I might add, is going to have a completely wasted journey because you simply bundled Harry into the ambulance and took him to hospital!'

'How do you know Dr Simpson is coming?' Eli said with a calmness which was infuriating.

'Because he *told* me he would!' she retorted. 'Did you want to talk to him yourself—is that what this is all about? You're piqued because the number cruncher took the phone call?'

'I'll ignore that,' he replied, his tone considerably harder than hers, 'but I will repeat, what proof do you have Dr Simpson is on his way?'

She stared at him blankly. 'What are you talking about? I phoned him—'

'Brontë, we *never* call a GP from a landline, or a mobile. If we need to speak to a GP, or a social worker, or a CPN, we ask EMDC to call them for us because then all the telephone conversations are recorded, which means if someone says they are going to attend they'd better.'

'But—'

'There are some wonderful GPs out there, some terrific social workers,' Eli continued, 'but there's a small minority who are more than happy to shunt all their responsibility onto the ambulance services rather than getting off their butts and doing what they're paid for. With no way of proving your phone call, we could be sitting in that house until doomsday waiting for your Dr Simpson, and he could deny he'd ever made that promise.'

Eli was right, Brontë realised with dismay as she stared at him, but knowing it didn't make her feel any better.

'Why didn't you tell me this before?' she demanded. 'If you'd just told me, kept me in the loop—'

'How was I to know you were going to do something stupid?'

Stupid. He thought she was stupid. He thought she was stupid, and silly, and a doormat, and the hurt she had felt ever since he'd thrown that last epithet at her, combined with the pain she still felt from realising all he had wanted from her was 'fun', brought tears to her throat. Tears she was never going to let him see.

'Okay. Fine,' she said with difficulty. 'You know everything, and I'm the village idiot, so in future I'll simply drive your ambulance, and the only words I'll speak will be, "Where to?"'

'And now you really *are* being stupid,' he threw back at her.

She didn't say a word. She simply started the engine, and drove off down the road, but she didn't get far before their MDT began flashing a message.

'Suspected purple in the Potterrow. Police officer in attendance. Young boy who doesn't appear to be breathing.'

Brontë's eyes shot to Eli's. A 'purple' was ambulance code-speak for someone who was dead, but that wasn't the word on the screen which had caused her to suck in her breath sharply. It was the word *boy*.

Please, don't let it be him, she prayed, as she shot off down the road, heedless of the icy, snowy conditions. Please let it be somebody else, anyone else. She knew Eli was thinking the same, could see it in the tense way he was sitting next to her. He had tried so hard to help John Smith, and if the young boy was him…

'I'm afraid there's nothing you can do here, folks,' the police officer said when she and Eli got out of the ambulance. 'Judging by how cold he is I'd say he's been dead for a couple of hours. No sign of foul play that I can see so my guess is hyperthermia, though on these streets it could well be drug-related even though he's just a kid.'

A kid who was wearing a pair of threadbare trainers, thin denim trousers, and a tattered wine-coloured jacket,

Brontë realised as she walked slowly towards the small figure lying huddled in the shop doorway.

Why did it have to be him? she wondered as she knelt down beside John, and took his cold, stiff hand in hers, automatically feeling for a pulse, although she knew there wouldn't be one. He had been so frightened of death, so afraid someone would kill him, and it hadn't been a person who had killed him. It had been the elements, and a society that had walked past him, ignoring his plight.

'Any pulse?' Eli asked, his voice gruff, and she shook her head.

'No, nothing,' she said, through a too-tight throat. 'Eli…'

He wasn't listening to her. He was already reaching for John and, when he'd lifted him up into his arms, he walked determinedly towards the ambulance, leaving her where she was, kneeling in the snow.

'If this weather doesn't change soon, I'm afraid we're likely to see more cases like this,' the policeman said sadly. 'And when it's a kid… It always hits hardest.'

'It hits hard no matter who it is,' Brontë replied, thinking of Peg, and the others at Greyfriars. 'And he wasn't just a kid,' she added. 'He had a name, and his name was John. John Smith.'

Wearily, she went to the ambulance but, when she opened the back door, what she saw there stopped her in her tracks. Eli was performing CPR on John. Desperately, and frantically, he was performing CPR.

'Eli…' She bit her lip. 'It's no use. He's been dead for at least two hours.'

'People can survive for longer than that if they're in a state of suspended animation,' he muttered. 'There are well-documented cases of people being pulled out of freezing rivers, and they've been brought back.'

But John hasn't been in a river, she wanted to point out, but she didn't. Instead, she climbed into the back of the ambulance, closed the door, and began affixing an Ambu bag.

'Epinephrine, and the defibrillator, Brontë,' Eli declared.

Obediently, she did as he asked, though all her professional knowledge told her neither things would help.

'Set the power to two hundred,' he ordered.

She did, and then she stepped back from the trolley and closed her eyes. She didn't want to watch this, couldn't bear to watch this. No power on earth could bring John back, and to see Eli's stricken face, to watch him frantically do everything he knew, try everything he could, required more courage than she possessed.

Three hundred, three hundred and sixty joules... Numbly she upped the power every time Eli asked her to but, eventually, she knew she had to say something and when, after twenty minutes, Eli reached for the paddles again, she put her hand on his arm to stop him.

'He's gone, Eli,' she whispered, her voice breaking. 'We have to accept he's gone, and nothing we do is going to bring him back.'

'I can't let him die, Brontë,' he replied, anguish thickening his voice. 'Maybe if I just keep on trying...if we keep on shocking him...'

'He's *dead*, Eli,' she said, her voice suspended. 'We're too late. You have to accept we're too late.'

For a second, she thought he was going to argue with her, continue with his attempts, then she saw his face twist and, when he sat down with his head in his hands, she gently kissed John's cold forehead.

'Be at peace now,' she murmured, fighting to contain her tears. 'Be at peace, and if there is a heaven be happy there.'

Impotently, she brushed the remaining flakes of snow from his hair. He looked so young, even younger than the fourteen years she'd guessed him to be, and, though she didn't want to do it, she carefully pulled a sheet up over his face, then turned slowly to Eli.

'I always say we can't win them all,' Eli said, his voice muffled. 'That sometimes the only victory we get in this job is if we can manage to keep somebody alive long enough to get them to hospital, and their families can arrive and say goodbye to them, but who was there to say goodbye to John, Brontë? *Who?*'

Instantly, she knelt down in front of him and tentatively covered his hands with her own.

'We were,' she replied. 'We were here, and though we didn't get here in time, I'm sure he knows you tried. You tried so very hard.'

'He ought to have his whole life ahead of him,' Eli exclaimed, raising his eyes to hers, eyes that were full of misery and pain. 'He ought to have a future, a home, a job, and now… Why, Brontë, *why?*'

'I don't know,' she declared. 'I don't know why some people open the wrong door, take the wrong corner.' She glanced over her shoulder at the small, sheet-wrapped figure. 'We'll have to take him to A and E, won't we, so his death can be formally registered?'

Eli nodded. 'And then his details will go to the procurator fiscal who will arrange for an autopsy.'

'Does there have to be one?' she protested. 'He's already been through so much.'

'I'm afraid it's the law. If someone dies unexpectedly, there's always an inquest.' Eli glanced towards the front of their cab, and let out a bitter laugh. 'Guess what, Brontë? Your bosses will be really pleased with ED7 tonight. You made that call in under seven minutes so you can notch John up as one of ED7's success stories even though he's dead.'

'*Don't*,' she begged, hearing the raw pain in his voice. 'Please, *don't*. I know how you're feeling, and this isn't how I wanted his life to end either. Eli—'

He slipped his hands out from under hers, and got to his feet abruptly. 'We'd better get going. There'll be other cases—people who need us.'

'Yes, but…' She scanned his face. 'Eli, I think after we've taken John to the Pentland we should log out, take the rest of the shift off to decompress.'

'I'm fine.'

'You're not,' she insisted. 'I know I'm not, and it's EMDC regulations that when you've had a very difficult job you should come off the road.'

Anger flashed across his face.

'If I say I'm fine, Brontë, then I'm *fine*.'

He wasn't—she knew he wasn't, and neither was she— but she had no opportunity to argue with him. They had scarcely returned to their ambulance after they'd taken John to the Pentland when their MDT flashed up a message.

'Code red. Two-month-old child. Not waking up. Number 108, Nicolson Street.'

'Oh, damn,' Eli muttered, and Brontë felt the same as

she put the siren on, and her foot on the accelerator despite the icy, snow-covered road.

It sounded very much like a case of sudden infant death syndrome. Every medic's worst nightmare, every family's worse fear. She hadn't thought this shift could possibly get worse, but it just had, and it got even worse when she reached Nicolson Street, and saw cars parked on either side of the road.

'I know,' she said as Eli opened his mouth. 'This is an emergency, so just park in the middle of the street.'

She did but, even as Eli pulled a medi-bag out of the ambulance, she could hear the sound of people crying from inside number 108. Crying was never a good sign. Crying meant they were probably too late, and they were. One glance at the baby was enough to tell Brontë the child had been dead for quite some time.

'She was all right when I put her to bed,' the young mother sobbed. 'She'd had her bottle, and she was fine—a little snuffly, but nothing else. She was fine, she was fine—and now…'

'I work nights,' her husband declared, rubbing a hand across his tear-stained cheeks, a muscle in his jaw twitching, 'and I just looked in, like I always do when I get home, and Jenny… She was just lying there, and I knew right away there was something wrong.'

Brontë looked helplessly across at Eli, but he was already scooping the baby into his arms.

'Hospital. This little one needs the hospital,' he declared, striding towards the door, and the child's distraught parents grabbed their coats and followed him. 'Blue us in, Brontë.'

Obediently, she hurried out of the house, but she didn't

get far. A middle-aged woman was standing beside their ambulance looking distinctly annoyed.

'Look, are you going to be much longer here?' the woman declared. 'I have to get to my night shift at the supermarket, and I can't get past.'

Brontë stared at the woman in stunned disbelief, but Eli wasn't similarly reduced to silence.

'Madam, we have a critical case here,' he replied, 'and it will take as long as it takes.'

'Can't you be a bit more specific, time-wise?' the woman protested, and Eli drew himself up to his full six feet two with an expression on his dark face that would have had Brontë backing away fast.

'Madam, do you have children?' he declared tightly.

'Well, they're teenagers now—'

'Then I'd like to know how you would feel if I couldn't park outside *your* door because some insensitive, uncaring individual felt I was blocking her way!'

The woman reddened, but she wasn't crushed.

'I want your name!' she exclaimed. 'I demand to know your name so I can make an official complaint!'

'If you can't read the name tag on my uniform, then I'm certainly not going to spell it out for you,' Eli retorted as he got into the back of the ambulance with the baby's parents.

'I'm going to report you—both of you,' the woman yelled after them as Brontë drove away.

Brontë fervently hoped she would. She would enjoy contesting that complaint but, as she drove to the hospital, she would have preferred, even more, to have been anywhere but where she was.

It was one thing to be in A and E when a SIDS baby was brought in, and quite another to drive through the dark

Edinburgh Streets with that SIDS baby in the back of her ambulance. She tried not to look in her mirror because she didn't want to see Eli performing CPR on a baby who would never laugh or cry ever again. She tried to stop her ears to the sound of the heartfelt, wrenching sobs from the baby's parents, but she couldn't do that either. All she could do was bite down hard on her lip, and pray she would get to the Pentland fast.

'That was the worst journey of my life,' she mumbled when the baby and its parents had been handed over to the care of the A and E staff.

'I know the regulations say I should have declared the child dead immediately,' Eli replied as he and Brontë left the waiting room, 'but those poor parents…' He shook his head. 'They need to know everything that could be done was done, and in hospital there are people who can help them rather than us just simply driving away, leaving them alone with their baby and their grief.'

He looked as upset as she felt, and she half stretched out her hand to him, only to withdraw it quickly.

'The woman in the street—the one who was complaining,' she said angrily. 'How can people do that, behave like that?'

'It doesn't happen often,' Eli declared. 'In fact, I've watched people park on roundabouts in an attempt to let my ambulance through. I've seen people trying to get themselves into almost impossible spaces so they won't hold me back. I've even scraped the sides of vans as I've tried to get to the hospital as fast as I can, and the drivers have just called after me, "Don't worry about it, mate, it's not important." The vast majority of the public are decent people, Brontë, but some…'

'But *why*?' she insisted. 'Why are some people like that?'

'Because those people live in a "me" world, Brontë. They truly don't care about anyone else, don't think about anyone else's feelings, just take what they want, and concentrate on themselves.'

And he was describing himself, Eli thought with sudden, appalled recognition. No matter how much he tried to deny it, no matter how much he didn't want it to be so, everything Brontë had said about him was true. He *was* arrogant, he *was* self-absorbed, he *was* blind to other people's feelings. How much damage had he inflicted on the women he'd had in his life without noticing it, or—even worse—caring? Okay, so he cared passionately about the homeless, about people who were down on their luck, people who were disadvantaged by circumstances, and society, but in his personal life...

All he'd ever thought about was himself, what he wanted, what made him happy, and he was horrified.

'Are you okay?'

He looked down to see Brontë staring up at him with concern.

'I'm fine—fine.'

'I really do think we should log off,' she said tentatively. 'You need time out—we both do—and—'

'Brontë, I've been doing this job a hell of a lot longer than you have,' he snapped. 'I don't need nannying, I don't need my hand held, so back off, will you?'

She wasn't going to, Brontë decided, as he strode away from her. She'd seen murder in Eli's eyes when the woman in the street had been complaining, and she knew that if she didn't forcibly take him off the road he was going to lose it completely.

'I could do with a coffee,' Eli muttered when Brontë joined him in their ambulance.

'Me, too,' she replied as she drove away from the hospital and turned right at the bottom of the road.

But not at Tony's. They would both have their coffees in their own homes because she was going back to the station and signing them both out whether he liked it or not. Yes, it would leave ED7 one ambulance short but, no matter what Eli said, neither he, nor she, could cope with anything else tonight.

Eli glanced out of the window, then back at her.

'This isn't the quickest way to Tony's.'

'I know.'

'Brontë—'

'We're not going to Tony's,' she continued determinedly, seeing the dawning realisation in his eyes. 'I'm taking us both off the road. No ifs, no buts, no argument,' she added as he swore long and volubly. 'We both need the rest of the shift off.'

'But—'

'My decision, Eli, my call,' she interrupted.

She could feel him fuming beside her, could sense his anger and resentment, but she wasn't going to back down, not even when they got back to ED7, and he got out and slammed the ambulance door with a look at her that would have killed.

'I'll see you tomorrow, then,' she called after him as he began walking away from her, but he didn't reply.

He just kept on walking, and she stared indecisively after him. She'd never seen him looking so low, so down, and part of her wanted to go after him, to say she felt the same way, she understood, and she took a step forward, only to stop.

Distance, Brontë, her mind warned, *you were going to keep your distance, remember?*

But he's so upset, she argued back, and what harm would it do to ask if he'd like some company, to maybe share a meal with her, rather than them both going back to their empty flats alone?

Mistake, Brontë, big mistake, her mind insisted, and for a second she swithered and then before she had even realised she had made a decision she was running across the forecourt after him.

'You're inviting me to your place for a meal?' he said slowly when she caught up with him.

'I just thought… It's been such an awful night…maybe you'd like some company,' she said, feeling her cheeks beginning to heat up under his steady gaze. 'It wouldn't be anything fancy—just what's in the fridge—but the offer's there if…if you want it, that is.'

She thought he was going to refuse—he looked very much as though he intended to—then, to her surprise, he nodded.

'On two conditions,' he said. 'Number one, I drive you home, and number two, we make a short detour to Tony's to pick up some take-away spaghetti and meatballs, and then neither of us have to cook.'

A take-away spaghetti and meatballs sounded wonderful, and it smelled even better when she'd unwrapped it in her small kitchen.

'What do you want to drink?' she asked, taking two plates out of her kitchen cupboard. 'I have a half-bottle of red wine left in the fridge, coffee, tea…?'

'Coffee, as I'm driving,' he replied.

'Comfy seats, and slobbing out in the sitting room?' she

said, switching on the kettle. 'Or hard seats with a table in the kitchen?'

'Comfy seats every time,' he declared, and when she led the way into the sitting room he smiled as he gazed around. 'Nice room.'

'The flat's rented, but the furniture's all mine,' she said, pulling a coffee table over. 'It's nothing special, or valuable, just bits and pieces I've picked up from second-hand shops, and car boot sales over the years.'

'You like old furniture?' he said, sitting down on the sofa.

'I like the idea of lots of people having owned something before me,' she said, unzipping her jacket and throwing it over one of the chairs. 'That they've polished something, touched it, maybe left a little bit of themselves, their hearts, in it.' She laughed a little uncertainly. 'And now you're thinking you're having dinner with a fruit cake.'

'A romantic,' he said firmly. 'I think you're a romantic.'

Did he mean that as a compliment, or a condemnation? She wasn't sure and nor was she about to ask.

'I'll see if the kettle's boiled,' she said instead. 'Don't wait for me—just start eating.'

He hadn't, she noticed when she returned to the sitting room. He'd taken off his jacket, but he was still sitting where she'd left him, lost in thought and, as she stood in the doorway, holding their coffees, a lump came to her throat. He looked so tired. Tired, and beaten, and she wanted to put down the coffees, and take him in her arms and say, 'I'll make everything all right,' but she couldn't. She couldn't make everything all right tonight, nobody could.

'Thought I told you to eat?' she said, all cheerleader bright, and he turned to face her with an effort.

'Sorry,' he replied. 'I was miles away.'

'Someone—a man who isn't always the smartest of men—once told me, Don't think,' she observed. 'And, on this occasion, I think he was right.'

Eli forced a smile. 'So, I'm a dummkopf now, too, am I, along with all my other faults?'

'Hey, why should I be the only one with a gazillion labels?' she protested, taking a seat opposite him, hating to see that forced smile on his lips. 'And you're not a dummkopf, just a very complicated man, and now eat something.'

'Yes, ma'am,' he replied, giving her a mock salute, and she managed to laugh, and picked up her knife and fork because she knew if she didn't she would put her arms round him anyway.

Because she didn't simply want to comfort him, she wanted him. Even though it would end in heartbreak, even though it would never be for ever, she knew she still wanted him, and she always would.

'Great meatballs,' she said, deliberately putting some in her mouth.

'Yup,' he said. 'I was wondering… Tomorrow's your last day at the station, so…'

'You can tell everyone at ED7 I'm giving the station a glowing report,' she answered, and he shook his head.

'That's not what I meant. I was wondering what you were going to do, whether you were going to stick with this job, or…'

'I think we've pretty well established I'm rubbish at it.' She smiled. 'So when I hand in my report, I'll also be handing in my resignation.'

He sat back in his seat, his face concerned. 'Christmas is a lousy time to be out of work.'

'Maybe one of the big stores will be looking for a spare pixie, or an elf, for their Santa grotto,' she declared. 'Having said which, I'd have to lose a bit of weight first. Pixies and elves tend to be slender.'

'You look perfect to me.'

Her gaze met his, then she looked away fast. Oh, hell. Why did he have to have such intense blue eyes? Why couldn't he have had ordinary eyes, eyes which didn't make her heart jump around so much in her chest?

'You've just broken one of your promises,' she said, mock stern as she determinedly took another fork of spaghetti. 'The no-flattery one.'

'I wasn't flattering you.'

Oh, double hell. Change the subject, Brontë, she told herself, and change it fast, but she couldn't think of a single thing to say, and he raised an eyebrow.

'Cat got your tongue?'

'Nope,' she replied. 'Just enjoying the food. As my mother used to say—'

She bit off the rest of what she'd been about to say. Mothers were not a good topic, not with Eli, and he clearly sensed her discomfort because he smiled a little wryly.

'What you said—about going to an agency to try to find my mother,' he began, and she cut across him fast.

'I'm sorry, I should never have suggested that. I can fully understand why you wouldn't want to go down that road—'

'I already have. I went to an agency two years ago because I thought…' He sighed. 'I don't know what I thought. Maybe I was looking for closure like you said, or maybe I just wanted to ask her, face-to-face, why she left me.'

'Did…did you find her?' she said hesitantly, not really wanting to know, but knowing she had to ask.

'I was too late. She… She died six months before I started my enquiries.'

Nothing could have prepared her for him revealing that, and nothing could have prepared her for the bleakness she could see in his face.

'Oh, Eli, I am sorry,' she said softly, 'so very, very sorry.'

'She took her reasons for leaving me to the grave, so now I'll never know why she did it,' he murmured, his eyes dark. 'Maybe if I was a "think the best of people" person like you, I could pretend. I could create a scenario, a perfect resolution, but I'm not like you.'

'You don't have to be,' she said, hating to see the pain in his eyes, wanting so much to ease it, but not knowing how, 'but I do think you need to let it go, or it will never stop hurting you.'

'Yeah, well… Sorry,' he added, 'I've really put a dampener on our dinner, haven't I?'

'I'm just flattered you felt you could tell me,' she said, and saw one corner of his mouth turn up in an attempt at a smile which didn't deceive her for a second.

'I thought you said flattery was a no-no?' he pointed out.

'Oh, very funny,' she said, 'now eat before all this lovely sauce gets cold.'

He did, and she did, too, but as they ate she knew she could have been eating anything for all the impression it was making because all she was aware of was him. Him sitting in her sitting room, him just an arm's stretch away from her. Every time he pushed his hair back from his forehead, she thought, *Let me do that, I want to do that.* Every time he moved in his seat she tensed, hopeful, expectant.

Stop it, Brontë, she told herself, *stop it*. He's just a man, just a very handsome man, but he wasn't just a man, and she knew he wasn't.

'Something wrong?' he asked, looking up and catching her gaze on him.

'No—absolutely not,' she said brightly, much too brightly, and, because she was nervous, she forked up too much spaghetti only to watch in dismay as some of it dropped off her fork and landed with a soft splat on the front of her shirt.

'You are a klutz, aren't you?' Eli chuckled. 'No, don't stand up,' he added as she made to do just that, 'you'll get it on the carpet.'

And before she realised what he was going to do, he had picked up his napkin, and begun wiping the sauce and spaghetti from her shirt.

And it was torture. The most exquisite form of torture as he wiped down the front of her shirt in a smooth, rhythmic movement, and she felt his fingers through the napkin, through the material of her shirt, hot on her breast, and she knew when he caught his breath because hers caught at exactly the same moment.

'I think…' She heard him swallow. 'I think you're re-spectable again.'

Slowly she raised her eyes to his.

'Am I?'

Even to her own ears her voice sounded husky, and she saw him crumple the napkin into a tight ball.

'I shouldn't have done that, and I think…I think I should go now,' he said.

She didn't want him to go. She didn't want him to leave. She wanted him, and it didn't matter to her any more if she could only have this one night with him. It didn't even matter if he whispered words he didn't mean, said exactly the same things to her that he'd said to dozens of other women. She had no pride left. She just wanted him.

'You don't have to go,' she said, saw his pupils darken, then he got to his feet fast, shaking his head.

'Brontë, I do. You want more than I can give—you know you do—and you deserve more.'

She stood, too, and, before he could evade her, she put her hands on his chest, and felt his rapid heartbeat.

'Right now, I want you,' she said softly. 'No strings, no promises, I just want you.'

'Brontë—'

She silenced him by standing up on her toes, and kissing him, with no reserve, no holding back, exactly as she'd kissed him in the snow what seemed—oh—like a lifetime ago now, felt him hesitate for a heartbeat, and then he was holding her tight, and kissing her back with a desperate, urgent need.

Heat, all she could feel was a pulsing, throbbing heat, and when he pulled her shirt free from her combat trousers, and slid his hand up underneath it to cup and stroke her breast, she shuddered against him, wanting more, so much more.

'Brontë, think about this,' he groaned as her fingers fumbled with his shirt buttons while she planted a row of kisses along his collarbone.

'I have,' she said, pulling his shirt apart so she could look at him, could see his beauty, his strength. 'And I have never been more certain of anything in my life.'

And she wasn't, she thought, as she claimed his lips again, and felt him slide her shirt down off her shoulders, felt her bra go in an instant, and then she heard his sharp intake of breath.

'I could kill the man who did this to you,' he said, his voice tight, vicious, as he stared at the ugly scar on her chest, but, when her hands instinctively came up to cover herself, he caught them, and pressed a kiss into each palm. 'He hurt you. He made you afraid, and I don't want you ever to be hurt, or afraid, again.'

And you'll hurt me so much more when you go, she thought, but she didn't say those words.

'Just make love to me, Eli,' she whispered instead. 'That's all I want and need right now—just for you to make love to me.'

And somehow they made it to her bedroom, and soon their clothes were gone, and they were skin to skin, on her bed, his body hard and muscular against her, and his kisses weren't enough, his touch wasn't nearly enough.

But he was hesitating still, she knew it, sensed it, knew he was holding himself back, and she knew why, and she kissed him harder, with greater intensity, and reached down to stroke him, stroke him, until he gasped under her fingers, and it was then he slid into her, hot, and hard, balancing himself on his elbows, his eyes fixed on her.

And he said her name, and it sounded almost like an apology, but she didn't want an apology. She arched herself up against him, forcing him on, so that he slid even deeper into her, and she bit her lip as he began rocking into her, over and over again, and she could feel it coming, feel the blood surging to her fingertips, her toes, every part of her, knew she was reaching the precipice, and she wrapped her legs round him, drawing him further inside her, and then she broke. Broke and began spiralling and shaking beneath him, and he came, too, and as he did, he laid his head between her breasts and she heard him give a sigh that was almost a groan.

CHAPTER SEVEN

Sunday, 9:30 a.m.

ELI lay on his back and smiled as he gazed down at Brontë. She was lying curled up against his side, her head resting against his chest, and gently he placed a kiss on top of her head, and tightened his hold on her.

Last night had been the most incredible night of his life. He'd made love to her twice, and each time it had been wonderful, but that second time… That second time had been special. Slower, less frantic, it had been like nothing he had ever experienced before. It had felt almost as though he had come home which was crazy because he'd never had a home, not a proper one, but Brontë had taken him somewhere he'd never been before, and it was somewhere he didn't want to leave, not ever.

She stirred in his arms, almost as though she had read his mind, then she stretched against him, her full breasts rubbing lightly against his ribcage, sending a tremor of arousal through him, and his smile widened as she opened her eyes.

'Morning, sleepyhead,' he said.

For a second, she looked confused, as though she wasn't

a hundred per cent certain where she was, then her grey eyes softened for an instant, and then, just as quickly, she looked away, and suddenly—and unaccountably—he felt cold.

'What time is it?' she asked.

Was it his imagination, or did her voice sound carefully neutral? Unconsciously, he shook his head. Imagination, it must be his imagination. He knew he had pleased her last night. Hell, just thinking about the tiny cries, and sighs, she'd given was enough to turn him on all over again.

'Nine-thirty,' he replied. 'Which means we have a whole day ahead of us before work tonight. A whole day in which we can do whatever we want, and I've already thought of some pretty interesting things we can do. For example…'

Gently, he slid his hand up her side and began brushing his fingers across one of her nipples. It hardened instantly but, when he moved to the other breast, she eased herself out of his arms, and moved further away from him in the bed.

'I'm afraid I have plans for today,' she said. 'Things to do, places to go and a report on ED7 to write.'

'If you need to go shopping, I can carry your bags, and as for the report, I can help you there, too,' he said, reaching out to cup her chin only to see her turn her head away.

'You can't help me,' she replied. 'The things I need to do… Only I can do them.'

'Okay.' He nodded, regrouping quickly. 'How about I keep you supplied with coffees all day, then rustle you up a delicious lunch, followed by an equally jaw-dropping dinner? You have to eat, and if you've got someone like me who—' he grinned '—is not only good in the bedroom, but also pretty damn good when it comes to wielding a saucepan, why not use me?'

'Today's not a good day for me, Eli,' she muttered. 'I've made plans—plans I can't cancel.'

'Then what about tomorrow—or the day after?' he said, feeling a chill begin to creep around his heart. 'I'll be on a three-day break because I'll just have finished a seven-day block, and if you're handing in your resignation I can check out Santa grottoes with you to make sure you don't end up working with a load of licentious pixies.'

She didn't laugh—she didn't even smile—and she still wasn't looking at him, he noticed.

'Actually, I thought I might go and stay with my sister for the next few days,' she declared.

'But, Brontë, you don't even *like* your sister,' he replied, and she shrugged.

'Yes, well, she's still family.'

If it had been anyone else he would have said he was getting the brush-off, but this was Brontë. Brontë who didn't play games, didn't toy with other people's emotions, so the fault had to be his, and he sat up, tucking the duvet round her so she wouldn't get cold.

'Brontë, listen to me,' he said. 'I don't know what I did wrong last night—'

'You didn't do anything wrong,' she broke in. 'It was great, just great, but I'm leaving ED7 today—'

'Which doesn't mean we can't see each other any more,' he protested. 'It doesn't mean this has to end.'

He saw her fingers grip the sheet.

'Eli, I had a great time last night—fabulous, truly—but can't we just leave it at that?'

'Leave it at that?' he echoed. 'Brontë, in case you've forgotten, we made love last night, and I think we should at least talk about it. I've obviously upset you in some way—'

'You haven't—not in the least. Look, as you told me before,' she continued as he tried to interrupt, 'there's mediocre sex, okay sex and great sex, and though the sex last night was pretty good, my feeling is we should quit while we're ahead, shake hands, wish each other well, and move on.'

They should shake hands and wish each other well? They'd had great sex, but they should quit while they were ahead?

She was making what they'd shared sound so clinical, so unemotional, and it hadn't been like that, at least not for him, and he caught hold of her chin with his fingers, and forced her to look up at him.

'Brontë, *talk* to me. Don't give me all these platitudes, all this…this crap. *Talk* to me.'

'I would if there was anything left to say,' she replied, her eyes meeting his briefly, then skittering away. 'We had a great time, but can't you just accept that's all it was? Now, do you want to use the shower first? I don't want to hurry you— make you feel I'm throwing you out or anything—but…'

She was throwing him out. No ifs, no buts, she was throwing him out, and he didn't want to be thrown out. He wanted to hold her. Not even to make love to her again, though his body would have welcomed that with unbridled enthusiasm; he just wanted to hold her, to try to recapture that wonderful feeling of belonging he'd experienced last night.

'Brontë—'

'So are you showering first? It's just, like I said, I have—'

'Things to do, people to see and a report to write,' he finished for her grimly. 'Fine. Absolutely fine.' He threw back the duvet, and stood. 'Do I get a cup of coffee before I go, or would that interrupt your schedule too much?'

'You know where the kitchen is,' Brontë replied.

And she turned on her side when she said it, so all he could see of her was her bare back which meant she was well and truly shutting him out.

Well, fine, he thought, angrily. If that's what she wanted, then that was just *fine*, and he walked out of the bedroom, and slammed the door and didn't see Brontë bury her face deep in her pillow so he wouldn't be able to see or hear her tears.

'I don't see anyone,' Brontë declared when she turned into Richmond Street. '"Elderly woman lying in the street," Dispatch said, but I can't see anyone.'

'Drive to the top of the road, then come back down again,' Eli replied.

It was on the tip of her tongue to say, 'And, like, *duh*, so you didn't think I was going to think of that?' but she didn't.

Perky, and upbeat, Brontë, she told herself. You are going to be perky and upbeat for the whole of this shift if it kills you, and quickly she drove up Richmond Street, then back down again.

'Well, unless she's the invisible woman,' she declared, 'I'd say she's either just wandered off, or it was a hoax call.'

'Someone's waving to us from outside that house,' Eli said suddenly. 'Pull over.'

Obediently, Brontë did as he'd said, and an Indian gentleman walked gingerly over the snow towards them.

'Are you looking for the lady who fell?' he asked, and when Brontë nodded he looked a little awkward, a little guilty.

'She is in my house. I know you are not supposed to move someone who is hurt,' he added as Eli sucked in his breath, 'but it is so cold out here, and my wife, Indira, she said we couldn't leave her, not in the snow, not when she was clearly in such pain. My name is Mr Shafi, by the way.'

'That was very kind of you, Mr Shafi,' Brontë said quickly before Eli could say what she knew he was itching to say. 'Can you tell us anything about her?' she continued, as she reached for a medi-bag.

'Her name is Violet Swanson,' he replied, ushering Brontë towards his home. 'The poor old lady… She had been to the chapel, to say her prayers, and she slipped on the snow on her way home. Indira…she thinks perhaps the lady's arm is broken.'

Violet Swanson's arm *was* broken, and she was clearly in considerable pain.

'So stupid,' she murmured. 'Such a stupid, stupid thing to have done. I know I should have waited until morning to go to church, but it's very peaceful there at night, very comforting.'

'You'll have to go to hospital,' Eli declared. 'I'm sorry, but you really must,' he added when Violet Swanson began to argue. 'That arm needs to be X-rayed, and put in plaster. Is there anyone you'd like us to contact, to say where we're taking you?'

'I'm a widow, dear, live on my own,' Violet Swanson replied, wincing sharply, as Brontë began to strap her arm across her chest to keep it secure. 'No family. Archie and I were never blessed, but then you don't always get what you want out of life, do you, so you just have to make the best of things.'

Which is what I'm going to do, Brontë thought, deliberately avoiding Eli's eyes. Last night… It had been the most wonderful night of her life, but she'd known it was just that. One night. One incredible night she would be able to look back on, and remember, and though she'd remember it with some pain—the pain of knowing he was the man she wanted, but could never have—it was better to walk away now than live with Eli for two months and then have him leave. That, she knew, she would never survive.

'Mrs Swanson, do you think you can walk?' she asked. 'We have a carry-chair—'

'Of course I can walk,' Violet protested, but from the way she swayed when she stood, it was patently obvious that not only was she in a lot more pain than she was admitting, her whole system had taken a severe shock.

'The carry-chair,' Eli said firmly.

'Thank you for helping,' Brontë told Mr Shafi and his wife, as she helped Mrs Swanson into the chair. 'It was very kind of you.'

The man shrugged. 'What else could we do? We could not leave the poor lady, turn our backs on her.'

A lot of people could, Brontë thought when they'd got Mrs Swanson safely settled in the back of the ambulance, and she set off for the Pentland. In fact, too many people did. Too many people walked on by, thinking, Someone else's problem, not mine.

'It's a pity there's not a lot more people in the world like that nice couple in Richmond Street,' she observed after they had delivered Mrs Swanson to A and E. 'People who are willing to put themselves out, to help others.'

'To be fair, some people prefer to keep themselves to themselves,' Eli replied. 'They don't want to let down their guard in case people encroach on their personal space.'

Like me, he thought, as he watched Brontë climb back into the ambulance. Always he had been the one who'd been in control in all of his relationships, the one who had decided when it was over, but this time…

For the first time in his life he was completely out of his depth. For the first time in his life he didn't know what to do. Maybe if he talked to Brontë again. Maybe if he waited until the end of this shift, then talked to her…

And said what? his mind asked.

That he didn't want her to walk right out of his life. That he wanted to spend time with her. A lot more time. That he'd miss her snippiness, and her laughter. He'd miss her silver-grey eyes, and her fringe which never would stay flat. He'd miss *her.*

But how could he get her back? His looks had always been his primary tool of seduction. His looks, and some well-practised flattery and flirtation, but none of that would get him anywhere with Brontë. He needed something else, and he would have to find it fast or she would walk right out of his life just as quickly as she'd walked into it.

'Code red. Male, aged twenty, collapsed and in pain. Number 82, Bristol Street,' the MDT screen read, and Brontë grimaced slightly.

Code red sounded ominous, but Eli hadn't said to switch on the siren. Actually, Eli hadn't said very much at all since they'd come on duty, but he was watching her, she knew he was. Watching her with a slightly puzzled expression in his eyes, as though he was trying to figure something out. She wished he wouldn't. She wished he would just take what she'd said this morning at face value, because it would be easier for both of them if he did.

Will it? her heart whispered as she drove down Melrose Street. *Will it really?*

It had to be, she told herself, because the alternative was so much worse.

'Turn left at the bottom of the road for Bristol Street,' Eli advised and, as she did, she blinked as she saw the row of elegant Georgian buildings.

'Whoa, but these houses are seriously stunning.' She gasped. 'I wouldn't be able to afford to live here even on a hundred times my income.'

'Money can't buy you happiness, or contentment,' Eli replied cryptically.

He was right. Number 82, Bristol Street might have been just as lavish inside as it was out, but its occupants weren't in the least to be envied.

'You the ambulance dudes?' a young man asked, his voice distinctly slurred as he opened the front door.

'Yes, we're the ambulance dudes.' Eli sighed. 'Where's the casualty?'

The young man waved his hand vaguely. 'Dining room, I think. Or it could be the sitting room. Dunno, really.'

'Great,' Eli muttered, pushing past him. 'Let's hope somebody in this house is in a fit state to answer some questions.'

Brontë very much doubted it. That the son, or daughter, of the house had decided to throw a party was clear. She could hear the thumping sound of music and laughter, and there was discarded food, and empty bottles, scattered everywhere.

'I wonder where the parents are?' she asked as she followed Eli over the parquet entrance hall, feeling her boots stick with every step.

'Winter cruise, shooting in the highlands, down in London to take in a few exhibitions?' Eli suggested, and Brontë shook her head.

'You'd think they'd have more sense than to go off and leave a bunch of youngsters with no supervision. So, what do we do?' she continued. 'Search every room, or what?'

They didn't have to. A girl who couldn't have been more than eighteen appeared, looking scared and worried.

'Gavin's through here,' she said, pointing to a door at the end of the hallway. 'He's acting all funny—not making any sense at all.'

Brontë wasn't surprised when she saw the young man. He was lying on a sofa, curled up into a ball, clutching his stomach and moaning, but it was the rest of his appearance which told her immediately what the problem was. His pupils were almost pinpoints, his skin was clammy, his fingernails and lips had a bluish tinge, and he was twitching uncontrollably.

'What's he taken?' Eli said, as he crouched down beside the young man.

'A few beers—maybe a shot or two of whisky,' the girl replied, and Eli exhaled with irritation.

'Look, give me credit for some sense,' he declared as Brontë began strapping a blood pressure cuff to the young man's arm. 'Is it crystal meth, cocaine, Ecstasy, or heroin?'

'Gavin doesn't do drugs,' the young girl protested. 'He's just had a bit too much to drink, that's all.'

'Sweetheart, he clearly doesn't know where he is, or even *who* he is, and you don't get muscle spasticity like that from booze,' Eli protested. 'So, I'm going to ask you again. What's he taken?'

'Eli, his BP is way too low, and his pulse is very weak,' Brontë murmured. 'We're going to have to tube him, and fast.'

'Did you hear that?' Eli demanded, and the young woman looked from Brontë to the young man in panic.

'I…I don't know anything,' she said.

'Look, what's your name?' Brontë asked, seeing Eli shake his head in despair.

'It's Joanna,' the young woman replied. 'My name's Joanna.'

'Joanna, Gavin is very sick indeed,' Brontë said, 'and, without wanting to frighten you, he could die. We need to know what he's taken so we know how to treat him,' she continued as the young girl let out a gasp, and tears filled her eyes. 'We're not here to make judgements, but to *help*.'

'My parents will kill me,' Joanna whispered. 'They don't know about this party, and when they find out…'

Out of the corner of her eye, Brontë could see Eli was beginning to insert an intubation tube into Gavin's trachea to help him breathe, but they needed to know what the young man had taken, and they needed to know it fast.

'Joanna, has Gavin had any seizures?' she asked.

'Seizures?' Joanna repeated blankly.

'Had a fit, thrashed about at all?' Brontë explained.

The girl nodded. 'He had one about half an hour ago.'

'Please, Joanna,' Brontë said softly. 'We need to know what Gavin's taken before it's too late.'

The girl bit her lip, then took a shuddering breath.

'Heroin,' she said, her voice thick. 'He's taken some heroin.'

'Do you know how much?' Brontë said, and the young woman shook her head.

'Brendan… He said it would make Gavin feel great. He's been feeling a bit down, you see. His parents have stopped his allowance because he crashed his dad's Mercedes, and it was just meant to pep him up a bit.'

Eli muttered something under his breath that was most definitely unprintable.

'How often has he taken heroin?' he demanded.

'I think this was the first time,' Joanna replied, 'but I don't know. I honestly and truly don't know.'

'Brontë, his BP is going down even more,' Eli said urgently. 'We have to go.'

'Can I come, too?' the girl asked. 'He's my sort of boyfriend, you see.'

A sort of boyfriend who might not survive the night, Brontë thought, as she helped Eli carry Gavin out to the ambulance, past youngsters who were still partying, apparently oblivious—or uncaring—about what was happening in front of them.

'Do you think he'll pull through?' Brontë asked after they had taken Gavin to the Pentland.

'We can but hope,' Eli replied, 'but the waste, Brontë, the damn waste of a young life, if he doesn't!'

'I know.' She sighed. 'All that money, all those advantages, and yet to be so stupid.'

'Yeah, well, I'm afraid all the money in the world doesn't buy you some plain, old-fashioned common sense.' Eli glanced down at his watch and sighed. 'And can you believe we've only been on duty for a couple of hours?'

Brontë couldn't. This shift felt endless, and it was about to get worse, she thought when a message appeared on their MDT.

'Gang fight in Princes Street Gardens. Police in attendance. All available ambulances to attend the incident. Repeat, all available ambulances to attend, and offer assistance.'

Her stomach lurched. A gang fight. That meant a crowd, and she was being asked to drive there, to get out amongst it, to offer help.

'Brontë…'

She heard the instant concern in Eli's voice, the gentle understanding, and breathed in again, hoping it might work, but it didn't.

'I'm okay,' she lied, hating the betraying wobble in her voice as she switched on the ignition. 'I'll…I'll be okay.'

She wouldn't be, she knew she wouldn't. Already her heart was racing at just the thought of being amongst a crowd, and her palms were so sweaty she could barely grip the steering wheel.

Failure, her heart whispered, *you're a failure. People could be hurt out there, and you can't do anything to help them.*

She wondered what Eli was thinking. *Liability,* that's what he was probably thinking, that he was stuck with a liability. Well, at least she would get him there fast, she determined. At least he wouldn't be able to accuse her of deliberately dawdling, but it was easier said than done.

'Look, I know you don't want to go there—that crowds freak you out—but couldn't you drive just a little faster,' he said softly, and Brontë glanced at him helplessly.

'It isn't me. I've got my foot to the floor, but we're losing power, and I don't know why.'

'You did make sure she was filled up?' he said, only to smile a little ruefully when Brontë shot him a withering glance. 'Sorry. Stupid question. The trouble is she's old, clapped out.'

'What do you want me to do?' Brontë asked. 'We're not going to be much use ferrying casualties to hospital at this speed, and what if it breaks down on the way to the Pentland with a seriously hurt person in the back?'

Eli chewed his lip indecisively, then seemed to come to a decision.

'Get as close to Princes Street Gardens as you can. At least that way I can be of use, help the other paramedics.'

And they looked as though they could do with all the help they could get, Brontë thought when she reached the garden and saw not just an array of police cars, and ambulances, but a seething mass of fighting youths.

'Stay where you are,' Eli ordered as he pulled a medibag out from behind him, and opened his passenger door. 'When I get out, lock all the doors, call Dispatch and tell them we have a problem with the ambulance, and stay where you are.'

'But—'

'Keep the MDT display on, and if anything urgent comes in, try and attract one of the policemen's attention, but do *not* get out of the ambulance.'

'But, Eli—'

He was gone before she could say anything else and,

for one brief moment, she saw him clearly, pushing his way through the fighting youths, head and shoulders taller than most of them, and then he was gone and she wrapped her arms around herself as a wave of nausea engulfed her.

Never had she felt so frightened. She could see the rival gangs quite clearly through her windscreen. Some were hurling stones, some were armed with bits of wood they'd clearly torn from garden fences, some were simply using their fists, and here and there, she saw the flash of metal in the moonlight. Knives. Some of them were armed with knives.

And the fight was moving closer to her now. Occasionally, somebody was thrown against the ambulance, and she could feel it shaking under the impact, could hear the thud of the body, see wild, enraged faces in front of her, and the noise…the noise…

She put her hands over her ears, and curled herself into a ball in the driver's seat, but it didn't help. She could still hear the oaths, the roars, the screams, and she wanted to put the ambulance into reverse, to get away, but even if the ambulance would go anywhere, Eli was out there, amongst all the mayhem, and he might need help, except she couldn't help him, she couldn't do anything but sit here, with her eyes tight shut, and wait.

A bottle crashing against her windscreen had her sitting bolt upright in panic. They couldn't get in, surely none of them could get in, and then—out of the corner of her eye—she saw something else. A young boy was lying beside one of the hedges. A young boy, with an ashen face, and closed eyes, who didn't look much older than John Smith had been. A young boy who had blood on his forehead, and blood dripping down from his fingers onto the snow below.

Desperately she scanned the melee in front of her. If she could just see a paramedic—any paramedic—maybe she could attract their attention, point out the boy, but all she could see was people fighting, The blood dripping from the boy's hand was forming a pool, and he was even whiter now than he'd been a minute ago. He was going to die. She knew as surely as she knew anything that he was going to die, all alone with no one to help him, and a sob broke from her.

Somewhere in the distance someone screamed, and she bit down hard on her lip until she tasted blood. If she'd been there when John had been dying she could have saved him, but she hadn't been there. She was here now, though, and that young boy lying so close to her needed her, and she could help him if she could only find the courage.

With shaking hands she dragged a medi-bag out from behind her, and took a shuddering breath. She could do this. She *had* to do this and, though her heart was pounding, she opened the ambulance door and got out.

Where the hell was she? Eli wondered, as he scanned the now almost deserted gardens. He'd told her to stay in the ambulance, not to move, but perhaps she'd got so frightened she'd just taken off into the night which meant she could be anywhere.

'You've not seen Brontë O'Brian, have you?' Eli asked urgently as one of the paramedics from ED12 passed him. 'Small, golden-brown hair, big grey eyes? The government number cruncher.'

The paramedic shook his head.

'Mate, I doubt whether I would have recognised my

own mother in that mob tonight. Bedlam. Sheer bedlam.'
He glanced over his shoulder. 'Maybe one of the cops
might have seen her.'

Eli nodded, and quickly hurried over to the small group
of policemen who were standing by one of the railings,
looking decidedly the worse for wear. One had a black
eye, the other's uniform was torn, and one had a badly cut
lip.

'I'm looking for my colleague,' Eli declared. 'Small
woman, short golden-brown hair, big grey eyes. Have you
seen her at all?'

'Can't say I have,' the policeman with the black eye
replied. 'Maybe she went off in one of the ambulances?'

It was a possibility—a remote one—but a possibility,
but as Eli turned to go, the policeman with the cut lip
suddenly frowned.

'A small woman, you said?' he declared. 'With short,
golden-brown hair?'

'That's her,' Eli said eagerly. 'Do you know where she
is?'

'If it's the same woman you're talking about, I'm
afraid she took a knife wound. Pretty serious, too, by the
looks of it.'

Eli's heart clutched in his chest. A knife wound.
Pretty serious.

No. No. *No.*

If she was badly hurt, if she was… No, he couldn't
think that—wouldn't allow himself to think that—but he
had to know, had to find out.

'Can you take me to the hospital?' he said.

'Sure thing, mate,' the policeman with the black eye
replied. 'Which one?'

The Pentland, or the Waverley? Eli desperately tried to think, but his brain didn't seem to be working. All he could see was Brontë lying white, and cold, and bleeding, on the snow. Brontë slipping away from him on a sterile hospital trolley, without him, and him never being able to say what he knew now to be the truth. That the indefinable emotion he experienced every time he was near her, was love. The feelings of protectiveness, the need, and the rightness, he had felt last night, was love. It was an emotion he had told Brontë didn't exist. An emotion he had denied for the past thirty-four years, and he couldn't lose it now. Simply couldn't.

'Hey, mate, you okay?' one of the policemen asked as Eli dashed a hand across his eyes.

'Yes, I'm…I'm okay,' Eli replied, trying to blot out the image of Brontë lying on a cold mortuary slab. 'Can we go now?'

'No problem,' the policeman replied, but as Eli turned to follow him he saw a figure emerging from the gardens.

A figure, whose short pixie cut was sticking up all over the place. A figure who had a smear of blood on her cheek, and who looked exhausted, and before he even realised he was moving, Eli was running towards her, his arms out-stretched, and when he reached her, he clasped her into his arms and enveloped her in a crushing embrace.

'Don't ever do that to me again,' he said, his voice breaking. 'Don't ever just disappear like that, not *ever.* When I got back to the ambulance and you weren't there…'

'I couldn't stay,' she mumbled into his chest. 'There was this young boy, and he reminded me so much of John, and I couldn't stay, just couldn't, and…' She raised her head to him, her eyes shining. 'I did it, Eli. I *did it*. I was terrified, and I thought I was going to faint—'

'Are you okay?' he interrupted, scanning her face. 'The blood on your cheek—is it yours?'

'No—no—it's someone else's,' she said dismissively, 'but did you hear me, Eli? I conquered my fear. After I'd treated the boy, I just kept going, and going, with other casualties, and I could do it, I could *do it*!'

'This past half-hour,' he murmured, not really listening to her, 'when I couldn't find you, and the policeman said someone looking like you had been taken to hospital—'

'That was Liz Logan from ED10. She got a nasty knife wound. I saw them take her away, but I think she's going to be okay because she was talking…' Brontë chuckled. 'Actually, she was swearing.'

Eli held her tighter. 'Do you have *any* idea how scared I was when I thought it was you?'

'You worry too much.'

'And you…' The relief he had felt at finding her safe turned to anger as he remembered the agonies he'd been through, fearing the worst. 'What the hell did you think you were doing? I *told* you to stay in the cab. Didn't I tell you to stay there, but, no, Brontë O'Brian thinks she knows best, so out she gets, completely disobeying my order….'

She pulled herself out of his arms, and glared up at him.

'Order? You didn't give me any order. You just suggested I should stay in the ambulance, but, Eli, it was mayhem out there—'

'All the more reason for you to stay put.'

'—and people were hurt, bleeding. I couldn't ignore them, and keep my self-respect, and once I got outside, once I started treating people, I was fine, I was okay. I *am* fine, I *am* okay.'

'I'm *not*,' he said with feeling. 'Brontë, get in the ambulance.'

'There's no point,' she protested. 'It's not going anywhere until the breakdown truck arrives.'

'No, but we have an audience,' Eli declared, suddenly becoming aware that the three policemen were watching them with various grins on their faces. 'And I have more to say to you.'

'More to chew me out for, you mean.' Brontë sighed. 'Don't you see what this means for me, Eli? It means I can be a nurse again, go back to doing what I love most. Or I could retrain, become a paramedic. Not at ED7, of course,' she added quickly. 'I wouldn't inflict myself on you—'

'I wouldn't mind.'

'But the big thing—the most important thing—is you said I'd get over my fear, and you were right, so, please…' She caught and held his gaze anxiously. 'Can't you be pleased for me?'

'I am pleased for you.' He nodded. 'But I still want you to get in the ambulance.'

'But—'

He wasn't taking any buts. He took her by the arm and steered her firmly towards the ambulance, and waited until she'd got in before he climbed into the passenger seat beside her.

'Look, I'm sorry you were worried,' she said immediately. 'I should have left a note or something—'

'Brontë…' He paused, and shook his head. 'You scared the living daylights out of me, but, believe me, what I'm going to say now is a hell of a lot more frightening.'

'Something's happened to one of the paramedics?' she said instantly. 'Liz Logan, she was hurt a lot more badly than we thought—'

'No, it's not Liz, or any of the other paramedics,' he interrupted. 'This…this is about me.'

'You,' she said with a frown. 'I'm sorry, but I don't understand.'

'I don't either,' he murmured with a wry and rueful smile, 'and, as I've never said this to anyone before, I'm probably going to mess it up big time.'

'Mess what up?' she declared in confusion. 'Eli, you're not making any sense.'

'I don't think I have since the first minute I met you,' he said slowly. 'You see…when I thought I might never see you again…when I thought I might have lost you for good… It was then I realised you're the most irritating, annoying, lippy, wonderful woman I've ever met, and I need you in my life.'

She blinked. 'Okay, I understood the annoying and the lippy part, but as for the rest…'

'I'm saying I love you, Brontë O'Brian.'

She didn't say anything. She simply stared at him blankly, and he felt his cheeks darken with colour. Surely he couldn't have got it so badly wrong? He thought—he was sure—she felt something for him, but maybe he'd been wrong.

'Aren't you going to say anything?' he said with an attempt at a smile that fooled neither of them.

'I'm waiting for the punchline,' she declared. 'What you just said… There's got to be a punchline.'

'No punchline.'

'But…' She shook her head. 'Eli, you've only known

me for seven days, and for most of that time we've shouted at each other, and you don't believe in love. You told me you didn't.'

'I didn't until I met you,' he said awkwardly. 'I've never wanted any woman to stay with me forever, but I want you to.'

'Is this another pitch?' she said, and he saw her lip tremble. 'Eli, if this is another of your pitches, another of your lines, I swear I will never forgive you.'

Never had he regretted his reputation as much as he did now when he saw tears shimmering in her eyes. Never had he so much regretted all the women he had dated, and then so carelessly discarded.

'No—absolutely *not*!' he exclaimed, reaching out to capture one of her hands in his. 'I wish I knew the words to say to convince you I'm telling you the truth. Brontë, I *love* you. I have never said that to a woman before, and I know I will never say it to any other woman. I love you, and I know I always will.'

'Is this about last night?' she said uncertainly. 'Because we slept together, you now feel guilty—'

'*No!*' He let go of her hand, and gripped her shoulders. 'Last night…last night you gave me something I've never had before. It wasn't simply sex,' he continued as she tried to interrupt. 'I've had enough sex to know the difference. It's not something I'm proud of, it's something I now bitterly regret—all the women I hurt without even realising I was hurting them—but I can't erase my past, can't change it.'

'Eli—'

'I told you once before you're one of a kind, Brontë O'Brian, and you are. Last night… Last night you made me feel whole, you made me feel complete, that I finally belonged, and I want you to stay with me for always, to marry me. If…' His eyes met hers. 'If you'll have me.'

For an answer, she reached out and caught his face between her hands, her eyes large and luminous in the dark.

'You're smug, and you're arrogant, and you're a bit of a prat.'

'And a true bastard.' He nodded. 'Don't forget that one.'

'No, that one I won't allow,' she said, her voice shaking, 'but I love you, too, Elijah Munroe. Even when you called me silly, and stupid, and a doormat—'

'I didn't mean that,' he said, alarm appearing in his eyes. 'I was angry, just lashing out—'

'I know you were,' she said softly. 'Don't forget I've called you some pretty rough things when I was angry.'

'I just…' His voice broke. 'I don't want you to leave me, Brontë.'

She could see the shadows of his past in his eyes, and vowed that, even if it took her a lifetime, she was somehow going to erase them.

'Eli, I'm always going to love you even when you're crotchety, even when you get right up my nose, and even when we argue as we're bound to,' she said, her voice trembling slightly. 'I am never, *ever* going to stop loving you, and I am never going to leave you.'

And to prove it, she tilted her head, and kissed him, giving him everything she had, holding nothing back, feeling his familiar heat, his strength, as he wrapped his arms around her to kiss her back, and this time it was even better than before because this time she knew it was for keeps, and they would be together, always.

'So is that a yes, you'll marry me?' he said breathlessly into her hair when they had to draw apart to breathe.

'What do you think?' She chuckled.

'I want to hear you say it,' he insisted. 'I want you to say, "Elijah Munroe, I love you and I'll marry you as soon as we can."'

'Kiss me again, and then I'll give you an answer,' she replied, unable to prevent herself from teasing him just a little.

And he did kiss her again. Kissed her until she had to clutch onto his shirt, feeling breathless and giddy, so when their MDT bleeped insistently she groaned against Eli's mouth.

'I told them we were off the road,' she protested. 'I told them the ambulance had broken down and we couldn't take any calls.'

Eli glanced down at the screen, then his lips quirked.

'I think you'd better read what it says,' he declared.

'Why?' she said in confusion, and, when his smile widened she gazed down at the MDT, then across at him in confusion.

There, across the screen, were the words, 'We can't stand the suspense. Are you going to marry him, or not?'

'What the…? How can they…? How do they…?' She faltered, and then her cheeks flushed scarlet and she frantically stretched across the dashboard, and switched off the radio receiver. 'Oh, criminy, Eli, did you realise the radio was still on?'

He shook his head.

'You must have left it on by mistake when you patched EMDC to tell them our ambulance was out of commission,' he replied, reaching for her again only to see her put up her hands to fend him off.

'But that means everyone heard what you said, and

everyone heard what I said,' she wailed. 'They were all *listening*, Eli.'

'I don't give a damn.'

'I do,' she protested. 'Oh, this is so embarrassing. Can't you see how embarrassing this is?'

'Only if you tell me you don't want to marry me.'

'But we're never going to live it down,' she declared, putting her hands to her hot cheeks. 'We must have sounded… Those kisses, do you think they heard those kisses?'

'I doubt they heard them.' He laughed. 'But I should imagine they managed to put two and two together during the long silences when we weren't talking, plus there was all that heavy breathing, of course.'

'It isn't *funny*, Eli,' she exclaimed, and he caught both of her hands in his tightly.

'Brontë, everyone heard me tell you I loved you. Everyone heard me ask you to marry me, so look on the bright side. I can't back out now even if I wanted to. Not if I don't want to be lynched.'

She stared up into his deep blue eyes uncertainly. 'And do you—want to back out?'

'Not now, not ever, so quit with the stalling, O'Brian. Will you marry me?'

There was love, and tenderness, and a great deal of uncertainty, in his face, and it was that uncertainty which tugged at her heart, and brought a tremulous smile to her lips.

'Of course I will, you idiot.'

And she leant towards him to kiss him again, but he put a hand out to stay her.

'Just one minute,' he said firmly, though his eyes, she

noticed, were gleaming, and he leant forward and switched on the radio receiver again. 'I don't want you to be able to back out of this either, so, in front of witnesses, Brontë O'Brian, will you marry me?'

'Yes, Elijah Munroe, I will,' she said, and saw him switch off the receiver again. 'So, it's official now, neither of us can back out.'

'Nope. We're stuck with each other,' he replied, and then the corners of his mouth tipped up ever so slightly. 'So, what now?'

'What do you mean, what now?' she asked, and saw his smile widen.

'Well, we're stuck in this ambulance with nothing to do until the breakdown truck arrives.'

'We can listen to the radio,' she suggested. 'Earwig on other paramedics.'

'Nope, that's not lighting my fire.'

'Or we could play I Spy,' she observed. 'I can think of some pretty fiendish ones.'

'I can think of better games to play,' he said, sliding his arm along her seat, and she shook her head.

'I'm sure you can, but we're not playing any of those, not in an ambulance.'

He stuck out his tongue at her. 'Spoilsport.'

'Realist, more like.' She grinned. 'I'm already notorious on the radio, and I've no intention of becoming even more so should the breakdown truck arrive.'

'We could just abandon the ambulance, go back to your place?'

She shook her head at him.

'Eli Munroe, you're a very dangerous man.'

He laughed. 'Nah. Big pussycat, me. So what do you

say—will we go back to your place? I mean, we could be sitting here all night, getting colder, and colder, and you have a lovely, warm and very cosy bed....'

It sounded so tempting, and his eyes were hot, and as he'd said, they had no idea when the breakdown truck would arrive. In fact, when she'd told Dispatch of the problem with the ambulance, the caller had been anything but encouraging.

'Okay, we'll get a taxi back to my place,' she said, but as she made to open her door, Eli stayed her arm.

'Just one question before we go,' he declared. 'Do you have a tape measure at home?'

'I...I think so,' she said, bewildered. 'In fact, I'm almost positive I do. Why?'

'Because there's one question you still haven't given me the answer to.' He grinned. 'So, in about half an hour's time, when I've got you naked in front of me...'

'Are you naked in this scene, too?' she said, her lips curving.

'Oh, absolutely.' He nodded. 'Most definitely.'

'So, when I'm naked, and you're naked?' she prompted.

'With your tape measure, I'll finally get to find out what your hip measurement is.'

'I promise you the results will be ugly.' She smiled. 'In fact, it might make you reconsider your offer to marry me.'

He lifted her hand to his lips, his blue eyes soft, and warm.

'Even if you turn out to have hips the size of a barn door—'

'*Hey!*'

'Nothing is going to stop me from marrying you,

Brontë O'Brian. We're a partnership now in every sense of the word, and we always will be.'

And as she gazed back at him, and saw the love in his eyes, she knew they would be.

Do you dream of being a romance writer?

Mills & Boon are looking for fresh
writing talent in our biggest
ever search!

And this time…our readers have
a say in who wins!

For information on how to enter
or get involved go to

www.romanceisnotdead.com

BACHELOR OF THE BABY WARD
by Meredith Webber

New to Jimmie's Children's Unit, anaesthetist Kate Armstrong is desperate not to fall for the sexy surgeon Angus McDowell – because she knows he'll be impossible to forget! But Angus' son has other ideas… All *he* wants is Kate to be his mummy…!

FAIRYTALE ON THE CHILDREN'S WARD
by Meredith Webber

Dear Santa, I've just learnt I have a daddy called Oliver, who works with my mummy Clare at Jimmie's Children's Unit. All I want is for my family to be together by Christmas Day! Love, Emily (aged 9¼)

PLAYBOY UNDER THE MISTLETOE
by Joanna Neil

Heartthrob Dr Ben Radcliffe is back in town and A&E doctor Jasmine knows she should stay well away, but it's impossible! As the snow starts to fall the village has their fingers crossed that the mistletoe at the village dance will work its Christmas magic!

OFFICER, SURGEON…GENTLEMAN!
by Janice Lynn

When Dr Amelia Stockton sees dashing naval surgeon and old flame Cole Stanley on board her ship, her heart calls mayday! Cole is aware of the Navy's 'no relationship' policy! But when it comes to the beautiful Amelia, rules are made to be broken!

On sale from 1st October 2010
Don't miss out!

Medical Romance™

MIDWIFE IN THE FAMILY WAY
by Fiona McArthur

Emma has built a beautiful life for herself and her little girl in Lyrebird Lake. Gianni has come to the lake for a whistlestop tour, but is soon enchanted by the beautiful Emma. Will he be able to leave when he discovers she's expecting?

THEIR MARRIAGE MIRACLE
by Sue MacKay

Doctor Fiona is about to face Dr Tom Saville, her new boss – and the husband she hasn't seen for years. They were separated by heartbreak, but is Tom's incredible smile enough for Fiona to find the courage to take this second chance at happiness…?

On sale from 1st October 2010
Don't miss out!

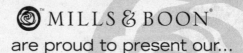

2 FREE BOOKS
AND A SURPRISE GIFT

We would like to take this opportunity to thank you for reading this Mills & Boon® book by offering you the chance to take TWO more specially selected books from the Medical™ series absolutely FREE! We're also making this offer to introduce you to the benefits of the Mills & Boon® Book Club™—

- **FREE home delivery**
- **FREE gifts and competitions**
- **FREE monthly Newsletter**
- **Exclusive Mills & Boon Book Club offers**
- **Books available before they're in the shops**

Accepting these FREE books and gift places you under no obligation to buy, you may cancel at any time, even after receiving your free books. Simply complete your details below and return the entire page to the address below. You don't even need a stamp!

YES Please send me 2 free Medical books and a surprise gift. I understand that unless you hear from me, I will receive 5 superb new stories every month including two 2-in-1 books priced at £4.99 each and a single book priced at £3.19, postage and packing free. I am under no obligation to purchase any books and may cancel my subscription at any time. The free books and gift will be mine to keep in any case.

Ms/Mrs/Miss/Mr _____ Initials _____

_____

Surname _____

Address _____

_____

_____ Postcode _____

E-mail _____

Send this whole page to: Mills & Boon Book Club, Free Book Offer, FREEPOST NAT 10298, Richmond, TW9 1BR